INNER DEMONS

STACIA STARK

CHAPTER ONE

Danica

My boxes were breeding.

Their box babies had also bred. And now I would forever be surrounded by the reminder that I was clearly the most disorganized person in this realm.

And it wasn't just boxes. Bags of files jostled with a few lone weapons, which competed for space with old spell stones, stationery, and various other crap.

Who knew I had so much *stuff?* And where had I been keeping it all?

I gazed around my new office, and despite the mess, I grinned. Mine. It was all mine.

Thanks to Keigan's generosity, I was going independent. My years working for the Mage Council had taught me everything I knew about investigating, and since they'd fired me, I would now put those skills to good use running my own investigative firm.

Okay, okay. Calling it a firm was an exaggeration. I was a one-woman band who only had experience working as a contractor. So I planned to take relatively easy jobs to start with, slowly building up my reputation. The small space was located in a strip mall off East Main Street, just a few minutes from my apartment. My office was wedged between a ballet school on the right and an insurance firm on the left.

I needed to reinforce the wards on my office, buy a desk, unpack, and get organized. I also needed to start advertising my services. I scowled. The Mage Council had been quick to distance themselves from me after firing me for saving Samael's life, spreading the word of my "betrayal" far and wide.

Luckily, I had some money up my sleeve. Mariam, the light fae representative, had paid me a hundred thousand dollars for finding some missing fae artifacts and saving her ass.

After I'd paid for the invisibility spell for the rowan arrow hanging around my neck, I'd had enough to set up my business and pay Keigan rent for my office for the next few months.

Then I was on my own.

Hence why I was unpacking and organizing at 9:30 p.m. The sooner I got this stuff unpacked, the sooner I could advertise my services and take meetings in here.

"Uh, hello?"

I'd left the door open to get some fresh air circulating in the office. Now, two women stood in the doorway, both of them gazing at the cramped, cluttered space.

From the matching orange-red of their hair and freckles, it was clear they were related.

Not sisters. Mother and daughter. The woman on the left had her arm wrapped around the older woman's shoulders, and both of them looked exhausted. The older woman's face was ravaged with grief, while her daughter's jaw was set in a way that told me she was barely holding it together.

"Can I help you?"

"You're Danica Amana," the older woman said almost dreamily, as if she was speaking from far away. Someone had given her a sedative.

I smiled. "It's 'Ah-muh-nuh.'"

"I'm sorry. We're looking for your help. You helped the light fae find those artifacts. And you found out who was killing Samael's demons."

"Yes."

"I should probably introduce myself." She gave a long, slow blink. "My name is Maeve Walsh, and this is my daughter Siobhan."

I glanced around. I didn't even have a chair to offer her, but my office had a small, attached kitchen. "Can I get you some water?"

"No thank you, I'm fine."

Siobhan squeezed her mom's shoulders and leveled a frank stare at me. "My sister has gone missing, and we need your help."

A solitary tear tracked down Maeve's cheek. With nothing else to offer, I pushed a couple boxes out of the way and sat on the floor, gesturing for them to do the same. "Why don't you tell me what happened?"

They both sat down, and Siobhan crossed her legs in front of her, studying my face intently. "We're members of the Allen coven."

I frowned, trying to place the name, but it must be a

small enough coven that I hadn't heard of it before.

"We're not large." Siobhan nodded. "Not even particularly powerful. We keep to ourselves. But we're a family. My sister is one of the most powerful witches in our coven. She'd never want to take a leadership position, but using her magic has always come easily to her."

Since I was watching for it, I caught the way Siobhan's eyes flickered at the words. A hint of jealousy there. As the sister of a witch who had also found it second nature to use her power, I got it. But I noted it anyway.

"My daughter has never been in any trouble," Maeve said. "She's a good girl."

I glanced at Siobhan. We both knew siblings told each other things that they would otherwise keep from their mothers. Especially sisters. She shook her head at me. Okay, so her sister wasn't secretly running wild.

"Riona went missing two days ago. No one has seen her since."

"How do you know it was two days ago?"

"That was the last time I talked to her, and we speak every day."

"Have you reported her disappearance to the human authorities?"

She nodded. "They've started an investigation, but we both know a witch will be at the bottom of the priority list."

Yeah. Unfortunately, while witches were technically human, most of the time, the human authorities focused their attention on humans without power.

"Please," Maeve said. "Will you help us? We have money."

I glanced around at the boxes. "As you can see, I'm kind of still getting this business off the ground. More importantly, I've never worked on a missing persons case. It would probably be a better idea for you to work with an investigator with missing persons experience."

Siobhan shook her head. "As soon as Riona went missing, I thought of you. I watched you on the news when the McCormick coven was harnessing demon power. And I heard about how you found all those artifacts for the fae. You were raised human, but you know the paranormal world. And unlike the human police, you give a shit. Besides, you traced and hunted bad guys, right? Is a missing persons case really that different?"

Yes. It definitely was.

I opened my mouth and snapped it closed at the desolate expression on Maeve's face.

"I'll look for her," I said, because how the hell could I not? "Is Riona dating anyone?"

"Not seriously. She was seeing a mage for a few weeks, but you can imagine how well *that* ended." Siobhan sniffed. "He was terrified someone he knew would find out he was with a witch, and he broke up with her before the relationship could even get off the ground."

I'd seen that before. My filthy half-witch blood had been allowed to walk the hallowed halls of the Mage Council only because I was a contractor. And because as far as everyone had known—myself included—my other half was human.

Low-level mages who were hoping to eventually get access to the mysterious power the Mage Council kept classified? They were expected to keep their personal life pristine. That meant no rubbing up against anyone who wasn't either a mage or human.

"What's his name?"

"Um. Jerry, I think. Let me check our messages." She pulled up her phone. Next to her, her mom stared blankly at the wall, and I wished again that I could offer her a cup of coffee or something.

"Yeah," Siobhan said. "Jerry."

"I know Jerry a little," I said. "I don't think he'd hurt Riona, but I'll talk to him. Take me through Riona's schedule the week before she went missing."

"She doesn't live at the coven's main house. None of us do," Maeve said. "I've been thinking about moving in, now that my children are grown and have lives of their own. But Riona has her own apartment. She always loved her independence."

I glanced at Siobhan. "What about you? Do you live alone?"

She held up her hand, and the rock on her finger caught the light. "I'm engaged. Riona was supposed to be at the party. That's how I knew something had happened. I hadn't heard from her on Friday, but I was busy with a new case at work—I'm an attorney. But when she didn't show at my engagement party on Saturday, I knew something was wrong. She never would've missed it." Tears filled her eyes, and she struggled to speak for a moment. Her mom took her hand and squeezed.

"I'm okay," Siobhan said, taking a deep breath. Then she looked at me. "Do you have a sister?"

"Yes."

"So, you know. No matter how mad you are about

the little things—occasional jealousies, old wounds, new annoyances…you show up when it counts. Riona never would've missed that party. Not unless she was hurt…or worse."

"When was the last time you heard from her?"

"Ah, she texted me on…Thursday?"

Siobhan handed over her phone.

Buying new dress for Saturday. Will Cam's hot friend be there?

Siobhan had replied a few minutes later. *He will. And according to the little birdy I'm marrying, he's into you. Spring for the matching heels, sis. You deserve it.*

Riona had sent back a line of heart-eyed emojis and used a charm that made them jump out of the phone and dance in the air above the message. We all watched them for a moment. Cute.

"Cam is your fiancé?"

"Yeah."

"Does Riona have any problems with him?"

Her eyebrows rose. "No. I mean, I think she finds him a little dull, to be honest. He's an attorney as well. Property law. But he's good to me, and she knows that."

"Was she having problems with anyone else?"

"No. Riona's a few years younger than me— she's only twenty-three. She likes to party, enjoys men, and attends coven meetings whenever she can."

"What does she do for a living?"

"Everything. She walks dogs, runs errands, drives for Uber and Lyft. She's always wanted to be an author, and she's been working on her novel for the last year or so. She said all the jobs were worth it if it meant she had a shot of living her dream."

"Does she have a schedule or calendar anywhere?"

"In her phone, probably. But she'd have that with her. I think maybe her calendar is synched to her work laptop."

"Do you have keys to her apartment?"

"Yes." She reached into her purse and handed them to me.

"I'm going to go take a look tomorrow. In the meantime, you guys can help by writing down everything you know about what she was doing in the days leading up to her disappearance. Anyone she was having problems with. Any guys who she'd broken up with recently, any difficult clients, anyone in the coven holding a grudge. Even if it doesn't seem important, note it down anyway."

"Thank you," Maeve said quietly. "Thank you so much."

"If the cops tell me to back off, I'll probably have to," I warned. "I don't work for the Mage Council anymore, so I don't have any jurisdiction."

"You have the demons."

I winced. "Not exactly. Listen, if you're here 'cause you think I can call up an army of demons to help…"

"We don't," Siobhan said. "We'll make you that list."

She got to her feet, and we all turned at another knock on my door.

Nathaniel poked his head in and nodded at Siobhan and Maeve. What the hell was he doing here?

Siobhan gaped at me. "Is that…"

"Yup." The werewolf Alpha in all his glory. I walked them out, and Siobhan took a good, long look at the Alpha.

I couldn't blame her. He was built like a Greek god, and he radiated both dominance and threat. Even a happily engaged woman couldn't help but notice.

Nathaniel nodded at the two women as they left. Then he sauntered in and sat down on the floor. He stretched out his long legs and glanced around my office. "I like what you've done with the place."

I merely raised one eyebrow. Seeing the werewolf Alpha out of his territory was a surreal experience.

Of course, the sheer alpha-ness of Nathaniel meant that if anyone walked into my office, they'd immediately assume it was his territory. The thought made me scowl.

"Danica?"

"Sorry. How can I help?"

"I have a proposition for you."

"What kind of proposition?"

"I'd like you to hire one of my wolves."

I gaped at him and gestured at the boxes. "Look, as you can see, this is a party for one. I can't afford to hire anyone until I have some money coming in the door."

His gaze stayed steady on my face. He wasn't giving me his alpha stare, but it still took everything in me to meet his eyes anyway. I suppressed the urge to tap into my power and give him a run for his money.

Werewolves.

He smiled slightly. "You don't need to pay her. Think of her like an intern."

"Why, exactly, do you need me to hire her? There must be plenty of places she could work if she needed a job."

"Kyla is a female werewolf."

"Explain to me exactly what that means."

He gave me a cool look at the order and I refrained from rolling my eyes.

"Female wolves are exceedingly rare. Think one-in-a-million. She's too dominant to be ignored, she's bored, and she's challenging male wolves above her in the pack hierarchy. Their responses range from refusing to fight a female to deciding to teach her a lesson."

"So she's a werewolf with authority issues and you thought *I* would be a calming, level-headed influence?"

He laughed. "That may be a bit much to ask."

"Look, Nathaniel, I'm the last person who should be working with anyone who has problems taking orders. Especially if you're hoping for her to level out some."

He smiled slightly at that. "Many of my wolves have positions working for human security companies or as firefighters and police officers. However, they have all been wolves for at least a decade. Their self-control is excellent."

"Kyla's isn't?"

"It is. However, she has been a werewolf for less than two years. She wishes she didn't need the pack, resents my authority, and craves a return to her normal life. She has threatened to leave the pack."

"That would make her a lone wolf."

Nathaniel nodded. "A female lone wolf is unheard of. She would be hunted by feral wolves looking for a mate."

"I'm assuming she's not an idiot. Why would she risk that?"

"As she likes to tell me, Kyla had a life before she

was changed. A good one. And now she is expected to follow the rules of someone she doesn't particularly respect."

I winced. As someone who was technically under a demon's authority right now, I could relate.

Nathaniel's gaze dropped to the intricate gold mark on my arm. The mark that proclaimed me as belonging to Samael himself.

He nodded. "I think it would be good for Kyla to see you working within the confines of Samael's authority."

I gritted my teeth at that. "As you've just reminded me, I live with Samael's *authority* hanging over my head. And I'm doing everything I can to remove that authority."

Nathaniel smiled. "I think you will get on well with my wolf."

"I don't have enough work for her."

"A missing person case will take a lot of grunt work."

So, he'd caught that. Werewolf hearing. But he was right, damn him.

I sighed. "I can't afford to pay her more than minimum wage. Human minimum wage."

"That's more than acceptable. Give her a chance. Make her see that she can have a place in this world. That becoming a werewolf doesn't have to mean her life is over."

I chewed on my lower lip. It wasn't like Nathaniel to put himself in anyone's debt, and I'd be an idiot to miss out on the opportunity.

But teaching a werewolf the ropes… It sounded like a lot of work.

"You'll owe me," I finally said. "You'll owe me big."

Nathaniel smiled. "I will."

He practically radiated satisfaction, the same way a certain demon did whenever he'd maneuvered me into a corner. I was ornery enough that his satisfaction made me want to immediately rescind my agreement.

Nathaniel got to his feet and offered his hand. "Thank you, Danica."

"She's on a trial," I said as I stood. "If she turns out to be a huge pain in my ass, she's gone."

He nodded. "Fair enough." His thumb blurred as he sent a text and within moments, he was opening the door to my office and murmuring to someone outside.

A gorgeous woman elbowed her way past him and stalked into my office, offering her hand.

"Hi," she said. "I'm Kyla."

I eyed her as I shook her hand. She eyed me back. She was a little taller than me, but fine boned in a way that made her seem almost delicate. Her skin was a rich, creamy brown I could never achieve no matter how much I baked myself in the sun, and her bright blue eyes were sharp and alert.

"Danica," I said.

My phone vibrated and I fished it out of my pocket. Evie was calling. It was almost 11:00pm and a pit of dread formed in my stomach.

"I'm sorry," I said, "I have to take this."

Both wolves nodded and moved toward my office door. It was a nice gesture, but they'd be able to hear whatever Evie said even if she was whispering on the other end of the phone.

"Evie?"

"You have to come. Please. They're dead. They're all dead."

Every muscle in my body tensed. "Who, Evie?"

She was sobbing, hyperventilating. "The coven. Come. Please."

I jolted, my body suddenly on full alert. She had to be mistaken.

"I'll be right there."

My eyes met Nathaniel's. His eyes had turned an eerie blue. "I'll come with you," he said.

If my sister was in danger, I'd be an idiot to turn down the werewolf Alpha. I glanced at Kyla and she nodded.

"Fine." I said. "Let's go."

CHAPTER TWO

Danica

The coven was based in Trinity Park— deep in witch territory. Flames engulfed the house, licking at the roof as smoke thick enough to choke on filled the air.

Human firefighters were already working to put out the flames, while a circle of witches I recognized as some of the coven's neighbors were standing nearby. They chanted softly, doing what they could to starve the fire of oxygen.

The house had been painted a butter yellow with white trim. The yellow was no more. What hadn't yet burned was black with smoke and soot, and a creaking sound wrenched through the air before a chunk of what was once the roof of the porch collapsed.

My stomach swam sickly. Anyone still in that house was likely dead.

I ignored the wolves as I frantically searched faces. Where the hell was Evie?

"Danica," Nathaniel's voice was low, and he pointed toward a fire truck. Evie sat in the back, her face ashen as she stared at the house.

Her gaze met mine, her face crumbling as she choked on another sob.

"They're gone," she said. "I think they're all gone, Dani."

I hauled her into my arms, stroking her hair. She could've been in that house. She could have been in that fucking house.

Evie coughed and I leaned back as a paramedic handed her the face mask she'd dropped.

"You need oxygen," he told her. She held it up to her face and her eyes turned blank as she gazed past me to the burning house.

A cop in plain clothes walked toward us, casting a wary look at Nathaniel as he approached Evie. It was unlikely that he knew he was within a few feet of the werewolf Alpha, but his instincts still warned him Nathaniel was a predator.

The cop introduced himself as Detective Trevor Roberts. "I'd like to take your statement if you feel up to giving it," he said to Evie.

I opened my mouth to object, but she nodded, a tear rolling down her cheek.

"Do you live in the house?"

She nodded again and he made a note on his notepad.

"And what time did you arrive back here?"

"About 11:00pm."

"Where were you tonight?"

"I'm dating a wolf from Nathaniel's pack," she said, glancing at me and then away. I attempted to ignore the stab of hurt that burrowed into my gut. Evie hadn't mentioned that she was seeing anyone when we had lunch last week.

"Name?"

"Liam…" she trailed off. "I can't remember his last name. I don't know what's wrong with me."

"You're in shock," I said. I glanced at the cop. "Does she have to do this now?"

"It would be best," he said, shooting me an unfriendly look. "I understand this is difficult."

He didn't understand, not really. Everyone in that house was Evie's family. Her words from one of our last arguments played on a loop in my head.

"Gemma was there when I got my first period. Noelle bought me chocolate when my first boyfriend broke my heart. Ainsley taught me how to ward."

Around a third of the coven were based in that house. Evie had lived with them since she was fourteen. And if they'd been inside, they were likely dead.

"Liam O'Connor," Nathaniel's voice was a low growl. His expression was carefully neutral as he approached us. But Roberts still shot him a wary look, instinctively averting his gaze and writing the name down as Nathaniel spoke. Roberts was too jumpy to do this job. Nathaniel's wolf likely saw him as prey.

"O'Connor," Evie murmured. "That's right."

Her eyes met Nathaniel's for a single moment and he nodded at her before turning to stalk away.

"Lia was in the house," Evie said, her eyes meeting mine. "I was supposed to keep her safe. I'm sorry."

My chest tightened and Evie wiped at the tears dripping down her face. I squeezed past Roberts and wrapped my arm around her shoulders.

For a moment I couldn't speak.

After one too many late nights, I'd decided I was a bad cat mom and given Lia to Evie to look after. I visited a few times a week, but now she was likely dead. If I'd just kept her, she'd currently be sleeping in my apartment.

Grief stabbed into my chest and twisted but I managed to swallow around the lump in my throat. I would mourn our sassy little cat later. "Don't think about that right now."

"What happened when you returned?" Roberts asked Evie.

"I smelled smoke as soon as I got out of the car a few blocks away. I ran toward the house. People were standing outside. They were just staring. A few of them had already started trying to fight the fire with their magic, but fire is the most difficult element to harness. I had some idea about running in and dragging them out."

She stared at the house. "I opened the door and something exploded. I guess it… knocked me out because when I opened my eyes, there was nothing but fire. Why didn't the smoke alarms warn them? Why did the wards fail?"

"We'll be investigating," was all Roberts said. "What happened when you came to?"

"I was screaming. One of the neighbors— Delia— pulled me up, told me she'd called the fire department and I needed to get away from the house. I tried to go in, but it was too hot. I tried…" her voice trailed off and she stared at me in horror. "If I'd gotten back earlier, I could've saved them."

I shook my head. "You don't know that, Evie. If

you'd been in that house, you'd likely be dead right now."

Her eyes were glassy, her face so pale she looked almost translucent. I glanced at the cop. "Are we done here?"

He ignored me. "I'll need your details in case I have any follow-up questions."

Evie rattled off her phone number and Roberts noted it down.

"Where will you be staying?"

She gave him a long, slow blink.

"With me," I said. I gave him the address for my apartment and Evie simply nodded, her gaze darting back to the house.

The flames were dying down now. Kyla appeared at my elbow and I glanced at her. She nodded toward my sister and then gestured for me to follow her.

"I'll be right back," I told Evie.

"I've been doing some eavesdropping," Kyla said. Her face was dark with soot. "It's definitely arson. Looks like the smoke alarms were disabled, and the fire burned too hot and too fast to be electrical."

I closed my eyes. I'd known it was arson as soon as I'd seen the house, but I'd hoped I was wrong.

"What are the police saying?"

"There's a fire investigator on scene. He's been writing his notes on a notepad. I can steal it if you want."

Despite the subject, I chuckled. Looked like Kyla was going to work out as my intern.

"That's okay for now. If you could hang around and keep listening, that would be awesome."

She nodded and melted away again. Across the

street, Nathaniel was talking to a firefighter. The burly guy lowered his head submissively in a way that told me he was one of Nathaniel's wolves.

"Dani?" Evie's voice was thin and thready as I walked back and sat next to her.

I took her hand and squeezed. "Yeah?"

"Do you think you could ask Samael to help?"

I winced. Demons had an affinity with fire. It was a good idea, but Evie didn't know what she was asking. For some strange reason, she often had hearts in her eyes when she talked about me and Samael.

It had been a few weeks since I'd seen the winged pain in my ass. The invisible arrow I'd hung around my neck felt suddenly heavy. The arrow contained rowan—the only known vulnerability when it came to high demons.

On top of the arrow, I wore a lanyard which held my Benchmade Nimvarus Cub II— one of my favorite knives. The lanyard was studded with real diamonds and had been given to me by the same high demon who'd driven me to protect myself by wearing the arrow.

Our relationship was complicated.

The truth was, he'd hurt me. Deeply. When I first met the demon, I was terrified and furious. Slowly but surely, he'd chipped away at my fear, until I'd realized he would never harm me.

Physically.

He'd sure as hell hurt me emotionally.

I didn't trust easily, and for a brief moment, we had something real. I'd hated demons, but he'd slowly cut through all my defenses and I'd allowed myself to…

hope.

I don't know what I'd been thinking. You don't *date* a man like Samael. He'd been alive for longer than I could comprehend. I was hopelessly out of my depth with him, and he'd toyed with me. He'd probably enjoyed keeping me ignorant about who and what I really was.

My jaw ached and I forced myself to stop grinding my teeth. At this rate, I'd need to see a dentist. One more thing to blame the demon for.

I sighed. Evie was still looking at me with a dull hope in her eyes. I'd only just gotten my sister back and she'd lost almost everyone she loved. If this was what she needed, I'd tuck my metaphorical tail between my legs and ask the demon for help.

I had no doubt he'd make me pay dearly for that help.

"I need you to tell me if you've noticed anyone hanging around the coven. Or the house itself. Someone you didn't recognize."

Evie's lips parted slightly. "You're going to find out who did this."

"I'll try my best. For now, I need a list of everyone who was in the house. We need to figure out if the coven was targeted as a whole, or if the killer specifically wanted one of them dead."

Evie nodded, her gaze turning blank again. "Gemma and some of the others went to New York to meet with a coven we've been exchanging spells with. Out of the witches who stayed behind and who lived in the house, I'm one of the most powerful. I should've been here."

Relief made my shoulders slump. The fire didn't get all of them then. While a healthy percentage of the coven lived in that house, the fact that they weren't all home was good news.

Tears streamed from Evie's eyes and I wrapped my arms around her as sobs tore through her body.

"I can't believe I wasn't here," she croaked out.

I eased away. "Listen to me. No, seriously, listen. This isn't your fault. Whoever did this, they would've been watching this place for a while. They picked a time when Gemma and the others would be gone."

This was the most powerful coven in Durham, and the witches who'd been slaughtered had been either knocked out somehow or trapped in a way that left them unable to use their powers. How the hell had the murderer accomplished that?

"Evie?"

I turned as a group of witches approached, automatically scanning and memorizing their faces. As far as I was concerned, anyone who hadn't burned to death was officially a suspect.

A witch I'd only spoken to a few times shuffled over to me. She'd joined the coven after I left, and for the life of me, I couldn't remember her name.

"I'm Freya," she said.

"Danica."

I glanced around. There were a bunch of witches from the coven standing on the street, many of them dressed in pajamas and robes, horror and grief written across their faces. A few of them walked over to Evie, talking in low murmurs.

"What do we know?"

I glanced at Freya. "Nothing yet. Does the coven

have any enemies who might've targeted the house?"

She shook her head, her eyes on the blackened destruction. "Not that I know of. I'm not exactly in the inner circle though. You'll want to talk to Gemma for that. She's getting on a plane from New York now."

A whoosh of air, a flap of wings, and Vas was suddenly standing next to me. Everyone in the vicinity went silent and most of the witches backed away, their expressions distrustful.

"I heard what happened. Thought I'd stop by and see if I could help."

"Actually, you can," I said before Evie could say anything. "Are you able to walk through the house tomorrow and examine it?"

He nodded. "Sure, if it helps. You'll want Samael to take a look though. He's much, much better than I am with fire."

I could feel Evie's eyes on me and I sighed. "I'll go see him tonight."

"He's not at the tower."

I blinked. He was always in the tower. "Where is he?"

"Away on business with some of the others. He's due back tomorrow morning."

"Okay. Tomorrow morning then." I glanced at the paramedic who was checking my sister's chest. He nodded at me.

"Rest and fluids."

Evie slowly got to her feet. "I don't want to leave yet."

"Okay."

We stood and watched as the firefighters conquered the blaze. At one point, I felt eyes on me and glanced around.

Hannah. Of course.

The black witch lived a few streets away, and I wasn't at all surprised to see her smiling merrily at the flames. If Evie saw the pleased look on her face, she was liable to punch her right in the throat, and I wouldn't blame her.

I left Evie with Vas, making my way through the gathering crowd to where Hannah was feeding on all the shock, pain, and anger.

Her curly, white hair was covered with a scarf, and she was using a walker, which I knew damn well she didn't need. But who was going to tell a defenseless old lady to move along when she'd come out to see what was happening in her neighborhood?

She glanced at me as I approached, and my expression must have told her exactly what I was thinking, because she raised one eyebrow, her watery eyes steady on my face.

My voice was very quiet. "Enjoying your dinner?"

"There's no need to be snarky, halfling. It would have been wasteful not to pay a visit. Besides, you've benefited from the spells I create with such power a time or two."

She had me there. While I'd always be creeped out by the way black witches fed on pain and suffering, I'd hired Hannah a few times when I'd needed someone with her expertise.

"Did you see anything when you got here? Anyone who looked a little too interested in the fire?"

She shook her head. "Whoever created the flames

was long gone. A shame, really. It was a beautiful house."

Now it was a house full of dead bodies. Trust Hannah to care more about the loss of the building than the people.

I left the black witch staring at the flames, her light-blue eyes glowing as she gathered the power. Waste not, want not.

And when, exactly, had I become so accepting about the way she fed?

Probably around the same time I'd started seeing Samael. My moral foundation was becoming increasingly shaky.

I made my way back to Evie, and we watched the flames together. There was nothing to say. All I could do was stand next to her as a silent support.

Finally, when there was nothing left but smoke, Kyla approached. She cast a sympathetic look at my sister and then leaned close to murmur in my ear.

"You may want to take her home. They'll be bringing out body bags soon. I'm going to stay and watch out for lookie-loos who seemed a little too entranced with the fire." Her eyes gleamed. "I watch enough TV to know arsonists often return to the scene of the crime."

I wasn't going to be able to justify treating Kyla as an intern. She was already proving herself. "Thank you. If you could meet me at my apartment in the morning, that would be great. Nathaniel probably has the address."

Kyla nodded.

"I appreciate it."

I walked Evie toward my car, pausing as Nathaniel approached. His eyes were very light, a sign he was finding it difficult to control his wolf. I wasn't entirely sure what the werewolf Alpha was still doing here, but people were beginning to send him wary looks. Their fear likely wasn't helping Nathaniel keep his furry self hidden away.

He took Evie's hand in his. "I'm glad you're okay."

She nodded, her gaze darting up to his face and then away. "Thank you."

Evie got into the car and I glanced at Nathaniel. "I'd like to talk to Liam."

I didn't think he was a suspect, but if he was dating Evie, maybe he'd notice if anyone had been hanging around the coven. Wolves had superior instincts.

Nathaniel angled his head in a way that was all wolf. "I'll make sure he's at the pack house when you're ready to speak to him."

He turned and loped away. I blew out a breath and got into my car, glancing at Evie. Her face was still pale, and she was staring at the burnt remains of her home.

I opened my mouth, but I had no idea what to say. Snapping it closed, I turned the key and slowly drove past the emergency vehicles still parked along the narrow street.

By the time we arrived at my apartment, each of Evie's blinks was longer than the next.

We were silent as we took the elevator up and I glanced at her as I unlocked the door.

"I'm not going to fall apart," she said wearily.

"I wouldn't blame you if you did."

I opened the door and pulled off my boots, before padding across the wide space that served as the living room and into my bedroom. My apartment was once a textile mill, and I adored the large rooms and tall ceilings.

"You can take the bed," I called out. "I'll just change the sheets."

"Don't bother. The sofa is fine."

I poked my head out the door. Evie had already crawled onto the sofa, fully dressed except for her shoes. I searched through my closest until I located a spare pillow and comforter and handed them to her.

"Can I get you anything?"

She blinked up at me, her eyes wet. "I could use a hug."

"Of course."

I leaned down and wrapped my arms around her. She shook silently with sobs and my own eyes burned.

"You're going to find whoever did this, right?"

I leaned back enough to see Evie's face. It looked ravaged by grief.

"You bet your ass I will. And when I do, they're going to pay. I promise."

Samael

"What do you have?" I asked Agaliarept as soon as he walked into the suite of the hotel. I had never been overly fond of Miami, although Ag seemed to enjoy it every time he came down here, spending as much time as possible at the beach.

Today though, he was scowling.

"Sit down, Ag," Lilith ordered, pulling her feet closer

to her so he could sit on the sofa.

He shrugged and sat. "My sources say Lucifer is doing everything he can to reverse his tie to the underworld without losing the power that binds him to the throne."

"Not unexpected," I said. It was the one place where we held the upper hand. Lucifer took my grandfather's throne by foul means, but he hadn't wielded enough power to hold it. So he'd bargained with the underworld itself. But I had no doubt that he'd be doing everything he could to remove that tie and hunt my little witch.

I couldn't even go to the underworld myself to challenge him. When Lucifer bound himself to the throne, sacrificing his ability to leave, he also sacrificed part of his power to restrict my abilities. That meant I was unable to access the power of the underworld while I was there. If I returned now, I would be as powerless as a human– unless I could kill Lucifer.

"You've been making plans," Lilith purred at my silence.

I got up to prowl the room. "The amulet that transported Danica to the library in the pocket realm gave me an idea."

Ag went still. My biggest struggle, and the flaw in all my plans, was my inability to use my alliance with Finvarra. He was willing to lend us his forces, but Lucifer had spent centuries building up his defenses, and if I attempted to get the dark fae army past Lucifer's sentries and guards and into the underworld, it was likely that the war would be fought far from Lucifer's palace.

My palace.

"I need a pocket realm attached to an artifact. One large enough to hold a few hundred thousand fae and demon warriors. And I need someone trusted enough by Lucifer to carry it with them into the palace."

Lilith raised one eyebrow. "Most of those artifacts are hidden deep in the light fae realm."

"Yes. And we need to find them."

"A few of the seelie owe me favors." She frowned. "Give me a few weeks to see if I can call them in."

Bael walked in. "Problems in Durham," he announced. "Danica's sister's coven has gone up in flames. Evelyn is safe," he assured me as I got to my feet. "Our people on the ground said she's waiting for her sister right at this minute."

"We leave tonight."

Ag shot me a pitying look but said nothing. I ground my teeth, well aware of what he thought of my obsession with the little witch.

"And then what?" Bael asked.

And then I would wait for her to come to me. Bael shook his head at whatever he saw on my face.

"Do you want her?"

"Of course I want her."

"Then you need to show her who you are."

I scowled at him. I was a demon with an obsession with vengeance and a penchant for turning my enemies to ash. That's who I was.

He heaved a sigh. "All she knows about you is that you compel her to do things she doesn't want to do and she can't escape a bond she never wanted."

Bitterness clogged my throat. If I had known who Danica was, who she would become to me, would I have risked her hatred by bonding her to me?

"What is it that you suggest?"

Ag shifted on the sofa but wisely kept his mouth shut.

Bael angled his head. "So far you have allowed her to skip Monday dinners. This gives her an excuse not to spend time in your company."

"That comes perilously close to forcing her again."

A shrug. "You are, after all, still a demon."

Yes, I was still a demon.

Lilith stretched like a cat in the sun across the room and I glanced at her.

"You have something to say?"

"Men," she said. "Always so black and white. All or nothing."

"Get to the point, Lilith."

She smiled. "You're forgetting that for most of her life, your little witch was raised as a human."

"And?"

"And humans like romance."

"Romance?"

She shook her head at me. "No need for that terror-stricken expression. Danica is, after all, the woman you want to be with, correct?"

I shifted, grinding my teeth. "Yes."

"But you've never taken the time to woo her. To romance her."

I frowned. "You believe these are the kinds of things human women enjoy?"

She shot a glance at Bael, who was very carefully not looking at her. "All women want to feel seen. Especially human women. Prove that you *know* her."

"At the very least," Bael said, "she won't be able to continue pretending you don't exist."

CHAPTER THREE

Danica

Early the next morning, I left Evie sleeping and drove to the 2000-foot-high tower that served as both Samael's home, and the headquarters for many of his various businesses.

Bael was standing in the lobby, chatting with a demon I'd never seen before. While most demons tended to have darker hair, Bael's white-blond hair stuck out like a beacon, and he kept it long enough to brush his shoulders. His eyes were the color of a frozen pond. The demon could occasionally see glimpses of the future, and he'd once told me that he couldn't see anything around me except pain.

Our relationship was a work in progress.

A group of unseelie were sitting on the new long, black sofas in the lobby, while several other armed fae gave me hard stares as I walked in. Why were so many fae guards here? I raised one eyebrow as I met Bael's eyes. He merely shrugged.

"He's in a meeting," Bael told me as I pressed the elevator button.

I took the elevator to Samael's penthouse and waited in his living room as I answered emails on my phone.

Finally, the door to his office opened and my eyes met burnished gold. The unseelie king smiled, and the hair on the back of my neck stood up. That explained the guards in the lobby.

"Danica Amana."

"Your Majesty."

"Please," he said. "Call me Fin."

He'd asked me to call him that once before. But the chances of me calling the dark fae king 'Fin' were slightly lower than the chances of me doing a strip tease on Main Street.

Samael appeared behind him, and I resisted looking at him for as long as I could as the two men murmured a few words and Finvarra strolled out.

Finally, it was just me and the demon.

Samael stepped back and allowed me to walk past him and into his office. I silently cursed him as his citrus and cedar scent wound up my nostrils, my thighs clenching as my mind took me back to the feel of his—

That was enough of that.

I took a seat, watching as he did the same. He leaned back in his seat, his silver gaze on my face.

He looked endlessly amused, and it pissed me off. His wings were hidden away, his clothes covered almost every inch of his hard body, but whenever I looked at him, all I saw was that hard body covering mine, the wicked lust on his face as he thrust into me.

"Danica?"

Our eyes met again and he smiled. He knew exactly what he did to me.

"I'm sure you heard what happened last night."

He nodded. "I did. I'm sorry I wasn't there."

"Where were you?"

Surprise flashed across his face and I shook my head. "Never mind." It was none of my business where the hell the demon was, and pretending to care would likely just give him ideas.

"Miami," he said.

I nodded, my gaze flicking past him to the glass doors which opened to a wide balcony. Outside, demons flew through the air, coming and going from the tower, their invisible wings making it appear like they were floating.

"What is it that you need, Danica?"

"I came here to ask you to help with the investigation."

"Is this a favor for you or your sister?"

"Both."

"Ah. Your sister asked you for my help, and you buried your pride long enough to come to me."

I stayed silent. He let out a low chuckle, the sound coated with a layer of bitterness.

"Of course, you would never ask for my help if not for your sister, isn't that right?"

"You lied to me."

He shook his head, raising one eyebrow. He looked remarkably composed. The last time we'd talked about this, he'd seethed with frustration. The emotion had almost humanized him for a few brief moments. He didn't look close to human now.

A few weeks ago, I'd discovered a human hate group who were hunting ancient fae artifacts. My friend Gary had almost been killed when the hate group traced a light fae amulet to his store. We'd recovered the artifacts. But the moment I touched the amulet. I'd been transported through a portal to a library.

At first, it was a good time. The library was filled with ancient demon lore, and I snooped until I found a bunch of books detailing Samael's history.

Unfortunately, those weren't the only books in that library.

As soon as I'd laid eyes on the book containing The Nephilim Prophecy, it was as if my body was no longer my own. No matter how much I fought the compulsion, I'd eventually opened the book and read the prophecy.

When the Morning Star goes to war with the Nephilim of his bloodline, only one shall survive.

I was the Nephilim, and my grandfather was Lucifer himself. The same man responsible for the slaughter of Samael's entire family and the theft of *his* grandfather's throne.

Opening the book had alerted Lucifer that I was alive. That meant that his people would be hunting me.

As if that wasn't bad enough, Samael had known who I was. Known, and kept it hidden from me.

Samael got to his feet, rounded his desk, and leaned against it, his gaze steady on my face.

"We will talk about this. And my reasons— which are valid. But I will wait until you are not so distracted. I will investigate this arson," Samael said. "I will visit the scene this morning."

I closed my eyes. Some small part of me had hoped he'd refuse, if only to keep me from needing to spend any time with him.

I tensed as he stepped closer. Samael did nothing without some kind of bargain.

"In return," he murmured into my ear, and I could feel him smile as my breath caught in my throat. "You will move into my tower."

I spun, my mouth dropping open. His gaze fell to my mouth and his eyes darkened.

"You've got to be kidding."

He shrugged and walked back to his desk as if unconcerned.

I let out a strangled sound. "Let's negotiate."

"Those are my terms."

My hands were fisted so tight, my nails were cutting into my palms. "Your terms suck."

He raised one eyebrow. His expression was the exact combination of boredom and languid amusement he knew I loathed.

"Directly after learning about the prophecy, you made me show you my memories of your mother's body," he said silkily.

I closed my eyes. "Stop."

Of course the demon ignored me. He'd never been big on respecting anyone's boundaries.

"You wanted me to hurt you. You wanted to prove to yourself that you shouldn't trust me."

"And I was right."

My eyes shot open as his scent beckoned me. He was suddenly too close. I took a careful step back. "Look. I just got Evie moved into my apartment. I can't leave her."

"You may wait until the investigation is concluded, however as of now, your attendance at Monday dinners is mandatory."

I scowled. Anyone bonded to Samael was expected at Monday dinners, and the idea of sitting that close to him for that long made me want to stab him with a fork. So far, I've only attended one. The demon knew exactly how I felt about him using words like 'mandatory,' and I wouldn't give him the reaction he wanted.

He raised one eyebrow at my silence. "I promise, it won't be as painful as you're imagining."

"Sure it won't," I muttered, barely resisting kicking out at his desk. Today was Monday, which meant I was going to have to somehow work his dinner in with everything else I had going on.

"If I move in here, I want my own room."

He made a noncommittal sound and I let out a low growl. "Why am I always on the back foot with you?"

Surprise flickered in his eyes and he slowly raised his hand, giving me enough time to block it if I wanted to. His warm hand cupped my face.

"You missed me," he said. His expression was hard, but his eyes glittered at me. "Say it."

I squirmed. He simply waited me out. "Samael–"

"Give me something, Danica."

I glowered at him, pushing his hand away.

"I missed you," I snapped before I was aware I was speaking. "I always miss you. Even when I shouldn't. But that doesn't mean anything. I can't trust you."

I wanted to slap my hand over my mouth. To rewind time and have a redo of the last few seconds.

Triumph, victory, arrogance, it all flashed across his face.

"You will forgive me for not telling you about the prophecy," he declared.

"I can't do that."

"You *won't*. There's a difference." He shrugged like it was unimportant. "But I'm a patient man."

I snorted. "We both know that's a lie."

His eyes lit with humor and I glanced away. When he was like this— when it was just me and him and nothing else to interfere, it was impossible not to be charmed. I'd reluctantly lusted for Samael from the moment I'd met him, but when I ignored all the history between us, I enjoyed simply spending time with him.

And I was a sucker. It was only a matter of time before he screwed me over again.

"My patience only stretches so far, little witch. I'm tired of watching you fight your feelings for me."

I narrowed my eyes at him.

"You're forgetting I've known you for less than six months. It takes longer than that to come to terms with any feelings I may or may not have."

His silver eyes gleamed. "Ah, Danica. We both know those feelings exist. But I will only wait for so long."

"And then what? You'll leave me alone?"

He slowly shook his head. "Never."

I didn't think I wanted to know what the alternative was.

"I'll go with you to the scene," he said, jolting me from my thoughts.

"When?"

"Now." He pressed a button on his phone. "Reschedule this morning's meetings."

"Yes sir," his assistant's voice was surprised.

I sighed. And just like that, he dropped everything to help me. Was it any wonder I was constantly off balance with the guy?

"We will fly," he said. I opened my mouth to argue, and he simply ignored me, throwing open the balcony doors.

"Why don't I take my car? There's no need for you to haul me around when I can meet you there."

He smiled over his shoulder at me. "Ah, but I so enjoy hauling you around. Why rob myself of the small pleasures in life?"

His mood had improved. And why wouldn't it? He'd gotten everything he wanted. Again.

His eyes glittered. "It's not often I get to see you pout. It makes me want to—"

I thinned my lips and gave him a dark scowl as I stalked toward him. The demon simply chuckled, gathered me in his arms, and knifed into the sky.

Flying with Samael was torture. On the one hand, I had a birds-eye view of Durham, the blue sky stretched out before me, and the breeze rustled my hair. On the other hand, the demon delighted in holding me as close as possible, nuzzling my neck and murmuring in my ear as he carried me across the sky. By the time he landed, I was a horny wreck.

He knew it too. My knees almost buckled as he landed, and he held on for a few extra moments.

"Careful now," he purred.

I was far too mature to respond to such obvious needling. I turned toward the house and an ache took up residence in my chest.

I'd done everything I could to avoid this house when I returned to Durham. The memories had been too painful. But I'd never expected that one day it would be gone. In my mind, the house would outlive all of us, standing against all storms.

And it should have.

Why had the wards failed? Why had none of the witches managed to get out?

I needed to get a copy of the autopsy reports. I slid a glance toward Samael, who was frowning at the black remains of the house. One more bargain to make with the demon. Awesome.

I followed Samael as he strode toward the blackened rubble. Some of the house's support beams had survived, and they stood like weary soldiers amongst the carnage of the rest of the house.

"The house will be unstable. Stay close, witchling." He closed his eyes briefly and I narrowed my eyes.

"What are you doing?"

"Removing any remaining heat." His hand waved through the air and then he nodded, gesturing for me to follow him. Human firefighters would love the ability to do that little trick.

The rubble was still wet in places. I gingerly picked my way across it, and Samael paused, frowning at something only he could see.

"The fire started in three places almost simultaneously."

"How do you know?"

He simply looked at me. Right. Demon.

"What places?"

"The third floor, the ground floor close to the entranceway, and that bedroom there."

"That was Evie's room. She wasn't home."

He nodded. "The fire wasn't electrical. I wouldn't be surprised if it was started by an unseelie or a mage. Or a human who convinced a witch to give them access to a spell that would do this kind of damage."

"Why a dark fae or mage?"

"I don't know many seelie who can access enough power to create a fire of this scale. The light fae would send a flood, or use their power to grow poisonous flowers which would bloom all at once, choking the residents in their sleep."

I pushed that image out of my mind. "A demon could create the fire."

He raised one eyebrow. "No demon would dare target this house."

"In that case, why didn't any of the witches get out? And how were the smoke alarms disabled?"

Samael shrugged one shoulder. "That's your area, witchling. But this attack was well-planned and executed by more than one person."

"Can you tell where the witches were located? I haven't gotten my hands on that information yet."

He gazed at the house and I could feel his power rising, hot and strong. It licked against my shields and I shivered.

"Eight witches were gathered in one room downstairs."

I swallowed around the lump in my throat. "Watching

TV, maybe a movie.”

“Two were in the kitchen. The others were spread throughout the rooms upstairs.”

“How many in total?”

“Twenty-two.”

Twenty-two women. Just living their lives, hanging with their friends and family. One minute they’re eating popcorn and watching a movie, and the next they’re staying put while their house burns down.

Samael took my hand and led me away from the rubble. I turned back, finding it difficult to take my eyes off the blackened reminder of what was once my home.

“I need a favor.”

Samael smiled. “As the witchling who lives with me, you have only to ask for what you want,” he purred.

I took a deep breath. No one could piss me off like this guy. No one.

“I need a copy of the autopsy reports,” I said through gritted teeth.

He waved his hand. “I will ask the medical examiner to keep you updated. She is an acquaintance of mine.”

I eyed him. “You bounced on her, didn’t you?”

He smiled “I did not, as you so charmingly put it, ‘bounce on her.’ I was involved with her sister a few decades ago.”

I rolled my eyes. “The human police aren’t going to cooperate with me. They’ll probably deal with the High Coven, maybe Gemma. But I need–”

“Access. Understood. Steve will be told to cooperate fully. All of my demons will help in any way they can.”

That was too easy. Of course, Samael loved watching

my debts pile up, and he particularly enjoyed when I had to rely on his people. I scowled at him and opened my mouth.

A rough meow sounded and I whirled.

"Lia?" I let out a wet laugh as I looked up. The small black cat was sitting in a branch of the huge oak, her white paws gray with soot.

Samael glanced at my face, and a gust of air slid along my skin as he rose on invisible wings, reaching for the cat who yowled at him. He handed her to me and I buried my face in her fur with a choked sob.

"I thought you were dead."

She bit me gently and let out another meow before purring wildly. Samael brushed a tear from my face.

"Your emotions are intense, bounty hunter."

"Because I'm human, Samael."

"Half. The other half makes you one of us. One of *mine*."

Lia reached out a paw and Samael glanced down. The cat wanted his attention and I laughed as she bumped his hand with her head.

"I have a missing witch and a dead coven to deal with," I said. "I'll see you later."

"Yes," Samael said, his tone a dark promise. "You will."

CHAPTER FOUR

Danica

A knock on the door sounded a few minutes after I got back to my apartment. Evie was still lying on the sofa, her eyes open as she stared at nothing.

She'd smiled for the first time when I placed Lia on her chest, her eyes popping open in incredulous joy. The cat was now nestled beneath the comforter, purring up a storm as Evie slowly stroked her head.

Kyla glanced at my sister as I led her in, sympathy written across her face. I didn't know the wolf, but so far, I liked what I'd seen. I still wasn't happy about taking on an 'intern' for my brand new business, but I needed all the help I could get.

Kyla sniffed at the air. "Coffee?" she begged, the desperation clear. I grinned and turned back to the kitchen, pouring her a cup.

"I'm going to hunt down whoever murdered the coven," I said. "But there's something else."

I filled her in about Riona. "Honestly, if this had happened after I knew the coven had been slaughtered, I would've said I couldn't help. But I gave her mom and her sister my word."

Kyla smiled. "Good thing you've got a brand new partner. Uh… intern." She winked at me, and I couldn't help but laugh. Then her face turned serious. "Where do we start?"

"I need to go check out Riona's apartment. There's a chance she was kidnapped, and if she's alive, she's counting on us to save her."

Kyla was studying my face. "You think she's dead."

"I think she never would've missed her sister's engagement party." I glanced at Evie, who was still staring at the blank wall as if it held the answers to the universe. "But we work it. She might've pissed someone off. Hell, she could've broken an ankle walking a dog and trusted the wrong person to help her. She might've been kidnapped by the guy she dumped. We look at all angles."

"And the coven?"

"Witness statements. Samael kindly ensured that his people and the ME will cooperate, but the cops aren't going to want to play nice with the bounty hunter who saved Samael's life."

Kyla raised one eyebrow. "I can see why that would be a problem."

Another knock on the door. It swung straight open, and Vas strutted in like he owned the place.

"You know, just because I matched your power to my wards doesn't mean you can just waltz in here," I griped.

He grinned at me, but it fell from his face as he glanced at Evie.

"How's she doing?"

"She can hear you," my sister said irritably. Vas

stalked over to the sofa and glanced down.

"Have you eaten anything?"

"I'm not hungry, Mom."

He glanced at me. "She's just like you. Can I have some of that?"

Evie ignored us, staring into space, and I poured Vas a cup of coffee. With another glance at my sister, he handed me a piece of paper before introducing himself to Kyla. They made small talk while I scanned the email, and every muscle in my body tensed.

Samael had come through with the preliminary details from the investigation.

The smoke detectors were fakes. Fakes with cameras planted inside. Samael's people would attempt to trace them, but they were one of the most common spy cameras available– easily purchased online.

I kept scanning the page until I got to information about the bodies. I froze.

Beheaded. The witch in Evie's room had been beheaded.

Bile burned my throat and little dots danced in front of my eyes. If Evie hadn't been out, if she'd been in that house, she'd be gone as well.

Not gone. *Dead.*

Vas cursed and steered me to the small table I'd positioned near the window, pushing me into the chair.

I barely paid him any attention as I scanned the rest of the email. The witch's name was Brooke Jacobs.

I knew her.

I'd sat in the kitchen and chatted with Evie and Brooke just a few weeks ago when they'd invited me to a party at Meredith's.

Beheading someone took skill, strength, and a strong stomach. But why behead Brooke and leave the other witches to burn alive?

Because if someone got to the other witches in time, there was a chance they could survive. Whoever did this wasn't willing to take that chance with Brooke.

I inhaled and let out a deep, shuddering breath. Then I handed the email to Kyla and steeled myself as I got up and crouched in front of Evie.

"Hey."

"Hey," she said, dragging her gaze from the wall to my face.

"I need to ask you some questions, and they're going to suck."

She pushed herself up slightly and shoved some of her hair off her face. "They'll help you find whoever did this. I want to help."

"Okay. I need you to tell me everything you know about Brooke."

Tears spilled silently down her cheeks. "Brooke was my best friend. She'd only been with the coven for a few years, and she didn't live in the house, but she spent most of her time there."

"Where did she live?"

"With her boyfriend. But they just broke up. She was staying at the house for a while."

"Was she staying in your room?"

"No, but she hung out there a lot. My room has a TV and hers doesn't. She knows she's welcome to watch whenever."

Evie kept slipping into the present tense, her brain refusing to accept that Brooke was gone.

"What can you tell me about her boyfriend?"

"He was kind of a dick. When I started hanging out with Liam, Brooke talked about how lucky I was because he was such a gentleman. Charles was kind of a slob, and Brooke did everything around the house. She *hated* that. It was one of the big reasons why she dumped him. She said if he refused to pull his weight now, it would only get worse if they settled down and had kids, and she had no desire to clean up after an extra child."

A shadow of a smile flickered across her mouth before it disappeared. "She said he was the kind of guy who'd probably refer to looking after his own kids as babysitting. I think she loved him for a while. But she wanted a family. She'll never have a family now. She would've been such a good mom."

The Brooke I'd seen had been ready to party. She'd seemed young. But Evie would know her best friend's deepest wishes.

I reached out and scratched Lia under the chin.

"Do you know his last name?"

"Walker."

"How'd he take the breakup?"

"Called her a heartless bitch. Brooke mostly talked about how she was better off without him." Evie stared at me. "You think he did this? He's a human."

"I don't think anything. I'm looking at everyone."

Evie wiped at her face. "I keep thinking I can't have any tears left. And then it all hits me again."

"I know. Listen, I'm going to do everything I can to

find out who did this to the coven, but Riona could still be alive."

She nodded. "I know, Danica. You need to prioritize her."

"I'm going to go talk to the mage she dated. Then I'll go talk to Charles Walker."

I hesitated and glanced at Vas.

"I'm hanging out here," he said before I could say anything.

"Thanks."

Evie didn't protest that she didn't need a babysitter. She simply closed her eyes and pulled her comforter over shoulders as Kyla and I walked out.

"Jerry will probably be at the Mage Council," I said as we stepped into the elevator. Technically, I shouldn't be allowed back after they fired me, but Keigan gave me guest access. There's no way I'll be able to get you in though."

"Makes sense. What do you want me to do?"

"Siobhan sent me a list of Riona's friends, and I'm going to forward them to you. A few of them work together at a clothing store… ah… Blast. Get as much out of them as you can and I'll text you when I'm done."

Kyla nodded. "I know Blast." She smiled slightly at my blank look. "It's a boutique store on Main Street."

"Okay. Take your car. We'll split up and I'll meet you outside the Mage Council."

Twenty minutes later, I ignored the furious beeps from a white SUV as I nipped into a parking spot on the street outside the Mage Council.

"Gotta be faster than that," I muttered as I got out.

The driver waited, still laying on the horn and I put my hands on my hips, allowing my t-shirt to slide up just enough to reveal the dagger on my hip.

Tires squealed as he took off.

As usual, both mages and contractors stopped and stared as I walked through the lobby. The first few times this had happened, my shoulders had automatically hunched, and I'd ground my teeth at the insult. Just a few months ago, I'd been one of them, risking my life to take down paranormals who turned on humans, and lesser demons who'd been summoned by idiots.

Now, I no longer had to pretend I didn't care. It was… disquieting to know that Samael's demons had treated me better than most of the Mage Council ever had, even knowing that I'd snuck into his private party, stole a dagger from his dragon's hoard, interrogated a demon who ended up dead in his nightclub, and just plain driven Samael crazy.

I headed up to the 5th floor to stop by Keigan's office.

"What the hell are you doing here, Amana?" Ben's voice was a low growl as he stuck his head out of an office close to Keigan's. He'd been promoted since I'd been gone.

I ignored him, well aware that it would only piss him off more.

"Hey, I'm talking to– ugh." Ben attempted to grab my arm and I evaded his grasp, sliding my elbow straight into his gut. He bared his teeth at me, and Keigan walked out of his office, likely hearing the commotion.

"Benjamin," he said, his tone cool. "Is there something I can do for you?"

Ben gritted his teeth, shooting me a look of hate, but even he wasn't dumb enough to piss off Keigan. "No."

"Then I suggest you get back to work. Danica, good to see you. Can I get you something to drink?"

"I'm good, thanks."

Ben colored at the obvious dismissal, and I sailed past him, slamming Keigan's door in his face.

Keigan smiled at me, gesturing for me to take a seat. "How are you doing, Dani?"

"I'm good. I've taken on an intern. She's my first official hire."

He raised his eyebrows. "Hiring staff already?"

I filled him in on Nathaniel's request and he nodded. "Ah."

"She's been a huge help. I got my first case yesterday. Missing person. And I'm also hunting whoever targeted the coven. Without Kyla, I wouldn't have a hope of juggling both cases."

"Let me know if you need some help. I can do some leg work."

I angled my head. "You're not busy with the Council?"

He sighed, taking a seat at his desk chair.

"I have been… considering leaving the Council."

My mouth dropped open. "You can't."

He gave me a look. "I assure you, I can."

I attempted to process that. Keigan was a Discipulus Mage. One of only five in the Triangle. It took training, commitment, and loyalty to work your way up to that level, and he was close to getting invited to join the waiting list to become one of the ten members of the Mage Council itself. Of course, being taken off the waitlist would require one of the other ten to die and leave a spot open.

The only reason Keigan hadn't already been invited was likely because Albert didn't like him. Keigan didn't do nearly enough ass-kissing to please Albert.

"Why would you leave?"

Keigan was silent for a long moment. "You're going to do great things out on your own. You've always been willing to stand for your morals, Danica. That's a trait that is becoming increasingly rare in this world."

"Uh… you know Albert fired me, right? It's not like I kicked his door open and told him exactly what I thought of him."

Keigan smiled. "He fired you because you refused to fall in line. You made the correct choice shielding your demon from the McCormick descendants. The streets would have run red with blood if they had lived, and everyone knows it. Albert has many qualities that make him a good leader. His inability to see the bigger picture is not one of them. For Albert, that bigger picture is often obscured by the dense fog of his own bigotry."

My mouth dropped open. Keigan gave me a faint smile. I'd known he didn't like Albert, but he'd never actively said anything about that dislike before. But if Keigan was thinking about quitting, maybe he just didn't give a shit anymore.

"Tell me about your missing person case," Keigan said, and I filled him in.

"I don't think Jerry had anything to do with it, but I need to talk to him anyway. Do you know where he is?"

"I believe he's in the library."

"Okay thanks. Uh, I wanted to thank you again for renting me your space."

He waved a hand, getting to his feet and crossing the office to open his door for me. Keigan's old-world manners had always both charmed and discomforted me.

"I know you'll do incredible things with it. Now go find your missing witch."

CHAPTER FIVE

Danica

I f there was one place I missed in the Mage Council, it was the library. It stretched across the entire 6th floor, the sturdy shelves standing at least ten feet high. Here and there, mages and contractors sat in various nooks, searching for information on their bounties or studying for their exams.

I'd sat in those nooks, learning the best strategies to take down a feral troll, an out-of-control banshee, or a lesser demon who'd killed their summoner.

And if Albert found out Keigan was letting me access the library as his guest, he'd have me thrown out in a heartbeat.

I smiled at one of the librarians, who nodded back as she passed me, a stack of books in her arms. Across the room, Cara was sitting at a table close to the restricted section, and she sent me a wave as I walked in.

Cara was a weapons expert who'd helped me figure out exactly why both a lesser demon *and* a high demon had been killed by what had seemed like a simple arrow. The answer was the rowan wood hidden within the arrow— one of the demons' only weaknesses.

I waved back but turned toward one of the small nooks near the window. Jerry was sitting with a contractor I didn't know well. His name was… Wes? Both of them glanced up as I approached, and Wes gave me such a look of hatred I almost glanced over my shoulder to check if he was really aiming that look my way.

As far as I knew, I hadn't done anything to personally piss him off.

"I need to talk to you, Jerry."

Wes narrowed his eyes at me. "We're busy."

I didn't have time for this. "Beat it, or I'll make you eat that book."

Wes slowly got to his feet, angling toward me in a way that told me it was *on*.

"Wes," Jerry sighed. "Give me a minute."

The other man hesitated and I merely waited for him to make up his mind. Finally, he glanced around him, as if remembering where the hell he was, then turned and stalked off.

"Well, that was interesting," I said as I sat in the chair Wes had vacated.

Jerry's jaw tightened. "How is it that you manage to piss off almost everyone you come across?"

"It's a natural talent. Plus, I've never gone out of my way to piss him off."

"He hates demons. What are you doing here, Danica?"

"I'm Keigan's guest."

He sat back in his chair, his eyes lightening. "Of course you'd get around Albert that way." He shook his head. "You're not the most popular person around here, you know."

"I've heard. Listen, I need to ask you some questions."

"I'm researching for a bounty. I don't have time."

"You're going to want to make time. Riona Walsh. When did you see her last?"

His brow furrowed. "Uh, a couple months ago maybe? I'd need to check."

"You dated her."

He glanced over his shoulder, lowering his voice. "You know I'm not going to admit to that."

I rolled my eyes. "I'm not here to out you for daring to date a witch, Jerry. She's missing."

His eyes widened slightly as he stared at me. "Riona's… in trouble?"

"Yeah. She could even be dead."

Sorrow and shock wrestled across his face as he turned his attention to the window, staring blankly out at the sky.

"Riona's a powerful witch. She can't be dead."

"Why don't you tell me the last time you saw her?"

"Uh, it was at Meredith's. We were sitting in the corner, having a few drinks, just talking. She said she was tired of us sneaking around. It had been fun at first, exciting, but she wasn't interested in being anyone's dirty little secret." His mouth twisted and I raised one eyebrow.

"And what did you say to that?"

"I said I needed to think. And then ten minutes later, Ben came in. He saw us in the corner."

I sighed. Meredith's may be neutral territory, but that didn't mean people were blind. "What did he say?"

"He came over and asked what I was doing slumming

with a witch. Riona didn't use her magic publicly— she was mostly good at warding. So I figured he must've had us followed. You know what Ben's like."

"Uh huh. So Ben comes over and talks shit about your girl, in front of her, and what do you do?"

His cheeks flushed. "I told him I was having a business meeting. Riona didn't say anything. Then Ben said I should be careful, or word about my 'meetings' would make its way to Albert."

Jerry pushed a hand through his hair. "You have to understand, I'm the first mage in my family. My parents are human, and my mom's sick, dad's on disability. They rely on my paycheck to pay the bills. Six more months, and I'll get benefits."

"So you broke up with Riona."

"It was mutual, I guess. As soon as Ben walked away, she gave me this look. She didn't say a word, but it was obvious she thought I was a coward."

"That was the last time you saw her?"

He shrugged. "I saw her around a few times but she ignored me. A woman like Riona… she's not going to chase after a guy, you know?"

I did know. And I was pretty sure any lady boner Riona might have had for Jerry likely disappeared the moment she saw him cower to Ben. Nothing killed a relationship like contempt.

"I need your whereabouts on Wednesday."

He gaped at me. "You think I'm a suspect?"

"No," I told him honestly. I had a feeling Riona would've kicked his ass if he'd even thought about getting physical with her. "But you know this is how it's done."

He was silent for a long moment. Then his shoulders slumped. "You need to cross me off the list so you can find out who might've hurt her."

"That's right."

"Okay. Wednesday. Let me think." He pulled his phone out of his pocket and scanned it. "I was here until maybe three. I'd pulled an all-nighter and I was going to go home, but some of the guys convinced me to go shoot a few hoops. Then we grabbed dinner and a few beers."

"When did you finish the beers?"

"Uh, maybe nine-thirty or ten?"

"I'm going to need the names of those guys."

He nodded and ripped a piece of paper off the pad in front of him, noting down a few names and their phone numbers. I slipped it into my pocket.

"What about after the beers?"

"I went home and slept for twelve hours. I was exhausted."

"Did you talk to anyone while you were at home?"

"No," he shook his head. "I just wanted to get some sleep."

I got to my feet. "Okay. Let me know if you think of anyone who was giving Riona trouble. Anyone who might've hurt her."

He nodded, his expression miserable. "Do you think she's alive?"

"I'm assuming she is unless I learn otherwise."

I mulled over what Jerry had said as I made my way back across the library. I didn't know exactly when Riona had gone missing yet, but the fact remained that Jerry had no alibi for most of the night.

"Hurry up, you dumb bitch."

I froze, slowly turning my head. Across the library, Bruce was once again tormenting Mella.

Her hands shook as she sorted through a set of files, and Bruce let out a low snarl.

"Fuck, you're stupid. How long have you been here, and you still can't do your fucking job?"

Mella dropped her files, chains rattling against the manacle around her ankle as she crouched to pick them up. A dull fury took up residence in my chest. I stalked toward them, visions of blowing Bruce's head off his shoulders dancing through my imagination.

I let my voice carry over the murmurs of anyone within a few feet of me. "It's been a crappy few days, asshole, and I'm more than happy to take my frustrations out on you."

He turned and bared his teeth at me. "Oh yeah? Try, bitch, I dare you."

"Someone needs to improve his vocabulary," I said to Mella. "Didn't he already just call you a bitch?" I smiled at Bruce. "You want me to buy you a word of the day calendar, pal?"

Mella ducked her head, clearly hiding a smile, and a dull flush worked its way up Bruce's meaty neck.

"You don't work here any longer, whore. That means I can make you hurt."

I let my smile widen. "Why don't you try and take on a woman who's not chained up, huh?"

He snatched the file Mella lay on the counter, narrowed his eyes and sneered at me. "Your turn is coming, bitch. Sooner than you can imagine. I can't wait."

I yawned. "Get gone." I stepped in front of him,

facing Mella as I turned my back on him. I studied her face, carefully watching for any indication that Bruce was stupid enough to attack me from behind, but it was only relief that shone in her eyes as he cursed and stalked away, his boots clomping loudly on the floor.

"Thanks," Mella said quietly.

"How often does he torment you?" I asked. "It seems like it's getting worse."

She shrugged. "Most days," she attempted a smile. "It's okay. He's all threat. He wouldn't really hurt me in here. The librarians would revolt."

Frustration wound through me, joining the general pissy mood that was driving me through the day. No one would speak about exactly what Mella had done to wind up here, but Albert had stolen her pelt— or skin— which kept the selkie chained up in here. Without her pelt, she couldn't shift to her selkie form, or access her power. The Naud chains clamped around her wrists and ankles only added insult to injury.

Whatever Mella had done, surely thirty years chained up in this library and dealing with fuckheads like Bruce was enough.

The worst part? I was pretty sure I knew where her pelt was. But there was no way I could get my hands on it.

"While I'm here, do you mind doing a quick search for me? I know I don't work here anymore…"

Mella shot me a grin. "Of course. Who are you looking for?"

"Riona Walsh. Anything you have on her would be great."

She turned to her computer and hummed, typing

the name into the system. The printer hummed, and she collected a few papers, handing them to me.

"No trouble with the law," she said. "Nothing on her that says she would be on the Mage Council's radar."

"Okay. Thanks anyway. Look after yourself, Mella."

"You too."

I had a text waiting for me as I got into the elevator. Kyla was done chatting to Riona's friends and waiting in her car. Perfect.

She was making a few notes in her notebook, but she opened her door as I approached.

"Hey. Any luck with the ex?"

I shrugged. "I doubt Riona would even call him her ex. The moment she made noises about no longer sneaking around, one of his fellow mages— and one of the banes of my existence— got involved. Ben threatened to out him to Albert, and boom, Jerry and Riona were done. Let's take my car so we can talk on the way."

Kyla slid out and followed me to my car. "Poor Riona."

I shrugged. "No loss, believe me. Jerry's a dick." I reached for my phone, sending a quick text to Steve before starting the car.

I angled out of the park. "We also need to stop by what's left of the coven's house at some point and talk to witnesses."

"Question," Kyla said.

"Answer."

"How come your sister is such a huge part of the coven and you're not? It wasn't your choice to leave Durham, right?"

"No. When my mom took me from the coven that day,

the witches who were present helped her. They used spells to hold Evie in place while Mom dragged me into the car with her magic. I never really forgave the witches for that, but Evie was just a kid. She was entering that pre-teen stage where nothing makes sense and you hate everybody. But at the same time, she desperately needed some normalcy. She lived with twenty or so witches, some of whom stepped into maternal roles."

"So she was able to move on."

"Yeah. I didn't visit. I was a teenager myself, and Mom had told me that if I saw Evie, she'd be in danger. I believed her at first, but eventually, I'd half decided my mom was crazy." I smiled. "I'd been training every day since we arrived in Austin, and with a seventeen-year-old's ego, I was certain I could protect both of us from anything."

"Of course," Kyla grinned.

"Then Mom died. I still don't know why she came back here. Maybe I'll never know. But I know she wouldn't have returned without a good reason. I was her next of kin, so I was notified first. They said it had been an accident. A hit-and-run. I wanted to tell Evie myself, so I came back."

"I'm guessing it wasn't the reunion you were hoping for."

"No. She didn't quite slam the door in my face, but it felt like it." I sighed. "The thing you have to remember is that, in Evie's mind, she was abandoned by the two people she loved the most.

"Anyway, I went back to Austin, figuring our relationship was done. Then I was sent photos of the crime scene. It wasn't a hit-and-run. I guess I kind of… snapped. I came back, spent four and a half years looking for any kind of leads, and then I heard about the dagger."

Kyla's gaze went to my hip. "So you decided to steal it."

I sighed. "At that point, I thought I had nothing to lose. Stupid, I know. You fucking always have something to lose."

"Ain't that the truth."

"The dagger helped, and after so long without any hope, I had a couple of leads. But both were killed in front of me. One of them was in Samael's club, which I'd snuck into. That's how the whole bond thing happened. The demon was *pissed*."

"But you're… *with* Samael now?"

"It's complicated. I think… I think there are some people who drive you crazy, even when you can't help but want them in your life. I don't think Samael and I will ever have a nice, normal, placid relationship. I guess neither of us would know what to do with one."

The thought made me frown. Then I glanced at Kyla. It wasn't like me to spill it all to someone I didn't know well. I needed a change of subject.

"What did Riona's friends say?" I asked, and Kyla scanned her notes.

"She worked at Blast for a few months herself last summer, but the shifts kept changing and she felt like she wasn't getting enough writing time in. None of them had seen her for a few weeks. They said their schedules never really meshed and they kept missing each other, but all three of them seemed really cut up when I told them she was missing.

I nodded. "Alibis?"

"Two of them were at work until late, and then they got a drink at Meredith's. The other was at her boyfriend's. I checked all of their alibis and they're clear."

"Okay." I blew out a breath. "Here's the plan. Riona lives close to Trinity Park, so we'll go check out her apartment. We could split up, but you have a superior nose. If you scent anyone in there, maybe you'll recognize them when we're interviewing people she knew."

"Good plan. Since we'll be in Trinity Park, I'm assuming you want to switch to the other case."

"Yeah. We'll split up there and talk to any witnesses who might've seen the fire. Then, we'll take Brooke's ex. Uhh, Charles Walker. He only lives a few blocks from my apartment."

Kyla let out a low whistle. "Your workload is insane. Good thing you hired me," she preened, and I chuckled. She wasn't wrong.

Danica

Riona lived in a three-story apartment building on North Duke St. Her apartment was on the third floor, and thanks to the outside staircase which led directly to her floor, there was no need to go through the main entrance.

"Not exactly secure," Kyla muttered.

"Yeah. She's a strong warder, I can feel it from here. But if she came home late at night…" I frowned. "Stand next to her door, will you? Pretend like you're unlocking the door."

Kyla raised one eyebrow but took her place while I examined the open-aired corridor. A few feet from Riona's door, there was a dented metal door which led to the inside staircase. I opened it and nodded.

"They get up here, all they have to do is wait behind this door. She's busy unlocking her own door, her wards haven't been tripped so she's not worried. Maybe she's been walking the dogs all day so her feet are sore. She's not thinking she could be targeted. All she wants to do is take her shoes off and stretch out on her sofa for a while."

Kyla nodded and pointed to the camera at the end of the corridor. "You think that works?"

I shrugged. "I doubt it, but we'll try and get access to any video from the neighborhood." I pulled the keys Siobhan had given me out of my pocket and handed them to Kyla. The door swung open and Riona's ward pricked at my skin warningly.

Samael could slip beneath my wards as if they weren't even there. Unfortunately, he hadn't taught me that little trick.

"What are you doing?"

"Trying to decide if I should break her ward. It could give her the mental boost she needs to hold on. And she'll know someone's looking for her."

"What about the police? They've probably been through here, right?"

"Wards can't be calibrated for humans— not without earning a fine or prison sentence from the Mage Council. Most witches risk it to some extent, but it sounds like Riona played by the rules."

"If I were her, I'd want to know," Kyla said. Her eyes

were intent. "If she's still alive, she's been missing for at least three days by now. She needs to know people are looking for her."

"Okay."

I pulled one of my throwing knives and sliced a shallow cut along my forearm. Then I raised my hand and focused. Riona's ward was a pretty lilac color, shimmering darker in spots. I raised my eyebrows.

Kyla watched, her eyes narrowed in interest. "What is it?"

"She's powerful. This ward was created to look mundane. So if someone tried to break it, they wouldn't put enough power into it, and they'd get slapped back." I grinned. "I like her already."

"You can break it?"

"Yeah, I can break it."

"It's pretty. The color."

I'd forgotten werewolves could see most magic. "Yeah, looks both pretty and easily breakable. Riona is smart."

I slammed my bleeding hand into the ward and *pushed*. The ward seemed to snarl back at me, but a moment later it popped out of existence.

"Will it stay down?"

"Unlikely. Most witches create their wards to reform after they've been broken, unless they're destroyed completely."

Riona's apartment was spotlessly clean. The front door opened directly into her living room, which sheltered a plush cream sectional sofa, a scarred wooden coffee table, and a rug patterned with whites, blues, and grays.

Flowers drooped in a vase on the coffee table, and a painting of horses galloping across a beach hung on one wall.

"Looks like her sister was right," Kyla said, pointing to the large box wrapped in silver and gold on the small table by the window. "That'll be the gift for the engagement party."

"Let's try not touch anything. The human cops might've dusted for prints, and if they haven't, we need to be careful. No sign of a struggle, and you'd be able to tell in this place."

"Yeah. She sure keeps it neat and tidy."

We both glanced around. I wasn't the neat and tidy type, and I was guessing Kyla wasn't either.

"You take the kitchen, I'll check out the bedroom."

Riona had indulged her love of pretty things in her bedroom. It was mostly done in light colors, with a frilly white comforter that drew the eye. A fluffy gray blanket was draped along the end of the bed. Her white side tables held girly silver lamps, the faux-crystal glass beads glimmering in the sunlight streaming in the window.

Nothing to indicate she'd been worried about someone targeting her. At least not at home.

She'd set up a small workstation in the corner, and it contained a laptop, a few notebooks, a folder, and a collection of pretty pens. What it didn't hold was a planner or calendar. I pulled on a pair of gloves and opened the laptop.

"No password?"

"She's obviously the trusting type," Kyla called and I rolled my eyes. Werewolf hearing.

The laptop had been sleeping, and Riona's schedule was open in one of her tabs. I let out a low whistle.

"You're a busy girl."

Her work schedule was intense. Most of her mornings were blocked off with the word 'manuscript,' and in the afternoons she drove for Lyft, walked dogs, and occasionally nannied. It looked like she also did both pet sitting and house sitting as well, and I made a mental note to check out the addresses.

Then I used her printer to print off a couple of copies of her schedule for the three-week period leading up to her disappearance.

"Nothing," Kyla announced when I walked back into the living room. "Towel in the bathroom is bone dry, plants need to be watered, and the takeout Chinese food in her fridge looks like an interesting science experiment."

"She has a packed schedule," I said, holding up the laptop. "I'm going to take this with us. We need to see if her car is downstairs."

"You think maybe she picked up the wrong person when she was driving?"

"I don't think anything yet." I took a final glance around. The wrapped gift, the drooping flowers, the high-heeled shoes sprawled next to the small TV… they made me sad.

Hold on, Riona. If you're still alive, just hold on long enough for us to find you.

I went still, my gaze stuck on a framed photo hanging on her wall.

"What is it?"

"Small world. I know that witch."

Kyla narrowed her eyes. "She looks familiar. Does she work at that bar…" she clicked her fingers. "Meredith's, right?"

"Yeah. I need to have a chat with her at some point." I pushed my hair off my face. "But first, we head to the coven's house."

Samael

Danica's smile flashed through my mind, the combination of love and shock as I gave her the cat. Her smile did something to me. It made me want to do everything I could to see that smile on her face every single day of her life.

And if I were to tell her such a thing, she would likely ask me if I was insane.

"Samael?"

"Yes."

Bael slid me an amused look from where he balanced his laptop on his knees in the seat across from mine. He placed the laptop on my desk and all amusement fled from his expression.

"How sure are you of Finvarra's loyalty?"

I raised one eyebrow. "He has no reason to double cross us."

"Not even for his revenge?"

I frowned. "Finvarra needs a scroll which Lucifer keeps close. Unless he's an idiot, he knows very well that if he betrays me, I'll burn it to ashes, along with Lucifer's office." And the unseelie king was many things, but he wasn't an idiot. "Where is this coming from?"

"Two of his inner circle were spotted speaking with Lucifer's right-hand next to the portal in Chicago."

"Contact him," I ordered. "I will hear his explanation."

If those members of his inner circle were attempting to betray Finvarra, they would die terribly. And if the unseelie king knew about the meeting, our alliance was over before it truly began.

My teeth clenched but I forced myself to put it away. "What else?"

Bael scanned his notes. "Our spies have been working on Garadiel. If we can turn him, it will be one of our greatest accomplishments yet. So far, he hasn't been receptive, however he loathes both Daimonion and Pischiel."

Daimonion was Lucifer's favorite assassin, and I had promised his death to Vassago. Pischiel had slowly become more and more powerful over the past century, occasionally going as far as to attend meetings in Lucifer's place.

Bael cleared his throat. "Some believe Lucifer is grooming Picshiel to be his eventual heir."

I smiled. "Lucifer can groom whoever he likes. Picshiel will be one more person for us to kill in front of him."

CHAPTER SIX

Danica

I got lucky, and there was an empty spot just a few cars down from the wreckage of the coven's house.

Kyla and I split up, each taking a side of the street. Most of the witches didn't want to talk to me, insisting that they'd already talked to the human authorities and would cooperate with the High Coven's investigators.

"You should be ashamed of yourself," Mrs. Baker snapped at me. "Coming around here and asking questions. It was probably your relationship with the demons that got them killed."

I wouldn't punch a seventy-year-old woman in the mouth, but I wanted to. I *really* wanted to.

"The demons are helping with this investigation."

She sneered. "The Mage Council said I don't have to talk to you."

Of course the council had poked at me again. It no longer surprised me when they took every opportunity to screw with me.

Mrs. Baker slammed the door in my face

and I turned, finding Kyla waiting for me on the street. I clomped down the porch steps.

"I hope you had better luck than me."

She attempted a smile. "Witches don't like wolves. We're immune to some of their magic. It pisses them off."

I wiped a hand over my face and she nudged me with her elbow. "I'm starving."

"I could eat."

We turned toward my car and Kyla went still. Her gaze was fixed on a teenager walking down the street toward us, and her head cocked in a way that was all wolf.

"I know that kid. I saw him last night. He was staring at the house while it burned."

The teenager lifted his head and froze. Then he promptly turned on his heel and headed in the other direction.

I raised one eyebrow. "Well, that's suspicious."

We stalked after him. He glanced over his shoulder and broke into a run.

One minute Kyla was next to me, and the next she was gone. I gaped. She'd already caught the kid, and she was holding him by his throat against a power pole.

I jogged up to them. "Jeez you can move," I said. It made sense, but I'd never seen a werewolf run. I'd bet she was even faster in her other form.

"Let me go, I don't know nothin'. Let me go!"

I surveyed the street. We had to get this little chat over with quickly, otherwise the local witches were going to decide to find out exactly what all the noise was about.

"Quiet." Kyla snarled. Her claws slid out as her hand tightened around the neck of his shirt.

The kid went chalk white and barely breathed. I sighed. Obviously I'd have to be good cop.

"Ease back a bit," I said, and she relaxed her hand slightly.

"Why did you turn around and walk in the other direction when you saw us?"

He strained against Kyla's hold on his shirt, his eyes rolling. "I realized I'm late for an appointment. You don't own the streets!"

"Uh-huh. What were you doing here last night?"

The kid started shaking. "Nothin'. Nothin', I swear."

I held up the Mistilteinn Dagger as it glowed red. "See this? It can tell when you lie."

He stared at the knife in my hand.

"You want me to slap him around?" Kyla offered.

I chuckled. As a werewolf, Kyla could probably lift my car. If she slapped a human, he'd likely be dead before he hit the ground.

"Don't let her hurt me. Please!"

I rolled my eyes. This kid wasn't a killer. But he might've seen something. I glanced at Kyla and she held her hands up and stepped back. The kid straightened his clothes and took a deep breath.

"You looked mighty interested in those flames last night," Kyla said, and the kid flinched.

"What's your name?" I asked.

"Greg."

"Look Greg, we're not going to hurt you. We're just trying to find out who might've wanted to harm the coven. Tell us what you know, and you can go about your day."

"I know you. You're the witch bonded to Samael."

His gaze dropped to my arm and I nodded.

"Yep."

Strangely, this seemed to relax him. "That means you have the demons backing you up, right?"

"To a point."

"Okay. Okay."

Terrified. The kid was terrified, and not just by the claws Kyla had flashed.

"You saw something, didn't you, Greg?"

His eyes filled with tears and I glanced around. Across the road, a lace curtain shifted in one of the windows facing us.

"Let's get off the street. You had lunch?"

He shook his head and my stomach rumbled at the thought. It was close to 3:00pm already. I gestured for him to follow us to my car. Now that he'd figured out we weren't going to hurt him, he relaxed enough to glance at the coven as we passed it. Fury flashed across his face.

"I hope you find who did this and make them pay."

"That's the plan."

We picked up burritos from the Mexican place on Duke Street and took them to Central Park. I handed the kid his Pepsi and we sat on a bench, watching a group of human kids play some game that involved a lot of shrieking and running.

I took a huge bite of my burrito. Flavor exploded in my mouth. "Mmm." I swallowed. "You wanna tell me what you know?"

Greg put his burrito down and picked up his soda. "There's this witch… her name is… *was* Maribel."

"You have a thing with Maribel?" Kyla asked,

reaching across to grab the guacamole.

"No. No. She's taking a few college classes at the human college. And I'm still in high school."

His shoulders hunched and I sighed. "You had a crush on Maribel."

He glanced up at me. "Yeah. I'd see her around sometimes. We talked about music. I knew she thought I was just a kid, but she was always nice to me."

"Okay. Did you come by the coven that night?"

He nodded. "I had… flowers. I was going to tell her how I felt. To convince her I wasn't just a kid. They were violets. Her favorite," he said softly.

Kyla stretched out her long legs. "That says a lot, you know. When a guy knows enough to give you your favorite flowers."

Greg eyed her. "You think?"

She nodded and he attempted a smile. Obviously there were no hard feelings about the way she'd accosted him on the street.

"So you showed up with your flowers," I said. "And then what happened?"

"I saw this car. I'd seen it a few times before, but I hadn't really noticed. A few guys got out of the car and walked up the street toward the coven's house."

"How many guys?"

"Ah, three."

"Describe them," I said, and he let out a shaky breath.

"It was dark. And they were all wearing black from head to toe. They had these caps covering their hair and they didn't look around. They didn't talk at all. They kind of… marched toward the house."

"Did you see any of their faces?"

"I was behind that huge tree on the other side of the road." Greg flushed. "I was trying to talk myself into walking across the road and knocking on the door. If I had, maybe they'd still be alive," he said miserably.

"If you had, you'd be dead," Kyla said around her next bite. "What about their skin color? Height? Anything you noticed."

"One of them was mixed. I think the other two were white. They were all taller than me. They had wide shoulders like they worked out."

"Any weapons?" I asked.

He shook his head. "Two of them carried bags. Like duffels."

"Okay. So you're standing behind the tree, and they walk toward the house. Then what happens?"

"Two of them continued up the path, and the other one split off. He went around the back of the house. I thought they were friends of the witches. They have guys around sometimes. Especially when the older witches are away."

His gaze met mine. "I thought they were friends. That they were maybe planning to surprise them or something."

"There was no way you could've known."

He just shook his head. "So I was standing there, feeling like an asshole with the flowers in my hand. I couldn't go in, unless I wanted a group of guys to laugh me out of there. I waited around for a while, hoping that the guys would leave, and then I ditched the flowers. That's when I saw it."

"What did you see?"

"Flames. In one of the upstairs bedrooms. And then in the living room. I called the fire department and the police, but I had to hang up, because the guys were coming out."

Greg swallowed and put his burrito down. His face was turning green. "They didn't say anything. Just marched back to the car."

"Which doors did they use to get into the car?"

"Huh?"

"Did any of them get into the driver's side, or was there a driver waiting?"

"Ah, one of them got in the driver's side. The others got in on the side away from the road."

"Take me through it again."

I took notes, and by the time we were done, Greg was pale but holding steady.

"I should've done something."

"Did you hear anything? Screams, yelling?"

"No."

"So there was no way to know, until you saw the flames. You did everything right."

"I should've gone in there, should've–"

Kyla angled her head. "Greg. If they'd seen you, they would've killed you. They wouldn't have thought twice."

Greg leaned down and put his head between his knees. I glanced at Kyla. She simply shrugged and took another bite of her burrito.

"Tell me about the car, Greg. Did it drive past you?"

He sat up. "Yeah. It was a black SUV. Maybe a Ford? It was dark."

"License plate?"

"Um. I tried to get it. They drove too fast. But the plate was from Tennessee."

"Okay. You've been very helpful. Thank you."

"I think… I think if I had been murdered, Maribel would have done everything she could to help. She was a good person." Greg closed his eyes.

"It sounds like she was. Give Kyla your details. If we have any more questions, we'll be in touch."

He nodded and added his number to Kyla's phone.

"We'll drop you at home," I offered.

"Thanks."

Greg lived near Trinity Park in Walltown, and we both watched as he walked up his porch steps.

Kyla slid me a look. "What are you thinking?"

"I'm wondering how the fuck they got through the wards."

"I'd forgotten about that. Powerful coven like that is going to have some pretty good wards, right?"

"Yeah. So how the hell did those bastards get through?"

Kyla looked slightly sick. "It might've been an inside job," she said.

"Yeah. Someone could've adjusted the wards so the murderers would be recognized when they tried to enter the house. They would've needed some kind of spell, or a ton of natural power to either hold the witches in place or send them to sleep. Otherwise, some of them would've gotten out."

"So we need to figure out if any of the witches wanted a chunk of their coven dead."

I nodded. "I want to go check on Evie and then I'll talk to Meredith. Do me a favor. Make a note of any cameras in the neighborhood and send the details to Steve. If he can't hack them, he'll send one of Samael's demons to get the footage so we can see if there's any sign of the black SUV. It'll be faster than us having to intimidate it out of the locals."

"Aw," Kyla gave me a mock pout. "I love intimidating things out of the locals."

"We don't have the time." I glanced at my phone. "God, where did the day go?"

"It disappeared in a blur of conversation," Kyla said.

"Yeah. I never had to deal with this much blah blah when I was a bounty hunter." I sighed longingly. "I solved most problems with my fists."

"Must've been nice."

I grinned. "It was, but I was working for the Council. Now, I get to work the kind of cases *I* want to work, even if these cases come with a lot of 'blah blah'. We're not going to have time to talk to Charles Walker today. I've been away from Evie for too long."

"I can go talk to him if you want."

"Tomorrow is soon enough."

My phone vibrated and I glanced down at it as I stopped at a red light.

"Fuck."

"What's wrong?"

"It's Vas. I forgot about Monday dinner."

I glanced at Kyla's confused face and sighed, holding up my hand. The gold gleamed in the sunlight. "It's part of dealing with Samael. Plus, he's helping me find out who's targeting the coven. I can't miss this one. Crap. Okay, new plan." I took the next right and headed back toward the Mage Council.

"I'll drop you at your car. If you get a chance, call Siobhan and ask for the contact information for any of Riona's friends. Look for anyone who might've seen her on the day she went missing. And check out any addresses where she was house sitting recently."

"You think whoever took her was related to her work in some way?"

I sighed. "It's all we have so far. We need to check every avenue." I reached behind me to the backseat where I'd stashed Riona's laptop and handed it to her, along with the information Mella had printed off about Riona.

"You'll have more time to go through this tonight since I have the stupid dinner. I printed off her schedule and I'll take a look at it, but it would be a massive help if you could check any other apps, her email, anything you can think of."

Kyla nodded. "Sounds good." She grinned at me as I pulled up next to her Nissan. "In spite of all the 'blah blah,' it was good working with you today, boss."

I couldn't help but grin back. "Ditto."

Danica

I made my way up to my apartment. Vas was sitting on the sofa next to Evie, Lia curled up on his lap.

He'd gotten a beer from somewhere, and he looked

almost like a human guy watching sports after a long day of work.

Evie was lying in the same spot, her gaze fixed on a reality show about a coven of witches. I winced.

Vas made a tapping motion on his wrist. We both had to be at Monday dinner in half an hour, and I really didn't want to leave Evie alone.

"We made a list of everyone who died and anyone they'd had a problem with recently," Evie said, her gaze still on the TV.

Vas held it up and I plucked it from his hand. "This is helpful. Thanks."

"How is the investigation going?" Vas asked.

"I interviewed a few people today. One of them was a kid with a crush on Maribel. He saw the people who went into the coven's house."

Evie slowly sat up. "Who was it?"

"Three men. Dressed in black. Tennessee plates."

"How can I help?" Evie asked. I opened my mouth and snapped it shut.

"I'm tired of lying around," she pushed her hand through her hair and it got tangled in a huge knot. We both winced.

"I should probably shower," she muttered.

Vas's lips twitched and she elbowed him.

"I didn't say anything," he said.

"Vas and I need to be at Samael's tower tonight," I said.

Evie's eyes met mine. "Because he's helping you. He's making you see him more often."

"Hey, the guy's chef makes all of my favorite foods.

You can come if you want. Or I can bring you back something to eat?"

She shook her head. "I'll shower. You don't need to worry about leaving me, Danica. I'm okay."

We all pretended we couldn't see the way Misty glowed on my hip. Evie got to her feet and stalked into the bathroom. I let out a shuddering breath and glanced at Vas.

"She may not be okay now, but she will one day," he said. "She's stronger than you give her credit for."

I shrugged and stole his beer, taking a sip. "That's terrible."

He laughed. "I like it."

"Speaking of beer, I have it on good authority that you have a thing for Meredith."

His face went blank. "I don't know what you're talking about."

I nudged him. "I was only teasing. We don't have to talk about it if you don't want to."

Vas cursed and got to his feet. There went his good mood. I was the worst.

"I might've had a thing for her."

"Past tense?"

He scowled. "When you and I first met, you knew who I was when I introduced myself."

"It took me a while to get it, but yeah, the name Vassago rang a bell."

"Known for discovering a woman's deepest secret, finding lost things, and foretelling the past, present, and future," he said, bitterness clear in his voice.

I wasn't surprised that he'd remembered my exact words. Demons were like that.

His eyes met mine. "Did you tell Meredith who I was?"

I shook my head. "I've been so busy over the past few months, I've barely had a chance to talk to Mere. What happened, Vas?"

The demon looked miserable, and I gave into the urge to give him a hug. He heaved a sigh and wrapped his arms around me.

"My power doesn't work all the time. I lose things constantly, and I sure as shit haven't ever been able to foretell the future. That's Bael's territory."

I opened my mouth to ask exactly why his power was so spotty and he drew back, dropping his arms. "I'll go into the reasons one day. My power didn't work on you, remember?"

I nodded and drew back. "But it worked on Meredith?"

"Not at first. But one day I was sitting in the bar and it came to me. Her darkest secret. It didn't matter to me," he said. "I didn't care. But we got to talking, and a few weeks later, someone must have figured out who I was and told her. She asked if I knew her secret."

Vas wouldn't have lied.

"I'm so sorry."

"She never specifically said anything, but she stopped talking to me. Had her fae bartender serving me instead. It's pretty clear that she no longer wants anything to do with me."

I swallowed. "Her secret… is it something that could get her in a lot of trouble?"

He nodded. "But I wouldn't let that happen. I'd protect her."

"She doesn't know you, Vas. From what I've seen, Meredith is fiercely independent. She works harder than anyone I've ever seen. The idea of a guy she barely knows having access to her darkest secret… I can't imagine how vulnerable she feels. In her mind, you're an axe hanging over her neck, and that axe could drop at any time."

Vas flinched. Then he got to his feet and turned, stalking over to the window. "So you're saying I don't have a hope. I should just forget about it."

"No, I'm not saying that at all. I'm saying that expecting Mere to be okay with you knowing her deepest, darkest secret, it's a lot."

His eyes were wounded when he glanced over his shoulder at me. "I'd never do anything to fuck up her life."

"I know. Maybe you need to let Meredith know that too. And give her time."

Evie appeared, her hair wrapped in a towel. She was wearing a pair of my old sweats.

"We should probably get you some underwear and stuff, huh?"

She attempted a smile. "Yeah. Maybe tomorrow I could go shopping."

"Sounds good. In the meantime, help yourself to anything. Clothes, weapons, toiletries, whatever you need." I glanced at my phone. "We need to take off. Are you sure you're going to be okay?"

Evie nodded and headed back toward the sofa. I eyed her. "There's a great Chinese place a few blocks away. They deliver. The menu is on the fridge."

"Thanks."

I chewed on my lip as Vas followed me into the

elevator.

"I'm worried about her," I admitted.

"Me too."

"My instincts are telling me she shouldn't be alone. I know you're probably busy, but would you mind hitting the mall with her tomorrow?

"I've already planned to."

"Thanks, Vas."

The elevator doors opened and I squeezed out first, picking up a stray feather that had fallen from his wings.

"Give that back before Samael loses his mind," Vas said.

I rolled my eyes and pinned it to the bulletin board in my apartment lobby.

The air was cooler than it had been for a while when we stepped outside. Fall would be here before we knew it. Vas gathered me into his arms and climbed into the sky, banking toward Samael's tower.

It stood like a beacon in the distance, looming over the entire city. Vas and I were both lost in our own thoughts as we flew toward it. I wanted to sit next to Samael for a couple of hours about as much as I wanted a root canal, but as always, I'd made a deal. And now I had to hold up my end.

"Deep thoughts?" Vas asked.

I sighed. "Always."

He shook his head, and I glanced up to find him frowning down at me.

"You know what your problem is?"

"No, but I'm sure you're going to tell me."

He ignored that. "You want to be happy. And you can

see happiness. It's so close you can almost touch it. But you can't get out of your own way long enough to reach out and take it. You're so wrapped up in who you thought Samael was, in the promises you made your mom, in your reputation, that you may just lose everything."

"It's not that simple."

"Yes, it is. Every time you get close, you leap away, as if he's on fire and you're afraid of being burned."

"Every time I get close, I learn more about how he manipulated me. Lied to me."

Vas shook his head, banking left toward the tower. "You're judging him by human standards again."

"I grew up human. They're the only standards I know."

"He's changing, Danica. I've known him for over seventy years and I've never seen him smile as much as he has recently. Never seen him make allowances for a woman or compromise the way he does with you. You need to make a decision."

I'd never been indecisive. Never questioned my decisions once I'd made them. Until now. And I hated it.

By the time Vas landed on one of Samael's balconies, I'd convinced myself that dinner wouldn't be that bad. I may not be excited about spending time with the demon who'd dented my heart, but it wasn't like it would be just the two of us. There were enough other demons there that I could focus on them and ignore the looming presence sitting beside me.

The balcony door opened and Samael's eyes met mine.

CHAPTER SEVEN

Danica

Vas excused himself and strode past Samael, calling out to one of his friends.

Samael raised one eyebrow as he swept his gaze over me, from the toes of my scarred leather boots, over my worn jeans, and along the t-shirt that had seen better days.

"I forgot to change, okay?"

"I didn't say a word. You look as beautiful as always."

I squinted my eyes at him, but the demon didn't seem to be fucking with me. He held out a hand and before I was aware I'd held out my own, he was drawing me inside.

Most of the others were already seated, although a few demons were standing close to the balcony, drinks in hand. Lilith angled her head and surveyed my outfit.

"Nice to see you made an effort," she said.

I opened my mouth to snark back at her, but Samael squeezed my hand. "Enough Lilith."

She merely nodded and turned back to Asmodeus. The demon grinned at me, giving me a wink.

Most of the usual crowd were here. Agaliarept had returned from doing whatever mysterious task Samael had asked him to do. The demon wasn't exactly my biggest cheerleader, and he gave me a sour look as I walked in.

Sitri nodded at me from where he was already seated at the long table and I nodded back.

A bell rang from somewhere in the kitchen, and everyone began moving toward their seats. Samael pulled my chair out and I plunked myself down.

A single red rose lay across my plate, the thorns removed. I glanced at Samael, who was deep in conversation with a demon whose name I'd forgotten.

I raised the rose and sniffed, charmed despite myself.

The menu was Italian and my mouth watered as the waiters began bringing out plates of food. I started with a caprese salad and mentally planned to inhale a bowl of pasta.

By the time the next course was served, the topic had turned to Lucifer. When there was a break in conversation, I reached for my glass and sat back in my seat.

"You guys are so powerful. How come you haven't taken Lucifer down before now?"

Bael gave me a steady stare. "Lucifer has survived fifty-four assassination attempts since we left the underworld."

Fifty-four. I swallowed. And somehow *I* was supposed to be able to kill him? Seemed unlikely to me.

"How sure are we about this whole prophecy thing?"

Several demons chuckled. Beneath the table, Samael took my hand. I allowed it.

"We could spend hours disclosing Lucifer's atrocities during his rule," Lilith said. "Just a few of those charming stories will give you nightmares. They won't make you strong."

"Ignorance won't make me strong either."

She smiled. "No. You must make *yourself* strong."

Ag took a sip of his wine and met my eyes. "Let's just say that Lucifer's cruelty is infinite. Ruling the underworld isn't enough for him, and he rules in such a way that those who are not in his inner circle are miserable. Even the hint of betrayal or rebellion is ruthlessly stamped out. As my brother learned."

Across the table, Vas studied his plate, then reached for his own wine and took a large gulp.

Samael squeezed my hand. "There are few who are *born* evil. Most are created, shaped by life until they choose to break people and ruin lives. But Lucifer was forever scheming. He always had one eye on the throne. And yet my grandfather trusted him for longer than he should, because he believed Lucifer's lust for power would never turn on him."

Samael shook his head. "Lucifer raised his son to think the same way. When he found out your father had visited this realm, he was furious. My spies reported the deaths of seventeen of his inner circle, who had been tasked with keeping your father in the underworld, where there was no chance he could create a Nephilim."

"My father knew about the prophecy and he went after my mom anyway?"

"Some say he was rebelling as a way to prove to Lucifer that he should be given more power. Others say he acted as the hope of our people, finding the only way he knew to kill Lucifer."

"But you said Lucifer didn't know I was alive."

"No. Your father returned to the underworld and was likely tortured. If he had disclosed his relationship with your mother, Lucifer would have found her well before she gave birth."

I struggled with that for a long moment. My father had abandoned my mother, knowing that if anyone found out what he had done, she was dead. And yet… if he'd withstood torture to protect us…

Samael poured me another glass of wine. I took a steadying gulp.

Bael shoved a bite of gnocchi into his mouth. "The rebellion against Lucifer's rule had begun long before we left our world. And yet, as the ruler of all demons, when he gave an order, it was almost impossible for us to *not* follow it."

Ag nodded. He sent Samael a look that might have been… affectionate. I resisted the urge to pinch myself at the hint of something other than his usual blank expression.

"We had heard rumors, of course. That the boy had survived. That he'd been smuggled out. We realized the rumors were true as we learned what had become of the men who had killed Samael's family."

It was my turn to squeeze Samael's hand. Thanks to the memory he'd shared with me, I could still remember how heavy his sister had been in his arms. And how his heart had broken in a million pieces when Lucifer's men killed her in front of him.

Samael had been a child, and he'd killed them all.

"Samael became a myth as he grew into a man. The ferryman had taken him to the unseelie realm to grow into adulthood, and when he returned, we believed the darkness would end." Bael's expression turned mournful, and I glanced at Samael.

"It wasn't until I returned to my homeland that I realized what Lucifer had done. He connected with the underworld in a mockery of the relationship it had once had with my grandfather. And he made a bargain. The underworld would remove any ability I had to access my power while Lucifer was the underking. In exchange, Lucifer tied himself to the underworld. He is unable to step through a portal without instant death. And I am unable to return without losing access to my power."

Lilith speared a baby tomato and popped it in her mouth. "The heir returned, and our people celebrated, only to realize he was powerless."

"And yet," Ag said, "the very fact that the rumors were true, and he was still alive… it was enough to keep our people going. To keep them hoping. We begged him to travel to another realm to stay safe until we were ready to move on Lucifer. He refused. For centuries, Samael stayed hidden within the underworld, and the rebels waited for their chance to strike."

"And then my parents were killed," Vas said, his eyes sad. "They were part of Lucifer's court, and he was furious to learn the rebels had managed to get so close."

"Their deaths were a lit match on a sea of gasoline. War broke out. But Lucifer had carefully hidden a secret alliance with the seelie king."

I gaped at him. "The *seelie* king helped the demons?"

"He was at war with the unseelie. Lucifer agreed to send his people to join his war in exchange for his troops."

Explained why Samael loathed the seelie king now.

"None of us were prepared to be fighting both our own people, and the seelie. Half of our army quit on the spot, slinking back to Lucifer and hoping for mercy."

From the sick look on Bael's face, they didn't find it.

Sitri angled his head. "Before the portals were opened, only the strongest demons were able to cross into this world. When the rebellion began, no one had any idea that a group of human witches would offer us a lifeline." He lifted his glass in a toast. "So we sacrificed power. Various amounts depending on the demon. We had lost the war, and our people were being slaughtered, so we had no choice. The most powerful among us gave our power so that those who would otherwise not be able to travel through the portals could. Ag sacrificed the most, as he had a baby he also needed to get out, and Vas hadn't yet come into any of his own power."

I glanced at Samael. "So some of the demons who are loyal to you also won't be able to return to the underworld?

"Correct."

Samael leaned over and nuzzled my cheek. He seemed to need the comfort, so I allowed it.

"Do not worry, little witch. My plans will account for these limitations."

The conversation switched to something lighter, and I finished the meal with the best tiramisu I'd eaten in my life. When dinner ended, I glanced at Vas.

"Danica will meet you downstairs," Samael said.

I ground my teeth, ignoring the amused looks a few of the demons threw me as they filed out.

Once the room was empty, I glowered up at the demon. "I'm tired. I don't want to talk right now."

He grabbed my arm as I moved to shove past him. "This conversation is necessary."

"Don't get handsy with me, Samael."

He squeezed warningly. Not enough to hurt, but enough to make it clear I was pissing him off.

Ditto.

I shifted my own hand to the rowan arrow hanging from the long, thick chain beneath my lanyard.

The movement only worked because I had the element of surprise. I stepped forward, one foot behind Samael's as I twisted, pushing him against the wall. He let out a startled laugh and pulled me against him.

Then he froze.

My arrow was positioned at his heart.

"Feel that?" I purred.

His eyes widened, but there was no fear. Just a strange kind of lust.

"Rowan wood," he murmured. "You continue to surprise me, bounty hunter."

"I could kill you right now."

"I know. I find the concept strangely… arousing."

My mouth fell open and his gaze dropped to my lips. He wasn't lying. I could feel him hard and thick against me.

"You won't kill me," Samael purred. "You want me too much. Your life would be dark and cold without me."

I pushed the arrow closer, until the tip was pressed against his skin. "My life was just fine without you."

"Lies only annoy me, witchling."

How the hell was I the one threatening Samael's life, and yet he still had the upper hand?

I could feel the arrow, hard and sharp in my hand. But I couldn't see it. It was disconcerting.

"Either kill me or kiss me, bounty hunter. Your current position is giving me a variety of interesting ideas."

I rolled my eyes and did neither as I stepped away from him.

He moved like lightning. Within half a second his hand was over mine, trapping the rowan arrow against my body as he backed me into the wall.

"Now it's your turn to listen to me," he said.

"Let me go."

"When I'm done. When I first met you, I didn't know who you were," he said. "My people were gathering information from the moment I bonded you. By the night of the pact with Finvarra, I had strong suspicions. Part of me hoped I was wrong, as you would almost certainly die. Another part hoped I was right, as you could free my people. I won't apologize for my plans before I realized what you meant to me."

My heart flipped in my chest. "I'm not asking you to."

"Quiet."

I ground my teeth and he narrowed his eyes at me.

"When I finally learned my suspicions were correct, I had to make a choice. A choice I knew could make you hate me. The demons I sent to guard you… they weren't just protecting you from threats in this realm. They were told to ensure you never took a portal to that library. So you could dodge your fate. I'd forgotten about the amulet, and it never occurred to me that the fae would be stupid enough to allow it to be taken."

"I told you. I don't believe in fate."

He laughed at that, but it was hollow. "Fate is a bitch who plays with mortals and immortals alike." His other hand found my shoulder and he shook me. "There was a chance. A slim chance that I could have kept you from finding that book. From setting this into motion. From getting on Lucifer's radar. If you don't know by now that I'll do whatever it takes to keep you safe, then you haven't been paying attention."

We were both silent while I processed that. I felt oddly weepy. Samael seemed to understand, because he nuzzled my cheek, his voice gentle.

"I knew you would face Lucifer one day. But after all these centuries, I was still willing to wait until you were stronger. I wanted you to come into your power, to wield it expertly, and to be ready when you met him."

If there was one accusation I could never throw at Samael, it was the idea that he wanted me to be weak. The demon had been pushing me to learn how to use my power since the moment he learned of the suppression spell containing it.

"Would you have ever told me?"

"One day, when you were powerful enough that you could *choose* if you wanted to help me take him down. But I don't need you to kill Lucifer. I've been planning my vengeance for centuries, slowly collecting allies and making plans. You're not critical to my plans, Danica." His mouth curved up in a crooked smile. "Only to me."

I stared at him, gobsmacked.

He watched me out of cool eyes. "What are you thinking?"

"Give me a minute."

If there was a chance I wouldn't have found the prophecy, that I wouldn't have ever popped up on the underking's radar… could I *really* blame the demon for keeping it from me?

Yes. Because he treated you like a child. He didn't think you had the right to know who you were.

Like a child? Or like someone he cared about? If it had been Evie who'd been fated to kill or be killed by Lucifer, would I have told her?

No. I would have taken that secret to my fucking grave.

Which meant I was being a hypocrite.

The difference? I loved Evie.

"Will you forgive me, little witch?"

I heaved a sigh. The truth was, hating Samael was exhausting. It no longer came naturally to me. I had to actively work at it, stoking the fires of my distrust and annoyance, constantly reminding myself of all the ways he'd messed with my head since I met him.

I leaned close. Suspicion entered Samael's eyes and I almost laughed. No wonder we were so evenly matched. But he allowed it, and I brushed my mouth over his. Once. Twice.

I kept my gaze on his, so I saw it. The helpless

frustration that flickered in his eyes before he slammed them shut.

"I forgive you." I nibbled on his lower lip and he sighed.

"Samael," I murmured.

"Hmmm?"

The words were out before I knew what I was saying. "Are you in love with me?"

He stiffened, and his eyes slowly opened. Cold fury. So cold I shivered as he drew away, his body coiled like a panther waiting to strike. His laugh was bitter.

"Clever, clever witchling. You wish to leave me with nothing?"

I trembled at the look of wrath on his face. For the first time in months, I was actively scared of the demon.

"Samael–"

"Leave."

I took a deep, shuddering breath, but he was already turning away, stalking to the balcony, where he snapped invisible wings open and leapt into the sky.

I was practically stumbling as I made my way into the elevator, my eyes blurry.

Not tears. There was no way I was crying over the demon.

Right, because you've never cried over Samael before.

I'd messed that up so, so badly.

Every time we were close to laying our cards on the table, one– or both– of us dumped the entire deck on the floor. Neither of us wanted to admit we were vulnerable, and so we danced around the subject, waiting for the other person to put it all on the line first.

"Are you okay? Danica, wait up."

Vas grabbed my arm and turned me as I strode from Samael's tower. "What's going on?"

"Nothing." I wiped my face and he simply raised one eyebrow.

"Uh-huh."

I couldn't help but smile, and more tears fell. "Why does it all have to be so fucking complicated? I spent over four years with one goal: Figure out who killed my mom. And then I met Samael and he's done nothing but complicate my life. But at the same time, I can't imagine *not* having met him. Ugh, listen to me, I'm all over the place."

Vas shook his head. "You're not."

We were both quiet for a moment as I attempted to pull myself back together. Then he sighed.

"I think sometimes it's meant to be complicated, for it to be worth it. Maybe the complication and the struggle and the heartbreak is the price you have to pay to have that one person who fits you."

I let out a shuddering breath and wiped the last of the tears off my face. "You really believe that?"

He shrugged. "I'm trying." He gave me a crooked grin. "You want me to drop you home?"

"I need to go to Mere's."

He stiffened and I winced. "It's only a few streets away. I was planning to walk."

"I'll drop you outside. I'm going that way anyway."

"Have you thought about talking to her?"

"She's made it more than clear that she doesn't want

to see me. Another one of those 'complications,' I guess."

"Vas…"

"It's fine. Let's go."

Vas stepped back, his wings rustling as soon as my feet were on the ground in front of Meredith's. "You want me to stay and wait?"

"Nah, I'll take a Lyft. But I'll still see you in the morning."

He nodded. "I'll bring breakfast."

"You don't have to do that."

"I sure do. You have nothing to eat in your apartment."

I laughed as he swept into the sky, flying faster now that he wasn't hauling me around.

Meredith's was a staple in Durham, located in neutral territory on Main Street. The bar itself was also neutral territory, and it was one of the only places in the Triangle where paranormals could let down their guard and relax. Infighting was banned, and anyone who started shit in Meredith's immediately paid for it.

Mere was pouring pints for a group of gnomes when I took a seat at the bar. She nodded to me and placed the last pint on a tray for one of her waitresses. Business was obviously doing well, because she'd hired more staff.

A few light fae women were flirting with some of Nathaniel's wolves in one corner. On the opposite side of the bar, several high demons I didn't recognize were playing cards with a few dark fae guys. One of the demons nodded at me and I returned the nod, turning back to the bar as Mere slid a vodka soda in front of me.

"You look like you've had a rough one."

"You have no idea."

"I heard about the fire. I'm so sorry, Dani. If there's anything I can do…"

"Thanks." I studied her face. Shit. I'd forgotten. Brooke had mentioned that one of the other witches… Jessica… was Meredith's bestie.

"I'm sorry about Jessica," I said.

Meredith's eyes gleamed with tears and she blinked furiously, glancing at a ticket on the bar as she reached for a fresh glass.

"I just can't believe I'm never going to see her again, you know?"

"I can't imagine."

A tear fell and she glanced around, wiping it off her face. "Jess was one of the few witches who was actually friends with me since I refused to join a coven. Oh, she kept trying to convince me to go talk to Gemma, but she never looked down on me. Some of the witches… let's just say they're happy to drink here, but they take my dislike of covens as a personal attack." She sighed. "Do you know anything yet?"

"No. I'll let you know as soon as I do. Uh, there's something else."

Mere's eyes met mine, the weariness evident. I got it. Losing a coven of local witches was bad enough.

"Riona," I said.

"What of her? Has she gotten in some kind of trouble? I won't believe it." Her smile dropped at whatever she saw on my face. "She wasn't in the house when it burned."

"No. No she wasn't."

Meredith put her hand on the bar and one of her bartenders, a light fae guy I'd seen a few times before, came over and rubbed her back.

"Mere. Are you okay?" He shot me a look and I gazed steadily back.

"I'm fine. Just tired." She met my eyes. "What happened to Riona?"

"She's missing."

"God, what is going on? Everything in this city is turning to shit."

"I'm going to find her."

"Yeah, but will she still be alive?" The words were bitter. I couldn't blame her.

"I hope so. Can you tell me anything?"

"I doubt it. I haven't seen her for a couple of weeks. I've been busy with the bar, understaffed as usual, and I had some personal stuff going on that I had to deal with."

I took a sip of my drink. "She never mentioned having any problems with anyone?"

Mere frowned but she thought about it for a long moment. "Not that I can recall. But let me think about it and get back to you."

"Okay. Uh, this isn't any of my business…"

Mere's eyebrow lifted and I blew out a breath. "Don't worry about it." She watched me. "This is about Vassago."

"I'm not going to get involved." I rolled my eyes. "I realize I'm literally getting involved right now."

Mere's lips trembled before she firmed them. "Just spit it out. You'll feel better."

"He's a good guy, that's all. And whatever's going on between you, I've never seen him this miserable. I just wanted to let you know that he'd never do anything to hurt you."

"Did he tell you what he saw? When he saw my secrets?"

My mouth dropped open. "God no. He'd never even think about doing that. Jeez, Mere."

Surprise flashed across her face, quickly followed by relief. She nodded, her shoulders hunched, and I backed off. I'd stuck my nose far enough in her business, that was for sure.

By the time I got home, all I wanted was my bed. It called to me like a lover as I took the elevator up to my floor. Evie had texted me and said not to bring back any food since she'd already eaten. That likely meant that she was having an early night.

I opened my apartment door and froze.

Gemma sat next to my sister, her arm around her, while Evie silently wept. Four other witches had made themselves at home in my apartment. I recognized Gail, Zoe, and Caroline. The witch I hadn't yet met looked down her nose at me in a way that made me want to slam my fist into her face. I ground my teeth but pushed the irritation away.

Evie lifted her head. "They just got back from New York," she said wearily. "I said they could come here."

"It's fine."

Gemma stared at me. "Evie says you've been investigating the fire."

"Yes."

"Well you can cease your investigations now that I've returned. I will be working to find whoever did this."

"I'll just keep fumbling my way through my

investigation, if it's all the same to you."

Gemma narrowed her eyes at me. My power decided to stroke against my shields, and the memory of holding Gemma in place while I questioned her rose up, taunting me.

"The coven thanks you for your help," Gemma said. "But it is unnecessary."

I raised one eyebrow. "How'd they get through the wards, Gemma? You want to tell me how three men managed to stroll through those wards and take down everyone in that house without them raising the alarm?"

Gemma's face turned gray.

I kept going. "And how come none of them got out? What kind of spell would do that to a coven of witches?

Evie stiffened. "Enough, Danica."

"No. Not enough. Because the coven owes it to those women to do everything they can to find out who killed them."

"The High Coven is investigating. So is the Mage Council."

I laughed at that. "You think the Mage Council gives a shit about a house of dead witches? I worked for them. This investigation has been passed to some rookie who has nothing better to do. And the High Coven? Where are they? Cause I haven't seen a single representative while I've been investigating."

Gemma slowly got to her feet. Evie opened her mouth, but the coven leader held up her hand, silencing her.

"You have a lot of nerve," she said softly. "Instead of rejoining our coven, you worked for the Mage Council for four and a half years."

"Yeah. And that means I know how to hunt people down. And unlike everyone else looking into it, I actually give a shit. You *know* this, Gemma. You know I'll find anyone who threatened Evie. Cooperate with me."

Zoe cleared her throat delicately. "She has a point," she said. "Most importantly, she has the demons."

I loathed that my relationship with the demons was seen as worth more than my years on the streets, but I was no dummy. I kept my mouth shut.

"She has no loyalty to us," the other witch said. "Everyone knows her psycho demon boyfriend turned most of the McCormick descendants to ash. Who's to say he didn't do the same to our coven and she's trying to cover it up?"

Evie jolted like she'd been electrocuted. Then she jumped to her feet. "Don't you dare, Marie," she hissed. "Danica's working herself to the bone trying to find out who killed our family."

To her credit, Marie took one look at Evie's enraged expression and nodded. I watched her as she took a seat at my dining table.

Gemma sighed. She looked her age, grief cutting deep lines into her brow. "You may investigate the fire," she told me.

"Great. I'll need to interview all of the coven members in Durham."

I'd expected her to argue, but she merely nodded, ignoring the protests from the witches sitting at the table.

"Give us a couple of days to mourn," she said, and I frowned. That would give people time to get their stories straight.

She shook her head at whatever she saw on my face. "We all need to get some sleep."

The witches filed out. Evie poured herself a glass of water. "I'm sorry they were assholes."

"I'm used to it."

She flinched and I sighed. "I wasn't poking at you. Christ, I'm tired. Let's shelve this conversation for the morning."

She nodded and I turned, wandering into my bedroom. Lia was stretched out on my bed and she opened one eye as I walked in and turned on the light.

I lay down next to her, petting her soft head. Then I forced myself to get up and find the calendar I'd printed at Riona's. I hadn't had a chance to talk to Mere, but Riona needed me to figure out what the hell could have happened to her.

I scanned her schedule as I lay back down. According to Riona's calendar, she had a dog walking job in Chancellor's Ridge on the day she disappeared. I made a mental note for the morning to check if Kyla had followed up on that. And then I dreamed of blood and swords and fire, and war.

Samael

I shook my head as I gazed at the exhausted witch, sprawled out on her bed next to her cat. The cat eyed me distrustfully and I leaned over, holding my hand out for her to sniff.

She let out a tiny meow.

"Quiet," I ordered in a sharp whisper, shaking my head at the sleeping witchling. She hadn't even taken off her shoes. I pried them off her feet and she came awake instantly, her fist swinging as her mouth opened. I caught her fist and slammed my other hand over her mouth as she glared up at me.

"You'll wake your sister." I slowly removed my hand from her mouth and she let out a low growl.

"What exactly are you doing here?"

I shrugged and pulled off my shirt. Her gaze slid to my chest, and I felt it like a caress as it drifted lower before she managed to pull it back up to my face.

"You're here." I smiled at her.

Her mouth fell open and my body stirred. She made a picture with her tangled hair, open mouth, and narrowed, distrustful eyes.

"How did you get through my wards?"

I lifted one eyebrow and she cursed.

"Have you gone mad?" Her voice was a low hiss, and I smiled.

"It certainly feels that way. Move over."

"You're not sleeping here."

Since Danica refused to move, I picked up the cat and lay down in her spot.

"This bed is atrocious."

"Yes," she said. "It is. You should go find your own, much bigger, much more comfortable bed."

I ignored that. It twisted something inside of me that I could no longer sleep well without Danica in my arms. If she knew, the witchling would likely laugh herself hoarse.

Turning, I gathered her close. One of her hands burrowed between us and she planted her fist into my gut. I smiled. "I'm happy to tussle, but we will wake your sister."

I could practically hear her grinding her teeth. But she relaxed in my arms. I drew her even closer, resting my chin on her shoulder. The scent of her both aroused and comforted, and my eyes were instantly heavy.

Demons could go a long time without sleep. It had been weeks since I had truly rested. If my little witch knew just how desperate I was for her, how I could no longer sleep properly without her in my arms…

She sighed, and her muscles turned limp. The cat butted at me, then stalked over my thighs and lay down between us.

"We're going to talk about this," Danica slurred, and I smiled into the dark.

"Go to sleep."

It made no sense– the indescribable *want* I felt for the little witch. The little witch who had armed herself with what she imagined was my greatest vulnerability. I couldn't feel the rowan unless it was pressed against my skin, but I knew it was there, invisible between us.

And yet *she* had been my greatest vulnerability from the moment I dragged her kicking and screaming into my life. My mood darkened at the thought of our last spat. She was the only person in this world who had the ability to hurt me. And every day, I fought dual urges to both clamp her to my side and remove that vulnerability from my life.

I was still furious after our latest argument. This woman challenged and infuriated me like no other. But I was self-aware enough to admit that I wanted to hold her in my arms more than I wanted to roam the sky thinking dark thoughts.

I nuzzled her neck, enjoying her shiver, and closed my eyes as my body finally decided it needed sleep.

CHAPTER EIGHT

Danica

I woke feeling more rested than I had in days, and it pissed me off. I would have thought I'd dreamed Samael had climbed into my narrow bed, but when I woke, a single black feather had been lying next to Lia.

That was a taunt if I'd ever seen one.

"Next time, you need to bite him. No more snuggling with the demon."

Lia opened one eye and then closed it again. I shook my head, climbed off the bed, and froze.

A brand new utility belt lay on my dresser, next to my battered, worn belt. I reached for it, opening a few of the pockets, where I found a few small pouches of wixbane, a new and improved first-aid kit, and a more powerful mini-flashlight. The utility belt had individual sheaths built in which could hold at least five throwing knives. The knives would lie against my left hip.

He'd even included a few spell-stones loaded with exploding spells and low-level pain charms. They were expensive as hell, and I'd been too busy recently to visit Gary's and stock up.

I stared at the belt for a few more minutes. Just a few weeks ago, the demon had attempted to drape me in jewels. He'd been confused and a little baffled when I'd declined the diamonds in favor of a visit to his dragon when her egg hatched.

So he'd taken a new route when he noticed that my utility belt had seen better days.

Something warm took up residence in my chest and I struggled to push it back down.

I mentally planned my schedule as I showered, fueled up, and checked on Evie. She was still asleep, but she roused at the scent of coffee.

"Caffeine," she murmured, her face still buried in her pillow.

I poured her a cup and placed it on the coffee table in front of her. She sat up, her eyes bleary. Since she wasn't mercilessly teasing me about my late-night visitor, she obviously hadn't heard Samael last night.

Sneaky demon.

He'd done nothing but hold me. I could've made enough noise to rouse Evie. I could've demanded he leave, but instead, I'd snuggled closer and slept like the dead.

"Dani?"

I glanced at Evie. She raised her eyebrow. "Mind elsewhere?"

"Just thinking," I blew on my coffee to cool it quicker and took a glug. "What's up?"

"I need to work."

I'd figured this would happen. Evie's world had been rocked, but I'd known it was only a matter of time before she was ready to face what had happened.

"I've had the locations of several cameras sent to Steve. I'm hoping one of them will have our black SUV on it and we can get the plate number. If you're up for it, I'll give you a list of the cameras we've already found, and you can search the neighborhood for anything we might've missed. Then, head to the tower and help Steve search through the footage."

"Okay. I'm going to run down to the mall and grab a few things and then I'll get to work."

"Vas will be here soon, and he'll take you. Text me if you need anything."

She nodded and I stuffed my keys in my pocket, reaching for my phone as it vibrated on the counter.

Kyla.

Swung by the dog walking gig. No luck. But I found a housesitting job for the night Riona disappeared. It was last-minute. No mention of it in her calendar but her texts were synced to her laptop. She'd house sat for their friends a few times and these guys asked her to fill in for someone else who had to cancel.

Finally. Finally, something we could use.

Send me the address. I'll meet you there.

Kyla instantly replied with an address in Rockwood. I'd managed to leave during rush hour, and I gritted my teeth as I bullied my way across town. Kyla was already leaning against her car, waiting for me as I pulled up to the house.

Rockwood was a mostly human neighborhood popular with white-collar workers and business owners. I turned and scanned the street. It was quiet in the suburban way that gave me the heebie-jeebies. I climbed out of my car and crossed the narrow road.

"Any signs of life?"

"No one coming or going. Feels empty to me."

We walked a few feet toward the front door and Kyla stiffened.

"I smell blood."

Fuck. I closed my eyes as dread climbed into my stomach and stayed there.

I took a deep breath and forced myself to keep moving.

"Door's unlocked," I murmured, trying the handle.

I pulled my Colt automatically, kicking the door open and scanning the entranceway.

Blood was smeared across the tiled floor, staining the grout crimson. An arc of red decorated the door behind me, while the first few stairs of the wide staircase had gotten the majority of the splatter.

It stunk of black magic.

I glanced at Kyla. "What do you smell?"

"A black witch. A human male. Riona was definitely here."

Shit. "The human male— how do you know it's not the human guy who lives here?"

"It's more recent." She took a deep breath. "The blood isn't human."

"Are you sure?"

She slid me a look. Okay, the werewolf was sure. I rocked back on my heels. There was still a chance Riona was alive.

"What kind of blood is it?"

"Dark fae. Some kind of lesser dark fae. Maybe gnome or goblin. I'm going to shift and see if I can track where they took her."

She stepped away from the blood and started pulling off her clothes. I turned around to give her some privacy.

Kyla chuckled. "I forget how shy humans are about nudity. It only took two years for that to be knocked right out of me."

I shrugged, studying the window, the long white curtains, now decorated with crimson droplets.

Sunlight spilled through the window and onto the floor, catching on something shiny. I crouched, examining the metal lighter.

"Well, well, well."

"What is it?" Something— likely her jeans— hit the floor as I carefully used a plastic bag to collect the lighter.

"Some spells require candles. Whoever was here had to clean up fast once Riona interrupted them. They missed this."

"Wouldn't a witch just like, wave her hand to light the candle or some shit?"

"Depends on the witch. If they don't have a natural talent for fire, they wouldn't attempt to use it when they're about to do a difficult spell that requires sacrifice." I shrugged. "Could be that they brought it as a backup. Who knows."

I slipped the bag into my utility belt. Fingers crossed they hadn't been wearing gloves.

Something nudged me and I froze, my head slowly turned.

"Whoa. Those are some fangs."

Kyla opened her mouth in a wolf grin, displaying those lethal-looking teeth for me. I blinked at her. "You're white as snow… How the hell do you hunt at night?"

She lifted her lip in a sneer, giving me a closer look at those gleaming fangs. My mouth trembled as she turned and sniffed at the blood. Her tail was extraordinarily fluffy.

Kyla was likely three times the size of an ordinary wolf. I didn't understand how the magic worked, or where all that mass went when she shifted back to human.

She made her way closer to the door, glancing over her shoulder at me. I followed her as she sniffed her way down the hall, then lifted one paw, pushing down on the door handle and nudging it open with her nose.

An empty garage.

"You think they took her out of here in a car."

She nodded, inching back and forth along the garage, then she led me through the rest of the house.

Nothing.

"I think Riona stumbled onto something here," I said once Kyla had shifted back. "We'll get in contact with the owners, but they're human, and it's more likely that someone knew they'd be out of town. People are idiots these days, bragging about their vacations on social media so everyone knows when their house will be empty. Whoever did a spell like this would've wanted a human neighborhood where the residents wouldn't be able to sense black magic. They weren't expecting a house sitter, so maybe Riona surprised them."

Kyla glanced at me. "You think she's dead."

"I don't know. She's a loose end. But they took her out of here, when they could've just left the body or staged it to look like she was the one casting black spells.”

“Might be easier for them to dump the body and make sure it doesn’t lead back to them.”

“Yeah.” I glanced at my phone. “I’ll give the lighter to Samael’s people to analyze in their lab, and we’ll go from there.”

“She could still be alive.”

I glanced around the crime scene, my heart heavy.

“If she is, they won’t keep her alive for long. I’ll get Steve to do a run on the owners of this house and anyone who may have known they’d be out of town.” I sighed. “Let’s go over the scene one more time. They got sloppy with the lighter, maybe they forgot something else.”

We spent the next half hour checking both the crime scene and the rest of the house, but nothing popped out at us. Kyla glanced at me as I closed the door behind us.

“Where to now?”

“Charles Walker only lives a few blocks away, near my apartment.”

“How convenient. He’s probably at work though.”

I shook my head. “He works from home. Web development or some shit.”

“How, exactly, do you have that information already?”

“I’ve got skills.”

Kyla glanced at my phone. “You mean you’ve got contacts.”

She wasn’t wrong. Steve had already sent me Walker’s details.

Kyla followed me in her car and I spotted Vas landing in my parking lot as we passed my apartment. I beeped and he lifted his hand in a wave. Gratitude made my chest tight.

When I'd fallen in love with my apartment, the location had been a huge part of its appeal. My windows had no view of the tower, and the building backed onto a series of largely human neighborhoods in East Durham.

Charles lived in one of those human neighborhoods, in a blue, split ranch in Wedgewood. I knocked, waited, and Kyla rolled her eyes at me. "He's in there. I can scent him."

I pounded on the door some more. When Charles finally appeared, he was wearing nothing but a pair of boxers, his hand wrapped around a can of beer. His eyes were red and puffy.

"What do you want?"

"We're investigating the fire at the coven," I said. "I'd like to ask you a few questions."

He glanced between us and gave a sharp nod, turning and walking back into the house. We followed him in, and I heroically didn't wrinkle my nose at the smell of old food, beer, and dust.

Brooke had been right. The guy was a slob.

And she'd never get the chance to meet another guy. Never feel the fluttering of butterflies in her stomach, never get to raise those kids she wanted. Life was damn unfair.

Charles sat on the sofa and glanced at me. He flinched and I forced a neutral expression onto my face. He gestured at a ratty armchair next to the sofa and I sat down. Kyla wandered the room restlessly.

There were signs of a woman's touch here. A bunch

of dead flowers sat by the window. The cushions were obviously new, patterned with cheerful floral covers. A vanilla-scented candle stood alone on the coffee table.

I forced myself to focus on Charles.

"Do you know of anyone who might've wanted to hurt Brooke?"

Charles ran one hand over his face, shaking his head. He took a swig of beer and his eyes locked on the candle.

"She loved those things. Burned them all the time. I've got candles in my bathroom, for Christ's sake. What kind of guy has candles in their bathroom?"

Kyla nodded. "She was making a home with you," she said, her voice soothing.

"She dumped me." Charles's voice cracked. "Because I never cleaned, never helped out. If she'd still been here, she wouldn't have been at that fucking house. She'd still be alive."

My heart twisted. "Nothing will bring her back, but we can find whoever did this and make them pay."

My intuition was telling me the guy had nothing to do with the fire. He wasn't organized or motivated enough to keep his house clean. But people did things that seemed out of character all the time.

"Are you going to be questioning everyone who knows the victims? Or just the exes? I know how this works. The cops were here earlier. They've decided I'm the only one with motive."

"You want to clear your name, tell us everything you can."

My hand dropped to my thigh sheath as Charles lunged to his feet, but he wasn't going for a weapon. He grabbed the candle and threw it at the wall, hard enough to leave a dent.

I slowly got to my feet. My turn to be bad cop. I glanced at Kyla. Hopefully she was able to pull off good cop, because I was running on far too little sleep.

"I can see why the cops were looking at you. You have an angry streak, don't you, Charles? What happened, you got pissed because Brooke wasn't coming home, and you decided to make her pay? Make the whole coven pay?"

His mouth dropped open. "No. I wouldn't."

"Then maybe you hired someone. Someone who'd teach the bitch that she shouldn't have left you, huh?"

"Don't call her that. She wasn't a bitch."

"Oh yeah? Cause I heard that's exactly what you called her when she left."

Charles' face turned red, and then slowly drained of color. He met my eyes for a long moment, and then buried his head in his hands. Kyla stepped forward and sat next to him.

"How about we all take a breath," she said softly. "Can I get you some water, Charles?"

He shook his head. "I wouldn't have hurt her." The words came out muffled and he lifted his head, his expression desperate as he appealed to Kyla. "I swear."

"I believe you," she soothed. "But these are the kinds of questions that have to be asked. Once you've told us what you know, we'll be able to move on."

"I wouldn't have hurt Brooke. I was going to marry her." Charles got to his feet and stalked over to the circular table in the kitchen where a small velvet box was sitting. He opened it and stared down at the ring.

"I was going to marry her. I was going to convince her to come back. I was going to go to therapy, do whatever she wanted."

"Okay," I said. "Did Brooke ever tell you about anyone she argued with? Anyone who gave her a bad feeling?"

"The guy at the corner store. Marty. He sold her some fruit that was bad. She said she wasn't paying enough attention, but they had words the next time she went in."

"Anyone else? Where's her family?"

"Dead. Her mom and dad were killed in a car accident. She said she'd found her family with the coven." His red eyes met mine. "If she'd never found that family, she'd still be alive."

Kyla glanced over her shoulder as we walked out of the house. "So what did you think of him?"

"I think he's a putz, but he's a putz who's grieving."

"You can grieve someone and still have killed them."

"Exactly. He goes to the bottom of the list, but he's still on that list."

She glanced at me. "But you don't think he did it."

"Nope." I rounded my car and opened the door.

"My trusty dagger didn't glow. He was telling the truth. I don't think he's smart enough or motivated enough to pull off the attack." I frowned. "I don't think corner store Marty did either, but we follow the steps. You never know who could've noticed someone watching Brooke."

Kyla followed me to the small store. A neon sign hung in the window, the word reading *Mart's*. The *y* wasn't lit.

Marty was standing behind his counter, wiping it

with a grimy cloth. I'd put him in his fifties or sixties, with deep frown lines carved between his brows, his mouth turned down as we stepped inside. Above the counter, a large white sign stated *No refunds!*

"We need to ask you a few questions."

"This is about that woman from down the street? I heard she was dead." Marty wiped his hands on his apron. Then he narrowed his eyes at me. "I know you. You're the witch who kept that demon alive."

"She also stopped an insane coven from rampaging through the city," Kyla said. "You're welcome."

Marty sneered at me. "She was a witch, too, that girl who died. Tried to hide it, but I know the signs. This is a good human neighborhood."

"Wow," I said. "You're a flaming asshole, aren't you, Marty?"

"I don't have to take this from you. You're not even a cop."

"Nope. Cops have all these rules and regulations around how they can treat their suspects." I gave him a wide, toothy smile. "I don't have any of those."

Marty paled. "I didn't do anything. You think this store runs itself? I ain't got time to go set a house on fire."

He was a bigot, but I doubted he was a murderer. "You ever notice anyone who had issues with Brooke?"

"That was her name? Brooke?" He shrugged. "She kept to herself most of the time. Usually polite, until she stalked in here and told me I needed to replace her fruit. I don't give refunds."

He pointed to the sign above him. "It's right there. People these days don't even fucking read."

I wasn't going to get anything out of him. I shook my head, bit my tongue, and walked out.

"She sounds like a normal woman who was just living her life." Kyla said as the door swung shut behind us. "It pisses me off."

"I know. But why take the other witches out? There were so many easier ways to kill her while she was alone. They could've set it up as a home invasion, a robbery gone wrong, or even a simple execution. Taking the rest of the coven out just means there are more grieving families. More cops, more publicity, more time on the news. Why draw that much attention to yourself?" I scowled. "It just doesn't make sense."

"What now?"

I sighed. "Now, we interrogate what's left of Gemma's coven. One of them is likely involved in the slaughter of the women who considered her a sister."

Kyla looked slightly sick. "Can't wait."

CHAPTER NINE

Danica

We stopped by my apartment building long enough for Kyla to leave her car so she could ride with me. That way, I could give her a rundown of what to expect from Gemma's coven. They were staying at the new boutique hotel off Main Street, and Kyla whistled when I said the name.

"I've always wanted to stay at Alchemy. So they're going to let you interview them?"

"According to Gemma they will. I'm not expecting most of them to be cooperative though. The Durham witches aren't exactly my biggest fans."

"Why?"

I took a right and scowled at the long line of traffic. "They need to do something about this fucking intersection." I sighed. "I guess they think I should've come crawling back to them and rejoined the coven when I returned to Durham. Instead, I joined the Mage Council."

I pulled into the parking lot of the hotel and sent Gemma a text. She replied instantly with her room number and we strolled into the lobby.

"Wow, this place is as gorgeous as everyone says."

"The coven has money."

We walked past the front desk, ignoring the speculative look from the staff. In my ripped jeans and beaten-up brown leather jacket, I didn't look like the type to stay in a five-star hotel. Kyla was wearing black leggings and an oversized t-shirt, although she somehow managed to look almost elegant.

Gemma opened the door herself as soon as we knocked, moving back so we could step into the suite. Her eyes were red-rimmed and tired.

"This is Kyla. She's helping me with my investigation."

Gemma narrowed her eyes, obviously unhappy that a werewolf was involved. I merely shrugged, and after a moment, Gemma stepped aside.

"We have gathered in the living room. We also have the suite next door, which you may use for your interviews."

I nodded. The witches were quiet when we walked in, a few of them eating lunch. There must have been ten or fifteen of them gathered together in small groups, some of them sitting on the floor. A few of them nodded at me, while most ignored us. Charming.

"I'll make this quick," I said. "We need to talk to everyone. The easier you make this, the faster it will go, and the more chance I have of finding out who did this."

One of the witches sneered at me. I recognized her from last night. Marie. I gave her a wide smile. "You're up first."

Kyla glanced at me. Technically, Marie was on her list, but I was just ornery enough to want to deal with her myself. Kyla glanced at her phone.

"Isabel," she said. "You're with me."

Isabel was in her eighties, and she merely nodded, slowly pushing herself out of her chair. I turned and walked out of the suite, plucking the keycard for the suite next door out of Gemma's hand.

Marie scowled at me as we sat in the living room next door. Kyla had taken Isabel into one of the bedrooms and closed the door.

"You have no right to do this," Marie said.

"You know, the more you protest about this investigation, the more I wonder if you had something to do with the fire."

Shock flickered in her eyes, instantly replaced by rage.

"I was in New York."

"Uh-huh. We both know that ward had to be messed with to allow the killers inside the house. All you'd need to do is introduce the house to their magical imprints."

The blood slowly drained from her face and I was small enough to enjoy it.

"You're not pinning this on me, you bitch."

"Right now, you're at the top of my suspect list. You've been an asshole since you learned I was investigating, you refuse to cooperate, and you were conveniently out of the city when the coven was killed."

She gaped at me. "You honestly think I had something to do with this?"

I shrugged. "Tell me why you didn't."

"Guilty until proven innocent, is that right?"

I showed her my teeth. "This isn't a human system of law." We both knew what would happen to whoever was found responsible for the murders. There would be no life sentence in a maximum security prison. Witch covens may include women in their nineties, but those women had lived through the Decade of Despair. The witches had carved out their territory and fought tooth and nail for every ounce of power they had in this country.

"Why would I want my family dead?"

"You tell me."

Her eyes were suddenly wet and she fixed her gaze on the wall behind me. "The love of my life was in that house."

The suppressed pain was obvious in her voice. "Who?"

"Heidi. We'd danced around it for a few years, both of us seeing other people. But eventually it was obvious that we were meant for each other."

"Did anyone have a problem with your relationship?"

"No. At least, not that I knew of. We snuck around for a few months, but we didn't really need to. It was more that we just wanted to keep it private. Then, on her birthday, Heidi had a few too many glasses of champagne and kissed me in front of everyone."

A tear spilled from her eye and she wiped it away, fixing her gaze on the wall again. "People teased us, but it was more of a 'how long has this been going on for?' kind of way."

"Okay. Take me through this trip to New York. Why did you guys go?"

"The coven leader is Gemma's second cousin. They've stayed in touch over the years. Most covens are… secretive. We don't trust easily."

Yeah, no shit. Marie was obviously choosing to forget

I was a witch, but it was no skin off my nose if it helped her cooperate.

"But Gemma has some kind of what… alliance with this coven?"

Marie sneered at me again. I was getting really tired of seeing that look on her face, and something in my expression must have communicated exactly that, because she lost the attitude.

"It's not an alliance. Just a friendship. Both Gemma and Louisa realized that a little cooperation could help both of their covens. Since they're in different states, they're not in competition for territory or power."

"What kind of cooperation are we talking about?"

"Spells, mostly. Some witches are just good at thinking on the fly and creating new spells."

I nodded. Evie was one of those witches. She'd always had a knack for magic, along with the kind of instinctive creativity that couldn't be taught.

"So you guys share spells?"

"Some of them. Sometimes it's spells, sometimes information about other covens, that kind of thing."

This was interesting. Gemma's coven had always been powerful, but there was no doubt that it had grown over the past few years. Maybe Louisa had regretted forming that alliance.

"Do you know anyone who might have wanted to hurt Brooke specifically?"

She frowned. "No. Why? You think Brooke was the target?"

"Just a question."

She gave me a look that told me she didn't buy what

I was selling. Not my problem. I'd tell Gemma what had happened to Brooke, and then it was up to her whom she told. With her contacts in human law enforcement, she'd likely find out soon anyway.

I glanced down at my list. "Tell Caroline she's up next."

A muscle clenched in her jaw at my dismissal and she got to her feet, stalking out the door. Pissing her off wasn't necessary, but I had to take my joy where I could find it today.

Misty was in my lap, and it hadn't lit up once while Marie was talking. She may not like me, but she wasn't lying.

Caroline clutched a wad of tissues in her hand as she walked in a couple of minutes later. Her blue eyes were huge and wet, and she sniffed, wiping at her nose as she took a seat on the sofa across from me.

"Hi," I said.

"Hi. Gemma said we needed to tell you everything we could think of, but it's just so hard."

"I know. All I need is for you to tell me what happened."

She sniffed. "Okay. Where do you want me to start?"

She took me through her history at the coven. Caroline was Gail's niece, but she'd lived in Houston for most of her life. She'd left her old coven five years ago, and Gemma had agreed to a trial run when she'd moved to Durham. Then she'd quickly become indispensable to the coven, thanks to her healing spells.

"I, uh, volunteer sometimes at the human hospital," she said shyly. "They always need healing spells, and I'm good at them. I've even come up with something that can treat the common cold. Not the cold itself, but I have a spell that can remove all of the symptoms."

Now that sounded like a spell I could use. She smiled slightly at whatever she saw on my face. "Let me know if you catch a cold and I'll give Evie the spell to try."

"That would be great, thanks."

I made a few notes on my phone and then glanced up.

"What can you tell me about Brooke? Did you ever see anyone hanging around? Did she ever mention anyone who was giving her trouble?"

Something flickered in Caroline's eyes at the question, and I went still. "You know something?"

"No, it's just…"

"You can tell me."

She was silent for a long moment. "She told me about this guy who was a real dick. At the corner store."

Disappointment made my shoulders slump. "Yeah. We've spoken to him. Thanks. Anyone else?"

More tears leaked down her pretty face. "No, but I'll let you know if I think of anyone."

I interviewed five more witches, and by noon I was desperate to get out of the hotel. I waited until Kyla had finished up with her last interview and then poked my head in the bedroom door.

"Anything?" I asked.

She shrugged. "No one seems to know shit. There's infighting and power struggles, but no more than your average human sorority. How that many women can live together and not want to kill each other is beyond me."

"Amen."

"It was sad though. One of the witches…" she glanced

at the notes on her phone. "Willow. She just sat there and cried."

"No one could've imagined their coven would end up like this." I frowned. "I need to get a better understanding of the power structure of the coven itself. From Gemma down."

"You think someone did this as a way to get more power?"

"I don't think anything, but I can't figure this shit out. If Brooke was the target, why can't we find any reason? Maybe she wasn't the target at all, and she was just in the wrong place at the wrong time. Maybe the sleep spell didn't work on her, or she woke up and discovered the assholes in her house and then one of them panicked."

Kyla's stomach chose that moment to let out a howl from across the room. I eyed her. "I should probably feed the hungry werewolf, before I end up losing a hand or something."

She laughed, but her eyes had lightened the slightest amount. I wouldn't have noticed if I hadn't been watching for it.

The day was getting away from me again. I pulled out my phone and sent Selina a text.

The witch had a touch of the sight. I met her when I first began working for Samael, and she used that power to tell me a little about the murderers. Since then, we'd struck up a… friendship. Once a week or so, she helped me learn how to use my power. The hope was, one day, I wouldn't need to worry about my power using me.

It was thanks to Selina that I was no longer battling the urge to use that power to tear someone to pieces when they pissed me off.

Well, not unless they threatened my life. I was still working on keeping my shit together when my adrenaline was high.

"Okay, let's head back to the house really quick. I want to see if a witch I know can sense what kind of magic was used. Then we'll get some lunch."

Kyla nodded, and I drove to Trinity Park, both of us lost in thought. Since Selina lived in North Trinity Park, she was waiting on the street when we arrived, her eyes sad.

Selina never failed to make me feel like I was a slob. And it wasn't like she wanted to make anyone feel that way, it was just that she was one of those women who always looked perfectly put together, but never like they were trying too hard.

Today, she was wearing jeans that fit like they'd been tailored, pointy black flats, and a gorgeous floaty shirt that was some kind of color between blue and green. Not aquamarine, but close. A trio of sparkly bangles were stacked on her wrist, her braids had been pulled up into a bun, and she wore intricate silver earrings that danced above her shoulders.

She turned her head and smiled at me. "It's good to see you," she said, "although the circumstances are terrible."

"They sure are. This is my newest employee, Kyla. Kyla, this is Selina."

They shook hands and Kyla leaned against the car. "I'll wait here. I want to write down some of my notes."

Selina and I walked closer to the blackened remains. She sighed. "This was a beautiful house. And the witches who lived here… you could tell they were close. Whenever they were in public, they always seemed to be laughing." She glanced at me. "Since there was no murder weapon left on the scene, I don't know if I will be much help. But I believe you should be able to get a sense of the type of power that was used."

I frowned. "That's not exactly in my skill set."

"Humor me."

I took a deep breath and focused on the remains of the house. My shields held strong as I slipped a spark of power through them, looking for anything that felt familiar.

"That's weird. It seems like a mishmash of several types of power. Witch, werewolf, fae?"

"I don't know exactly how that could be," she frowned. "I wouldn't think that these factions would work together to take down the coven, as the power vacuum will likely impact everyone in this city." She glanced at me. "You've been practicing."

"Yeah. Night and day. It's become almost instinctive to hold my shields while using my power now."

Because if I ever went up against Lucifer, I couldn't face him with power that flared with emotion but was otherwise tucked away, deep beneath thick shields. The more I worked with my power, the less it rose up with a vengeance when I was dealing with strong emotions.

"I'm proud of you."

I shifted uncomfortably and she laughed. "That embarrasses you."

"No… I'm just not used to it, that's all."

She took my arm, leading me away from the burnt remains of the house. Vas had arrived while we were talking, and he was leaning against my car, chatting with Kyla. He still looked miserable.

"Your circle is growing."

I glanced at Selina. "My circle?"

"The people you care about."

I sighed. "Yeah. I used to be able to count those people on one hand. A few fingers, really. Now I have all these people in my life and I have to deal with all their drama."

Selina laughed. "And your life is better for it."

Kyla reached into her pocket, offering the demon a stick of gum. He shrugged and popped it into his mouth.

Selina gestured at the house, and I turned my attention back to her.

"I've never heard of multiple factions working together to take down a coven. It's curious."

It was curious alright. Why would the fae and werewolves work with witches? Either way, this was just bolstering my theory that it was an inside job. That meant I needed to look at any other covens competing for territory and power in Durham.

"With Gemma's coven decimated, which coven would be the next most powerful?"

"Now that's an interesting question," Selina frowned. "I would say either the Jefferson coven or the Blake coven."

I made a note on my phone. "Thanks. I better get going."

"Where are you off to now?"

"The morgue."

"You lead an interesting life."

"Yeah, it's a barrel of laughs."

CHAPTER TEN

Danica

Vas had already disappeared when I headed back to the car. I glanced at Kyla.

"What did he want?"

"To tell you he has a few things to do for Samael this afternoon and Evie is hanging in the tower working with Steve."

"He could have texted me."

"Yeah. I think he was sad."

I sighed. "Romance problems." I had to put it out of my mind. "You okay going into the morgue?"

She slid me a look. "You think I'm going to get peckish and go for the corpses?"

"Ew." My shoulders hunched. "I don't know anything about wolves, jeez."

From Kyla's narrow-eyed stare, I should've kept my ignorance– to myself.

She heaved a sigh. "If it was a building full of hurt prey… *people*… I would have problems. At this point, I still need to have eaten a meal before I step into a hospital, for example. But cold, dead flesh doesn't appeal to werewolves."

"Okay. Ah, I'm sorry. That was rude of me."

"I'm used to it."

I winced and she laughed. "Don't worry about it. I know nothing about either witches or demons, and you've answered plenty of my stupid questions."

"True. Okay, There's another witch… Freya. She lives near the coven but she wasn't at the hotel today. I talked to her briefly the night of the fire, but I want to talk to her again. Let's stop at her house on the way to the morgue."

Freya lived two streets west of the coven, in a cute Victorian-esque house that was on the smaller side of Trinity Park.

Her eyes were exhausted, her face pale when she answered the door.

"Hi," I said. "Do you mind if I ask you a few questions?"

She shook her head. "Gemma asked us to cooperate. Come on in." She turned suddenly green and held a hand up to her mouth, pointing through a doorway to a small sitting room to the right. "I'll be right back."

I glanced at Kyla and we both strolled into the sitting room. The wallpaper was old and peeling, and someone had painted a few swatches on the wall, all in various shades of white and off-white.

Freya returned a few minutes later, sipping a glass of water. "Can I get you something to drink?"

"No, we're fine." I wanted her to sit down. She looked like she was going to pass out.

She smiled at whatever she saw on my face. "Morning sickness."

"Oh, wow. Congratulations."

"Thanks. I haven't told the father yet. It's… complicated. Anyway."

She sat down, crossing her long legs in front of her. Unlike most of the witches, she didn't practically radiate contempt when she looked at me.

I ran her through the night. One of the neighbors had called Freya when she'd spotted flames, and Freya had contacted the rest of the coven as she made her way to the house.

"How come you didn't live in the main house?"

She shrugged. "Personal choice. My grandmother left me this house and I've been slowly doing it up. I'm an introvert, and while I love visiting the coven, I get way too overwhelmed with the constant talking, fighting, laughing, and everyone poking their nose into everyone else's business."

"Fair enough." I glanced at my notes. If Freya had anything to do with the fire, I'd eat my pretty diamond lanyard. But she could probably help me with a few other questions.

"I'm interested in the power levels of the witches killed."

Freya clammed up, shooting me a suspicious frown. "You should ask Gemma about that."

"I'm not looking for your secrets. I'm looking for motive. Tell me who was left behind when Gemma and the others went to New York."

"Um, most of the coven. It was really only a few who went. Originally, Nellie was going to go to New York and Gemma was going to stay here. Gemma decided to go a few weeks ago. I guess she just wanted to get away for a few days.

"I think Gemma had a word with Evie— sort of told her that even though Nellie was staying behind, Evie needed to keep an eye on things." A smile trembled around Freya's lips. "Nellie was getting a little cantankerous in her old age. She mostly wanted to be left alone with her plants. God, I can't believe she's gone. Can't believe they're all gone."

Kyla shifted, drawing Freya's attention to her. "Were there any grudges within the coven? Any threats, or bad blood?"

Freya smiled. "You're talking about a large group of women, all of different ages and power levels, who *have* to get along for the good of the whole. When we do, it's amazing. There's nothing like female friendships, you know? But it can be bad, too. The power hierarchy changes as people grow in power, and others retire or stop practicing magic. The coven has grown substantially over the last few years as we got a reputation for being both stable and powerful."

"Any other covens threaten that stability?"

She shrugged. "Not really. We keep to ourselves for the most part. Gemma says she's too damn old for territory disputes. I have to ask, why are you investigating this?"

"Evie could have been in that house. She asked me to help."

Freya shook her head. "You could have told her no. Insisted it was too sticky with the coven. But you care." She was silent for a moment and then heaved a sigh. "Not all of the witches in that coven hated you, you know. Some of them missed you, thought you'd come back one day. I just thought you should know that."

I didn't know what to say. Freya seemed to understand, because she offered me a sympathetic smile. The smile dropped as her face went pale and she got to her feet, striding toward the bathroom. "You guys mind letting yourself out?"

Kyla winced. "Nope. Good luck."

My eyes burned as I got into the car. Kyla offered me a tissue she pulled out of somewhere.

"God," I said, wiping at my eyes. "It's easier to think of them all hating me. It's easier to remember hating *them* for old wounds. We'll never get to talk now." I sighed and turned the key. "And it's not about me."

"You're a witch. Someone who knew some of the dead. And even if you didn't, it would be impossible not to be impacted by the murder of so many women. Hell, I didn't know any of them and I'm ready to find whoever did this and rip them apart."

"Yeah." I finished wiping my face and took a deep breath. "Okay, time to go to the morgue."

We hit a drive-thru on the way to the morgue, and Kyla ate seven burgers and two large fries. Werewolves.

My phone vibrated as I parked.

"Siobhan. Hi."

"Hey. I heard about the fire at Gemma's coven. I know you must be so busy juggling two cases, and I'm sorry to hound you, but I needed to check in. Do you know anything?"

"You're not hounding me. We're going through Riona's schedule. Kyla, my... employee—" and didn't *that* feel weird to say— "has been interviewing all her friends and neighbors. We're looking for anyone who saw her the day she went missing."

"Okay. Okay. I know you're doing everything you can. I've been going over the last time I saw her, trying to remember if she said anything that I should've found concerning. But I was so focused on the engagement party and the wedding…" Guilt dripped from Siobhan's voice.

"She seemed excited for the engagement party. And I bet she loved hearing about your wedding plans."

"Yeah. Yeah she did." Siobhan blew out a breath. "Thanks Danica."

"Look after yourself."

I hung up and finished the rest of my Pepsi.

"It's gotta be hard," Kyla said.

"Yeah. I don't know what I'd do if it were Evie who'd gone missing. Do you have any siblings?"

Kyle was silent for a long moment. "I have a brother. I haven't seen him since I was turned. He'd be so disappointed if he knew what happened to me."

"I'm sorry."

She sighed. "Yeah. Me too."

The human morgue was a sprawling, concrete building located directly behind the Durham Police Department Headquarters on East Main Street.

The Decade of Despair had been good for the morgue. It now took up almost an entire block, with entrances on all of the surrounding streets. I parked in the lot on Elizabeth Street and dumped our trash in the garbage can as we crossed to the main entrance. The temperature plummeted as we walked through the sliding doors and into the small waiting area.

Several red plastic chairs and a water cooler occupied one corner of the room. Directly opposite the chairs, double swinging doors led further back into the morgue. To the left, a long marble counter stood between us and the lone guard, who was already giving us a hard stare.

"We have an appointment with Amy Wilson," Kyla said.

"Identification."

We handed over our licenses and the guard heaved himself to his feet, favoring his left leg as he shifted to the printer to make copies.

He held onto our licenses for a long moment once he was done, glancing between our IDs and our faces as if damn sure we were both suspicious characters.

"Wait here," he said. "I'll tell Wilson you've arrived."

We sat in the cheap plastic chairs for barely two minutes before the tap of heels on linoleum sounded. The wide doors swung open, and a curvy blonde appeared, her blue eyes examining us in a way that made me feel very much like one of her dead bodies.

"I'm Amy Wilson," she said. "I'm slammed today, so this will need to be brief."

I nodded as we got to our feet. "We won't take up too much of your time."

"Samael said you were mostly interested in the body that had been beheaded," she said as she led us down the corridor. Earrings swung from her pointed ears as she walked.

The scent of antiseptic and death wafted up my nostrils and I shuddered. Wilson shot a sympathetic smile over her shoulder. "You get used to the smell."

From the way Kyla wrinkled her nose, she wouldn't be getting used to the smell any time soon. I was suddenly grateful for my dull half-human senses.

Wilson pushed open the next door and we stepped inside. I suppressed the sudden urge to run, to leave and never come back. I didn't want to see Brooke like this, burned and in pieces.

Wilson paused in front of the steel drawer. "Are you okay?"

"I'm fine."

"Did you know the victim?"

"Yeah. Not well, but I knew her."

Wilson studied my face and her blue eyes turned darker with pity. She moved away from the drawer and to the desk in the corner of the room, opening her laptop.

"I have the report here. Why don't I go through everything you need to know, and you can ask any questions you have?"

"That's very kind of you," I said. I wasn't going to argue. I already had enough nightmares.

She merely nodded and turned back to her laptop. "No defensive wounds. Nothing to indicate that she was aware of what was about to happen."

"It looks like everyone else in that house was spelled. Either held in place, or incapacitated with some kind of sleeping spell."

Wilson nodded. "Her head was removed with one thrust. That means the killers used a sharp, heavy blade. They were likely experienced."

I couldn't bring myself to say anything and Kyla

stepped forward next to me.

"Anything else?"

"It would have been quick. She didn't suffer."

I swallowed. "She was in her home, she thought she was safe. They all thought they were safe."

Wilson nodded. "I hope you find whoever did this. We're still working on the other victims. So far, it appears that most of them died from smoke inhalation. I'll be in touch if I find anything unexpected."

"Appreciate it."

We moseyed out of the morgue, ignoring the guard who watched as we walked past him. The humid air hit me like a punch to the face but I inhaled as it cleared the scent of death from my nostrils.

"That was nice of her to condense it like that," Kyla said when we got back into the car.

"Yeah."

"Are you okay?"

"No."

"You've figured something out."

"Yeah. I can't be sure, but my instincts tell me Brooke wasn't the target."

I'd met her only a few weeks ago, and I'd liked her. At the time, I'd noticed how similar she looked to Evie, with her curvy, toned physique and long, blonde hair.

Every inch of my body came to attention as my mind struggled to process what now seemed almost obvious. "Everyone's been focused on Brooke, looking into any possible motives for her murder, but what if we're looking in the wrong place? She was in Evie's room. She looked like Evie. So much so that anyone who'd been given a description would probably assume they had the right person.”

“Fuck.”

I was trembling, I realized distantly, and my hands were clamped so tightly around the steering wheel that my knuckles had turned white. “Yeah. I feel stupid not figuring it out sooner, but I can’t see why anyone would want Evie dead either. At the same time, she’s the one with a sister who’s been sleeping with a demon. She’s the one who’s dating a werewolf.”

“You think it was a hate crime?”

“I don’t know what to think.”

I pulled the car into the parking lot of my apartment building.

“I’ll go see the wolves in the morning. Evie’s been seeing one of them—Liam.”

Kyla nodded. “He’s a good guy.”

“Yeah, I thought so too, but he’s been suspiciously absent since her life fell apart. And I caught a hint of wolf at the scene. I’ll text you when I’m done there, and we’ll figure out our next step.”

She slid me a sympathetic look. “I’m sorry, Danica.”

“We don’t know for certain that she was the target.”

Kyla was quiet as we got out of the car, and I blew out a breath. “Yeah, I’m sorry too. I’ll see you tomorrow.”

My mind raced as I made my way up to my apartment. I needed to get Evie out of here. If I was right, she was in danger if she stayed in Durham.

We had a cousin in Chicago. I hadn’t seen her since I was a kid, and she was a loose cannon, but she’d take my sister in.

And there was no way Evie would go. I wouldn't if I were in her shoes.

I pushed open my apartment door and Evie jumped to her feet.

"I learned something very interesting today," she said quietly, and I bit my tongue to hold back a deluge of curses.

"What did you learn?"

"I learned that Brooke was beheaded."

"Yeah." Fraught silence stretched between us and I sighed. "I was planning to tell you. I just didn't know how."

"Why, Dani? Did you think I couldn't handle it?"

I threw up my hands. "Yeah. I thought you couldn't handle it. Because I can barely handle it, and I've only met her a few times. It's horrifying, and you shouldn't have to handle it."

Evie stared at me. "You lied to me."

"I didn't. I just didn't tell you everything."

"Because you think I'm fragile."

"No," I pressed the heels of my hands against my eyes for a long moment. "Because what you've been through is so awful, I wanted to spare you from more pain for as long as I could. I tried to protect you from the truth, and I'm sorry. But there's more." Hiding my suspicions from Evie would only piss her off. If I were in her shoes, I'd be tempted to take a swing at me for even considering it.

"Tell me."

"I can't find anyone who could want Brooke dead, and believe me, we're looking. She lived a normal, quiet life. But she looked like you, Evie. She was in your room. You need to be careful, because there's a chance that someone was trying to kill you. And by now, they would've learned that they fucked up."

Evie collapsed back onto the sofa, burying her head in her hands.

"She died because someone thought she was me?"

I walked over and sat next to her. "She died because she was in that house. Even if she hadn't been mistaken for you, she would have died in the house with everyone else."

She was silent for a long moment. Finally, she leveled me with a hard stare. "Take me with you. Make me a proper part of this investigation. If someone's trying to kill me, I deserve to be involved. You know that."

She did. And I knew damn well that I'd be raising hell if it were the other way around. "Okay. I'm going to talk to the wolves in the morning. Selina and I sensed werewolf power at the coven as well."

"I'll be ready whenever you need to leave."

I took a shower and climbed into bed, my mind racing. An hour later, I was still wide awake. I punched my pillow, ignoring the meow of annoyance Lia let out from the foot of the bed.

"Stupid demon."

I couldn't fall asleep, and I had a sneaky suspicion it was because Samael wasn't next to me. All it had taken was one night wrapped in his arms, and I craved him once more.

He probably knew exactly what he was doing. Give me just enough to make me want him, but not enough to truly get my fix.

I let out a low growl and slumped back onto my bed at a knock on my door. Evie cracked it open.

"Can't sleep?"

"Am I keeping you awake? Sorry."

"No, I can't sleep either." She crawled into bed next to me. "I just keep thinking about how they never saw it coming. They never got a chance to fight."

"Yeah. It's fucking insulting is what it is, and when I find out who did this, I'm going to make them hurt. I promise you."

"I know you will. How come you can't sleep?"

I chewed on my lip. How exactly did I tell her that it wasn't because of the dead coven, but because of the demon who drove me crazy?

She let out a low laugh next to me rolling onto her side. "It's Samael, isn't it?"

"Yeah. Sorry, I know–"

"Don't be stupid. I know you care about the coven. I know you're doing everything you can for them. But you're a woman too."

I heaved a sigh. "Why can't I just let it go? I feel like every time I decide I'm done with him, something draws me back."

"I've never seen two people with your kind of chemistry. Whenever you're in the same room together, it just sizzles."

"Yeah, we have incredible chemistry, and the sex was better than I could've ever imagined. But you can't have a relationship based solely on chemistry."

"Is that what you think it would be?" Evie shifted

and Lia got to her feet, strolling up the bed until she was positioned between us. "I don't think I ever told you this, but I had to go to Samael's tower once."

"When was this?"

"Before you got back to Durham." Her voice was very careful. Neither of us wanted to open up that can of worms.

"Why were you there?"

"The coven hired one of the accounting firms which rents offices on one of the lower floors in Samael's tower. Anyway, I was walking across the lobby and I felt all the hair on the back of my neck stand up. It was like my body suddenly knew it was prey."

"Yeah, I remember that feeling." It was exactly how I'd felt when Samael caught me in his ward.

"I glanced up, and our eyes met for just a second. There was nothing there, Dani. He had the coldest, deadest eyes I've ever seen. He was just walking out of the elevator, his eyes scanning the lobby, and that single look made me want to run out of there screaming."

"Yeah, he's a scary bastard, all right."

"But that's the thing. He's not with you. Not even with me anymore. Not with those kids. He was so good with Cil and Zip, and he did everything he could to make us feel safe. The first time I saw him look at you, I almost didn't recognize him as the terrifying son of a bitch I'd seen in that lobby. His eyes weren't dead anymore. When he looked at you, they were full of all kinds of things."

"Why are you telling me this? It only makes it harder."

"Because he's in love with you. I think he never

expected it, and he probably hates you a little for it. But I think you're in love with him, too."

She'd told me this before, right after I left Samael the last time, when I found out how he'd lied to me. How he'd known about the prophecy. I hadn't wanted to listen then, and I didn't want to listen now.

I punched my pillow again and Evie laughed softly.

"How are *you* doing?" I murmured and she shifted.

Thankfully, she allowed the change of subject. "This is going to sound weird."

"Go."

"When I'm not thinking about everyone who died, and how scared Brooke must have been, and how I should've been there–"

"Evie."

"When I'm not thinking that stuff, I feel like something weird has happened. It feels almost like a huge weight has lifted off my shoulders. I feel… free."

From the heaviness of the guilt in her voice, she didn't exactly want to feel free.

I couldn't blame her.

I fell asleep next to my sister and dreamed of silver eyes and obsidian wings.

CHAPTER ELEVEN

Danica

The next morning, we had our windows wound down as I drove toward wolf territory. This time, I'd made certain to let Nathaniel know we were coming, and the sentries let us pass without any issue.

"It's so quiet out here," Evie murmured.

"I know. I'd go crazy in two days."

"I kind of like it. Not for forever, but sometimes it's nice to get away from the city."

"Hmmm."

"I'm sorry I didn't tell you about Liam," she said suddenly, and I glanced at her. Her gaze was on the forest and I shrugged.

"It's okay."

"It's not that I didn't want to tell you. It's just that it's so new, you know? I had the biggest crush on him when we were younger, and then he suddenly left. Seeing him again, it was like opening an old wound and healing it at the same time. We're taking things slow. He's giving me space right now because I need it, even though it's hard for him with those wolf instincts."

"I'm glad." I hadn't brought it up. Hadn't wanted to let her know I was hurt that she hadn't told me.

"The night the coven... I drove out here to hang with Liam. He lives at Nathaniel's with some of the other pack, but they have another small house which they can use occasionally when they want privacy. We watched movies and ate popcorn, and then he kissed me. I drove home, parked the car, and smelled the smoke."

"I'm sorry."

She shook her head as if attempting to push away the memories. "I just wanted you to know that I wasn't keeping anything from you. We'd hung out a few times, but that was the first night we kissed."

"I'm glad you have that with him. Really."

If my instincts insisted Liam wasn't the one for Evie, then I'd ignore them. He was a cute guy who obviously respected my sister.

Even if I wondered where the hell he'd been the night of the fire, and why he hadn't been around supporting Evie.

Nathaniel lived at the end of a cul-de-sac on the edge of Duke Forest. His huge, ranch-style home seemed to be part of the surrounding forest itself, in spite of the floor-to-ceiling glass windows which had been treated so no one could see inside.

I parked outside the Alpha's house, and Liam immediately opened the front door. He strode toward the car, his eyes intent on my sister. The moment she stepped out, he was wrapping her in his arms.

"I'm sorry," he murmured. "I'm so sorry."

"Hey. Hey, it's okay. What's wrong?"

"The night of the fire. I wanted to come to you, to help you. But when I heard what had happened, I turned." He pulled away, his shoulders hunching as a flush swept up his cheeks. "I lost control and I'm sorry for it. Nathaniel's second grabbed a few other wolves and they locked me in the basement."

That basement must be seriously reinforced if it could hold an out-of-control werewolf.

Evie was murmuring to Liam and I looked away, meeting Nathaniel's eyes. He nodded at me, glanced at Evie and Liam, and went back inside.

I followed him into the house, giving the couple a few moments of privacy. Although, Nathaniel could likely still hear everything they said.

I took a seat, watching as Nathaniel did the same, stretching his long legs out in front of him. The werewolf Alpha had the strangest colored eyes— a dark blue that lightened when he was fighting his wolf. Today, they seemed lost in thought.

Evie laughed at something Liam said as she walked in, and Nathaniel froze. Then he let out a low snarl.

The hair on the back of my neck stood up, I shot to my feet as Evie flinched.

"What the fuck, Nathaniel?" I demanded. He merely strode toward Evie, brushing past me as if I wasn't shielding my sister with my body.

"You smell wrong."

She scowled at him. "I showered, jeez. I can't help it if it's hotter than Lucifer's balls outside."

I cracked up. First, because it was the first time I'd seen a hint of my sister's attitude since before the fire, and second, because those balls technically belonged to my grandfather, and that was fucking disgusting.

Nathaniel leaned close, catching her hands in his when she raised them to push him away. Next to her, Liam let out his own long, low growl of threat.

"Quiet, pup."

Liam merely growled louder, and I slid him a look. My hand found the handle of my Nim Cub. I'd never seen a wolf shift that much and still remain human, but the sight of all those pointed teeth crowding for space in his human mouth was making me both nervous and queasy.

Nathaniel didn't seem worried, so I took my attention off Liam long enough to glance at Evie. She was glowering up at the Alpha, who currently had his nose buried in the space between her shoulder and her neck.

No wonder Liam was pissed.

Nathaniel slowly drew back, releasing Evie's hands.

"I've been wondering why there was something that struck me as wrong in your scent. I first noticed it the night of the fire, but now it feels like inhaling acetone."

She frowned. "I can't help what I smell like. If you don't like it, don't smell me."

"Evie smells perfect," Liam growled. He shoved past Nathaniel and stepped between them, until they were almost pressed together, Evie at his back, Nathaniel at his front. Since he'd shifted entirely back to human, and since I'd seen the way Nathaniel could control his wolves, I shoved my knife back in my sheath.

Nathaniel's face turned blank as he took a large step back.

"You're a new wolf," he said. "Your sense of smell is

nowhere near as honed as mine.”

Then he lowered his voice slightly as he addressed Evie, speaking over Liam's shoulder as if he wasn't there.

“There is something hidden beneath your skin near the back of your neck.”

I frowned. “What kind of something?”

“I don't know. I've never sensed anything like it. But it's close to Evelyn's spine. Removing it could be dangerous.”

He said Evie's name like a caress, but she was already turning to pace the room. “I want it out.”

I blew out a breath. “Let's take a minute here. We need to figure out where exactly it is, how big it is, and if it can be removed.”

Evie nodded. “We need a witch.”

“Yeah. Depending on how much power is required, we might have to use Gloria.” And I sneered at the thought of the black witch Samael kept on retainer.

Evie's lips twitched and I shot her a look. She found my silent war with Gloria hilarious.

Since no one was going to fight, I sat back down on the sofa. Nathaniel sat in his usual, delicate chair across from me.

Evie and Liam stayed standing, and Liam pulled Evie close, wrapping his arm around her. Aw.

“Have you noticed anyone following Evie or watching her a little too intently?” Liam shook his head. “No. And I would've noticed. But… we're pretty new.” He squeezed Evie and she smiled.

I glanced at Nathaniel. “We found a weird magic signature at the coven,” I said. “A mixture of witch, fae, and werewolf. Do you have any idea what it could mean?"

Nathaniel frowned. "I don't. Werewolves don't typically collaborate with other paranormals. And we certainly don't want to wage war against the witches."

"Would you know if there were any feral wolves in town?"

"Yes. One of my people would scent them. They would be hunted down and brought to me."

So this was a bust. Well, not entirely a bust. "You said you noticed something strange about Evie's scent when the house was burning."

He nodded. "Yes, although I didn't consciously know there was something in her neck. I just knew that her scent seemed wrong. Different."

"And now that the house is basically nothing but ash, you can sense the exact location of whatever it is that's in Evie's body."

"That's right. You believe the two are connected."

I shrugged. "I'm grasping at straws here. But I think it's interesting."

We wrapped things up relatively quickly after that.

Evie was quiet on the way home and I couldn't blame her.

"Are you okay?"

"I dunno. I can't explain it, but the moment that house burned down, it was like a weight off my shoulders. But I loved that house." She frowned. "And what the hell is in my neck? I feel like I'm constantly the last person to know what the hell is going on, and I'm tired of it."

"I don't blame you. We'll figure it out, Evie. Whatever it is, we'll get to the bottom of it."

She attempted a smile. "Thanks. And thanks for being here, for everything. I couldn't have gotten through this without you."

"Of course."

I was deep in thought as we made our way up to my apartment. My ward felt… wrong, and I pulled my Colt, using my other hand to unlock the door.

"Stay behind me."

Evie had already pulled the knife she'd likely found in my collection, and she simply sneered at me. Cool.

The apartment felt empty, but I did a full sweep anyway.

"Dani? You might want to look at this."

I stalked into my small kitchen, where Evie had opened the fridge.

The fully stocked fridge.

Fruit, vegetables, meats and cheeses jostled for space amongst full meals that had obviously been pre-cooked so we could heat them up. I opened the freezer, finding several pints of both of our favorite ice creams.

The pantry was the same, loaded with easy snacks, protein bars, nuts, and anything else we might need.

"The demon doesn't miss a trick," I murmured. He'd known I was low on food and likely wouldn't have a chance to hit the grocery store. And instead of using it as one more reason for me to move in with him, he'd taken it off my to-do list.

I blew out a breath and opened the freezer again. It was eleven A.M. but I needed ice cream.

I dug into a pint of chocolate fudge ripple, ignoring the smile that hovered around Evie's mouth as I handed her the butter pecan.

"What's the plan now?"

"Kyla's asking the witches a few more questions. In the meantime, I thought I'd go see Gary, maybe see if he's heard any rumors from his contacts."

The gnome sold weapons, spells, and, most importantly, information.

Evie smiled. "I can't wait to see the kids."

Danica

Gary's store was on Main Street. I'd only visited a couple of times since I took down the group of humans who had almost killed him, and he'd still been in the process of restocking.

Today, though, his store looked good as new.

"Wow," I said as I stepped inside. We were the only customers, and Gary stood on his stool next to the counter, reading a newspaper. He lowered it and smiled.

"Dani and Evie. The boys will be excited–"

His smile widened as the kids sprinted out from where they'd likely been up to no good in his stockroom. Cil and Zip talked a mile a minute as they hugged us both, pulling us toward the stockroom to show us something.

I couldn't help but grin down at them. "Hold on, you guys. Show Evie first, and I'll take a look in a sec. I need to talk to your dad for a minute."

Gary hopped off his stool and closed the stockroom

door. "This is about the fire at the coven."

"Yeah. Evie was nearly there too."

His expression darkened as he climbed back up on his stool. Gary refused to lower the counter, instead keeping it at the height of most of his customers.

"Bad business, that is. She got lucky that night."

"Yeah. But she might not always be so lucky unless we find out who might want her dead."

Gary narrowed his eyes and I leaned on the counter, keeping my voice low as I filled him in.

"You think whoever killed the witch in Evie's room was after your sister."

"I think there have been a few weird things going on in the last few days. It could be related to whatever the werewolf Alpha sensed under her neck."

"I'll keep my ear to the ground. I haven't heard anything, but I'll ask around."

"Thanks, I'll owe you one."

He merely shook his head. "After what you did for me and my boys, you'll never owe me one."

I smiled and glanced around. "This place looks better than it ever has." I'd offered to help with the cleanup, but Gary had insisted I leave him to it. The gnome wasn't known for being gracious at accepting help.

"Yeah, it's taken a while, but it's getting there."

I eyed him. I hated the thought of him being in a financial hole after being targeted by extremists.

"Listen, Mariam paid me for that job. If you need a loan–"

He instantly shook his head. "I don't. Truth is, I was going to go to Ridick." I winced and he laughed. "Yeah.

The interest would have crippled me, but I didn't think I had much choice. And then another party made me an offer. With zero interest. So I'm okay, Danica. I promise."

I angled my head. "Tell me that other party wasn't Samael."

He clammed up. "I signed a non-disclosure agreement. And my finances are none of your business."

I ran my hand through my hair. He was right, but the idea of him being in debt to Samael…

"I have very good lawyers," he said. "Don't worry about me."

Samael had bailed Gary out. With zero interest. And he'd made him sign a non-disclosure agreement, which meant he hadn't done it as a way to endear himself to me. There was literally nothing in it for him, but he'd done it anyway.

And that just plain confused me.

The demon I met just a few months ago… He didn't care about anyone but himself. Or at least, that's how he'd appeared.

I pushed the thought away. "Okay. I'm going to go see what the kids want to show me."

"I'll let you know if I hear anything."

The kids had grown their collection of 'treasures', and they solemnly took us through the newest additions— a long, pretty ribbon, a chunk of amethyst, and a shiny lock and key.

I waved to Gary as we left, and he nodded from where he was talking a witch through some of his best-selling charms.

Evie glanced at me as we drove back to my apartment.

"You're quiet."

"Just thinking. Let's grab some lunch at home, and then I need to go meet Kyla at my office."

"Do you get a buzz when you say that? Cause I get a buzz when I hear it. *Your* office. So professional. I'm proud of you, Dani."

That was the second person who'd said they were proud of me this week. I must be doing something right.

"I couldn't have done it without Keigan. He pushed me into it, truthfully. I owe him big time."

"He believes in you. It's nice."

"Yeah. It is."

I parked and we walked toward my apartment lobby. "Listen–"

The world went dark. Dark and quiet. I reached for Evie. Our fingers brushed as I fumbled for her hand. She disappeared, her scream echoing within the darker-than-night spell.

CHAPTER TWELVE

Danica

"*Fuck.*"

I reached for my Colt, then changed my mind and pulled my Mark II. It was better for up-close fighting, and I wouldn't have to worry about accidentally shooting Evie or an innocent bystander.

My power brushed against my shields and I focused, softening my main shield enough to let it through. My demon side wanted to rip and rend, which made it as dangerous as lighting up the parking lot with a gun.

I slid my knife gently against my forearm and my blood activated. The parking lot lit up in purple and gold. The dark-as-night spell was still active, shielding us from the view of any bystanders, but the dim light from my ward at least allowed us to see.

"Evie?" I turned, scanning desperately.

My feet left the ground as someone slammed into me. I gasped uselessly for air, winded from the bad landing as we rolled. We came to a stop with the guy straddling me.

Purple light caught the edge of a knife as he raised his hand. I stabbed my Mark II into the asshole's abdomen and he screamed. But it didn't slow him down as his knife arched toward my throat.

My power roared up without warning, throwing him off me. He flew twenty feet and slammed into the side of my apartment, crumpling to the ground.

Neato.

"Dani!"

I turned as a tall, bearded man attempted to pull Evie into the back of a black SUV. She slid on the ground, kicking out at him desperately. I charged toward them, my legs pumping.

Evie lifted her hands and his shirt caught on fire, but he simply pulled it off with one hand and then slapped her across the face.

This time I reached for my Colt. Evie could be trusted to hit the ground when she saw what I was doing.

Movement in the corner of my eye.

I ducked as a meaty fist slid inches from my face. If he'd connected, it would've put me me down for good. His other hand hit my inner elbow and my arm went instantly numb.

My gun flew from my hand, landing several feet away.

I whirled, burying my other fist into his gut. He didn't even grunt, simply baring his teeth as he advanced.

He probably had a hundred pounds on me, and he was fast. I bobbed and weaved as he advanced, keeping my gaze on his shoulders. They telegraphed his movements before his eyes, which were so dark they appeared black.

Who the fuck were these guys, and why did they want my sister?

I ducked again and this time Black-Eyes kicked out, almost making contact. I ground my teeth. My ward was keeping the darkness at bay, but whatever spell they'd used was strong. I was unused to using my power for more than a few seconds while keeping a ward up, and I could feel it sapping my strength.

If I dropped the ward, Evie would be in the dark. And I'd bet these guys could see through whatever spell they'd used.

So no magic.

Fine.

The next time he swung, I dodged left. My mind was across the parking lot, but I had to trust Evie to look after herself.

Black-eyes snarled, pulling a blade. "Kill you, cunt."

I faked a yawn. "Get on with it."

Two people fighting with knives usually meant two idiots were about to end up dead.

On the ground behind him, my Colt waited for me. My hand itched. If I could get to it, I could end this quick. But Black-eyes wasn't exactly going to let me tip-toe past him and shoot him in the back.

My new utility belt had five of my throwing knives lined up in individual sheaths along my hip. They wouldn't kill him. It was unlikely I'd even be able to seriously hurt him. But I could piss him off. Pissed off people were distracted.

I threw the first knife and he lunged to the side, giving me the space to throw a quick glance behind me at Evie.

She was still on the ground, kicking out at her attacker, but even from here I could see she was using the movement to cover the way she reached for her knife.

Time slowed down, until everything came into startling focus. The bearded guy snapped something at Evie, reaching for her wrist again.

She allowed him to take it, and he pulled her up from the ground. My ward glinted off her blade as she used the momentum to bury her knife in his thigh.

She ripped it free, and the guy stumbled, momentarily confused as blood sprayed. Evie had been training. That guy wouldn't be dragging her into the car.

And I was going to end up full of holes if I didn't focus. Black-eyes struck out with the side of one fist, immediately following up with his knife. I dodged the fist but the knife caught my shoulder, drawing blood.

I ground my teeth as the scent of my own blood reached my nose. Burning pain slid through me, but he hadn't hit anything vital. Most importantly, my arm would still work.

Black-eyes grinned at me and I threw another knife, immediately following it up with another as he dodged.

This one landed, sinking in right below his collarbone. He cursed and I threw a roundhouse kick. The trick was to pivot on your back foot and twist your hips, so the kick had as much power as possible.

He was off-balance and hadn't tensed his abdominal muscles. I didn't have a chance to enjoy the 'oof' of his breath leaving his lungs as I darted close and shoved my knee into his groin.

He swung out with the knife, but I was already gone,

and he was getting frustrated. Add testosterone and the fact that this little rendezvous wasn't going anywhere close to the way he'd thought it was going to, and there was no longer any critical thinking happening.

He slashed downward with the knife this time, and I slid to the left, using my right arm to guide it away from me. I swept out a leg, slid it behind his knee and gave him a shove.

He fell, and I lunged toward my Colt.

Black-eyes caught my foot, taking me down. I hit the ground hard, pain exploding in my shoulder as I kicked out at him.

It was like kicking concrete.

In this position, he had the upper hand, already on his knees as he grabbed my other foot. My body was leaving the ground as he pulled me toward him. I reached into my utility belt, cursing as my spelled stones went flying out of the pocket as he lifted me higher.

New plan. I grabbed the first pouch I found, clawing at it with my nails to break through the plastic.

I widened the hole, wiggled my fingers inside, and pulled out a handful of powder. My eyes slammed shut and I threw it over my shoulder.

Black-eyes screamed as the wixbane attacked his vision, and the steel clamp around my ankle was suddenly gone. My knees burned as I scrambled along the pavement. My hand fumbled for my Colt, and I rolled onto my back as he made it to his feet.

I shot him in the head.

He must have been tied to the darker-than-night, because it was suddenly daylight again.

"Evie!" I screamed as he fell.

"I'm fine," she called back, and I groaned as I slowly got to my feet. Bearded guy was lying beside her, still bleeding out, and Evie was leaning against the SUV, her face ashen.

I let my ward drop. I had no idea how the hell I'd even held it for that long, but I was exhausted.

It took a powerful witch to tie a human to a darker-than-night spell.

I glanced around us. Close to the apartment entrance, an old woman was crumpled on the ground. I made it to her in seconds, but it was obvious she was dead, her neck broken.

The assholes hadn't wanted to leave any witnesses.

I made my way over to Evie, and she threw her arms around me, both of us silently holding on for a long moment.

"One of them is still alive," she said.

"Yeah." I squeezed her tighter. "We'll question him."

The sun disappeared above us for a split second, and I glanced up.

The demons were here.

Samael landed a few feet away, his wings out, dripping with fiery embers. His silver eyes glowed with icy rage.

Evie was momentarily stunned, her gaze wide as she stared at him.

"Christ," she said, and I shrugged.

Samael's gaze found the man bleeding out next to the black SUV and he lifted his hand.

I bolted toward him, catching his arm and pulling it down. He looked through me. It was as if no one was home.

"No smiting," I told him. "I need their bodies, and I need that one alive for as long as possible."

He ignored that, still gazing past me as if I wasn't there, retribution burning in his eyes. Shit.

I reached up, pulling his head down. I'd caught him off guard, which was the only reason it worked, but as I pressed my mouth to his, he was still for a long moment.

"No smiting. I mean it," I whispered in his mind.

He tensed, and I felt the moment he transformed from the cold, remote demon to the hot, flesh-and-blood man.

Our kiss deepened, and my mind went blank as he wrapped me in his arms, his tongue stroking mine.

"Safe," he said in my head. *"You're safe."*

"I am. I promise."

"Uh, guys?"

Vas sounded amused, but when I slowly pulled away from Samael, I found the younger demon's gaze on the bearded guy currently bleeding out.

I pulled myself together and stalked toward him. Evie was already leaning over him, slapping his cheek to make him open his eyes.

"Who are you?" she demanded. "What do you want?"

"Monstrosity," he gasped out. "Miscreation. You… are an atrocity that should never have been born."

All of the color drained from Evie's face and Vas pulled her away. Samael stepped past me and leaned over the asshole.

"If you think she is an atrocity, you have yet to see what I can do to a human body," he purred. "You will tell us what we need to know, or my people will patch you up and break you down until you beg for death."

As far as threats go, it was a pretty good one. But the asshole merely smiled, raising his hand as he shoved something in his mouth. Samael grabbed his jaw, squeezing so hard I heard something crack, but it was too late. The guy's mouth foamed as he convulsed, his eyes rolling back in his head.

"Cyanide," Samael stepped away, his eyes cold. "I didn't anticipate it. I apologize."

"It's not your fault."

I glanced over at where Bael was checking the pockets of the dead guy I'd slammed into the apartment wall. Sitri landed and Samael gestured for him to do the same for the guy I'd shot, while I took the one who'd been dragging Evie into the car.

I emptied out his pockets, finding a wallet, a parking receipt, and a chip from a casino.

"I need to go through the car," I said, and Samael took my arm. "My people can do that," he said carefully. I opened my mouth to argue, and he gestured at where my sister was staring at the dead guy. She looked shocked, worn out, and a little unhinged, my knife still in her hand.

"Okay. Okay."

I turned and paced for a couple of moments, and then glanced at the demon, whose eyes were glued to my face. "We're moving in with you. Let me just pack and get the cat, and we'll figure things out once Evie is safe."

To his credit, Samael didn't show the smallest flicker of satisfaction, even down the other end of the bond. He merely nodded, his expression grim as he took in the scene.

"I will come up with you."

I didn't argue. Samael followed Evie and me into the

elevator, which meant we were practically standing on top of each other as we jostled for space amongst his wings. He hadn't bothered tucking them out of sight yet, although they were—thankfully— no longer dripping with sparks. I had a feeling he'd left them out because he knew studying them was giving Evie a tiny distraction from everything that had just happened.

My sister still only had a few clothes, so it barely took her a couple of minutes to pack them up. I hauled a suitcase out of my closet and loaded up on weapons, clothes, and toiletries.

I glanced at Samael, and my gaze got stuck. He was looking out my bedroom window, his wings tucked in behind him. He glanced over his shoulder at me, his silver eyes glinting, and I was struck by the picture he made, both completely out of place but somehow at home in my bedroom.

"Um, I wanted to thank you. For the food. I don't like the thought of it going to waste."

He smiled as if I was the cutest thing he'd ever seen. Then he stepped toward me. My room was so tiny that within a second we were practically pressed together.

"I'll have it sent to someone who needs it."

"Thank you."

He raised his hand and cupped my face. "I would like to point out that I have not slung you over my shoulder and hauled you back to my tower where I can be certain you are safe."

I eyed him. "And I suppose you want brownie points for that?"

"Brownies are annoying little creatures. No, I want

you to acknowledge that I am attempting to live up to your expectations of me."

I winced. "Samael…" I didn't want him to have to live up to my 'expectations.' That wasn't how relationships were supposed to work.

"I'm attempting to be a better man. For you."

"I'm not asking you to change who you are."

He smiled but there was no humor in it.

I hunched my shoulders and he brushed his mouth over mine.

"Come, bounty hunter. No matter the circumstances, I must admit I'm pleased to be able to sleep beside you in my own bed once more."

I rolled my eyes at that, but Evie and I followed him back downstairs, where the human police had already arrived.

I groaned as I spied Detective Roberts walking toward me. He was with another cop, who nodded to me as they approached.

"This is my partner, Detective Nelson. We have a few questions to ask you."

Nelson seemed to be in his early thirties. His skin was a golden tan, and his dark green eyes said he'd seen it all before, and was anticipating worse around the corner. He nodded to me and I nodded back, glancing at the uniformed cops who were going over the crime scene. I had to hope that the demons had already gotten everything they needed.

"Did you take anything from the car?" Roberts asked, his tone biting.

"Us personally, or the demons?"

He sneered at me and Nelson shot him a look. I had a

feeling he didn't like his partner much.

"How about you question the human witnesses?" Nelson suggested. Roberts shook his head in disgust but stalked off.

I glanced at Samael, but he was near the SUV and paying the cops no attention as he spoke to Bael and Sitri.

"This isn't really a good time," I started, and Nelson angled his head.

"A human was killed," he gestured to the woman who was still crumpled on the ground. I wished I could move her, even as I knew the body couldn't yet be touched. "Not to mention your attackers."

Evie let out a choked sound and I reached for her hand. Nelson shot her a sympathetic look.

"They're working with paranormals," I said. "They used a darker-than-night spell."

"Investigations involving both humans and paranormals can get messy," Nelson acknowledged. We both know this can easily devolve into a pissing contest. So I have a suggestion."

"What kind of suggestion?"

He gave me a faint smile. "You show me yours, and I'll show you mine."

It wasn't suggestive, more teasing, and I hadn't expected it from the hard-faced cop. I laughed.

Tell the detective if he continues to flirt with you, I will remove his head from his shoulders.

My laugh turned into a choked gasp as I turned my head, finding Samael's eyes narrowed on Nelson.

"Don't be ridiculous," I snapped, turning back to Nelson.

I shivered as Samael did something to the bond between us. It felt like a caress. I frowned over my shoulder at him, but he was deep in discussion with Vas again. Insane demon.

Nelson was staring at me curiously and I shrugged. "Look, we don't yet know who these guys are, or why they attacked us."

"Chances are high that the attack is connected to the fire at the coven's house."

Evie tensed and I squeezed her hand. Nelson shook his head at me. "Come on. I've been doing this a while now. Either one or both of you are the targets. Since you're both *friendly* with the demons, I'm assuming you won't want police protection, but whatever is happening, it's spilling out onto civilians. Human civilians."

I closed my eyes. "I know. Look, we don't know why they're coming after us. All I can tell you is that they tried to get Evie into the car."

It was likely he'd get his hands on a recording from either the public or one of the cameras in the parking lot, so he'd see that anyway.

"Any idea why?"

"No."

His attention shifted to Evie. "What about you, have you pissed anyone off recently?"

"No more than usual," she said wearily. "We don't know why this is happening."

I squeezed her hand again. "Samael's people will take the bodies, and we'll let you know what we find."

Nelson opened his mouth and I shook my head. "You don't want to get in a pissing contest with the demons," I advised him. "I'll pass on any information I can."

His jaw tightened but he nodded. "Fine. Look, I know the demons will want to handle this, but it makes sense for us to collaborate. Too many murderers are getting away with their crimes because humans and paranormals refuse to share information."

"And you want to change that." Despite myself, I was impressed. Paranormals were a secretive bunch, and humans typically treated any crimes against them as unimportant, just as paranormals did with most crimes against humans.

"Some cities are creating joint task forces between humans and paranormals. Rates of violent crime are dropping."

I liked the guy. I dug into my purse and pulled out one of my new business cards. I'd had them printed the day after Keigan gave me his office.

"You can contact me at that number," I told him. "We'll be in touch."

Vas met my gaze as I walked toward Samael. He offered me a grin. "You just can't stay out of trouble, can you."

"Ha ha."

"I just heard from one of the techs at Samael's lab. We have a print from the lighter."

It took my brain a moment to understand what he was talking about.

Riona. The metal lighter found at the house she'd been supposed to house sit at.

"Who is it?"

"A guy called Troy Burker. He was in the system

thanks to a drunk and disorderly a few years ago, but nothing since."

"Address?"

He nodded. "I doubt you're going to find anything there."

"No, they'll be gone. But I have to check anyway."

He pulled out his phone and I felt mine vibrate in my pocket. "You've got it. You need some help?"

"I'll pull in Kyla. She'll be pissed if I move without her. And I need you guys to focus on these assholes."

The back of my neck tingled and I glanced at Samael as he approached us. "You need a healer," he said. "Don't argue with me, I can smell your blood."

It would take Kyla a while to get here from Duke Forest.

"Fine."

He reached out and pulled me to him, uncaring of all of the eyes on us.

"I'm sorry this happened," he murmured. "I wish I had been here."

Pure vengeance dripped from his voice and I smiled against his chest. "We did okay."

"You certainly did."

I took a moment to breathe him in. Beneath the cedar and citrus, I could scent burning wood in winter. That was his 'recently pissed off' smell.

"Right," I said as I wiggled out of his arms. "I've got places to go and people to harass. Don't wait up."

CHAPTER THIRTEEN

Danica

By the time Eldan, Samael's seelie healer, had taken care of the shallow knife wound on my shoulder, along with the various other cuts and scrapes, Kyla was parking on the street outside my apartment. Roberts and Nelson had arranged for the parking lot to be sealed off with crime scene tape.

Evie was on her way back to Samael's tower and the demon had merely given me a dark look and told me he expected me to return to him without any further damage.

Kyla prowled toward me, carrying two takeout cups. "One of my friends recently opened a small cafe in our territory." She handed me a cup and I gulped at the coffee.

"Bless you."

She smiled. "You wanna tell me what happened?"

"Holy crap this is good coffee. I'll tell you on the way. You mind driving?" I was still achy, and my body was insisting it was time for a nap after Eldan's healing.

"Nope. Let's go."

Kyla glanced at me as we walked toward her Nissan. "I know we figured Brooke wasn't the target, but last night I spent a few more hours looking into her, just in case. I couldn't find any nefarious characters in her life, or any motive for killing her and taking down the rest of the coven."

"You kept working last night? You looking for a raise?"

She slid me a grin as we got into her car. "Always."

I wracked my brain, attempting to figure out how the hell I could afford it. Kyla's blue eyes laughed at me over her coffee.

"I'm only kidding. I plan to prove I'm indispensable first. I don't want you to be out of pocket for doing a favor to Nathaniel."

She'd already proven pretty damn indispensable. There's no way I would've been able to juggle both of these investigations without her.

"Address?"

I rattled it off and she put it into her phone and started the car. "They're not going to be there," she said.

"It's unlikely. They might've realized they left the lighter behind. Even if they haven't, they'll know people are investigating. But we might find something that can help Riona."

"She was just trying to get by. Working as much as she could while keeping her dream alive."

"We'll make them regret it."

"Fucking aye."

The apartment building was in South Durham. It had two parking lots— one in the front, and a smaller one in the back.

"Let's take the back," I decided.

A couple of suspicious characters exchanged small packets near the dumpsters behind the buildings.

"Hey ladies," one of them whistled. "Why don't you come party with us?"

"Fuck off before I make you eat pavement," I said, and the one on the left cupped his crotch.

"You too scared to handle this, baby?"

A low, threatening growl sounded, and I shivered. Both men froze as they stared at Kyla. Her lips were pulled back from her teeth, her eyes had lightened eerily, and the growl was coming from her throat.

"What the fuck, what the fuck, that's a she-wolf!"

"They don't exist, dumbass. Hey bitch, you wanna growl some more, I'll– fuck!"

Kyla had stepped closer to the building. The sun was setting, but one of the outside lights highlighted her feral expression, lengthened canines, and glowing eyes.

"She's hungry," I said mildly. "I suggest you get gone."

They took off.

"She's hungry?" Kyla said as we stepped into the small, dank space that passed as the building's lobby.

"I mean, you usually are, right?" She laughed and I glanced at her. "I heard it's difficult to partial shift like that."

"It is for most wolves. Well, difficult to do it and not

shift all the way. It's a control thing. I've never had an issue. Go me. We need the third floor."

The elevator was broken, so we took the stairs. The pungent smell of urine hit me and Kyla cursed under her breath as we clomped up to the second floor. "I've got Riona's scent."

My pulse quickened. "You sure?"

She narrowed her eyes at me as we swung around the corner and started up the stairs to the third floor. "As sure as I can tell you this building should be condemned."

"Even I'm sure of that."

A baby wailed like it was being tortured in the apartment across from Troy's as we examined the flimsy door of the apartment. "You want me to kick it in?" Kyla whispered.

Even I could kick it in. The door looked like it would fall apart if we knocked on it too hard.

"I don't want to piss off the neighbors. The cops show up here, we'll be trespassing. Give me a second."

I pulled out the small case of tools I'd slipped into my new utility belt and crouched in front of the door. The lock was stiff, but I channeled patience and the door swung open a few minutes later.

"You wanna tell me how you know how to do that?" Kyla asked.

"I'm naturally skilled."

I pulled my Colt, gesturing for Kyla to follow me in. She gave me an unhappy look but fell into step behind me. Sure, wolves were tougher than humans, but I wasn't getting her killed three days into working for me.

Troy Burker didn't live well. The living room

boasted a single, sagging gray sofa and a scarred coffee table. He'd hung old sheets up in front of the windows in a useless attempt to block out the light.

I poked my head into the bedroom, which housed a single mattress on the floor. The kitchen was the worst of it, takeout cartons littering the kitchen counter, holding a variety of old food. A single roach climbed out of the sink, and I backed out of the kitchen like my ass was on fire.

"She was definitely here," Kyla said. "I can smell her."

"Why would they bring her back here?" I frowned. "Maybe they panicked. They weren't expecting her to walk in on them. She's a witch who's good with wards, so they probably didn't sense her approaching the house."

I used one hand to massage the back of my neck. "They're going to know we found their flop. If she's still alive, she won't be for long. You take the bedroom, I'll take the living room."

Kyla wrinkled her nose but nodded, and we methodically searched every inch of the apartment.

"Yo," Kyla said a few minutes later.

"One sec." I was kneeling in front of the sofa, peering beneath it. I used the light from my phone to search the floor, but all I found was enough dust to be a health hazard.

I got to my feet and met Kyla in the bedroom.

She'd shifted the mattress— and she deserved hazard pay just for that. I crouched, examining some kind of bone. It was long— about the length of my forearm— and had been smoothed, polished, and wrapped in some kind of silver cage which was attached to a gleaming silver handle.

It was a bone wand. And I really didn't want to pick it up.

"Someone wanted some insurance in case the witch turned on him. We might get lucky and get a print or two off this, but I highly doubt it." I said. "If not, maybe we can take it to Selina. She can sometimes see things when she touches certain objects."

I pulled a clean plastic bag out of my utility belt, turned it inside out, and used it to pick up the bone.

"Let's have a chat with a few of the neighbors."

I took the apartment on the right, while Kyla took the one on the left. I knocked, waited, and knocked again.

Nothing.

I closed my eyes, sending a trickle of power through my shields. I had no idea if it would work but—

There. Movement.

I slammed my fist on the door a few more times, making it clear that I wasn't going anywhere.

Finally, the door swung open.

"Are you fucking kidding me, bitch?"

The woman wore nothing but a t-shirt, panties, and a vicious scowl.

"I need to ask you a few questions."

"Who the fuck are you?"

"My name is Danica Amana. I'm investigating a kidnapping."

She leaned against the door. "So you think you can just wake people whenever you please? I don't see no badge, bitch."

I hadn't quite pushed my power back behind my shield. With a wide smile, I slid the trickle toward her, wrapping her in darkness.

She couldn't see it, but she could feel it. My power wrapped around her wrists and ankles, holding her still.

"What the fuck?"

"Call me a bitch again," I said.

Silence.

"Answer my questions, and I'll leave."

"Fine."

"Your neighbor. Troy Burker."

"I didn't know his name. What about him?"

"He's a suspect. I need you to tell me anything you know about him."

"I work the night shift. I sleep during the day. Something you're interrupting."

I gave her a steady stare and she scowled. "He's a fucking creep. Always slithering around here, obviously up to no fucking good."

"What makes you say that?"

"Dead eyes. The guy has dead eyes. Except when he's checking me out, and then he has rapey eyes. You know what I mean?"

"Yeah, I know what you mean. Has he had any visitors?"

She shrugged. "None that I remember, and these walls are fucking cardboard. But I work at night. You might want to ask the old bitch who lives on the other side of him. She never keeps her nose out of anyone's fucking business."

Charming. I held up a picture of Riona. "Have you seen this woman? Anywhere?"

She studied it. "She's pretty. Looks soft. If she

drew his attention, she's probably in an unmarked grave somewhere. Look, can I get back to sleep now?"

I wasn't going to get anything else out of her. I handed her my card, well aware that she'd rip it up the moment she closed her door. "If you see him, give me a call."

She sneered, but her lips firmed as she studied my face. "You think he really did kill that girl?"

"He's a person of— yeah. I do. If you see him, call me. Don't get close to him, or anyone he's with."

I pulled my power back behind my shield and she slammed the door.

I glanced at Kyla, who was still talking to the old lady on the other side. She shook her head at me, and I walked back down to the apartment opposite Troy's.

The sound of wailing grew closer, until it assaulted my ears. A second later, the door opened.

The woman looked exhausted, with dark circles beneath her eyes. She had spit up on her shirt, and a baby in her arms.

"Can I help you?"

"Danica Amana."

"Michelle Polter." The baby screamed louder and she did the bouncy thing people did in an attempt to make her stop. It didn't work.

"I'm sorry to disturb you. I just need to ask you a few questions about your neighbor across the hall."

"I don't know him, really." The screaming reached new heights and I managed not to wince. "I'm sorry, she's teething and it's miserable. Look, we keep to ourselves around here. Most people who live here don't exactly want to be here, you know?"

I nodded. "He's a suspect in a kidnapping. Can you tell me if you've noticed him with any visitors recently? Or anything else out of the ordinary?"

"A kidnapping? Shit. No, I stay away from him for the most part. He's an asshole. I was taking the stairs a few days ago and he was coming up from the basement. He told me I needed to keep my fucking brat quiet before he gave her something to cry about." Her hand slid up to the baby's head and she pressed her lips against her cheek. "Who says that about a baby?"

"An asshole." I held up Riona's picture. "Have you ever seen this woman?"

"No, and I'd notice her around here."

I handed her my card. "Will you call me if you see Troy? Don't get anywhere near him, just tell me if you see him. Or this woman. Her name is Riona Walsh."

Michelle nodded. "Of course."

I slid my hand into my utility belt and pulled out a pain charm. Michelle's eyes lit up as I offered it to her.

"Jeez, they're so expensive. Are you sure?"

"I'm sure. Hopefully it'll give you a few hours of rest."

She blinked back tears. "You're an angel. Thank you."

Kyla was waiting for me at the end of the hall. "No one on this floor had anything good to say, but they didn't give me anything important. Guy sounds like an–"

"Asshole. Yeah. He also sounds like a dumbass. We're heading down to the basement."

She frowned. "You really think he'd be that stupid?"

"I think no one in this building visits the basement except maintenance, and let's be real… no maintenance is going on here."

We took the stairs down to the first level, crossed the hall to the west side of the building, and surveyed the door marked *Basement*.

Kyla froze. "Her scent is here too."

I tried the door. Locked. "*Now* you get to kick it in."

The door flew off its hinges as Kyla aimed for the spot right next to the doorhandle.

The ward glowed a muddy brown. I'd seen a ward like this before. Black witches could try to hide their affiliation as much as they liked, but their wards always gave them away.

I used a throwing knife to cut the back of my forearm, took a deep breath, and slammed my hand into the ward.

"Holy shit, this witch is powerful," I ground out. I pushed more power into it, straining until my head spun.

It popped, and I stumbled weakly. Kyla grabbed my elbow, hauling me back before I fell down the stairs.

"Thanks."

Below us, someone whimpered.

Our feet thudded against the stairs as we ran down them. At the bottom, I took a few steps, peering through the lilac ward.

A woman was tucked into a ball, the handcuffs around her wrists connected to a long chain, which was attached to a steel pipe. A few feet away, another pipe dripped water.

"Riona?"

She slowly pulled her hands away from her face.

"I need you to drop your ward."

Terror flashed across her face and she shook her head.

Kyla crouched down, inches from the ward. "Your mom and sister sent us. We've been looking for you for days. Siobhan was worried when you missed her engagement party."

Suspicion warred with hope in her dark eyes. I needed a different tactic.

"I talked to Jerry. What the hell did you see in him, anyway? Guy's a coward."

Riona's eyes widened. "He is," she croaked out. She dropped the ward, and her eyes rolled back in her head.

Danica

We bundled Riona into the car, Kyla sitting with her in the back seat. I called ahead, and a team of doctors and nurses met us outside as we pulled up to the ER. Kyla pulled Riona out of the backseat and stalked toward the gurney, laying her down before stepping out of the way.

I glanced at Kyla. Her eyes were so light they were almost white. I jerked my head and she nodded, slipping back outside.

The medical team took off with the gurney, and I jogged behind them. One of the doctors met my eyes as they lifted Riona onto a table.

"What happened to her?"

"She was kidnapped and locked up in a basement.

There was a leaky pipe within reach but she'll be dehydrated, and I'm betting she hasn't eaten for days. She's a witch and she held a ward for days at a time as well."

He nodded and responded to some medical jargon, then turned back to me. "We'll notify the human police. She has blood under her nails. Might've swiped whoever did this to her."

"God, I hope so. I need to talk to her when she's ready."

"That won't be for a few hours, minimum."

I nodded and pulled out my phone as I walked out and into the fresh air. I'd called Siobhan on our way here, but I needed to borrow one of Samael's demons to stay on Riona's door once they got her up to a room. I couldn't risk the black witch coming back for her.

Kyla cleared her throat from where she was leaning against the wall. "Uh, sorry about that."

"Nothing to be sorry for."

We both turned at the sound of footsteps. Maeve and Siobhan hurried across the parking lot, almost at a run. Maeve's eyes met mine and her lips trembled before she managed to firm them, throwing her arms around me as she reached us.

"You saved my baby."

I patted Maeve's shoulder and she eased herself back, tears streaming down her face.

I glanced at Kyla. "It was a joint effort. The uh, the demons helped too."

Shock widened Maeve's eyes but she smiled, taking Kyla's hand too. "I can't thank you enough. There will never be enough.”

“I’m glad we found her in time.”

Siobhan stepped up to us, pulling me into a hug as her mother released my hand. She repeated the gesture with Kyla and blinked back tears.

“I thought she was dead. I wouldn’t admit it. Not to myself and certainly not to Mom. But I thought she was dead. I thought I’d walk down the aisle without her. Have children without her by my side. I thought… I thought…”

“Hush,” Maeve pulled Siobhan into her arms and rocked with her. “You held me together when I couldn’t do it myself. Thank you, my darling.”

They walked into the hospital and we got into the car.

My chest was so tight it felt like I could barely breathe. I couldn’t even imagine what it would be like to have my mom around, but every now and then, the grief, the longing… it reached out and punched me in the throat.

“You okay?”

“Yeah. I’m just tired.”

“You’ve had a hell of a day. Look, Riona’s unlikely to wake up anytime soon. Why don’t you head back to the tower and get some rest?”

I nodded. “We’ll give her the night to sleep and tomorrow to be with her family.”

Samael

"Evie's sleeping," Danica murmured as she shut the door to one of the guest bedrooms in my penthouse. "I left Lia with her. I don't know what to do for her, Samael."

I stepped forward and wrapped her in my arms. My little witch had come here, of her own free will and at her own suggestion. She'd allowed me to protect her, trusted me to keep both her and her sister safe.

"We will find out why they want her. I promise."

"Any clues in the car?"

I shook my head. "The man who used cyanide to end his life was carrying an encrypted phone. My techs are attempting to decrypt the information now. Hopefully that will lead us to his employer."

"He called her an abomination and worse."

"I know."

Her green eyes looked haunted, her face pale, and I leaned down, gently brushing her lips with mine.

"You're so tired."

"I know. I'm not ready to sleep yet. I just need…"

I studied her face. If she needed a distraction, I could provide her with one she would enjoy. Anything to remove the exhausted misery from her eyes.

"I have a surprise for you."

Her eyes instantly cooled with suspicion and I felt my lips curl. Was it any wonder I was entranced by this woman?

"What kind of surprise?"

"A secret surprise. You'll enjoy it."

My phone buzzed and I reached for it, frowning as

I read the text. "I need to go take care of something, but I'll be back soon and I'll take you to that surprise. Make yourself at home."

She nodded absently. "I might take a shower."

"Take a bath. Relax."

She attempted a smile. "Maybe I will."

The thought of her lounging in my tub made it almost impossible for me to leave, but I forced myself to stalk out to the balcony. I dropped down to the lobby, where I took the elevator down two more floors, underground.

The doors opened to the cool rooms we used as a morgue. Gloria stood next to one of the bodies, her hands over it as she muttered to herself. Vas leaned against a wall, eyeing the witch with a similar suspicious expression to the one Danica liked to give her whenever they were in the same room.

"What do you know?"

"Whoever is in charge of these men was using these to track them," she took a knife and slit open the human's neck to reveal a tiny silver bar. With deft movements of the knife, she pried the bar free and held it up to the light.

"What is it?"

"It would allow their masters to know exactly where each of these men were at all times. It would also likely provide information about their vital signs. It was inserted in a dangerous place, and I wouldn't be surprised if that was deliberate. It could be that it can self-destruct or send out an electrical charge if the host is deemed no longer necessary. I'm unhelpful here, as the magical scent makes no sense— a mixture of wolf, fae, and something else. Your tech team will need to take one of the other bodies and examine the devices themselves.”

“The werewolf Alpha believes there is something in Evelyn’s neck.”

Gloria’s brows shot up. “In that case, I will need to search the grimoires for a way to neutralize it, and we will need an experienced healer on hand to pry it out. It would be prudent to also use a surgical team.”

“What are the consequences if the device is left alone?”

“They’ll certainly be tracking her, as evidenced by their attacks. However, these men must not have had access to her location in real-time, or they would have killed Evelyn while she was on her way back to the coven. Likely, they were simply pointed in her direction by whoever is pulling their strings, which is why they assumed the witch in her room was their target.”

“They may not have known they were being tracked.”

Gloria nodded. “Precisely.” She studied the device. “Whoever is after the witch has deep pockets indeed.”

CHAPTER FOURTEEN

Danica

Samael's tub was ridiculously large, and I lounged amongst the bubbles for long enough that when I pulled the plug, the water had cooled.

I'd solved my first case. And more importantly, I'd saved a life. It felt better than I could have imagined.

Riona would make it her sister's wedding. She wouldn't be sacrificed by a black witch who saw her as nothing more than meat and bones and power.

When Keigan had offered me his space to use as an office, all I'd known was that I had a limited amount of time to start making money, or my business was nothing but a pipe dream.

I hadn't expected the sense of achievement. The *pride*. The knowledge that I'd directly contributed to something good.

I climbed out of the bath and dried off, feeling more relaxed than I had in days. Samael pushed open the door to the bathroom as I was tying the belt of his robe around my waist.

The robe was so large, I'd trip on it if I wasn't careful. His lips twitched as he took me in, his gaze taking in the draining tub.

"I was hoping to be back before you got out."

"Next time," I said lightly, and his eyes narrowed on my face.

"I'll hold you to that."

Something was wrong. I could sense his disquiet down the other end of our bond. "What is it?"

"Gloria found some devices in the necks of the dead humans. Chips. Likely for tracking."

"You think whatever's in Evie's neck is the same thing?"

"Yes."

I wrestled with that. "If they're tracking her, they know she's here."

He nodded. "This is the safest place for her until we have the device removed."

"Is it safe to remove it?"

"We don't know. Gloria will check the grimoires for a spell that could be used. However, it will be a delicate procedure. We need a fae healer and a surgical team."

I turned and paced. "What are her chances, Samael? Don't sugarcoat it."

Strong arms caught my shoulders and he leaned his forehead against mine.

"I will not let her die," he vowed.

I blinked back tears. "From what you're saying, you might not be able to control what happens."

"I will be in the room every step of the way. We will

have the best healers, and if, at any time, it looks like the device can't be removed, we will abort."

"And then she'll be hunted by whoever is after her for the rest of her life."

"If it can't be removed, we will find a way to make the device inert."

He sounded so sure, I couldn't help but breathe in some of that confidence.

"Okay," I said. I buried my hands in his hair and pulled his head down so I could brush his lips with mine. "Thanks."

I'd have to talk to Evie in the morning, but I knew what she'd say. She wanted the device taken out, and if she had to, she'd risk her life to make it happen.

I needed to talk to Harriette. The light fae was cagey as hell, but she'd once been my mom's closest friend. There was a chance she would know what was in Evie's neck. If my mom had told anyone, she would have told her.

In the meantime, I was standing in a robe next to the demon, who had a hungry spark in his eyes. I peered up at him from beneath my lashes. "You said you had a surprise."

"I do. You're going to like it."

"What is it?"

He merely grinned, and I blinked. It wasn't often that Samael smiled, but when he did, it lit up the room.

"Come on," I wheedled. "Tell me."

"Scylla's egg has hatched."

I squealed. There was no other word for it. Samael threw his head back and laughed as I elbowed past him, hurrying into his bedroom and throwing open my suitcase.

I was going to see a baby dragon.

A. Baby. Dragon.

Samael watched as I got changed, his wings rustling. He still hadn't hidden them away, and I couldn't help but wonder if it was because he wanted me to see. Wanted me to accept who and what he was.

His eyes were liquid silver as I pulled a t-shirt over my support tank.

"I've never before found it particularly arousing to watch a woman dress."

"Yeah, I'm full of surprises. What are you waiting for? Let's go."

He raised one eyebrow and dropped his gaze to my bare feet. I scowled and reached for socks and boots.

A few minutes later I was pushing my hair out of my face as Samael soared through the air. We were headed toward the portal located behind what was once a human university.

The plethora of portals dotted throughout the Triangle had attracted many of the paranormals who made their homes here. While most of them could only be used by the most powerful paranormals around, that didn't stop even the most magically dead human from occasionally attempting to cross through a portal or using it as a quick way to take their own lives.

The Mage Council had made noises about setting guards on all of the known portals in an attempt to dissuade the kind of people who were fascinated by paranormals. This idea was quickly shot down by every paranormal in the triangle with enough power to cross over.

No one wanted the Mage Council knowing exactly which portals they were using and when.

The portal was beautiful. I could almost understand the humans who were drawn to it even if they had no power. The center was a blue so light it was almost white, darkening to azure, sapphire, and finally, a blue so deep, it reminded me of the night sky. The portal hummed, shimmering as if it was alive.

The first time I'd thrown myself through this portal, I'd been looking for the Dagger of Truth on my hip. It had felt like my limbs were being dunked in acid, my every nerve exposed and set on fire.

The last time had been much easier in comparison. Sure, the pain had ripped into me, but it had been over quickly.

This time, Samael didn't hesitate. He knew I hated traveling by portals, so he merely tightened his hold on me and flew straight through.

It hurt, but it was over in a few seconds. I opened my eyes to find Samael watching me. He smiled.

"As the suppression spell crumbles, your power can finally protect you the way it should."

Pure, unrelenting wrath danced in his eyes for a single moment at the reminder of the suppression spell and I tensed.

I hadn't told Samael exactly who had put that suppression spell on me. The demon was greatly offended that anyone would dare magically neuter one of his demons, especially since it had meant he hadn't known exactly what I was for a while. As much as Harriette annoyed me, I wouldn't be letting Samael know she'd had anything to do with the suppression spell.

I shivered as we flew toward the cave entrance. The

sun was high in the rust-colored sky, but it was still cooler in this realm. Samael clutched me closer, and I shivered for a different reason as he nuzzled my neck.

"Wait here," he said as he landed. "I'll check that Scylla is in the mood for visitors."

Good plan. The dragon didn't like me, mostly because I'd snuck into her cave and stolen Misty from her. It offended Scylla's dragon sensibilities that Samael had let me keep it. But she *adored* the demon.

He was gone for less than a minute, and then he stepped back out of the cave, holding out his hand. I took it, and he led me inside.

This wasn't any ordinary cave. The ceiling was so high that it defied the rules of physics, and I half expected the inside of the mountain to come tumbling down at any second. To the left, a collection of bones warned visitors that continuing to walk deeper into the cave was a very bad idea.

Scylla lounged in the middle of the cave, her tail flicking back and forth along the dirt floor like a cat's. The dragon's scales ran the gamut from violet to a deep purple so dark it appeared black in places. Her bright gold gaze was currently steady on my face as she silently warned me not to come any closer.

She stretched, her long, serpentine neck arching as she turned her attention to Samael. He let go of my hand and stepped closer to croon softly to the dragon, scratching her under her chin the same way I scratched Lia.

My breath caught in my throat as a tiny form shuffled forward, moving into the light.

"Oh my gosh," I breathed.

Samael glanced at me and smiled. "This is Scylla's daughter, Nuri."

The baby was about the size of a golden retriever. Like her mother, her scales were shades of purple, darkening to black in places. Her wings were oversized, almost comically big compared to the rest of her body, and they draped on the ground as she opened her mouth, revealing small, sharp teeth.

Two bright gold eyes gleamed at me as she took a stumbling step closer.

And tripped over her wings.

I stepped forward, as she face-planted, with some weird idea of helping the dragon to her feet. Scylla let out a warning snarl. I froze.

Nuri got to her feet, blinking wide eyes at me, as if shocked by her fall. She cocked her head, examining me from head to toe.

I fell a little in love.

My gaze slid toward Samael as the baby stepped even closer, this time managing to keep her feet. Scylla watched closely, but as long as I kept still, she didn't seem to have a problem with her baby exploring.

Nuri was incredibly cute, but she was still a dragon, and I was a warm pile of meat to her. A bead of sweat ran down the back of my neck as she tripped again but this time she stayed standing, moving forward until she was close enough to touch.

I heroically kept my hands to myself, caught between fascination and terror.

"Uh, should she be doing that?"

"She's merely saying hello."

Samael didn't seem at all concerned. In fact, it was amusement I could hear in his voice as I kept my eyes on the baby dragon. I ran through a few exit strategies as I watched her. She was cute and all, but she was also a predator with extremely sharp teeth.

Nuri leaned her head up, until she was staring right in my eyes.

"Uh, hi," I said.

She snuffled my belly, and it chose that moment to let out a grumble. Nuri jumped, and a tiny growl left her throat as she bared her teeth at my stomach. I couldn't help but laugh and she narrowed her gold eyes as she watched me.

Unlike her mom, who was all sharp planes and spikes, Nuri had tiny nubs where her horns would grow, and her head was rounded.

An image popped into my mind and my mouth dropped open.

Samael frowned as my eyes met his. "What is it?"

"She… showed me something."

"Interesting." He glanced at Scylla, who was still watching closely. "Dragons don't usually attempt to speak with demons until they are much older."

I'd forgotten. It was my demon side that allowed me to have a connection with dragons. If I was wholly human, Scylla likely would've eaten me by now.

"What did she show you?"

"Ah, a bone, sliding across the floor."

Samael glanced at Scylla again and laughed. "Her newest toy. Apparently she played with it last night."

Nuri was tired of being ignored and she butted my hand with her head, not unlike the way Lia did when she wanted to be petted.

I glanced at Scylla. "Can I touch her?"

She lay down, yawning massively, in a way that communicated how much I bored her, while also displaying her rows of sharp teeth.

I shrugged and raised my hand, slowly brushing it over Nuri's head. The dragon's eyes went to half mast, and I almost had to pinch myself as my gaze met Samael's.

His eyes gleamed. "You're happy."

"Are you kidding me? This is incredible."

His smile was crooked, a combination of what looked like surprised vulnerability and smug satisfaction. My heart melted for the second time in five minutes.

Nuri toddled back toward her mother, who stretched out a wing and tucked her daughter beneath it. I glanced at Samael.

"According to our deal, I owe you dinner."

"It will be ready when we get back to my tower." He turned and lay his hand on Scylla's snout, murmuring something to her that I couldn't catch. And then we were walking out of the cave and his arms were around me once more as he shot into the sky.

He banked right and both my lanyard and my rowan arrow slipped out from beneath my shirt.

The rowan must have touched Samael's skin because he hissed and repositioned his arm further down my body. I tucked it away.

"Sorry. I didn't know it could hurt a demon just from touching it."

It certainly didn't hurt me, and it lay against my skin all day.

"The more powerful the demon, the older they are, the greater their susceptibility. But even you would die if you were to fall badly and end up with it lodged in your heart. I'm tempted to take it from you."

I gritted my teeth and refrained from saying the vicious words dancing on the tip of my tongue. After a deep breath, I managed to regain control, pausing long enough to steel myself as we flew back through the portal.

Just a few months ago, the demon likely would have yanked the rowan from around my neck and burned it to ash, all in the name of 'protecting me.'

He was trying.

Still, I'd never reacted well to threats.

I opened my mouth but Samael was already murmuring in my ear. "Don't ever let Ag know you have rowan," he warned.

"Why?"

"As my second, it's his job to protect me. He considers it his duty to keep me safe— not just as his king, but as the future of our people. If he learned of it, he would remove that rowan from around your neck. If necessary, he could likely even convince himself that it made sense to murder you if he needed to remove you as a threat. I'd kill him for it, but you would still be dead."

I swallowed. "So why aren't you taking it from me then?"

"I've been surprised to learn that I enjoy a dangerous woman," he purred. "Besides, you wouldn't use that on me. You like me too much."

Unfortunately, the demon had a bloody good point.

CHAPTER FIFTEEN

Danica

Samael landed on the balcony and placed me on my feet. I felt a hint of something like nerves from his end of the bond as he reached out and opened the balcony door.

"After you."

I stepped into the room, inhaling the heady scent of flowers. Red roses had been placed in vases, which covered every available surface in his penthouse. The lights had been dimmed, and silver candles provided a warm glow.

A small table sat by one of the windows, silver domes covering two plates. Next to the plates, a bucket of ice held a bottle of champagne. I glanced at Samael but he was already walking toward the table and pulling out one of the chairs.

I followed him over and sat down.

"I dismissed the staff. They left dessert in the fridge in my kitchen. I would prefer to spend this time alone with you."

His tone, his words, for whatever reason, they

heated my cheeks and he smiled. Then he leaned over and plucked the dome from my plate, revealing steak, mashed potatoes, and green beans.

I couldn't help but laugh. "This is the meal you tried to feed me when I first woke up in your bed. God, it feels like years ago."

"You took a bite of each and then disappeared. I thought maybe you'd like to finish the meal."

I marveled at it, my stomach growling again. "You thought right." I covered my mashed potatoes in enough salt to make Samael wince, added butter, and took a mouthful, then I tried the steak.

"Mmm. Good."

"You never told me how you managed to sneak out of my tower that day," Samael said as we ate.

I swallowed and reached for my glass of champagne. It slid down my throat, cool and refreshing. I slid him a look. "Promise you won't lose your mind?"

He raised one eyebrow but finally nodded.

"Misty."

It took him a second and then his gaze dropped to my hip. I took another sip of champagne. "Since I'd so kindly fed it with blood from the hellhound, it was able to replicate a look-away spell."

He winced and I nodded. "Yeah. It wasn't ideal, but I felt trapped. I would've done almost anything to get out of your tower."

Samael sat back in his seat and watched me out of dark silver eyes. "And now?"

"Now I'm enjoying a very excellent meal and drinking champagne with the demon I thought I wanted dead. Life is weird."

He laughed and butterflies danced in my stomach at the sound. Maybe that was the champagne.

I spent the rest of the meal interrogating him.

I wanted to know more about what made Samael tick. More about the events and experiences that had shaped him into the man he was today. I'd had a glimpse of the horror that had sliced through his life when he was just a kid, but Samael had been alive for so long that it gave me a headache attempting to wrap my head around it.

I wanted to know more about the demons bonded to him. How did he make decisions? Was any of it a democracy? Did he outsource some of his rule, or did he micromanage his people?

"I learned early on that when you trust people to do their jobs, they rarely disappoint you," he said at one point. He sipped his champagne and the candlelight danced over his face, highlighting the strong line of his jaw, the gleam of silver eyes.

He smiled at me, looking content, relaxed, and… happy.

It hit me like a punch in the face.

This whole time, I'd fought this thing between us because I thought I'd lose myself. Whenever Samael did something that proved he wasn't close to human, I'd used it as evidence that we could never work. Even though *I* wasn't even entirely human.

Samael may not be the man I'd expected to find one day. But he was more than I'd ever imagined. And even when I had doubts about our ability to be together without constantly wanting to kill each other, I knew one absolute:

he loved me.

There was no other explanation for the way he came when I needed help, protected my friends and family, and taught me how to use my power to protect myself. I'd seen the baffled surprise on his demons' faces every time he involved himself in my life. For a demon as old and powerful as Samael was, it was likely unheard of.

He'd told me he was a patient man and I'd laughed. But he *must* be patient. He'd watched me take two steps forward and three back every time I fought what my heart had known for weeks now. Vas was right. I could see happiness, and I'd been refusing to reach for it.

"Little witch?"

I was in love with him. Wildly, inescapably, and *always* frustratingly in love with him. I was finally admitting it to myself, without reservation.

"Danica?"

"Uh, sorry, daydreaming."

"You look a little sick," his brow creased with concern. "No dessert then?"

My inner child wrestled with the grown-ass woman who had eaten far too much. "Maybe later?"

He studied my face, then got to his feet and held out his hand. "Let's take our drinks out to the balcony."

I could still see the first time I'd fought with Samael out on this balcony. I'd attempted to shove him, and the tips of my fingers had met soft, plush feathers for a fraction of a second. He'd warned me not to touch what wasn't yet mine.

"What are you thinking?" Samael nuzzled my ear and I sighed, arching to give him more access.

"I was thinking about the first time I stood on this balcony with you. I told you that you'd never have my loyalty."

He smiled against my neck, brushing gentle kisses along the spot that made me shiver. "And now?"

"I guess you proved I was full of shit." I frowned and he gently spun me.

"Attempting to convince you to trust me has been one of the greatest challenges of my life."

"Oh yeah?"

He brushed his mouth against mine. "Yes," he murmured against my lips, then slowly drew back. "You want me to change. I'm trying."

I blinked. Where did that come from?

"That's not what I want."

"You want me to be less like a demon and more like a human male."

Was that what I'd been doing?

You couldn't change people. Not really. And trying to change the person you were with was a good way to ruin any chance of happiness for you both.

"I don't want to change who you are. I know you're always going to be a bossy, domineering, control freak."

He nodded his head in agreement and I couldn't help but laugh.

"But... you don't have to be those things with me. At least not all the time. I'm not looking for someone to run my life. If you want to be with me, you have to accept that I'm going to do things sometimes that won't always please you. I'll occasionally be in dangerous situations. And I'll make decisions you won't always agree with. But

I promise, when I need help, I'll come to you. It's called compromise."

He ran his tongue around his teeth. "Compromise," he said as if tasting the word for the first time. "I compromise with you, and you'll stay with me?"

I sighed. I was kidding myself if I thought I could walk away from him at this point.

"One day, I'm going to ask you to remove the mark on my arm, and you're going to do it."

His wings flared, the expression on his face dark, mouth twisting in instant denial.

We stared at each other in silence for a fraught moment. Finally, I sighed.

"I'm in love with you," I blurted out.

Samael's expression shuttered and he drew back. "You would play with me even now?"

I frowned at him. "I didn't expect it to happen. God knows I didn't want it to. You infuriate me, challenge me, annoy the shit out of me. You're bossy and controlling, and dealing with your ego is no fucking picnic, let me tell you."

He raised one eyebrow and I threw up my hands, turning away to pace.

"Just a few months ago, if someone had told me I'd fall in love with you, I would've told them to get their head checked," I muttered.

"I'm not sure if that's complimentary."

I ignored that. "And now… I miss you when you're not around. I had to actively fight with myself not to come to this tower every damn day."

"Danica–"

"I want to fall asleep next to you, and fight with you, and fuck you, and complain to my friends when you're being your usual, overly possessive self. I want to be yours. But only if you're mine, too."

Strong hands gripped my shoulders, turning me, and Samael's mouth crashed down on mine. He buried his hand in my hair and the world faded away as I lost myself in the feel of him surrounding me. My demon. Mine.

"Is that a yes?" I mumbled against his mouth.

"Say it again," he ordered, and I rolled my eyes. Bossy demon.

"I love you."

He let out a groan and then he was lifting me in his arms, stalking through the doorway, into his penthouse, and through to his bedroom, where he slowly laid me down on his bed. He handled me so gently, it was as if he thought I was suddenly breakable.

"This doesn't mean you can tell me what to do all the time."

"Quiet." He nibbled on my lower lip.

"And I'm not going to give up my career for you."

He laughed. "Of course not." He pulled back long enough to strip off his clothes and my mouth went dry. I forced myself to raise my gaze to his face in an attempt to get my point across.

"I'm serious, Samael."

"I know." He let out a frustrated groan as he pulled my shirt and tank-top over my head. "So many clothes in my way." His gaze got stuck on my breasts and the next groan that left him was a different sound entirely.

"I want *you*, little witch. Not a woman who will do

everything I say without question. Although that might be an interesting experience for a few days."

I narrowed my eyes at him and he laughed, nuzzling my breasts. He unhooked my bra with deft movements, and a dark possessiveness slid into his eyes.

"I've had centuries of women doing as I said," he told me. "None of them could hold my attention for more than a few weeks. You? You will be mine forever."

I must be crazy, because the idea of being with the demon forever no longer scared the crap out of me. Well, only a little.

He tweaked one of my nipples, teasing it to a hard peak. "And if you didn't know I'm already yours, you haven't been paying close enough attention."

The words sent a thrill down my spine, but the way he lowered his mouth to my breasts sent a deeper, darker thrill through my core. I gasped and he murmured something I couldn't catch. He ran his tongue over my nipple, then gently used his teeth to tease and play.

My thighs clenched, my stomach muscles tightened, and I shifted restlessly, every nerve in my body on edge.

"I want you inside me," I murmured.

"You won't rush me, little witch."

I let out a breathless laugh as he slowly kissed his way down my body. He paid special attention to the sensitive spots that made me moan, while also learning about new spots which seemed to delight him.

"Show me," I ordered.

He didn't ask what I was talking about. His wings appeared, a dark curtain above us and I lifted one hand, stroking soft feathers. He moved further down my body, pushing my legs open as he lowered his head.

The sight of his dark head between my thighs, the obsidian wings jutting out of his wide, muscled shoulders, while his strong hands caught my hips, holding me still for him…

I lifted my hips, craving him.

He lowered his head and pressed gentle kisses to my thighs, nuzzling them in a move that was somehow achingly sweet, while also toe-curlingly sensual.

His gaze met mine. He sent me a filthy grin, and then his lips and mouth and tongue and— oh god— the edge of his teeth were caressing every inch of me. One finger pushed inside, while his mouth found my clit, and he let out a hum that made me arch my hips.

The bastard laughed.

I'd thrown my head back, and I glowered down at him. He sent me a wink and then slowly circled my clit, pushing another finger inside to join the first.

A moan left my throat as he hooked his arms beneath my thighs, pulling me closer for him.

He licked me. Again and again, paying special attention to the spots that made me tense, made me gasp, made me writhe.

Then he lowered his mouth, sucking on the sensitive bundle of nerves that made me jolt. His fingers caressed my g-spot.

My mind went blank, my breath caught, and I melted. Pleasure crested, engulfing my body until I was limp beneath him.

Liquid silver eyes met mine. Lust had tightened the muscles in his jaw. My demon was barely holding himself together. It was a powerful feeling.

I held out my arms and he covered me with his body, positioning himself at my entrance.

We both gasped as he thrust into me.

"God you're good at that."

He twisted his hips. "Say it again."

"God, you're–"

"Not that." He raised his head and nipped my chin. I laughed, and the sound turned into a strangled moan as he ground against me, hitting my clit.

"You say it first."

He narrowed his eyes. "I love you," he said.

"Well, you don't have to sound so pissed off about it."

His hips stopped moving.

I slammed my foot against his butt and he merely waited.

"I love you," I laughed. "Now, *move*."

He moved. He knew the exact spot to hit for the friction to drive me wild. Each time I was on the edge, he'd change his position slightly, until I was clawing at his shoulders.

"You goddamn sadist."

He laughed and then he was gone. I gaped, but he'd already lifted me onto my knees, spinning me around until my elbows hit the mattress.

His next thrust made me yelp. He was suddenly so deep I was sure he couldn't get any deeper. His hand slid beneath me, finding my clit, and my legs spread, welcoming him. He pounded into me, until all I could feel was each slide of his cock, my body tightening. He shifted his angle, and the combination of his clever fingers caressing my clit and his thick cock rubbing against my g-spot...

I was so close.

"Samael," I gasped, and he let out a low growl. Several hard thrusts, and then my climax hit me, climbing up my spine and sending shockwaves through every inch of my body. Behind me, Samael growled once more, flooding me with heat.

We both collapsed onto the bed.

Sometime later, I felt Samael stir. My throat was dry as a desert, but I couldn't bring myself to move. He nuzzled my ear, sending a delicious tingle through my body, and then he was returning with the champagne and a cool glass of water.

He held the water to my lips, placed the glasses on the bedside table, and hauled me into his arms.

He stroked my back, and I ran my nails along his abs, pleased when he shivered in response.

The gold glimmered on my arm, contrasting with his darker skin beneath mine.

"Why the bond, Samael?"

He tensed, and he was silent for a long moment. Then his arms tightened around me.

"That night we first met, I thought to humiliate you. And with you, the Mage Council. It is not often that I'm surprised by my own cruelty. That night, I was unable to look my reflection in the eye."

"What exactly do you mean by that?"

"Our bond is only reserved for bondmates. Those who choose to tie themselves to each other for life."

I slowly pulled away from him. "But why? You hated me."

"I enjoyed the fact that you would forever feel me at the end of the bond. I could easily block you, and would suffer none of the effects of the bond myself."

"Diabolical," I murmured. "But wouldn't that mean you would never be able to take a real bondmate?"

He shrugged. "I never felt the need to form that kind of bond with a woman."

"Seems like short-term thinking to me, but you do you, boo."

The corner of his mouth turned up. "At first, our bond was a way to put you in your place. To take you from Albert and make you do my bidding. And yet I had the strangest urge to listen to the words that leapt from your sarcastic mouth. I would attend meetings and wonder what you would think of my plans. As I watched you over the coming weeks, I became more and more sure that the bond was the right choice.

"When I realized who you were, I was... elated. Not only did I have the means to kill Lucifer, but I would need to protect you until you were strong enough. I had a reason to keep you close. To keep you safe."

He stroked my hair, pushing a tendril behind my ear. "I believe my deeper instincts knew you on some level the moment I saw you. Call it fate, or intuition, or whatever you like, but never have I done something as foolish as create a mate bond before. No matter how furious I have been over the centuries. Bael knew. So did Vassago. Ag didn't want to know, but he saw what was happening."

I had a lot to think about. I laid my head back on his

chest, and we were both silent for a long time. I opened my mouth and then snapped it closed. Samael pinched my chin. "What is it?"

"Why me?"

"Excuse me?"

I lifted my head. "I'm not being insecure. At least, I hope I'm not. I'm just curious. You could bone any woman in any of the realms. You've probably already worked your way through half of them. What made you so into me?"

Samael smiled and pressed a kiss to my neck. "Perhaps because you're so charmingly unaware of your own attributes."

I rolled my eyes. "I know and like my *attributes* just fine."

He laughed. "Ever since you gave me back my mother's bracelet, I've wondered what she would think of the man I have become. She was gentle and kind. She would go out of her way to help others, and she tempered my father, ensuring that he never gave into his brutality, like so many male demons. She would like you."

He'd told me that once before and I shook my head. "I'm not gentle or kind."

"Not gentle, perhaps. But your kindness pushes you to take risks for those you love. It makes you take on a missing person case, while juggling both your sister's grief, and the investigation into the fire. You're not soft and graceful, but that wouldn't have pulled me in the way you have."

I opened my mouth and he gently placed one of his fingers over my lips.

"You've never been impressed by my status. Or anyone's. You treated the unseelie king the same way as you would any suspect you came up against in the course of an investigation."

"He's a dick," I muttered.

He ignored that. "Once you give your loyalty, you don't rescind it. And you sacrifice for those you love, even if it hurts you. You're beautiful, you're strong, and you make me wish to be the kind of ruler you'll be proud of one day."

Tears filled my eyes. I attempted to blink them back, but one of them dropped to his chest. Samael jolted as if he'd been shot, his arms pulling me further up his body so he could see my face.

We didn't say anything, but he gently wiped the tears from my face until I'd managed to get a hold of myself.

"A while ago, at Merrill's funeral, you said I didn't know how to trust. Because of Mom, and because of the coven."

He brushed his lips over my temple and held them there for a long moment. "I shouldn't have said that."

"No, you were right. I thought about this a lot recently. Trusting doesn't come easy to me at the best of times, and Mom always insisted we stay away from demons. Now, I know it was because she assumed it was the best way to prevent Lucifer from finding out I existed."

I blew out a shaky breath. "When she died… the last thing I said to her was angry, hateful. Once she was gone, and I was hunting for her killer, I felt like I'd failed her. I figured I could at least do that one thing for her, you know?"

He nodded. "I understand, witchling. Your mother would be proud of the woman you've become."

I didn't think so. He must've read my thoughts on my face because he pinched me. I laughed, snuggling into him.

Tomorrow, I'd have to deal with the fact that was officially all-in with my domineering demon. But for now, I was going to simply enjoy the feel of his arms around me.

CHAPTER SIXTEEN

Danica

I woke to find Samael's silver gaze on my face. His arms tightened around me and I smiled at him.

"Were you watching me sleep like a creeper?"

Humor sparked in his eyes. "Merely listening to the sweet sound of your snores."

I scowled at him, slipping my hand between us and poking him lightly in the gut. My finger met nothing but muscle.

"Lower," he said, and I laughed.

"I don't have time for your games this morning. I need to talk to Harriette."

His eyes narrowed slightly at that. "The light fae woman."

"Yes. The one who was friends with my mom."

I yawned. The demon had kept me up late enough last night that it was a struggle to keep my eyes open.

He gave me a sleepy, very smug smile. He

looked disgustingly attractive and incredibly relaxed.

And now I was waking up next to him in his bed.

The idea of moving in with him had freaked me out. I'd been convinced I'd lose my independence. But I was too stubborn to let the demon steamroll over me. Ever. Our relationship was destined to be a power struggle until the end.

At least we'd never be bored.

"I want you to let me train you," Samael said, and I slowly turned my head. He was lying on his side, playing with my hair.

"How long have you been holding that in for?"

"I understood— when you didn't want me to train you after the incident with the witch descendants."

I eyed him. "Incident?"

"But now you're mine." I opened my mouth and he smiled, bopping me on the nose with the tip of one finger. "And I'm yours."

I slitted my eyes at him. "Try that again, and you'll lose that finger."

His smile widened, but his eyes turned serious. "You chose to be mine. And that means you'll allow me to do everything I can to protect you. My instincts urge me to tie you to this bed and keep you here, safe from Lucifer's reach."

I gave him a sweet smile. "It's a good thing you've had centuries of dealing with your instincts."

He gave me a dark look. "Not these instincts. These feelings are all new to me, and I wrestle with them every day. But I understand that as much as I need to protect you, you will insist on encounters with some of the most dangerous creatures in this city, all while Lucifer now knows you're alive."

I chewed on my lower lip. I mean he wasn't *wrong*. "So your solution is to train me?"

"If I can't be with you every moment of every day– and believe me, that's a hardship– you will allow me to protect you the way I know best. By teaching you as much as I can about your power. You have your witch friend, and she has done miracles in the time she has had— don't think I haven't noticed your shields." Pride entered his words and warmth unfurled in my chest. "But you need a demon to teach you how to use your powers."

"Okay," I said. Surprise flickered in his eyes, and I smiled. It wasn't often I could surprise the demon. He studied my face as if waiting for me to say 'psych' and I rolled my eyes.

"Despite what you must think of me, I'm not an idiot who acts without thinking," I said. He raised one eyebrow and I scowled. "Unless someone I love is in danger." He nodded as if that was exactly his point. "And," I said through gritted teeth, "I always loved learning from you. I just hated how you would never ask me to do something. You ordered. And of course, I was continually distracted by the warring instincts to either punch you in the face or jump your bones."

He grinned, the infrequent, almost boyish grin I loved.

Over the past few weeks, I'd thought a lot about the prophecy. About Lucifer. In fact, I'd had a pity party for weeks. But I didn't have time to feel sorry for myself. Lucifer knew I was alive, and that meant it was only a matter of time before he was coming for me.

I shifted and winced. My entire body ached. Most of it was a pleasant 'you sure got some' ache, but Samael had a gleam in his eye that told me if I didn't get out of his bed, I'd be walking with a limp.

I had to time this perfectly, because if he put his hands on me, I was destined to roll around with him for the next few hours.

I was weak, damnit.

"Will you pass me that water?

The demon reached over to grab it, and I took the opportunity to roll out of the bed.

"Psych."

He glanced back at me, his eyes darkened, and I realized I was standing in front of him, naked like a juicy steak in front of a lion.

"Come back here," he purred.

I shivered. "Don't even try to use your sex voice on me. I've got shit to do."

He slowly sat up, readying himself to pounce.

I took off toward the bathroom, slamming the door shut before he could open it.

"My cooter can't handle any more of your attention," I told him when he attempted to open the door.

"I'll have the healer look at you." I could hear the smirk in his voice and I scowled.

"You will fucking not." My face heated in mortification at the thought and he laughed. I turned on the shower and decided to ignore him.

By the time I made it into the dining room for breakfast, Evie was up and eating a bagel.

She seemed… energized. I was pretty sure she was fueled on pure rage, and at this point, I couldn't blame her. But I'd take rage over shell-shocked grief any day.

"I talked to Samael." I told her. "Gloria is our best bet for figuring out how to remove the device in your neck. Samael's giving her access to his grimoires, which apparently are necessary for this kind of spell."

Evie nodded. "Good. I want it out."

"I know. Here's the thing, though. You're going to have to be put under. We need a surgical team, and we need to make damn sure they're not going to kill you in the process."

She paled slightly but nodded. "Whatever it takes."

The door opened and we both glanced at Samael as he walked in.

"Ladies."

"Coffee?" I offered. My head spun at how weirdly domestic it was to be eating breakfast with my sister in Samael's penthouse.

"No thank you." He smiled at me, and the look in his eyes was both heated and intimate. Next to me, Evie fanned her face. I shot her a look and she grinned.

"How are you doing this morning Evie?"

The sparkle disappeared from Evie's eyes but she took a deep breath. "I'm doing okay," she told Samael. "It helps to know that I'm safe here."

Samael nodded. "Gloria is currently refining a spell she believes will work to keep the device in your neck inert for long enough to remove it without alerting whoever could be tracking it," Samael strolled over to the table, stole my coffee and took a sip.

"Get your own," I snarked.

"Yours tastes better," he said, and I narrowed my eyes at him. Evie snorted.

This was just weird.

"Nothing is happening before I talk to Harriette," I declared. "There's a chance she'll know what the device is."

Evie nodded. "I'm coming with you."

Samael glanced at me. "I will come as well."

I raised my eyebrows. "Don't you have work to do?"

He simply gave me a look and I shrugged. He knew no one tracking Evie would dare attack if he was with us.

My phone vibrated and I glanced at it. Gary.

"Hey."

"Danica. I heard about the attack. Are you both okay?"

"Yeah, we're fine. Thanks for checking in."

"I heard they used a darker-than-night spell."

"That's right.

"I sold one a few days ago."

I froze. "You did?"

"Yeah. It didn't seem like a big deal. Humans come in here all the time, looking for allergy charms and shit like that."

"Dad!" a little voice said in the background. "Bad word!"

"Sorry, Zip." Gary gave a long-suffering sigh and I chuckled.

"What did they look like?"

"That's why I called you. Three human men."

"Tell me you have camera footage."

"After what happened to my store? I have the best setup money can buy. Your man arranged for that."

I glanced at Samael. He merely smiled at me. My heart flipped in my chest and his smile widened.

"Can you send it to Steve? He'll check it out."

"Of course. Make them pay, Danica."

"You know it."

I hung up as someone knocked on Samael's door. Vas strolled in, nodded at both of us, and poured himself a coffee. "You needed me?" he asked Samael.

Samael filled him in, and within a few minutes, we were all soaring through the air, Samael's arms around me, while Vas carried Evie.

I needed a moment alone with Evie to warn her not to tell Samael that Harriette was partly responsible for the suppression spell that had been placed on my power. The spell offended Samael on a deep, primal level, and while it crumbled more every day, the demon wasn't the forgive and forget type.

If I wanted Harriette to stay alive, Samael couldn't know she'd been part of the decision— and execution— of that spell.

I felt a little bad as we landed outside Harriette's house. She'd always been terrified of demons, and some of that was likely thanks to the fact that if they'd ever found out that she'd helped my mom hide me from them, she would have been in deep shit.

I knocked on the door. No answer. Samael merely raised a hand and the door flew open.

"What the hell?" I demanded.

He ignored me, and I followed his gaze.

"Oh fuck."

Evie retched, and I barely suppressed the urge to do the same. We wouldn't be getting any answers out of Harriette.

She was hanging from her glittery chandelier, the soft light from the stained-glass windows turning her body into a gruesome display.

She hadn't died quickly. Deep scratches surrounded the rope that had been used to hang her, and even amongst the dark purple of her face, it was easy to see she'd been tortured.

My gaze was drawn to a pile of *something* beneath her body and it was my turn to heave.

Her eyes and her tongue. The message was clear.

Samael's face was hard. "This is a crime scene. The light fae will want to send their own investigators to look for prints and other evidence."

He was right. Like every other paranormal faction, the light fae were extremely territorial. They wouldn't thank us for poking our noses into this without asking. I'd ask Mariam if she could keep me updated.

I took a final glance around, my heart heavy. I hadn't particularly liked Harriette, or her way of dancing around the truth and only giving me half of the information I needed at any one time. But she'd been our only real tie to our mom.

We waited outside Harriette's house until a seelie team arrived. They were all dressed in white, and the guy in charge had long hair the exact shade as his shirt. His expression was placid as he approached Samael.

"My name is Aitri. I understand you found the

body. We may need to contact you both for a statement depending on what we find," he said.

Samael nodded and glanced at Vas, who gave Aitri a card. We watched as one of the fae stood in the doorway and lifted her hands, her body stiff.

"What's she doing?" Evie asked.

"Occasionally, she is able to get an imprint of the scene from any natural elements in the room," Aitri replied.

Then, with one last nod at us, he turned and followed his team into the house.

Samael nodded, and we were all silent as we flew back to the tower. I had no doubt that the same people who'd killed Harriette were the ones responsible for the device in my sister's neck.

"I should've put the pieces together," I murmured. "I should've warned Harriette."

"She had been dead for several days," Samael said as we landed. "They were tying up loose ends before you knew Evie was a target."

He was right, but it didn't make me feel any better.

"Since she's already dead, I may as well tell you, she was partly responsible for the suppression spell on my power."

Samael nodded. "I know."

I gaped at him, and he glanced down at me long enough to smile at my reaction before turning his attention back to our route. "While I may have wanted to punish her severely for daring to do such a thing, I knew you wanted her to live, if only for your mother's sake. The moment you decided that tie was no longer necessary, neither was the seelie.”

“You’re a scary bastard, you know that?”

Gloria was waiting for us in Samael’s penthouse when we arrived. I had the weirdest territorial instinct when it came to her, and I had to suppress an automatic sneer as she eyed me.

“No killing the witch until she has outlived her usefulness,” Samael said in my head.

I glowered at him. He simply smiled and gestured for us to move further into the living room, where we sat on his huge, U-shaped couch.

“I have found a spell that I believe will work,” Gloria said.

“How sure are you?” I demanded.

“A seventy percent chance that the device can be removed without death or paralysis. That chance rises with an extremely skilled surgical team and Samael’s fae healer.”

Seventy percent. I buried my face in my hands. Next to me, Evie nudged me with her elbow.

“It’s not bad,” she said lightly. “I have no choice, Dani, unless I want these guys to keep coming.”

“I know.” But I didn’t have to like it.

Samael got to his feet. “I have ensured that some of the best human surgeons in the country are being flown in. Eldan is also here and will be ready as soon as they arrive.”

Eldan was Samael’s personal light fae healer, and I’d seen him work miracles. I nodded, massaging the stiff muscles in the back of my neck. A strong hand took over and I nearly purred as Samael’s clever fingers expertly worked out the tension.

My phone vibrated and I glanced at the screen. Kyla had messaged me. Evie nudged me again with her elbow.

"Go get back to work," she said. "We have a few hours, and you need to talk to Riona."

"I want to know as soon as the surgical team arrives."

"I'll text you."

"Okay." I left them sitting on the sofa and texted Kyla to meet me at the hospital.

Want me to swing by and pick you up?

Shit. I'd left my car at my apartment. Samael must've felt me stiffen because he leaned over and read my text.

"Take one of mine," he said.

"Mind your own business."

He merely raised an eyebrow and I sighed. "Fine."

Kyla was sitting on a bench outside the hospital, her long legs stretched out in front of her as she played with her phone.

She glanced up at me as I approached, and got to her feet. I nodded at her phone.

"You're on Portal?"

She shrugged. "Every now and then. Most guys aren't interested when they learn I turn furry and could rip them to pieces. Funny how that works."

"Some men just aren't ready for a strong, self-sufficient woman."

She laughed. "Ain't that the damn truth."

"Ah, are you going to be okay in here?"

"I ate a huge breakfast. I'm fine."

Maeve and Siobhan were sitting on either side of Riona's bed when we walked in. Siobhan smiled at me.

"She's doing much better. She might even be released tomorrow. Keeps talking about all the calories she gets to eat to make up for the starvation diet she was on."

Her eyes gleamed with tears and she blinked them back. Maeve reached across the bed and squeezed her hand.

Riona's eyes opened, bleary and confused. She scanned the room and her gaze landed on me. "Hey," she croaked out. Siobhan handed her a cup of water and helped her adjust her bed until she was sitting up.

"We have a few questions if you're feeling up to it. If you're not, we can come back tomorrow."

"No. No, I want to get it over with." She glanced at her mom and sister. "You guys don't need to hear all this again. Why don't you go down to the cafeteria and grab some food?"

Maeve looked like she wanted to argue and Riona smiled. "I'd love it if you could bring me back something sweet."

"Of course, darling." She kissed her daughter on the forehead, smiled at me, and walked out.

Siobhan hesitated. "Are you sure you don't want me to stay?"

"I'm good. Promise."

She nodded and followed her mother. Riona reached for the controls to her bed and sat up a little more.

Kyla and I took the chairs on either side of her bed.

"I walked in on the spell. I was answering a text when I opened the door, paying no attention. Stupid."

"You housesit there a lot, right? You had no reason to believe anything bad was going on."

"Yeah. I guess they'd gotten wind that Mary and Jim would be out of town. They would've drawn attention in an apartment, and they needed a human neighborhood so no paranormals would figure out what they were doing."

"What were they doing?"

She swallowed.

"They had everything they needed for a Spell of Three," she murmured. The blood drained from her face. "I saw it. I walked in, and it was all right there, by the front door. I smelled the blood."

My mouth went dry. As if we didn't have enough problems right now.

"What's a Spell of Three?" Kyla asked.

"It's one of the most dangerous– and deadly– spells in existence," Riona said. "It's been banned by every law enforcement agency around, along with the leaders of every magical faction in our world."

I nodded. "The spell gained popularity after the Decade of Despair. And unsurprisingly, it turned out that no one would risk hunting the bad guys if they knew their power could be reflected back at them– times three."

Kyla gave a low whistle. "Can you tell if someone has used a Spell of Three?"

"Nope," I popped the P. "It made it exceptionally dangerous for mages who were going after black witches. They'd use their power, with no way of knowing that it would be reflected back at them. Since it was their own power, their shields were useless against it. Most of them died. Badly."

"How difficult is it to create a Spell of Three?" Kyla asked.

I shrugged and glanced at Riona. Her eyes had slid closed again, but she managed to push them back open.

"Difficult. It requires a sacrifice of something living— usually something sentient. It's that sacrifice that makes the magic multiply." Her eyes filled with tears. "In this case, they used a gnome. That's where all the blood came from."

She took a deep breath and blew it out in a steady stream. "They obviously didn't know the owners had asked me to housesit. I was… stupid. I realized I'd made too much noise walking in and I turned to go. The witch looked at me. Something hit me from behind and the next thing I knew, I was chained up in that basement.

"My hair had fallen in front of my face, so I cracked open my eyes. The black witch walked in and I swear to God, I thought I was dead right there. She looked at me like I was already no longer breathing, and I heard them talking about the spell while I pretended I was still unconscious. She told the human guy that I could at least be useful as the sacrifice for her next spell."

"What did he look like?"

"Um. Young. Maybe mid-twenties. White guy, dark hair. He had a scar on his upper lip. It was deep."

"What about the witch?"

"She was old. I'm not great with ages but probably somewhere between seventy and ninety. I only got a glimpse of her when I walked in the apartment, and when she first looked at me in the basement. M-most of the time I was too scared to even look at her. It felt like she was a cat, and I was a terrified mouse hoping not to draw her attention."

"How did you stay alive?"

She attempted a smile, but it fell from her mouth. "I'm one of the best warders in my coven. When I woke up in the basement, I raised a ward and she couldn't get through." Tears rolled down her cheeks and she wiped at them.

"She didn't care. We all knew it was only a matter of time before I had no power left and my ward would fall. It would happen before I starved to death, and she'd still be able to use me for her next spell. A sacrifice was a sacrifice. You guys saved my life."

Kyla smiled at her. "It sounds like you saved your own."

I let out a long breath. Riona was alive, but we weren't finished. We needed to find why someone had created a Spell of Three, and what they were planning to do with it– before they created anarchy in Durham.

Danica

Evie was waiting for me in Samael's medical center when I arrived. The demon had an actual surgical theatre in his tower. I was no longer surprised. For now, we'd wait in one of the smaller medical rooms until they were ready for Evie. Butterflies fought to the death in my stomach at the thought.

My sister sat on a hospital bed and swung her legs. "How did it go with Riona?"

I filled her in and she gaped at me. "A Spell of

Three… it's illegal to even buy most of the ingredients."

"Well, the sacrifice is also illegal, and that didn't seem to bother them any. They used a gnome."

"Who do you think it is?"

"I don't know. All Riona knew was that it was a black witch, but she was so traumatized, all she remembers is her eyes. She only saw her once. She was waiting until she dropped her ward so she could sacrifice her for a spell."

"You're worried it's Hannah."

I glanced away. "I'm really fucking hoping it's not. Anyway. How are you feeling?"

Evie blew out a shaky breath. "Terrified," she admitted. "But… resolved. I won't live with this hanging over my head. Or my neck," she smiled. "I'm in good hands. Your demon won't let anything happen to me if he can help it. He loves you too much."

"I want to be in there."

She shook her head. "They're cutting me open, Dani. You don't need to see that."

"I don't care."

"I do."

We both looked up as the door opened and Samael and Eldan walked in. The light fae healer smiled at us. "It's time."

My pulse was so loud I could hear it in my ears, but I attempted a reassuring smile.

"It'll be out before you know it," I said.

Evie nodded. "As soon as you know I'm not going to die, you need to get back to your investigations. You need to find the black witch with the Spell of Three, and we need to know who betrayed the coven before they try again."

I was silent for a long moment and she narrowed her eyes at me. "I mean it. No sitting by my bedside waiting for me to wake up. Get to work, Dani."

I rolled my eyes. "Fine. But if you die, I'm going to be really pissed off."

She grinned. "Same."

I wrapped my arms around her and held just a little too tightly, for just a little too long. Evie squeezed me back and then took a deep breath.

"I'm ready."

Eldan led her out of the room, giving me a moment alone with Samael.

"I'll be in there the whole time. I'll keep you updated."

I nodded, turning away to pace, and then I was in his arms, my head buried in his chest.

"Please Samael…"

"I swear to you, I won't let her die."

I swallowed around the lump of my throat. "Even I know you can't control death."

"The ferryman owes me a favor."

I gaped at him, and he gently untangled himself from me, brushing his mouth against mine. "I need to go supervise."

"Watch Gloria closely, just in case she decides to pull any dodgy tricks."

He shook his head at me and strolled out of the room, leaving me to pace.

Focus on something else.

Like it or not, but if someone was planning to use a

Spell of Three, the Mage Council needed to know about it. I fired off a quick text to Keigan and considered my duty done.

There was a whiteboard on one side of the room, and with nothing else to do, I crossed to it. Something had been niggling at the back of my brain for the last day, and I couldn't put my finger on it. Maybe if I got my thoughts out, I'd be able to organize them.

"She's under," Samael's voice was a comforting presence in my head. *"Everything is looking good."*

"Thanks."

I spent the next couple of hours pacing and updating my board with my thoughts. When the door opened, and my eyes met Samael's, panic climbed up and ripped the breath from my lungs.

He instantly crossed the room, pulling me close. "She's fine. Just resting. I thought you'd want to see her."

"Oh God. They got it out?"

He nodded. "My people are examining it now."

"Okay." The feeling of the adrenaline draining away was enough to make me want to toss my cookies. I sat on the bed for a moment and shoved my head between my legs.

Samael stood silently next to me, slowly running a hand up and down my back until I collected myself enough to get to my feet.

Then he took my hand and led me down the corridor to my sister.

Eldan smiled at me as he wrote something on a chart. "She came through swimmingly. I've healed most of the damage already, but the healing will make her sleep for the next day or so."

"Thank you."

Evie looked young and very fragile in the large hospital bed against the white sheets. I turned at a knock on the door.

Liam. He gave me a crooked smile. "I just heard. Wondered if I could come check on her."

"I'm sorry. She probably didn't want to worry you. It all happened so fast, but we should've let you know."

He shrugged, walking toward Evie and taking her other hand.

"I forget how delicate she is when she's not awake and raising hell," he smiled.

I laughed. "I was just thinking the same thing." I glanced at Samael. He'd allowed a werewolf entrance to his territory, solely so he could be there when Evie woke up.

"Thank you."

"You can show your appreciation by eating something."

I frowned and he raised one eyebrow at me from where he leaned against the wall across the room.

"When was the last time you ate?"

I shrugged, and my stomach rumbled at the thought of food.

"I'll have something brought up." He glanced at Liam. "For the wolf too."

"Thanks."

"I have a meeting, but I'll be around if you need me."

I sat in the chair next to Evie's bed. Within twenty minutes, food arrived. Liam scented the air and grinned at the woman wheeling the cart as she handed him a plate of some kind of hearty soup with bread.

"Appreciated."

We ate in silence for a while, and then Liam cleared his throat, his green eyes serious.

"I know we don't know each other well, but I wanted to let you know that I care about your sister," he said. "I thought about her most days after we moved. I was angry at my parents for a long time because I thought I'd never get a chance with her. When I was turned, I lost everything— it never occurred to me that your sister would be connected in any way to the pack here. Or that she could be interested in a werewolf."

"My sister doesn't discriminate when it comes to who she cares about. I'm glad she has you."

"But you don't trust me."

I sighed. "It's not that. I've seen firsthand how difficult it is for a relationship to work between a human and a paranormal— and I'm half demon. I think you can make it work, but Evie has a lot going on right now. She's being hunted, Liam. And we don't know why."

His face drained of color. "I won't let anyone hurt her," he vowed. "Kyla's on her way," he said, obviously scenting the wolf.

She poked her head in the room a few minutes later.

"How's Evie?" She nodded at Liam and he nodded back.

I blew out a breath. "Holding steady. She's really just in a deep sleep right now." I got to my feet. "If she were awake, she'd be telling me to get back to work. I've been working on the whiteboard in the other room. Come take a look.”

I glanced at Liam and he smiled his crooked smile. “I’ll stay with her.”

“Thanks.”

Kyla trailed me to the room I’d waited in, and I gestured for her to take a seat. She shook her head and stared at the whiteboard.

“This is the hierarchy of the witches in Durham.”

I nodded. “I don’t believe the Jefferson or Allen covens have enough motive, but I’m keeping them on the suspect list.”

“Why don’t you think they have enough motive?”

“It’s one thing to gain power, it’s another to hold it. Maybe if the Jefferson and Allen covens worked together with a third coven, they could hold onto the power Gemma’s coven had, but they’d be holding onto it with their fingertips.” I scowled. “You bet your ass, black witches from across the Triangle will be considering moving into Gemma’s territory right about now.”

And I couldn’t think about that. It would have to be a problem for another day.

“Do you think Gemma will be able to build the coven back up?”

I shrugged. “She lost a lot of them, which means she lost a lot of power. I guess it depends on how powerful her remaining witches are. Okay, here’s what I’ve got so far.”

I stared at the list on my board some more. On one side, I’d written a list of covens. On the other, I’d written Gemma’s name, followed by Nellie, who was followed by Willow and then Gail. Next was Noelle, Ainsley, and Evie, followed by the rest of the witches in the coven.

I crossed off Nellie, Noelle, and Ainsley while Kyla watched, her eyes narrowed.

"Gemma was going to stay in Durham. She decided to go on the trip at the last minute. But let's say for a moment that she had stayed and died."

I crossed her name off. Willow was now at the top of the list as coven leader. Gail, Noelle, Ainsley, Evie, Caroline, Marie, Zoe, and Freya were all shuffled into order.

"I don't know about the remaining witches at the top, but from what I can tell, they're mostly young or relatively new to the coven. Or, they've been members for a while but they don't live in the house— they're not interested in the internal politics."

Kyla nodded. "It's the same in the pack. You've got the wolves who keep to themselves but need to be members of the pack. Like me. And then you've got the wolves who are involved in the day-to-day running of the pack.

"Right." I frowned. "I don't know Willow well. And she never struck me as someone who wanted power." I pulled up the notes on my phone. "Gemma took her in a few years ago when her relationship fell apart. Before that, she didn't have much to do with the witches."

"Maybe someone figures she'd step aside if Gemma was dead."

"Yeah. You interviewed Willow, right? What do you have on her?"

"She sure didn't like being interviewed by a werewolf, but that's normal. She said the witches who'd died were her sisters and while we were wasting time interviewing the coven, whoever had killed them was likely flying to some island somewhere to drink mojitos on the beach."

"I'd pick margaritas myself. Family kill each other all the time, just ask the cops."

"Truth. Once she got that off her chest, she just cried, Danica. It was one of the saddest things I've seen."

I sighed. "We need to do a deep dive into the top five witches who are left, including finances, prior brushes with the law— both human and witch, and anything else that jumps out at us. First, we start with Willow."

CHAPTER SEVENTEEN

Danica

Early the next morning, I checked on Evie, but she was still sleeping in the medical ward. Then I made my way down to Steve's office on the third floor.

He sent me a look. As usual, his clothes were rumpled enough that he might've slept in them.

"You."

"Me."

"Ever since you hooked up with the boss, I've worked more hours than I have in years."

I managed to suppress my smirk, then ruined it with my smart mouth. "Aw, are you missing out on your day drinking?"

He scowled at me and turned away, and I used that as an opportunity to wander into his office. "This space is tiny."

He grunted. "Samael offered me a bigger one. I like it down here. A small office means you don't have to deal with constant *guests*."

I plonked myself in the chair across from his

desk. "I'm about to make your day."

"Is that right?"

"I need a deep dive on some witches. And I'm not going to ask you to do it since I know you're busy. But I am going to ask you to load whatever programs or websites I'd need onto my laptop, along with any passwords you'd feel like sharing."

He gaped at me. "Is that all?"

"I thought about hiring a guy. Or finding a contractor to deal with all this computer crap. But I'm not an idiot, and if you give me access, I can do it myself. I won't need to hit you up for help every time I need a run."

"And what does Samael say about this?"

I shrugged and he shot me a look. "I'm not risking my job without the boss's approval. Even if you are his–"

He cut himself off at the look on my face, and I had a pretty good feeling whatever he was going to call me wasn't complimentary.

"His what?" I purred.

Silence.

"How about I ask him right now," I tapped one finger to my temple.

Curiosity lit in Steve's eyes as he pushed his glasses further up his nose and focused his attention on me. The curiosity shifted to amusement, and I had a feeling I still had a tendency to look constipated whenever I attempted to speak to Samael through our bond.

"Samael?"

Silence. Maybe I was doing it wrong. I poked at the bond with my power and received a caressing stroke back.

"Yes?"

He sounded extremely pleased with me, and I'd have to deal with the smug, arrogant demon later. He was always happy anytime I showed a hint of initiating any kind of intimacy with him.

"You mind if I get Steve to download some programs onto my laptop and give me access to some of the systems he uses when tracking people for you?"

"No. As long as you never use that information against me or my people."

Something like hurt tightened my stomach. Since we were connected even more closely than usual, Samael must have felt it, because he made a low, soothing sound.

"I don't believe you would, little witch. But I am responsible for every demon in my territory. I would be a poor ruler if I did not ask for your promise."

"I won't use anything against you or your people. Even if you piss me off, which you do almost every day."

A low laugh. *"Very well. I've messaged Steve, and he'll allow you access."*

Steve's phone beeped at that moment and he glanced at it, his eyes widening.

"That was fast." He sighed. "Okay. Let's get you set up."

It didn't take long, even with my constant questions. Half an hour later, I picked up my laptop, thanked Steve, and made my way back up to the penthouse.

Lilith was stretched out on the huge sofa in Samael's living room when I arrived. She wore designer jeans and a pink t-shirt which read 'Girl Power.'

She nodded at me before returning her attention to the magazine she was flipping through. I made myself at home on the other side of the U, stretching out with my laptop.

I wasn't finding anything suspicious in Willow's bank accounts. No large deposits or withdrawals. No hidden accounts— although I'd probably have to get Steve to check that. So far, I couldn't see any bumps in her criminal record either.

Kyla was currently keeping a close eye on the witch, and I sent her a text, checking in.

All quiet here. Willow hasn't left the hotel except to go for a quick walk around the block.

I frowned. *No stops?*

Zero.

"Well this is cozy," Samael smiled at me as he stepped into the room.

Lilith glanced up at him. "I'm redecorating. I needed some quiet."

"My place is yours. Although there are a few empty suites downstairs…"

She shot him a look and his smile widened. He sat next to me, arranging his wings over the low back of the sofa before wrapping one arm around my shoulders.

He was right. This was cozy.

"We need to talk," he said.

I should've known. Cozy never lasted.

I closed my laptop. "What is it?"

"Until now, Lucifer has been very careful to keep his high demons out of my territory. They use other portals when they wish to visit this realm, as they know my people will kill them on sight if they dare arrive here without invitation."

"I'm guessing that's no longer the case."

He slowly shook his head. "One of Lucifer's people crossed several nights ago. He killed two of my demons. Unfortunately, they were ill prepared for his attack." Samael's mouth twisted.

"Do I know the demons?"

He shook his head. "We believe the demon who crossed was Daimonion."

I frowned. "I know that name. How do I know that name?"

Lilith closed her magazine. "Daimonion is the man who killed Vassago's parents."

"Fuck. Does he know?"

Samael shook his head. "I will tell him later today."

If Lucifer hadn't allowed his demons to enter Samael's territory during the past seventy years, and he was allowing it now...

"He knows I'm here."

Samael's jaw tightened. "Yes. We believe he was merely testing the waters." His arm squeezed me to his side. "My people were unprepared. Next time, we will be ready for him."

I could feel the blood draining from my face. My hands shook enough that I linked them together. I'd known Lucifer would find me, but I hadn't expected it to be this fast.

"I will keep you safe," Samael said, reaching out and taking my hand.

I needed to keep myself safe. "I guess we need to start that training sooner rather than later."

We were silent for a long moment. Lilith went back

to her magazine, and I stared into space, my mind racing.

"Samael…"

"Yes?"

I blew out a breath. "If something happens to me… if Lucifer or one of his people take me out… I need you to promise you'll protect Evie."

Samael went very quiet. And when he looked at me, there was nothing even remotely human in his gaze. I watched him, refusing to look away.

"I'm asking you to do this for me," I said quietly.

"If I was a better man, I would tell you I would protect everyone you loved. Everyone who loves you."

"You can do that."

His eyes were pure ice. "I suggest, bounty hunter, that if you want your friends and family to stay safe, you concentrate on staying unharmed."

I stared at him. He wanted me, but every now and then, he hated me for it. Because I made him vulnerable in a way he hadn't been for a long, long time.

He got to his feet, turned and walked away.

My chest burned and I realized I'd been holding my breath.

I glanced at Lilith. "He'd protect them. I know he would."

"I believe he would too. If he remembered who they were. If he was still capable of reason."

"What's that supposed to mean?"

"I suggest you stay alive. Because what Samael would do to this world if you died…" she shivered, and for the first time since I'd known her, true fear flashed across her face. "People would be speaking of the Decade of Despair with longing."

"Neat." I got to my feet and stalked toward the window, glaring down at the city below us.

"You knew what you were taking on with Samael," Lilith said, her voice amused. "This is just a small glimpse of what you'll be dealing with for centuries to come. You're a braver woman than I."

"Yeah yeah. You're not helping."

We were both silent for a long moment, each lost in our own thoughts. "Question," I said.

"Hmm?"

I glanced at the demon, who was once again reading her magazine.

"Samael has made it clear to everyone that I'm his. I guess he did that back when we could barely tolerate each other," I held up my arm, and we both looked at the swirling gold mark which decorated my skin, proclaiming that I belonged to the scariest demon around.

"Yes?"

"If I wanted to do the same… to prove to everyone that he was mine, how would I go about it?"

Lilith laughed. "Believe me, every demon in this world knows he is yours."

I frowned and she rolled her eyes, waving one elegant hand. Her gold nails flashed in the light.

"Offer him food in front of his people."

I raised one eyebrow. Samael had attempted to serve me once at our first Monday dinner, but I had a pretty good feeling he'd just been playing with me in front of his people. He'd given me food numerous times since.

"So it's the public offering that makes it meaningful?"

Lilith nodded and stretched. "When you offer him food in front of his people, you tell them 'this man is mine, and it is my privilege to serve him.'"

I scowled at that, and she smiled. "And by accepting, he says 'this woman is mine, and I accept her offering.'"

"And you think Samael will enjoy that?"

She waved her hand again. "It's an old custom, no longer fashionable. But Samael is a very old demon, and he would likely be charmed by your public claiming."

It would be a way for me to make my own claim. To make it clear that while Samael might have all the power, I wasn't meek, and I certainly wasn't going to live for centuries with his people believing he had me firmly in hand.

"I'll think about it."

"Fine. Now leave me be. I have a need to know what this human actress wore to the award ceremony."

I shook my head but left Lilith flicking through People.

CHAPTER EIGHTEEN

Danica

I spent the rest of Sunday and most of Monday investigating Willow. When I wasn't checking out the witch, I turned my mind to Riona's case and began looking into the ingredients for the Spell of Three. In the meantime, Kyla was staking out the hotel.

Since I was already at Samael's, I arrived early for Monday dinner, just in time for cocktails. I found Vas on the balcony, beer in hand as he studied the city below.

"I heard about Daimonion," I murmured, stealing his beer for a sip.

He shrugged as I handed it back. "Never known the bastard to dare enter this territory."

"I'm sorry."

Another shrug. "I've always known he was out there. My plans haven't changed."

I couldn't speak for a moment, my heart racing at the thought of Vas taking on Lucifer's assassin. He'd killed Samael's parents when he was just a baby. If Vas took him on now…

"I'm stronger than you think, Danica."

I turned my head. He was watching me. "Vas–"

"My powers are weakened outside of the underworld. So are Ag's."

"Why?"

"Dinner is served," a voice said, and Vas held his arm out for me to link with mine.

"We're talking about this later," I said.

"Not tonight. Tonight I need to drink enough to forget."

I frowned at that, and he smiled. "Don't worry about me, Dani."

The theme was Greek tonight, and Samael pulled my chair out for me, gently pushing it back in before leaning down to press a kiss to my cheek.

Aw.

I took a deep, steadying breath and glanced at Lilith. She gave me a reassuring nod. Who would've thought I'd be looking at her for support?

The servers put the platters and bowls on the table, and everyone got busy loading up their plates. Samael watched, and I lowered my shield enough to feel him down the other end of the bond. Pure contentment. Having dinner with the people he considered his family made him happy. He glanced at me and raised his eyebrow, and I felt the contentment deepen into something like tenderness.

Here goes nothing. Butterflies danced in my stomach, climbing up my throat until I was pretty sure I was going to toss my cookies.

Now that would be a gesture.

My heart stuttered in my chest as I reached for the closest dish. Some kind of Mediterranean rice. I took a spoonful and leaned over, plopping it on Samael's plate.

He tensed. I couldn't look at him, but I could feel him next to me, so still he barely breathed.

The chatter was quieting, and I wished everyone would go back to their own business. But I reached for a fish dish next, laying a spoonful next to the rice. Finally, I took some roasted vegetables and added them too.

Silence claimed the room. I squirmed in my seat, a combination of mortification and vulnerability making my legs twitch with the urge to get to my feet and bolt toward the elevator.

From the shocked possessiveness I was feeling from the other end of the bond, Samael wouldn't tolerate that.

I blew out a long shuddering breath. I wasn't a coward. If I was going to make the gesture, I had to at least see how it was received.

He was staring at me, his silver eyes alight with that tenderness, a brutal kind of lust, and… love. I glanced away, but he took my hand and I understood. While I was almost ashamed of my own vulnerability, Samael had absolutely no problem showing me how he felt about me.

My throat tightened, and his gaze softened at whatever he saw in my eyes.

The tension was thick enough to chew on. Finally, Samael picked up his fork and took a single bite.

Raucous applause sounded. Lilith grinned at me while Vas popped open a bottle of champagne, immediately filling glasses. Bael smiled at me, and even Ag gave me an approving nod. Would wonders never cease.

Vas kept the toast simple. "To Samael and Danica."

I took a sip of champagne, the bubbles warring with the bubbling in my chest. Samael understood. He knew I hated public attention, so he merely raised his glass.

"Thank you, my friends," he said and took a sip. Beneath the table, his hand squeezed mine.

Then he ate every bite of his food, his gaze continually shifting to my face.

No one hung around when the meal was over. Lust glittered in Samael's eyes, but I couldn't find it in me to be embarrassed by the fact that everyone knew what we were about to be doing.

Demons could sense lust. They'd known how much I wanted their boss since the moment I met him.

Actually, maybe I could find it in me to be embarrassed after all.

"What are you thinking?"

I filled Samael in and he laughed as he flew me up to the penthouse.

"Demons aren't quite as prudish as humans," he told me. "We tend to embrace the baser emotions."

I batted my eyelashes. "Oh yeah? Why don't you tell me about those baser emotions?"

He opened the balcony door and steered me straight toward his sofa, his mouth finding mine as his clever hands divested me of the short cocktail dress I'd worn to dinner. The dress hit the floor, and I would've tripped on it, but I was already in his arms.

My back hit the sofa and his heated gaze explored my body while he ripped off his own clothes.

"I didn't know I could feel such pride and pleasure

as I did tonight," he murmured, kicking his pants away.

His cock hung at my eye level, and I lifted one hand, crooking my finger.

He complied, stepping closer, and I wrapped my hand around him. He jolted like my hand was a live wire and I smirked.

"Now you have me, witchling, what will you– ah…"

I slowly slid my mouth down the length of him, using my hand to help since he was far too large for me to take all at once. Samael wasn't complaining. He threw his head back, and a few feet away, something fell off a table and hit the floor with a crash. I laughed around his length. His wings had snapped out in an obvious loss of control.

I licked around the head of his cock, enjoying the feel of him, hard and hot. My tongue found the sensitive underside and he groaned.

Then his eyes shot open and I was suddenly pressed against the sofa.

His claws cut through my bra and panties and I gaped at him, but he was already positioning himself at my entrance.

"You drive me wild," he growled in my ear, and I shivered as he slowly thrust into me.

I wrapped my legs around his waist, pleasure unfurled in my belly as he moved, and I arched my neck when his lips found my throat.

"I want you to feed from me."

He froze. "Danica…"

"I'm serious. When is the next time you need to feed?"

"Several weeks from now."

I glowered at him. That meant he'd fed recently.

He shook his head. "No, I didn't feed through sex. I have been… sipping from my club whenever possible."

Great, so the demon was half-starved. But the idea of him feeding from a single person… if I'd had wings, they would have flared in offence.

Samael nuzzled my cheek. "I love that you have finally accepted what I feel for you. What you feel for me. However, this is something you can't take back. We will wait until I need to feed and then we will have this conversation."

I frowned. "You don't want to feed from me?" Hell had frozen over.

Hunger swept into his gaze, and I shivered at his feral expression.

"I wish to feed from you more than I wish to take my next breath. But I won't rush you, Danica. Now that you have accepted that you're mine, I want to savor the experience. When I feed from you, there will be no reservations left in your busy brain. You will want to feed me because it's something you crave, not because you're worried I will feed from someone else."

I sighed. "I guess I can understand that."

"Good." His adjusted his angle and I groaned as he hit just the right spot. Then I was spinning through the air and I blinked. I was suddenly sitting on top of him.

"Ride me, witchling."

Challenge accepted.

I lifted my hips and we both sighed as I dropped back down, taking him inside me once more. Lust sparked in his gaze as it swept over my body, lingering on the place where we were joined before returning to my face.

He pulled me close and took my mouth, his hands sliding down to my hips, fingers squeezing as he urged me on. His lips found my neck, and one hand slid down to brush lightly against my clit.

I clenched around him and we both groaned. He thickened inside me, both of us on the edge.

He flicked my clit again. Once. Twice.

My climax washed over me, and he lifted his hips, thrusting up before he followed me over. I slumped against him, my breath coming in harsh pants.

He wrapped his arms around me and made a sound somewhere between a purr of satisfaction and a growl of contentment.

I could have fallen asleep right there, but Samael kissed my forehead and gently lifted me off him. I blinked up at him, and he pulled me to my feet. "I have something to show you."

I raised one eyebrow at him and gestured at myself. The underwear he'd torn from me was caught around one of my heels— still on my foot. My other heel was gone, my bra was in pieces, and my dress was nowhere to be seen.

"I think you showed me plenty."

He sent me a wicked grin and I couldn't help but grin back, as if we were two conspirators who'd gotten away with something they shouldn't have. "I'll get dressed–"

"We're not going far."

He pulled one of the soft throws from the sofa, wrapping it around me.

I was officially curious now. I followed him through

the living room and into his office. I'd thought the door on the left led to another bathroom, but he threw it open and gestured for me to go in.

I took a moment to focus on our bond. His expression was blank, but beneath it he was… nervous.

I walked into the room and frowned. "I don't understand."

The room was almost a twin to his office, only with a slightly smaller desk. A state-of-the-art computer gleamed silver on that desk, and a collection of filing cabinets stood against one wall. A door on the opposite side led to a bathroom, which led back out to the living room.

"I know you have your own office. But sometimes, you might want to do some paperwork here. Or get some research done on the weekend. You don't have to use it if you don't want to. The room was sitting empty."

He gave a languid shrug, as if unconcerned, but I could still sense his nervousness, warring with frustration and… trepidation? The demon was worried this would freak me out.

"When did you do this?"

"This afternoon."

Of course. Samael merely had to snap his fingers and he'd have a gorgeous office set up within a few hours.

He'd seen me working on his sofa, laptop balanced on my lap, and he'd immediately decided to offer me something better.

My heart melted and I opened my mouth, unsure exactly what to say.

He merely nodded at my silence and turned to walk away.

"Hey!"

He glanced over his shoulder at me, his expression haughty. I almost laughed.

"Are you seriously going to give me a workspace in your apartment and not bang me on the desk?"

He stalked toward me, pushed the throw off my shoulders and lifted me in his arms. My butt hit the desk and he smiled against my mouth.

"You like it."

"Damn right I do. You didn't have to do this, you know."

"I want you to be happy here. I want this to be *our* apartment. And if you want to move somewhere new–"

I slid my hands up his chest, marveling at the feel of his muscles beneath my palms. "I want you," I said. "Just you."

His eyes darkened and he cupped my breasts. "I want you too."

He spent the next few hours showing me exactly how much he wanted me, until I was limp, exhausted, and curled up against him in his bed, Lia purring between us.

Samael

My little witch opened bleary eyes the next morning, glancing at the clock on the nightstand.

"Shit, I need to get ready."

"Where are you going?"

"I need go stake out the witches. One of them is a

killer, Samael."

She frowned, and I ran a finger over the tiny lines that appeared between her brows.

It didn't surprise me in the slightest. Creatures of all stripes had been betraying each other for millennia. But this was the first time my little witch had seen such a betrayal firsthand.

"You will find the killer," I said.

Danica smiled. "I like your confidence," she studied my face and her eyes flashed. "You look very smug."

I smiled and stretched next to her. "And why wouldn't I be? *My* little witch slept where she belongs all night."

I reached out and snagged her wrist, pulling her until she fell on top of me. "Well, hello there."

She pushed dark hair off her face, green eyes flashing. "I don't have time to roll around on you right now."

I hardened further beneath her. Was it any wonder I couldn't get enough of this woman?

Her eyes went momentarily blurry as I arched my hips.

"What about now?"

She blew out a frustrated breath. "You play hardball." Her gaze slid to the alarm clock and she shook her head. "I promised Kyla I'd bring breakfast. I'm not making the werewolf hungry so I can bone."

She slid off me and I watched her with a frown.

Then I glanced down at my naked body. Still perfect.

Danica took one look at me and burst out laughing. "Not used to watching a woman walk away?"

"Any way I answer that is likely to piss you off, so I'll keep my silence in this matter."

She gave me a look. "Good idea."

She strolled into the bathroom and I forced my body to cool down. Immediately, my mind went to my plans. To death and betrayal and horror.

When Danica was nearby, I wasn't thinking about Lucifer's head on a spike. I wasn't mentally swearing to my father, my mother, my sister, that they would have their vengeance.

No, with my little witch I was strangely… content. I laughed, I teased, and I loved.

I had thought the worst possible outcome in my life would be never retaking my throne. Now I knew the truth. The worst would be watching my little witch die. Never hearing her laugh, never marveling at her smart mouth. Never seeing her smirk, her joyous smile, or her wide grin.

"Hey." Danica appeared in the doorway, wrapped in a towel. "Are you okay?"

With our new intimacy, our bond had grown stronger. She was feeling more of my emotions, which meant she was aware of the sick terror that clenched my chest.

I fought it back as she made her way over to the bed.

"Do you want to talk about it?"

I threw the sheets off and stood. "No. Just… be careful today."

"I'm always careful."

I gave her a look and she smiled. "I'll be fine."

I lowered my head, taking her mouth. I was sure she felt my desperation, my fear, but she parted her lips, taking everything I had to give.

She wrapped her arms around me, and I pulled away,

burying my face in her neck. Her hair was damp and smelled like the lightly floral shampoo she used. If she knew how much the scent comforted the ancient demon she slept next to, she would likely laugh.

My lips curled and I forced myself to release her.

"Are you sure you're okay?" Danica worried her lower lip with her white teeth and my gaze caught on her mouth. "I can text Kyla if you need me to stay for a while."

"I'm fine. Now put some clothes on before I convince you to get back into bed."

She grinned at me, let her gaze drop to my chest and lower. "You probably could convince me," she mused.

I reached for her and she danced away with a giggle that made my chest clench.

"Harpy."

She laughed some more as she pulled on her clothes. I found a pair of slacks and my lips twitched.

"I can feel when a woman is gawking at my ass."

"I bet you can," she said darkly. "Just remember I walk around heavily armed."

A surprised laugh left my throat. The possessiveness was… unexpected, but welcome.

"Laters," Danica called as she strolled out of my bedroom.

I wandered into my living room to watch her leave and frowned as I walked past the closet that held my safe.

The wards had recently been disturbed. I swung the safe open and lifted my eyebrow.

One of the grimoires was gone. Gloria knew the rules. The black books were only to be used with my permission, and were to be immediately returned.

The witch was becoming far too bold. I had allowed her too much slack, and she was forgetting who held her leash.

She would need to be reminded.

Danica

Kyla left her car in the parking garage beneath Samael's tower and we took my car to Alchemy.

I bullied my way through Main Street and glanced at Kyla. "Did Willow do anything except take a walk yesterday?"

She shook her head, wincing as I narrowly missed colliding with a goblin in a Mazda who shook his fist at me.

"You okay? You seem a little… on edge."

I scowled. "I want to put this to bed, you know? I want to know who would betray the coven, but that's mostly for them. I want to know who would betray Evie, and that's for me."

"How's she doing?"

"Still asleep. Whoever is hunting her will know she's in Samael's tower, but she's safe there."

I pulled up down the street from the hotel's entrance. Close enough that we could see who was coming and going, but far enough back that they wouldn't immediately spot us.

Then I slid my seat back, stretched out my legs, and settled in for a few hours of boredom.

Kyla did the same, unbuckling her belt and twisting in

her seat to face me. "What I don't understand is why they'd kill the witches. Why not just leave and start a new coven?"

"That takes money, relationships, and power. It's not unheard of, but Gemma would never allow it in her territory. And honestly, neither would the other large covens. They'd have to move somewhere without a large witch population."

Kyla nodded. We were both silent for a moment and then I slid her a look.

"Can I ask you something?"

"Of course."

"Nathaniel said you had a few… authority issues."

She rolled her eyes. "Do you know what it's like to have to sit in the hall while a man, your *Alpha* asks someone to hire you? To keep you out of trouble?"

I winced. "No. Why did you put up with it?"

She was quiet for a long moment. "I never really needed anyone, you know. Not really. I was mostly a loner, with the exception of the occasional boyfriend. And then I was turned into a werewolf, and once Nathaniel found me, I had this sudden longing for family. For *pack*. It's not something I want, and if I could rip that need out of me, I'd do it in a heartbeat. I've tried to leave a few times, but each time, Nathaniel just kept dragging me back. It's not *safe* for a female werewolf, after all," she sneered.

"I can't imagine what it's like."

"No? Not even with your demon?"

"It feels different. Maybe because there are all these other feelings involved. Samael is my lover, but before that, he didn't even make me go to his Monday dinners until recently— other than once when he first bonded me. Don't get me wrong, I resented the hell out of the bond— out of the fact that he *could* make me if he wanted."

I frowned, working it through in my head. "He hasn't changed the way he acts with anyone else. He's still the same domineering psycho who expects everyone to follow his orders or accept the consequences. But he's trying with *me.*

"I guess what it comes down to is he wants me happy. And he knows I'll never be happy if he wraps me in cotton and makes me stay in his tower. I'm guessing Nathaniel can't afford that kind of leniency."

"No. Not if he wants to remain Alpha." She waved a hand. "No one here would attempt to take his position; he could easily fight off most challengers. But there are a few other Alphas looking at our pack. We're one of the larger packs, with a reputation that's survived since the portals opened. If an Alpha from New York or Chicago could take Nathaniel, they'd have our pack as well as their own."

"Do you mind if I ask how you were changed?"

She gazed out the window. "I was living in Michigan at the time. My boyfriend liked to hunt and he'd gone away on a guys' trip with his closest friends. They were attacked by a feral wolf. He was the only one who survived."

Her face had turned ashen, and I reached behind my seat for an unopened bottle of water, handing it to her. "You don't have to talk about it. I was just being nosy."

She attempted a smile. Outside, a group of tourists walked past, bags swinging on their arms.

"No, it's okay. He went missing for a few days. They all did. We'd reported them missing, and one of the search parties found the bodies. Joel was nowhere to be seen. I think I knew then, but I couldn't face it. I'd half convinced myself that he'd gotten away."

I couldn't imagine the dread. The mix of hope and terror.

Kyla stretched, pointing her toes. "A few days later, I got home from work and he was waiting for me. He tried to pretend he was still human. That's what I still can't wrap my head around. He moved differently. His face was sharper, his eyes hungry. And he was trying to pretend he was human."

"You must have been terrified."

"Yeah. I played along for a while. I figured I needed him to relax, and I'd sneak away. But wolves… we can smell fear. I'd forgotten that. He was the one playing with me."

"The son of a bitch."

She let out a choked laugh and some of the tension left her face. "Yeah. Anyway, female wolves don't survive the change. Most people know that. Especially in Michigan. There are a lot of werewolves in that part of the country. The odds of a guy surviving the change are incredibly small. The odds of a woman?" Kyla smiled and it was bitter. "He bit me, knowing that. Knowing that I would likely die, but willing to take the chance anyway. So he wouldn't be alone, and I wouldn't move on with my life without him."

"Scum."

"Yeah. I turned. And when I turned, I went half-feral. There was no one dominant enough to help me regain control. Just the man who'd almost killed me, who'd stolen my life from me. And it turned out he miscalculated, 'cause I was more dominant than him. I killed him."

"Good."

Kyla laughed. "Most people would think twice about

working with a werewolf. Especially one who killed her ex."

I rolled my eyes. "You're talking to a half-witch, half-demon ex-bounty hunter. What happened after you killed him?"

"I was more than half feral. I'd shifted for the first time, and I was running wild in Michigan. One of the local werewolves saw me and attempted to catch me." She grinned. "I'm fast."

My mind jumped back to the way she'd moved when she'd chased Greg down the street. "You sure are."

"He reported me to his Alpha and then the chase was on. It got around to all the packs that there was a female werewolf. Nathaniel joined the hunt."

I winced and she shook her head. "A lot of packs, they see a female wolf as a kind of status symbol. But Nathaniel wasn't like that. He found me in Kentucky. Honestly, I'm lucky I hadn't killed someone by then. I was half-starved. He didn't seem to give a shit about status, he just wanted to make sure I was okay. He knew I was lost and afraid and as the word spread, I'd be hunted by every pack on this side of the country."

"I can't imagine."

"Yeah. Anyway, Nathaniel had important shit to do, but he tracked me down and dragged me back here. Spoiler alert, I wasn't exactly pleased by that turn of events," she said, and I laughed. "But within a few months I could control my shift most of the time."

She sighed and stared out the window for a long moment. "I guess that's why I can sit outside a room and listen to him ask you to hire me. That's why I've stayed so long, even though it chafes to live under his control. At the end of the day, he saved me."

She glanced at me. "I guess I had to talk it through to get to that place. So thanks."

"You're welcome." I tensed as one of the witches walked out of the hotel's lobby. "Willow's on the move."

"Probably for a walk around the block. Get a bit of fresh air, clear her head."

I started my car. "We follow her anyway. The same with any other witch who leaves. I want to know what they're up to."

I waited until she'd gotten to the corner and slowly pulled out of my spot as she turned left. She was walking slowly, her face turned up to the sun, as if savoring the feel of it.

I hit the gas to turn on the green, and was forced to slam my foot on the brake as a white van ran the red. I laid on my horn, and the van jumped the curb, smashing into Willow.

I was out of the car and running before I realized I'd moved.

Willow flew into the side of a building. I pulled my gun, aiming for the tires but the driver was already pulling out.

I threw my keys at Kyla. "Follow the van! Go!"

She caught them, her body a blur as she launched herself toward my car. I made it to Willow and dropped to my knees.

She was a mess. Her chest didn't rise, her heart didn't beat. I started CPR, and a hand on my arm stopped me.

"She's gone, Danica," a voice said. "Her neck is

broken."

I stared up at Gemma. So fast. It happened so fast, and out of nowhere. I'd been thirty feet away and I hadn't seen it coming.

Goddamn it.

Kyla appeared, her eyes burning with wrath. "Lost him."

"Did you get the plate?"

"They'd covered it up. Taped a piece of cardboard over the license plate. There are cameras in this neighborhood, Danica. We'll find him."

"It's a man?"

She shook her head. "I don't know. I guess it could be a woman."

The other witches were arriving, along with an ambulance. I got to my feet and stepped out of the way, watching Gail as she crouched next to the body, tears rolling down her face.

Either she'd just arranged for someone to kill a woman she'd lived with for years, or she was the next target.

We spent the next few hours questioning witnesses and gathering as much camera footage as we could find.

As usual, approximately half of the witnesses said they saw a man, while the other half insisted it was a woman. We noted down every description, but our biggest lead was likely to be the car.

"You think it could be a rental?"

"I hope not." We walked back to my car. "They're not going to fucking get away with this."

CHAPTER NINETEEN

Danica

I danced.

Twirling, flying, strong arms holding me close, keeping me grounded and spinning me faster at the same time.

I looked up into Samael's face, and he smiled down at me as he led me across the dance floor.

"I can't wait to dance with you once more."

I turned as the dream began to fade. Samael now stood a few feet away. The music quieted to a low hum, and while everything else in my dream was blurred at the edges, he was sharp and... real.

"Are you in my dream, or am I in yours?"

He smiled. "I am visiting your dreams."

I gaped at him. "And how exactly does that happen?"

"Your subconscious reached for me. I obliged."

Heaviness on my chest. Something sharp poked me in the boob and I yelped.

"What the fuck?"

Samael's smile widened. "I think the cat wants to be fed."

I opened my eyes, meeting amused silver. Samael had pulled the cat off me, and she was purring in his arms as he stroked her.

"How long have you been able to visit my dreams?"

"That was the first time."

Relief. Pure, unrestrained relief swept through me, strong enough that I knew Samael could feel it when he narrowed his eyes at me.

Then he laughed. "Someone has been dreaming of me," he purred. "Tell me, little witch… what kind of filthy, indecent things did I do to you in those dreams?"

My cheeks were turning red, goddamn it. I could feel them burning.

"I have no idea what you're talking about."

Lia jumped out of Samael's arms and sauntered across the wide bed, butting her head against my thigh until I scratched between her ears.

Samael watched me. "You're sad."

Somewhere along the way, I'd stopped ruthlessly holding my shields between our bond.

"Yeah. These women are Evie's family. Not only is she going to have to attend a bunch of their funerals, but one of them sold her out. Sold them all out."

Samael got to his feet, circled the bed, and pulled me up and into his arms. "I'm sorry."

I snuggled in, still shocked that I could find comfort here, in the arms of the demon I'd once planned to kill. Life was fucking weird.

His cedar and citrus scent enveloped me, but beneath that, he smelled like snow and burning wood. His voice rumbled in my ear as he spoke.

"Gail either had something to do with this, or she is the next in line to be killed."

"Yeah. She's the only witch I can see who could have benefited. Willow's new enough that she would've been expected to step aside, but she couldn't risk it. Take out Gemma, Nellie, and Willow, and she's the top dog."

"The top dog in a coven she likely cannot hold."

"Bet she thinks she could hold it. I need to check all her accounts today, along with some of the other witches. See if there's anything suspicious."

I sighed and raised my head, and Samael's mouth found mine. Desire curled through my stomach and my body said *yes, we need a distraction.*

I smoothed my hands down his chest and he pushed me back down to the pillows.

His phone buzzed and he ignored it, pulling the shirt I'd fallen asleep in over my head.

It buzzed again.

"Samael—"

His eyes practically glowed silver as he threw off the sheets, staring at me spread out beneath him. Paws hit the ground as Lia took off, clearly pissed that she was no longer the center of attention.

Samael's hands dropped to his pants.

"Drop it," I murmured.

He knew I didn't mean his pants, although he sent me a wicked grin. Whatever power hid his wings disappeared and they were suddenly visible, magnificent.

His phone buzzed again. I bit my lip. "Maybe you should–"

Pure male frustration darkened his eyes, and he pointed at me. "Stay where you are."

I raised one eyebrow and he pulled his phone to his ear, leaning down to run kisses along my belly. I shivered.

"I believe it's your job to handle that, Azazyel," Samael's voice was cold, and I winced. Poor Azazyel. No one wanted to interrupt the boss when he was about to score.

Samael's eyes turned hard, his jaw tightened, and he cast my naked body a look so mournful, so filled with regret, that I couldn't help but laugh as I rolled away.

I sauntered into his shower, feeling his eyes on my butt.

Samael followed me into the bathroom, leaning against the doorway and watching me as I dunked my head under the water.

"Perve."

He smiled, but it dropped from his face as he heaved a sigh. "Fine," he told Azazyel. "I'll be right there."

"It's hard work being the boss," I said as he hung up.

"It never seemed difficult until I had you waiting naked and wet in my shower."

I grinned at that, running my gaze down his chest and to the bulge in his pants. "I guess we'll continue this later."

He stalked toward me, reached into the shower, and pulled me close, ignoring the water as it sprayed him.

"You can count on that," he said. His mouth slammed down on mine, and then he was gone.

I increased the heat of the hot water, hoping the numerous showerheads would coax me fully awake. I'd stayed outside the hotel until the early hours of the morning to give Kyla a break, but by 2am, Samael had been displeased. He'd sent Bel— one of his demons— to take over, so Kyla and I could both get some sleep.

I couldn't complain.

I finished showering, pulled on jeans and a t-shirt, and checked on Evie— still sleeping. She'd been moved down into Samael's spare room. Liam had wanted to stay with her, but Samael wouldn't allow a werewolf alone with my sister in his penthouse.

I texted Kyla. Guilt made my stomach churn. As important as our investigation was, I needed to talk to Gemma about a different subject. It was time to ask her some difficult questions about my sister.

Once I was done, Kyla would take over watching the hotel— and Gail, and I'd get to work looking into their finances and criminal backgrounds.

I blasted the A/C as I drove, thankful I wasn't driving my old Toyota. I parked the car on the street outside the hotel and the nape of my neck turned damp with sweat as I walked toward the lobby. It was supposed to get into the 90s today, and the humidity would be brutal.

Caroline, Gail, and a few of the other witches were quietly eating breakfast in the living area when I walked in. They nodded at me, but the atmosphere was bleak. Someone had found pictures of every witch who had been in the house— and Willow— and taped them up on the wall as a makeshift memorial.

I knocked on Gemma's door.

"Enter." Her voice was hoarse and when I swung open the door, she was sitting next to one of the beds in an armchair, staring down at the city below. Her cane leaned against the chair a few inches from her hand.

Gemma's eyes narrowed intently on my face. "Have you found anything?"

"We're working on it."

She nodded and looked away. I helped myself to the armchair on the other side of the small coffee table.

She surveyed me. "I was only twelve when the portals opened."

Jesus. I mean I guess it made sense. That put her at eighty-four today, and right now, I could see the years weighing on her.

"How did you create the coven so young?"

"My parents took me out of the city. I returned when I was seventeen. By then, I could see hope. Over the next five years, I built friendships and alliances. By the time the factions had ceased warring, our coven was ready."

She turned her gaze away once more, staring sightlessly out the window. "And now most of my people are dead." Bitterness clouded her words. "Speak child. If you haven't come to inform me you've found whoever did this, you've come to talk about your sister. Evie texted me before her surgery. How is she?"

"She came through it and she'll sleep for a couple of days. I need to know why she's being targeted, Gemma."

She looked at me. "Taking your mother in was my biggest mistake as coven leader. I knew it was a mistake at the time, but even I couldn't know that it would lead to this."

I opened my mouth, but I couldn't make a single word come out.

She sighed. "And yet still, how could I have made a different choice? When your mother first approached the coven, I wasn't interested in adding another witch. Especially not one with two young children. Evie was a baby, and you looked like you'd be a pain in my neck." She narrowed her eyes at me. "I was right."

I ignored that. "What made you decide to let her join?"

"She was powerful."

I angled my head and let the silence lie between us. Gemma scowled. "And she begged for my help. She said if I didn't help her hide your sister, you were all dead."

"Why?"

"I don't know."

"Don't even try that shit with me. A desperate woman comes to you with two kids, says she's in serious trouble, and you don't even ask what that trouble is?"

"I assumed she was fleeing an abusive partner. She had cuts and scrapes on her, and she owned nothing. Gail was the one to convince me that it was our duty— both as women and witches— to take her in."

"What did you do to Evie?"

"Your mother insisted that she could be tracked. She said that if she was found, she would be taken, likely killed. I believed she was being overdramatic. But when I examined the child, I knew there was something different about her."

"Different how?"

"She held many 'threads' of magic. It was as if your

mother had laid with men from several different factions—fae, werewolf, demon— and they had all fathered the same baby. Impossible, of course. But I understood why your mother was so afraid. She was friends with a light fae woman who had urged her to seek out the most powerful coven she could find and ask for assistance. If the baby's father had found her, I had no doubt that he would take such an unusual child."

"So you agreed to help."

"Yes. We needed a way to cloak the baby if she was being tracked— and I certainly believed your mother about that. A child so unusual would be valuable to every faction. There was only one way we could think to hide her. Our house had been fed magic by hundreds of witches since the portals opened. We created a spell— one that had never been attempted before. It would tie Evie to the house in an almost... symbiotic relationship. She would be shielded— both by every witch who lived in the house, and the house itself.

"I hadn't expected the side effect. Evie is powerful enough that we no longer needed to renew the wards except to adjust them once every few years. If she'd been there, it's likely the house would have been able to fight the fire."

That creeped me out. "You say that like it was sentient."

"It didn't have true awareness, but it had been so heavily spelled for so long, it should never have burned."

"She can never know," I said. Gemma gave me a sharp nod. With this, at least, we were in agreement. If Evie knew that the house likely wouldn't have burned if she'd been home, that all those witches would probably be alive if she hadn't gone on her date… my chest ached at the thought.

"If the house is now magically dead, is it going to have an impact on Evie? On her health? Or her power?"

Gemma shook her head. "Not her health. I'm unsure about her power. She was so young when the spell was placed. And it will no longer hide her from those who were hunting her."

I leveled her with a hard stare. "The spell you created ensured that Evie would want to stay home most of the time."

Gemma was silent. I ground my teeth. "I'm right, aren't I?"

"She needed to be within range of the house for the majority of her life in order for the spell to hold."

"When were you going to tell her? Were you going to just let her grow old in that house, never knowing that she was under a compulsion to spend most of her life there?"

She sighed, suddenly looking so old and tired that a frisson of alarm went through me.

"We saved her life, girl."

"And I'm thankful for that. But now she's an adult, with no idea why she suddenly feels like a weight is suddenly off her shoulders– which is obviously confusing as fuck since so many members of her family are dead. She's completely unprepared for whoever is hunting her."

"She will learn. You will teach her. And now, she will have you, and all of the demons behind you to keep her safe. I have done my job."

"Did you know there was a suppression spell on my

power?"

She shook her head. "Your mother had taken care of that before she arrived. We never would have sheltered a half-demon child."

"Lovely."

She gave me an impatient look. "If the demons had known we had one of their children— so rare and so precious— they would have burned our coven to the ground years ago."

CHAPTER TWENTY

Danica

I left Kyla parked outside the hotel so she could keep an eye on the witches' coming and goings.

My mind raced as I drove back to Samael's tower. Misty was on my hip, and the dagger hadn't glowed once while I was talking to Gemma. She'd been telling the truth as she knew it.

I nodded at the demons in the lobby and took the elevator to the top floor.

Lia rubbed up against my legs as I entered Samael's penthouse. I crouched down and stroked her.

"You've got free run of this place, huh? And how's Evie doing?"

I poked my head in her room. Still asleep. But she was tossing and turning some.

Lia let out a meow and jumped at my legs. I walked into Samael's kitchen, where someone had set up her food bowl.

I gave her a hard stare. "I know damn well

you've already been fed this morning."

Her hard stare was better than mine. I sighed and poured a little dry food into her bowl.

A few minutes later, I slipped into the office Samael had designated for me, armed with a coffee and the cat, who'd clearly decided I was back in her good graces. I opened my laptop and turned on the computer on the desk.

Samael had arranged for Steve to load all of the programs I needed onto the desktop, too.

I sat behind the desk. While I was looking forward to setting up my main office, I had to admit Samael had hit the mark here. All because he'd seen me working with my laptop on his sofa.

Lia jumped up on my lap and I winced as she began kneading my thighs with her claws. I reached for my phone, hoping Steve had gotten lucky somewhere.

"Yo."

"Did you find anything in the video Gary sent you?"

He let out a frustrated growl. "Nothing we can trace. They knew they were being recorded. One of them glanced up at the camera and smirked as they walked out. Smug bastard."

"They're not smug anymore."

"There is that."

"What about the hit and run? Any luck with the cameras?"

"We have the color and make of the car, but the license plate was covered. I'll get back to you once we've narrowed it down."

"Thanks."

I ended the call and got to work.

Three hours later, I felt nauseous. There was no mistaking the recent transfers from one of the witch's accounts.

I picked up my phone to call Kyra, then froze, turning my head at movement out the corner of my eye.

Lia jumped off my lap to wind around Evie's feet.

"How are you feeling?"

She smiled. "A bit groggy and out of it, but pretty good considering. I'm mostly relieved."

"Same." I took a deep, steadying breath. "Can you sit down? I need to tell you something."

She frowned but perched on the edge of the chair in front of my desk, her eyes sharp.

"What is it?"

"I talked to Gemma. She told me there was a compulsion tied to the house's spell. For the spell to work, and for your power to be hidden, you had to stay in the house most of the time."

The blood drained from her face. "So they turned me into a homebody?" She attempted to come to terms with that. "How much of my personality is because I really like to stay home, and how much is because I was spelled to need to be in the house?"

"I don't know. I'm sorry, Evie."

She shrugged and glanced away, watching as Lia wandered the room, sniffing at furniture that caught her attention.

"Every morning I wake up clearer. You know I've never had a real job? Just part time stuff, easy, no-fuss jobs that paid for dinners out and clothes. It never occurred to me to have a career. To do anything other than work on my magic, date occasionally, hang out with my friends and *stay in that house.*"

Her voice broke and she lifted a hand to wipe at the tear that rolled down her cheek. "I'm glad it's gone. I wish the others weren't dead, but I'm glad I never have to see that house again."

"They didn't do it to hurt you, Evie."

"I know. They did it to protect me. Because whoever is coming after me would probably have killed me as a child. I don't blame the coven, Dani. They likely saved my life, and I got most of them dead."

"Evie–"

She got to her feet. "I'm going to shower and grab something to eat. And then I need you to put me to work."

"Okay."

I blew out a long breath as Lia followed her out of the room. Then I grabbed my phone again.

Kyla answered immediately.

"What did you find?"

I scowled at the information on the screen in front of me. "Regular payments to an offshore account. Ten thousand a month for the past seven months."

"Who is it?"

"Gail."

"Shiiit. You think she was preparing to get out of here if it all went belly-up?"

"Depending on who the account belongs to. If it's hers, then that's exactly what she was doing. If it's not, then she's been paying someone off. I'll need you to stay on the coven. I'm going to try and trace the account, but I may need some help from Steve."

"Sure. I don't get it, why would Gail do this?"

"She's one of the longest-standing members of the coven. She may not be one of the most powerful, but she'd have some loyalty there."

"But there are so few of them left."

I put my phone on speaker and got to my feet to pace. "Anyone who can pull off this kind of attack? You bet your ass they have alliances lined up with other witches. She probably has a bunch of new recruits ready to go. Witches are lining up to join that coven. She could rebuild the house, or move to a new one, and boom. She's suddenly in Gemma's spot."

"Wow. It's twisted, but it makes a sick kind of sense. All those deaths just to take out the top three witches?"

I shrugged. "Covens have strict rules of ascension. While Nellie was old and crotchety enough that she may have eventually stepped down as second, Gemma could live another forty years, fifty if the coven is particularly good at healing spells. Unless she suddenly decided she didn't want the responsibility of the coven anymore, Gail would never have the opportunity to step into her shoes."

"And Willow?"

I shook my head. "She never would've gotten the chance to be coven leader. She would've abdicated immediately, well aware that a newbie in the top spot would never fly. But she was a loose end that needed to be cut, just in case."

I studied the list some more. "I'm going to have to take this to them. And they're not going to like it. But if I don't take it to them, Gemma could be dead in the next few days."

"A few of the witches are exiting the hotel," Kyla announced.

"Is Gail one of them?"

"Nope. You want me to follow them?"

"She could have some of them doing her dirty work. See where they go."

"Okay, laters."

Someone stepped into the room. and I turned. Steve practically radiated excitement.

"Wanted to come up and tell you in person. We decrypted the phones of the assholes who attacked you and Evie. We know where their base is."

Anticipation made my hands fist. "Where?"

"Tennessee. If I were you, I'd put a team together and go in ASAP."

"You're damn right I will."

Steve stepped to the side, coming to attention as Samael appeared.

"I will help you with that team."

I opened my mouth to argue automatically. I knew of several mercenaries I could hire. He raised his eyebrow and I snapped it shut. If the demon wanted in, I could definitely use his people.

Samael watched me deliberate. He angled his head, his eyes on my face. "If you think I'll allow you to go without me, we will need to have a talk."

I ground my teeth. Silence stretched between us. Across the room, Steve cleared his throat.

"I'm coming too," he said. "You may need a hacker."

Samael nodded and Steve turned, hurrying away.

"If this is going to work, you need to strike the word

allow from your vocabulary," I told the demon.

He merely set his jaw. Of course it wouldn't occur to him that the a-word was a no-no. It was going to take a lot of time and effort to bring the demon's attitudes into the 21st century.

"Tell me," Samael said, and I told him everything Gemma had said, along with the payments from Gail's account.

"You'll need some help finding the owner of the overseas account."

"Yeah. It's in the Caymans. I could probably do it myself. but it'd likely take weeks."

"I'll have my people look at it while we are in Tennessee."

I frowned and he smiled. "Steve isn't the only person I employ who is skilled at that type of thing. In fact, he and Sitri have an ongoing war when it comes to preventing hacks and tracing them back to their source."

My lips twitched. "A war, huh? I bet you laid the groundwork for that."

"A little healthy competition can build a strong foundation for a good relationship." His silver eyes glittered. "Just look at us."

I laughed. "Healthy competition? Is that what you'd call it?"

He smiled. "I'll have one of my planes readied. We'll need to take our equipment with us for this little excursion."

While we'd been talking, Samael had pulled something out of his pocket, and he was idly playing with it as he talked to me.

He flipped it in his hand, and I raised one eyebrow.

One of my throwing knives, the blade wrapped in leather.

"Where did you get that?"

He glanced down, as if surprised to find it in his hand.

"You threw it at me months ago when you attempted to shield Vas from my wrath. My skin had healed around it by the time I pulled it out."

I smirked at him. "Guess you shouldn't have pissed me off." I held out my hand. "Gimme."

"I don't think so." He tucked it back in his pocket and I blinked at him. "It turns out that I'm a sentimental fool. I consider it a token of your affection."

My heart flipped in my chest and I cleared my throat. "Weird, violent, and yet so uniquely us."

He sent me a wicked smile. "Indeed. You'll need body armor, and since your sister will likely demand to come with us as well, I'll have some sent up for her also. We'll leave in an hour."

"Do you need me to be here for that hour?"

He raised his eyebrow. "Not particularly, but I imagined you'd want to be involved."

"I do, but I need to tell Gemma about Gail. I'd never forgive myself if Gail took her out while I was out of town."

"You could call her."

I shook my head. "This is the kind of information that should be given in person. We'll look into the accounts, but in the meantime, she should know."

I walked toward the door and hesitated, turning back to the demon, who was watching me carefully. I took a step toward him, buried my hand in his hair, and pulled his head down so I could brush my lips against his. It felt slightly awkward, kissing the demon as if we were a normal couple who did normal couple things.

But the pleasure gleaming in his silver eyes made it worth it as I pulled away. His arms encircled me, and then his mouth crashed down on mine, the kiss deepening until my mind went blank.

When he slowly pulled away, his expression was carved in lust, but his mouth curled. "Now that's a goodbye kiss. Be careful, little witch. If Gail is behind the murders, she's dangerous."

"I think I can take one crazy woman with a bad hip and a worse attitude."

"I've had to learn not to underestimate crazy women with bad attitudes."

I rolled my eyes. "Ha ha."

His gaze was steady on my face and I heaved a sigh. Overprotective demon. "I'll be careful."

Danica

Kyla was leaning against her car when I arrived. "Anything?"

"The group of witches I followed went down the block for ice cream. One of them spotted me and flipped me off. I don't think she likes me."

Kyla gave a mock pout and I laughed. "Yeah, I bet you're real cut up about that. Let's go make them like us even less."

We walked through the lobby, and something like dread took up residence in my gut. Gail was one of Gemma's closest friends.

"This isn't going to go well," Kyla murmured as we walked across the marble floor.

"Yeah, no shit. But I'm not going to pussyfoot around it just because it's something they don't want to hear. A good chunk of their coven is dead."

"Listen, you want me to wait outside the room?"

I glanced at her as we got into the elevator. "Are you scared of the witches?"

She shot me a look. "Just because most of their magic doesn't work on me doesn't mean I want to piss off some of the most powerful witches in Durham. Besides, they're less likely to cooperate if I'm in there."

She had a point. "Fine. Wait outside and be ready to come in armed if you hear me screaming."

Her eyes widened and I grinned at her.

Freya opened the door when I arrived. She hadn't been here earlier, but I was guessing most of the witches who didn't live in the main house were spending as much time with the rest of the coven as they could.

"You got anything?" her voice was low and her eyes widened when I nodded.

She stood back to let me in. Gail, Gemma, Ainsley, and Caroline were sitting around a coffee table, cups in their hands.

Gemma nodded at me.

"I have some news," I said, and Gemma got to her feet, reaching for her cane.

"Well, don't keep us in suspense," she snapped.

"I'd like to speak to you alone."

She glanced around at her witches, and I saw the moment she realized I was about to point the finger at one of them.

"Fine."

I followed her into the bedroom and closed the door behind us.

"I have no clear evidence," I began. "But I'm about to head out of town, so I needed to bring this to you. I spent some time looking at the structure of the coven. To attempt to figure out who would benefit the most from murdering everyone in that house."

"You assumed it was Willow."

"Yes. And then I looked at the next in line."

Gemma scoffed. "Gail? She told me she said a few harsh words to you while you were investigating the demon murders. If this is some kind of sick revenge…"

I stiffened. The last time Gail and I had actually spoken, I'd been sitting in my car, staking out a witch's house. Gail had told me I didn't belong in the neighborhood, ordered me to leave, and followed it up with a reminder that my sister didn't want me there.

Did I think she'd been a dick? For sure. Did that mean I'd incriminate her for no reason? I rolled my eyes.

"You clearly don't know me at all," I said softly. Gemma's eyes glinted with what could have been unshed tears and I gave her a moment as she turned away. Then she glanced back over her shoulder, her eyes dry.

"I won't believe it."

"I'm not expecting you to. I'm in the process of

gathering more evidence. All I'm asking is that you stay aware. Gail has been transferring ten thousand dollars to an off-shore account for the past seven months."

Gemma's face paled but she waved her hand. That hand shook. "What Gail does with her money is none of my business."

"You know better than that, Gemma. Seven months. You can't ignore that timing."

I turned to go, cursing as I met Gail's eyes. She'd stepped into the bathroom from the other door, and was now standing in the doorway staring at us, her face gray.

"You think I did this?"

"Someone let them in. Someone adjusted the wards. We have to look at who would've had the most motive. Gemma was supposed to stay behind, and you would've conveniently been out of the state and alibied."

Gemma took a sharp breath. "This is ridiculous. I won't believe it."

Freya stepped up behind Gail, narrowing her eyes at me. I didn't know why I'd attempted to talk to Gemma alone.

"If Gail had done this, she would've been the first to know that Gemma wasn't going to stay behind. Why would she keep the plan in place?"

I shrugged. "Maybe whoever she was working with insisted on it and it was too late to change those plans. A few months down the line, Gemma has a horrific accident, and Gail ends up in the same place. But the only reason the murderers would work with you would be because they needed access to Evie." I looked Gail in the eye. "You need to tell me why."

Gail stared at me. She looked very fragile, but Hannah had managed to look just as fragile several times, all while feeding on terror and agony.

"I will... do a truth test."

"You will do no such thing," Gemma snapped. She turned to me, her mouth a hard line. "Get out."

I shook my head. "You're making a mistake. One that could cost you your life."

"Leave now. Don't come back here."

I shook my head. The room was silent as I walked past the witches, who glared at me with varying levels of hate and disgust. Caroline stared at me, her face ashen as tears silently tracked down her cheeks.

Kyla gave me a sympathetic look as I stepped out of the hotel room.

"You got all of that?"

She tapped her ear. "Wolf hearing."

I pressed the elevator button. "Must be nice."

"Sure doesn't suck. Are you okay?"

I swallowed around the lump in my throat as the elevator doors opened. "Not really. But I did my duty. Gemma can't say I didn't warn her, and if Gail has an explanation for the money, Gemma will want to hear it."

We were both silent as we rode the elevator down and walked through the lobby. Once we got to her car, Kyla leaned against it once more, pulling her sunglasses off her head and sliding them onto her nose.

"What now?"

"Now, I need to go to Tennessee."

She gaped at me. "Why?"

I filled her in and she pouted. "You're going to want

me to stay here while you have all the fun."

I winced. "Yeah. Sorry. We need to keep a close eye on Gail. If she is behind the murders, the walls are closing around her."

"Say Gail's telling the truth and someone is framing her. Who could do it and why?"

"As soon as I get back, I'll be looking into that. Samael has his people tracing the account Gail's been transferring money to. If it's not hers, we'll know exactly who wanted to take the coven out."

"Fine. Don't have too much fun without me."

"I'll try not to."

CHAPTER TWENTY-ONE

Danica

The lab was in the middle of nowhere Tennessee— a few hours northwest of Nashville.

Other than a few stray pieces of paper which danced around in the breeze, the parking lot was empty.

Sweat dripped from every part of my body. Both Evie and I wore helmets and bulletproof vests— at Samael's insistence. Evie crouched next to me as we both took in the long, gray building.

"I can barely move in this thing," she griped.

"Same. But a bullet in the head or heart would really fuck up our dinner plans."

"Ha. It doesn't look like there's anyone there."

"Yeah. If we'd found it a little sooner, we might've been in luck. But they realized we were onto them and cleared out."

Evie hauled herself up to her feet.

My lips twitched and she smirked back at me. "You look just as stupid."

On the other side of Evie, Bael sighed. "Whole lotta nothin' out here."

I refused to let everyone else's piss-poor moods rub off on me. This was it. We were finally going to get some answers.

I sent Bael a sunny smile. "Aren't you glad you guys have us to bring you along on all our fun adventures?"

He sent me a sour look. "Nothing fun about it. There's nothing alive in there, which means I don't get to kill anyone."

Okay then.

Vas winked at me from where he leaned against the vans we'd taken from the small airfield nearby. As always, he looked completely relaxed, his dreamy eyes at half-mast while he basked in the sun like a cat.

The tiny diamonds glinted in my sister's ears as she moved her head. She caught me looking.

"You're wearing them," I murmured.

She nodded. "I was wearing them the night of the fire too. They were annoying me. Itching, burning. I'd half-convinced myself I was having an allergic reaction. Then I started thinking about Mom. I was so pissed off, I decided Liam would be a great distraction."

She smiled slightly at the look on my face. "Yeah. I think they might've helped save my life."

We were both silent for a while, a few of Samael's demons surrounded us, talking shit— demon style.

Finally, Samael returned, giving us a nod.

"I sense no signs of life."

I sighed. "Let's see what we find anyway."

The entrance reminded me of the morgue, with its

long counter and seating area. But instead of swinging doors, there was just one locked door with a keypad next to it.

Steve stepped forward with some kind of scanner. He worked his magic on the keypad and, a few minutes later, the door swung open.

More papers fluttering on the ground. Samael nodded at one of the demons and he turned, ordering some of the others to collect everything they could.

"We scared them enough that they fled like little bitches," Evie murmured. "I guess I should take some comfort in that."

"That's the spirit."

I shivered as we stepped into the corridor. Concrete walls caged us in on either side, and the first door was open. I peered inside and went still.

Measuring about six by six, it was a stone box. On the right and left wall, rings were attached every two feet or so. One of them had a chain dangling from it, the metal rusty with blood. Some kind of holding cell.

Evie stepped up next to me, staring around at the small space. She looked half-sick, but she turned, her footsteps echoing as she walked further down the corridor.

I glanced over my shoulder at Samael.

"Do you guys get claustrophobic? What with the wings?"

He stepped closer and tucked a strand of hair behind my ear. "Many of us could level this place with a thought. No concrete, human building could hold us."

"That's a no."

He smiled at me. "You need to learn that no concrete

human building could hold you either."

I attempted a smile back and squeezed past him, following my sister further into what we had thought was a lab.

But was really a prison.

"Why would whoever's in charge here come after Evie?" I murmured.

"I have my suspicions," Samael said. I glanced at him and he shook his head. "Let's collect what evidence we can, and then make our determination."

The next room was a small medical room, as were several others after that. Restraints dangled from each bed, and by the time we'd worked our way down the corridor to the first set of stairs, the hair on the back of my neck was standing up.

We followed Evie down toward the basement. Samael's people had already broken the security on the door, and we walked past cell after cell, furnished with nothing more than a steel toilet, sink, and a concrete bed with a thin mattress.

Hundreds of cells. Some of them showed signs of recent use. A pair of thin boots in one. Blood smeared on the floor in another. And always, an echo of hopelessness. People had been held in here. Where the hell were they now?

Another set of stairs waited for us at the end of the cells. We took it up, past the ground floor, where the corridors became white on white.

"Medical floor," Evie said, a few steps in front of us.

These cells were larger than the ones downstairs, mostly to fit the equipment. Cameras were positioned in the corner of each cell.

The third floor was one huge lab. It stretched the length and width of the building, the first quarter home to fifty or so workstations, while the rest of it was blocked off with more security.

Bile climbed up my throat as we walked through what were once secure doors.

Examining tables complete with stirrups, and more restraints. I'd seen some of that equipment at my gynecologist's, only I sure as hell hadn't been tied down for my checkups. The next section made me catch my breath.

"Babies," Evie said. "This is where they kept babies."

Tiny bassinets, some of them enclosed and surrounded by huge lights. They'd tried to destroy this room, but it was evident that this was a place for newborns.

Samael's demons walked through each room, collecting what they could.

The fourth floor had been designated for offices. More workstations, only this time without any scientific equipment. These were the drones. We passed them, heading toward the closest corner office.

Someone had been shredding documents. The shredder was full, and larger pieces of paper littered the floor, as if someone had panicked and attempted to destroy as much evidence as they could with their hands before they fled. A steel filing cabinet hung open and half-empty. Whoever's office this was, they hadn't had a chance to completely clear it out before they ran for their lives.

We left Evie searching through the filing cabinet and walked through the rest of the floor. "Half lab, half prison,"

I said. "They were experimenting on people here."

Samael nodded, and we spent the next half hour walking through the floor. I couldn't go near the lab, but I stared at the photos on the cubicles. There was something about seeing family photos in this place that turned my stomach. The people who'd worked here had treated it like any other job. Were they blind to the suffering or did they not care?

Maybe they'd enjoyed it.

Samael stepped away to murmur to Bael and I turned as Evie appeared. Her face was ashen, her hands shaking as she gestured for me to follow her back into the office.

She'd been piecing together some of the larger documents, and she had the first third of what looked like some kind of physical description. A photo had been stapled to the corner of one of the pieces and Evie's hand shook as she pointed to it.

"He looks just like the dark fae guy Mom was half in-love with when we were kids. But his features are slightly different. His eyes are darker too. Maybe his brother?"

"Maybe."

"Look at this one."

Every cell in my body came to attention. This document had obviously been stapled to the other page—they were torn in the same places. Mom's face looked out at us and the world seemed to stop as we both stared down at the photo. She looked impossibly young and incredibly scared.

Beneath the photo, they'd noted specific details. Height, weight, physical characteristics.

"One live infant," Evie read over my shoulder and

pointed. "Look at the date."

I'd been two and a half years old by then. The infant was Evie. Our mom had been here, and she'd likely given birth to my sister in this lab. I raised my head and we stared at each other for a long moment.

"What the hell am I, Danica? Some kind of sick experiment?"

"Don't be ridiculous," I snapped, and she shook her head.

"Even you can't explain this one away."

Samael ran his hand along my lower back, a silent show of support. He studied the papers over my shoulder, expression grim.

Sitri approached, his expression even more grim.

"Looks like most of the prisoners were killed, Boss. Slaughtered in the outdoor 'exercise yard.' It's a sea of blood, but no bodies. We think some of them were loaded out and transported, but we have no idea how many."

"Can you tell when they left?" I asked.

"Bael is the best at sensing that kind of thing, but it's not exact. Best he can tell is we missed them by a few hours."

Evie's hands shook. "I think we need to involve the police."

I stared at her. "Seriously?"

"We can take what we need, let Samael's demons process the scene first— if that's okay with you," she glanced at Samael and he nodded. "But we need to tell the human authorities what happened here. There are so many more of them than there are of the demons, and they can spread the word and do their own investigations."

I glanced at Samael. He didn't look at all concerned at the thought of the human police stepping on his toes.

"Nelson did seem like good people," I mused. "He's trying to increase cooperation across the factions. Mentioned some cities are creating joint task forces between paranormals and humans. The problem is that this is way outside of his jurisdiction."

Evie shrugged. "At the very least, he might know who to get in touch with, right?"

She had a point. "Okay. I'll call him."

I walked a few feet away as Evie went back to poking around. We needed more help. Samael had incredible resources, that was for sure, but as far as I could tell, there was no real downside to involving the human police at this point.

"Hello?" Nelson's voice was gruff.

"Were you serious about that whole cooperation thing?"

He was quiet for a moment. "Ms. Amana?"

"Danica. Did you mean what you said?"

"Yes."

"We have reason to believe that the people who attacked the coven are connected to a lab in Tennessee. We're here now, and there are no signs of life, other than some bloodstains."

He let out a bitter laugh. "So you went in, fucked up the crime scene, removed any important information, and now you're throwing the humans a bone."

I winced. "Yes, that's exactly what we did, but we're not throwing you a bone. We're wearing gloves, and being careful. You'll have access to everything we found, along with the recordings from when we accessed the lab. It'll all be transported to the tower.

Silence.

I waited him out.

"I want to see the lab myself. Then we'll talk about the evidence you're removing."

"Fine."

I found Evie in the office, a collection of papers in her hand.

"This is the shit they don't care if we find," she said. "They would have destroyed any evidence that could lead to them."

"We'll find them."

I watched Evie as she scanned the paper in her hand.

She was turning distant, her eyes unfathomable, her mind continuously elsewhere. If she was anything like me, it was vengeance that caused her eyes to sharpen occasionally as she stared into space.

My fun-loving, curious, mischievous sister was fading away.

"Don't let this make you hard and cold," I whispered. "Don't let it make you a predator."

She finally pulled her attention from the papers in her hand. "They wouldn't have targeted me if they didn't think I was prey."

I didn't know what to say to that. She handed me a stack of papers.

"They were mixing DNA, Dani. Look. Some of these were werewolves. They must've kept them drugged and starved or they would've torn this place apart. What do you want to bet that some of the chains in this place are Naud chains?"

I flipped through the papers, bile crawling up my throat. They had designations. Witch, wolf, fae, even demon.

This is why I sensed the weird power imprint when Selena was with me at the wreckage of the house. They kept all kinds of creatures here, likely using them to create their spells. They experimented, and at least during the time Evie was born, they'd been creating babies.

Danica

As soon as we landed, I met Kyla back at the hotel. She was sitting in her car, plowing through a burger as I slid into the passenger seat.

"You hungry? I have some fries."

"I'm good. Any movement?"

"Nah. Boring as hell."

I grinned at her. "Welcome to stakeout life." I studied the hotel entrance.

My phone vibrated and I answered it.

"Steve?"

"We got lucky," he said. "The driver took a left turn on Main and he took it fast. The corner of the cardboard covering the license plate lifted up. We have the last three digits and we managed to narrow down our list of potentials."

"Whoever was driving the car was both desperate and stupid. Needed to take Willow out and couldn't wait for an area with fewer cameras."

"Yeah. The car is registered to a Vicky Hanson. She lives in South Durham."

"Thanks."

"I'll stay here," Kyla said when I ended the call. "If the witch responsible for the murders finds out we've found the car, she may attempt to make a break for it."

"That's true."

"If the driver's at that address, he's going to be desperate. You need backup."

I frowned. "He's human."

"You don't know what he's involved in. If he's targeting a witch, there could be other paranormals there."

"Okay, you have a point." I lifted my phone. "I'll see if Vas is available."

Sorry, out on demon business. I'll send someone else.

As long as that someone else wasn't his uncle. I'd rather take on a bunch of rabid redcaps alone.

Thanks.

I chewed on my lower lip. Samael had dropped everything over the past few days, sending his demons whenever I needed them. I appreciated it, but I didn't want to rely on his people. When this case was over, I needed to touch base with some of the mercs I knew who did good work, kept their mouths shut, and didn't mind that I was bonded to a demon.

It would be a small pool, but most mercs I knew loved money more than they valued loyalty.

I left Kyla eating her fries. Realistically, if one of the witches wanted to make a run for it, they could go out the back exit. However, they'd have to climb a fence to get onto the street.

I drove to Vicky's, then leaned against my car and checked my emails. I was already sweating like a pig in this heat, may as well soak up some vitamin D at the same time.

The flap of wings announced a demon was landing and I raised one eyebrow. "What are you doing here?"

Samael smiled. "I had a few hours free, and I thought I'd spend them with my witchling." He glanced around the neighborhood and winced. "Although, I'd prefer a more romantic atmosphere."

I elbowed him. "Snob. You didn't have a few hours free. I've been sucking up all your time over the past few days."

"My time is infinite," he said.

"I guess you've got a point there. No sign of the car, and I doubt there's a pack of rabid redcaps waiting in the house."

"Rabid redcaps?"

I shrugged. Those redcaps were no joke. I still had nightmares about the time I was double-crossed and forced to fight my way out of their territory after dark.

"I'd decided I'd rather deal with them than work with Ag."

Samael laughed, catching my hand and pulling me in for a kiss. The kiss turned deep, heat coiling in my belly.

"Get a room!"

I pushed away, glancing over my shoulder at the kid on the bike. He grinned at me, then his gaze traveled past me and he went sheet white.

"I've never seen anyone pedal that fast," I said.

"Alright, let's get this over with."

The door swung open when I knocked, and my gaze dropped down to waist height.

"Can I help you?" The brownie angled his head, then glanced behind me at Samael and bared his tiny teeth.

I didn't know exactly what brownies had against demons, but it was amusing.

"We have a few questions for Vicky Hanson."

The brownie sniffed. "Mrs. Hanson is resting, Ma'am. She is unwell."

"This won't take long. But it's extremely important."

The brownie narrowed his eyes at me, but after a minute of contemplation he nodded his head and stepped further back, gesturing for me to enter.

I didn't bother asking his name. Anyone who named a brownie would no longer benefit from their hard work when the magic tying them to their position fled.

My gaze scanned the cramped living room. Someone was sleeping on the sofa, which had been folded out, blankets piled on top of it. Everything else was spotlessly clean, the faded carpet recently vacuumed. On the floor near the TV, a bowl of cream or milk sat, proving that Vicky Hanson knew how to ensure the brownie would stick around.

"How is it that you came to work here?" I asked.

Typically, only the wealthiest human families could afford a brownie. The brownies themselves weren't paid, of course, but the dark fae hired them out.

"The unseelie king has made recent efforts to improve his... reputation," the brownie said. "He has created a charity to benefit the humans, and has tasked some of my people to go to work for those less fortunate than we would typically work for."

The brownie glanced at the sofa and despite myself, I felt sorry for him. Cleaning, keeping a home tidy, they were compulsions for brownies. Whoever was sleeping on that sofa had asked the brownie not to touch it, and the poor thing must have been on edge all day every day.

Samael stepped forward, something like pity in his gaze as he glanced around the tiny house.

"Where is your master?" he asked.

The brownie puffed his chest out. "Mrs. Hanson is very unwell. I'll ask you not to upset her," he said to me, ignoring the demon completely. My lips trembled at the brownie's affronted tone, as he pretended Samael was invisible.

"I'll try my best," I said.

Vicky Hanson was lying in bed, an oxygen mask strapped to her face. Her eyes whirled as we arrived.

"My son. Something happened to my son," she croaked out, attempting to sit up. Her gaze slid past Samael, obviously not recognizing him. I couldn't blame her. Who would expect him to be hanging out in a human neighborhood?

"As far as we know, your son is fine. We just need to ask you a couple of questions."

Sitting up a few inches had exhausted her, and her face was pallid. There was no way this woman was getting behind the wheel of a car.

"Ask," she croaked out.

"When did you last see your son?"

"Two days ago. I've had the brownie contact the

police, and I've called all his friends, but no one's seen him." Her voice hitched and I took a deep breath.

"Your car was involved in a hit and run."

"But that's impossible. Peter is the only one who would've been driving my car. He wouldn't hurt anyone."

"Was your car stolen recently?"

Tears filled her eyes as she slowly shook her head. "Peter hasn't come home. Oh god, he had an accident and he didn't want me to know."

How exactly did I break it to her that her son was a murderer? Samael placed his hand on my shoulder and stepped closer to the bed. "Your son killed a witch. He jumped the curb and aimed for her."

Vicky gasped for oxygen, tears rolling down her face. When she'd caught her breath she shook her head. "He wouldn't have done that. Peter's a good boy. He volunteers at the hospital whenever he has a chance. You're lying. You're lying about my son."

Pity welled, even as I took a step closer. "Which hospital, Mrs. Hanson?"

"It's none of your business. He's a good boy. He works so hard to pay for my treatments."

My stomach churned sickly, but I had to find him before he targeted another witch.

"You know what will happen to him if the High Coven finds him. If we find him first, we can negotiate for leniency."

Tears fell in a steady drip and her breath hitched. "He wouldn't. He wouldn't." She closed her eyes, steadying herself in long, slow breaths.

"If he did anything, it was for me. Seeing me like

this… it was breaking his heart."

"Where would he go?"

"He was seeing a girl. Lori. If he's not with her… we used to visit Emporia when he was small, to see my mother. I always wanted to take him back as a teenager, but I was sick by then. Leave me. Leave me now. Please."

We let ourselves out and I stalked toward my car, kicking out at the tire. "Goddamn it."

Samael placed his hand on my shoulder. "You had to tell her. You had to ask."

I shook my head. "That woman has one good thing in her life and I just took it from her."

"Her son did that."

"Yeah. And now he'll die in prison— if he's lucky, while his mom dies alone."

Samael pulled me close, and I gave in, burying my face in his chest as he wrapped his arms around me.

"You have a miserable job."

"Not always. But the past couple of weeks have been as bad as it gets."

"We'll take a few days off after you've closed your case."

I stepped back and eyed him. "The workaholic demon will take a few days off?"

"If it means I can have you to myself."

I needed to set up my new office— the one Keigan had given me, where I'd be seeing clients. I needed to start advertising… screw it.

"Deal," I said.

"You'll be looking for the son."

"Yeah. His information says he lives in Wisconsin,

but I'm guessing he moved back here when his mom got sick. Unless he's an idiot, he's ditched the car, but he might've kept the phone."

"Are you sure?"

"He may not be answering, but that's probably because he can't face what he did. His mom's dying. You'd have to be ice cold to ditch the only way she has to contact you. I don't think he's cold. I think he's stupid and desperate, and he panicked."

"You know who got to him."

"Yeah. I can't prove it until I find him. But it all goes back to the fucking hospital." I kicked out at my tire again and then turned to face Samael.

"I need to ask you for a favor."

"Eldan is already on his way."

My heart squeezed in my chest and I had to swallow around the lump in my throat. "Thanks."

"The woman may be too far gone. But at the very least, he may be able to reduce her suffering."

CHAPTER TWENTY-TWO

Danica

Samael left to get back to work and I called Kyla on the way back to the hotel.

"I'm going to talk to Peter Hanson's girlfriend. Evie and I also have some of the funerals later tonight. Steve is going to trace Hanson's phone, although it's probably turned off. But his mother says he might be in Emporia. It's a couple of hours from here…"

"Virginia, right? I'm there." Relief warred with eagerness in her voice. Kyla was obviously excited to do something that didn't involve staking out the hotel.

"His Majesty decided he would prefer for me to be at the tower tonight, so he's sending one of his demons to take over from you."

Kyla laughed. "Sounds good. I'll update you when I get to Emporia. Did his mom have any idea where he'd be?"

"They used to visit the grandmother. I'll find her address and get it to you. Keep track of your expenses and I'll take care of them when you're back."

Peter's girlfriend Lori worked at a restaurant called Pixieland. The restaurant was light fae themed, boasting a small pond and waterfall inside, surrounded by plants and flowers. It smelled like a tropical forest, but the real draw was the pixies who made their homes amongst the greenery.

There were more pixies here than the last time I'd visited, although I'd only eaten here once when Evie and I were kids. Mom had decided she didn't like the place.

The pixies were notorious for playing tricks on diners, but it was part of the attraction for humans. They watched wide-eyed as the pixies fluttered by their heads, splashed their feet in their drinks, and tied their shoelaces together.

I breathed in the mossy, floral scent as I headed toward the hostess. "I'm looking for Lori," I said.

The hostess took one look at the mark on my arm and her eyes widened. "I hope she's not in trouble."

"She's not. I just need to talk to her."

"She's due for a break soon. Um," she glanced around. "Do you mind waiting at the bar?"

"Nope."

I took a seat on one of the wooden stools and shook my head at the bartender as he raised an eyebrow. A pixie sauntered across the bar in front of me, placing his hands on his hips.

"I know you," he said. I wracked my brain and then it hit me.

"You were at Mariam's office, right?"

He nodded, his wings fluttering behind him as he

rose a few inches into the air. "When you finished your investigation, the humans who were mean to us no longer came to clean. The one with the sucking machine disappeared. The new humans are nice."

The woman had been threatening the pixies with her vacuum. "I'm glad they're not being mean to you anymore."

Pixies saw and heard all. May as well give it a shot. "Have you heard anything about the fire at the coven?"

He shook his tiny head. "They say it was an inside job though. Not many people could get through the ward on that coven."

"Yeah."

"You wanted to speak with me?"

I turned on the stool. Lori had long, braided hair and dark eyes. Her smile was incredibly sweet, and a pixie hung to one of her hoop earrings. He narrowed his eyes at me curiously.

"Do you enjoy working at this place?"

Lori flashed her sweet smile. "I like it here. If you're nice to the pixies, they're nice to you."

We both turned at a shriek from the tables near the pond. A pixie zipped between a waitress's feet, tripping her, and the tray she was carrying went flying as she hit the ground. The pixies surrounding her laughed, the sound like bells.

"I'm guessing she's not nice to the pixies."

"Hates them," Lori said, her hand sliding up to cover her mouth. "She's on parole. Couldn't find a job anywhere else."

People were rushing over to the waitress to help her

to her feet. I turned back to Lori.

"I'm investigating a hit and run. I just have a couple of questions to ask you if you don't mind."

A tiny line appeared between her brows, but she sat down next to me. "Wow, it's good to be off my feet. I don't have a car."

"We're investigating Peter Hanson."

Lori stared at me. The pixie hanging from her earring gave me a vicious scowl.

"Peter wouldn't do anything like that. He hates violence."

"When was the last time you saw him?"

"Um," the line between her brows deepened. "A few days ago. We were supposed to hang out last night but he never got back to me. I ended up picking up an extra shift."

"You weren't worried when he didn't answer?"

She shrugged. "We're not serious. We only just started dating. I figured he was busy and he'd text me later."

"Did he?"

"No." She bit her lower lip. "You think he hurt somebody?"

"I do. Did he ever mention anywhere that he liked to go during the weekends? Any place he'd use to clear his head, or visit friends?"

Lori adjusted her earring, and the pixie lifted into the air on incandescent wings, making itself at home in her braid instead. "He has friends who have a place in Myrtle Beach. But they usually rent it out unless they're all going down there."

"Do you have the address?"

"No, but if you get in touch with his friend Jordan, he'll be able to give it to you. I doubt he'd go there, but I guess it's worth a try."

I pulled a pen and notepad out of my utility belt and wrote down my number. "If he gets in touch, I need you to call me."

Instant denial flashed across her face. I frowned. "If the witches find him before I do, he won't get a chance to explain himself."

The color had drained from Lori's face. "You really think he hurt someone?"

"I know he did."

"The Peter I know would never want to hurt anyone. I hope it's a big misunderstanding, but I'll let you know if he contacts me."

I ran through it in my head as I made my way back to the tower. By now, Peter had to know that every witch in the triangle would be looking for him. He'd be panicking, and he likely didn't have much money for an extended period of time on the run. His biggest threat was the witch who'd convinced him to do her dirty work. And if he wasn't careful, he'd be one of the loose ends she tied up.

I parked my car in the underground garage when I got to the tower, and took the elevator to the 49th floor. The floor was currently untenanted, so the demons had arranged for all of the evidence to be brought up and organized for processing.

The elevator doors slid open and my gaze immediately found Nelson, who was watching Azazyel bring in boxes of papers.

He gave me a hard stare. Okay, he was pissed.

He made his way toward me, and I glanced behind him as the balcony doors opened. Samael stepped into the room, his eyes warm as they met mine. They chilled significantly as the detective approached.

"The good detective is unhappy," Evie mused. I glanced at her. She was standing next to a table filled with boxes of chains, ready to be sent to the lab.

Nelson narrowed his eyes at us.

"Next time, we'd very much appreciate if you gave us a chance to enter the building with you." His tone was icy, and I sent Samael a warning look. He turned away, speaking to Azazyel, but I had no doubt that he was still listening.

"Look, Samael's people have their own labs, which aren't as backed up as yours. They took prints, we wore gloves, and every step inside that place was documented."

"You don't know what you might have missed. The demons aren't cops."

"No, but we had to move quickly. If we'd been even quicker, we might've gotten to that lab before they killed most of the people who'd been in it."

"And human cops would have slowed you down." The tone was bitter and I winced.

"Honestly, it didn't occur to me to contact you. All I can say is that next time it will."

His gaze was steady on my face. Finally, he hooked his thumbs in his belt loop and rocked back on his heels as he nodded.

"That's all I ask. I apologize for my tone."

I opened my mouth, but Evie stepped in. "No, you

don't. Why would you? We took evidence that you wanted to be left at the crime scene. You don't need to kiss our asses to be invited to share our toys, Nelson."

He stared at us for a moment and then threw his head back and laughed.

"I like you guys. God knows why. I understand this is personal," he glanced at Evie, "but in the future, I politely *request* that you allow us into the crime scene before you remove evidence."

I nodded. "Fair enough."

He scanned my face. "You've done good work to get this far."

"I couldn't have done it without the demons."

He nodded. "According to my sources, you're getting quite the reputation as an investigator."

"I wouldn't go that far. Let me know if we can get you anything, detective. Evie, you good here?"

She nodded, studying a blood-smeared handcuff. Likely, she was picturing it wrapped around our mom's wrist. I was attempting not to do the same.

I made my way over to Samael. He glanced at me, and I narrowed my eyes at him.

"Are you okay?"

"Of course. I only visited to check that everything was being processed according to my orders. I have a meeting I need to get to."

My eyes squinted further. "Are you… lying to me?"

Confusion wrestled with the tiniest glimmer of hurt. Samael likely felt it, because he cursed, taking my arm and pulling me out onto the balcony. A quick flight later, and we were stepping through the doors to his penthouse.

He let me go and I took a few steps back. My phone vibrated and I gritted my teeth, pulling it out.

"I'm sorry. I have to take this."

"Kyla. What's up?"

"It's Riona."

"Is she okay?"

"She's fine. But listen, before I headed out of town, I had a thought. I figured I'd show her a few pictures of as many local black witches as I could to see if she recognized any of them."

"That's a good thought. I should've had it."

Kyla laughed. "You've had a lot going on."

I closed my eyes. "It's Hannah, isn't it?"

"No. It's Gloria."

My eyes popped open and I hissed. "And Troy Burker?"

"Gloria's cousin's great nephew. The cousin is dead, Burker's mom wants nothing to do with black witches, but her kid was apparently obsessed with power. I talked to his mom. He disappeared and she's convinced Gloria killed him."

"Shit. Thanks Kyla."

I hung up. Across the room, Samael was very still, but there was no mistaking the wrath which radiated from him. Good. If he hadn't given a shit that Gloria had kidnapped and mentally tortured Riona… I didn't think we could come back from that.

Fury spread from his end of the bond. A deep, dark fury so encompassing that it scared the shit out of me, and I knew without doubt that he'd never hurt me.

"I will find her," he vowed. "Give me a few moments

to alert my people."

I wandered into the kitchen and poured a glass of water while he had his mind-to-mind conversations with his people.

When I came out, his eyes were still cool. "I have arranged for Asmodeus to stay outside the witch's hospital room. If Gloria learns she has identified her, she could take revenge."

My heart flipped in my chest and I took a few steps closer to him. I wanted to reach out, but he looked strangely remote. "Thank you. I appreciate that." I studied his face. "What's your problem, Samael?"

"There is no problem."

"Uh-huh. Play another tune, demon—"

I gasped as he was suddenly in front of me. He'd moved so fast he was a blur.

"Perhaps I need to remind my witchling who she belongs to," he purred.

His mouth slammed down on mine, and his hands reached for my jeans, deftly undoing the button.

His tongue was in my mouth, and one of his hands slid into my jeans. His laugh was low and satisfied.

"Already ready for me, little witch?"

I tensed, my hands rising to push him away. "Piss me off, and you won't get any, Samael."

He pulled my jeans off and I slapped at him as he tore my t-shirt in half.

I was furious, annoyed, and hopelessly aroused.

My bra disappeared, and his fingers plucked my nipple while his hand slid down and shot me to a vicious orgasm. I blinked.

"What the—"

He hoisted me into his arms, pushed me against the wall, and thrust inside me. My eyes rolled back in my head as his pelvic bone slid against my clit and I gasped as he twisted his hips, fucking me like I was his salvation.

He wound his hand into my hair, angling my head until I was looking up into his eyes.

"Who do you belong to?"

I showed him my teeth. He snarled back.

A thrust that stabbed into me, making my thighs quiver. I was so close…

"Who?"

"You," I cried out, my hands sliding beneath his wings to claw desperately at his back.

He buried his head in my neck and pumped his hips, I writhed, arching my back, straining against him. With a series of deep thrusts, pleasure overtook me and I quaked in his arms.

He growled out his pleasure and gasped against my shoulder as I stared unseeingly over his back.

Holy god.

Samael took one step and stumbled. I clutched onto him and the sudden breeze told me he'd used his wings to catch himself. He gently lowered me onto the sofa, stepping away, and I caught his hand, pulling him back to me.

"Not that I didn't just have a lot of fun, but would you like to tell me what that was about?"

"I'm sorry. I was rough."

"Don't apologize for mind-blowing sex. But clearly something's bothering you, Samael."

He opened his mouth and I scowled at him. "You would never let me lie to you, so don't piss me off by doing it to me."

He sighed and sat next to me.

"It was merely an ancient demon encountering jealousy for the first time."

I gaped at him. "*What* are you talking about?"

"You don't see it." He laughed, but not like it was funny.

I pushed both hands into my hair, frustrated behind reason. "See what?"

"He is the kind of man you would have chosen. One day when you were ready. He is the type who would be loyal and honorable, he also works a demanding job, and he would understand yours. You have chemistry."

I gaped at him, searching my mind for this mythical man. Samael had gotten pissed in the evidence room. "Nelson and me? Are you drunk?"

"Not chemistry like ours. Not even close. But a spark. A spark that would be a comforting fire on a cold night if given the chance." He bared his teeth. "You will never have that chance."

"I didn't ask for the chance!" I threw my hands up in the air. "You're being completely unreasonable. You're mad because of some imagined chemistry with a guy I've met a few damn times."

His wings rustled. "Don't negate my instincts. I *know* you."

I blew out a breath. It wasn't just anger or jealousy I could sense from him. It was... hurt.

"I don't want anyone else. You're the most frustrating

man I've ever met, but you're mine. And I'm yours."

I shifted closer to him, raising my hand until it rested on his cheek. "What is this really about?"

He was silent for a long moment, lost in thought. I waited him out, and he finally heaved a sigh, raising his own hand, until it mirrored mine, warm against my cheek.

"I will forever know that you didn't come to me on your own terms. That I had to force you into a bond you never wanted, and chip away at your defenses one by one. That I wore you down until you admitted you had feelings for me. That I pushed my way into your life and refused to leave."

"Well, yeah. What's your point?"

A ghost of a smile crossed his face, but his eyes were serious. "It is… unnerving to know that I did it all wrong with you. That no matter how much longer I've been alive, I failed to see the signs that I wanted you for myself, the moment I saw you."

He glanced away. "I know what everyone says about us. That you were forced to be mine, and that if you could, you'd be free. And I know that even if you asked for your freedom, I could never let you go."

I shook my head. "I don't believe that. Maybe at first, but you've changed. You do things because you want me to be happy. If you really thought I'd be miserable with you for eternity, you'd let me go."

He frowned at me. "Maybe I'd take you any way I could, even if it meant we were both miserable."

I smiled up at him. I was forgetting that this was all new to him too. Feeling vulnerable. Being in love with someone so completely different. He'd been alive for so long, and the time he'd known me was merely a blip during that long life.

"I don't want some human cop," I said carefully. "I'm sure, in some alternate universe, there's a reality in which you and I never meet, and I settle down with a nice, normal man one day. Just like there's a reality in which you fall in love with a gorgeous, long-lived woman like Lilith or even Mariam. But we *did* meet. We have enough issues to work on without thinking about what-ifs."

He was silent for a long moment. "I never wanted to feel this way."

I laughed. "Well, me neither."

"But it's worth it. For you."

"Right back atcha. Are we okay?"

He nodded. Then he wrapped his arms around me and buried his face in my neck. My possessive, terrifying demon held me for a long time. And I held onto him right back.

Samael

I should have felt remorse. Should have worried that letting my little witch see the depths of my desperation for her would give her the upper hand in the ongoing power struggle that was our relationship.

I should have been wary of spooking the woman who had barely accepted me. The woman who hadn't come close to accepting what I felt for her.

I'd barely accepted it myself.

And yet all I felt was a deep, all-encompassing satisfaction after proving to her that she was mine.

At the same time, the need to tie her to me was like a set of claws digging into my spine.

My black heart couldn't contain all that I felt for her.

Part of me hated her for the weakness she caused in me. A larger part knew that if anything ever happened to her, this realm would burn.

A knock on the door. I turned, finding Bael and Ag waiting for me.

Bael glanced around the living room, and it was obvious he knew what had just happened. Whatever he could see on my face warned him not to say a word.

"Our people have been searching for the black witch. She has disappeared."

Rage swept through me at the thought. After she'd 'borrowed' the last grimoire, I'd changed the code to my safe and sunk more power into my ward. Some part of me had known she was not to be trusted.

And yet, over the past decade, I'd trusted the witch enough to allow her into my home. Worse, I'd allowed her to have access to Danica while she was unconscious. I'd even trusted her with Danica's sister's life.

"She's a black witch," Ag said. "It was only a matter of time before she betrayed us. You made allowances for that when you decided to work with her."

"She's either dead or in the underworld. Have you flipped Teremos yet?" Another demon we hoped to sway to our side.

"I believe so. Lucifer killed his beloved. If Teremos could get through the portal, he would, but now he is willing to lose his life if it means Lucifer loses his."

"Find out if Gloria is there."

Ag nodded. "If she's stupid enough to turn to Lucifer, she deserves everything she will get."

Gloria knew nothing that could truly harm us, had never been privy to my plans. Yet she knew things about Danica's family that Lucifer would find *very* interesting.

Hopefully, Lucifer would have one of his rages and kill her when she showed up without the grimoires. But I would need to plan for other eventualities, just in case.

Danica

The funerals began at sunset. Some of the bodies had already been taken by relatives, back to their hometowns. Those who had no other families, or who had otherwise made their wishes clear, were given a joint funeral.

The coven had its own plot in Maplewood Cemetery. There had been protests earlier in the week regarding so many witches being buried on consecrated ground— even white witches–- but the local authorities had quickly put a stop to that.

No one wanted to piss Gemma off right now.

The coven had already formed a circle, and the witches were surrounding the coffins when we arrived. Evie stepped past me and joined the circle, clutching Freya and Marie's hands.

Those who weren't coven members surrounded the circle, heads bowed as the coven mourned their dead.

The coven had been a mainstay in Durham for years, and representatives from all factions had taken the time to pay their respects.

On the other side of the circle, Gary nodded at me, Cil and Zip by his side. Selina stood nearby, her eyes sad as she watched the proceedings. Nathaniel, Liam, and Kyla were positioned a few feet away, and even Mariam had taken the time to show her face.

Other covens had shown up too, including witches from both the Jefferson and Allen covens, along with several other covens.

Samael, Vas, and Bael stood next to me, and I idly wondered when the last time so many paranormals and humans had been gathered in the same place at the same time, without it turning into bloodshed.

Meredith stepped up next to me, her delicate shoulders hunched. Her best friend was being buried today. I wrapped my arm around her and gave her a quick hug.

Vas glanced at Mere once, and then looked at everyone but her for the rest of the ceremony. Subtle.

The witches' voices rose, the low chanting taking on a new life. The hair stood up on my arms as a cool, unnatural breeze swept over everyone in attendance.

"Today we send our sisters to the afterlife," Gemma's voice carried over the chanting. She released the hands next to her and stepped forward. Behind her, the circle formed once more.

"We call on earth."

Several humans looked spooked as the ground shook beneath us. A trickle of dirt raised up from the ground beneath Gemma's feet and into the air, slowly circling the coffins.

Ainsley stepped forward. A small basin of water waited near her feet. "We call on water," she said, lifting her hand as she continued to chant. Her face flushed with the effort, but the water slowly rose from the basin in a long stream, formed a ball above her head, and then began to whirl around the circle, as if chasing the dirt.

Freya stepped forward next. "We call on air."

The breeze kicked up again, leaves from a few nearby trees flying into the circle. What looked like a mini tornado formed within Freya's hands and I raised one eyebrow. She had power. A lot of it.

Evie stepped forward next. A candle was waiting at her feet, and Caroline leaned down to light it for my sister. Her hand shook, as she flicked the lighter a few times. Finally, Evie gave a tiny shake of her head and raised one hand.

"We call on fire," she said, her voice clear and confident.

I tensed as her hand sparked, and suddenly, a small ball of fire appeared in her palm. It slowly rose to join the other elements, lazily circling the coffins.

Shocked murmurs began, and I couldn't help it, I reached for Samael's hand.

Gemma sent one glance over the crowd, and the murmurs ceased.

The rest of the ceremony passed without incident. Each witch in the coven spoke about a memory they had with one of those who had been killed. By the time it was over, most of our faces were wet.

Once the coffins had been placed in their graves, Evie found me. "It feels real now," she said, her eyes dark. "It felt almost like a nightmare before."

"I know."

Liam approached, nodding at me. "How are you doing?" he asked Evie.

"I'm okay. It's… a lot."

"How's the neck?"

She attempted a smile. "Better now."

Nathaniel stepped toward us. Since I was looking at him, I caught the moment the wind changed. He stared at Evie, and his eyes turned such a light blue they were almost white. Next to me, Samael tensed. He'd seen it too.

Nathaniel gave me one sharp nod, turned, and stalked away.

CHAPTER TWENTY-THREE

Danica

I groaned as my phone rang. Next to me, Samael nuzzled closer, sliding his leg along mine and I nestled further into the soft down of his wing.

I groped for my phone. Kyla.

"Yeah?"

"Got him. I'm on my way back from Emporia."

God she was good. And she was definitely getting a pay raise. "How'd you find him?"

"Swung by his mom's house on my way out of town after I saw Riona. Took one of his hoodies. The brownie wasn't pleased. But I showed Peter's picture around once I got here. Place is tiny, and once I caught his scent, I found him sleeping in his car."

"Not the one he used–"

"Nah, he sold that. Probably the one smart thing he did out of all of this, but we'll be able to find it. Where do you want me to bring him when I get back?"

Samael lifted one hand and pointed a finger

downward.

"Samael has some cells and interrogation rooms below his tower. If we give Peter to the Council, they'll hand him over to the High Coven. I want to hear his confession first."

"Got that. I'll see you in half an hour."

I dropped my phone on the bed. It was 1:00am. I'd fallen into bed and had approximately two hours of sleep. Samael looked fresh as a fucking daisy.

I scowled at him. "How is it that you look so good?"

His smile was smug. "Superior genes."

I rolled my eyes, pushing my tangled hair off my face.

"Other than the funeral tonight, Evie's been avoiding the coven, likely because she blames herself. But she needs to be there when they find out it was Caroline. She'll have to live with the fact that Caroline was happy for her to be killed if it meant she'd have more power in the coven."

Interest lit Samael's eyes. "Why Caroline?"

I frowned. "I think my subconscious knew when I met her at the hotel. Something about her annoyed me, and I figured I was just being cynical, so I looked in every other direction. I had no reason to suspect her, but she was too helpful, too… *earnest*."

I blew out a breath. "I ignored my instincts. But it all ties back to the hospital. Caroline had motive, opportunity, and she used a desperate human as her patsy."

He pressed a gentle kiss to my cheek. "Go wake your sister. I'll send for coffee."

I swung my legs out of the bed and padded over to

the chair where I'd dropped my jeans. I raised them, gave them a good sniff, and slid them on.

The demon watched, clearly amused before he strolled to his bedroom-sized walk-in closet.

Since he was occupied, I pulled on a tank with a built-in bra, and rounded the bed to the floor where I'd dropped his shirt after pulling it off him last night. I lifted it and slid it on. It was huge on me, but worth it as I rolled up the sleeves and his scent wound up my nostrils.

Today would be a shitty day. I'd take my comfort where I could find it.

Yeah, I was wearing the demon's shirt. A few months ago, I'd done everything I could to hide the mark on my arm, and now I was declaring myself his. Life was weird but I was tired of fighting it.

I pulled the rowan arrow over my head, shoving it beneath the shirt, and then followed it with my lanyard and Nim Cub.

Samael stepped out of his closet as I was strapping on the rest of my weapons. He was dressed in black slacks and a white shirt, and as soon as he saw me, he went still.

It wasn't easy to surprise the demon, but his eyes widened, before glittering with lust as he stalked toward me.

"Nuh-uh." I put my fingers up in the sign of a cross like someone warding off a demon in an old horror movie. He merely ducked around me and his mouth slid over mine.

"It pleases me that you wrap my scent around you, little witch."

"Yeah, well today is going to suck a lot more than

most."

"You resist my mark, yet you wear my shirt."

"Wearing a guy's shirt is normal. Wearing a glittery gold tattoo on your arm is not." I ducked around him. "I need to wake up Evie."

He sent me a look of such wicked promise that my thighs clenched. I escaped the room before we started something we wouldn't have time to finish.

"Evie?"

Light spilled out from beneath her door and I knocked.

"Come in."

She sat up in bed, her cheeks damp and I crossed to her, wrapping her in my arms.

"Couldn't sleep?"

"No. It was… hard seeing how few of us are left today."

"We'll have the witch responsible for this by sunrise."

She went still and I pulled back so I could look at her. She wiped tears off her face. "You know who it is."

"Yeah. We've found the guy who killed Willow. We're bringing him in now. If you want to watch us talk to him, Samael can set you up with a monitor so you can observe."

"Yeah. I want to watch. Dani, I just want to say… I know this has been a lot. Juggling Riona's kidnapping with this. I know the witches haven't made it easy and it probably brought up all kinds of feelings and memories. But this is why I asked you to do it anyway. I knew you'd find out who did this." She smiled and gestured to the shirt

I was wearing. "When you love someone, you're all-in."

"Look, the coven may not be my family now," I said carefully, "but they were once. Mom took us to that coven and they sheltered us. They may not have done it the way we would've wanted them to, but they helped save your life."

"I'm trying to remind myself of that. I'm so mad at Gemma for never telling me the truth. I feel like I can barely look at her. But I have to go back for this. I have to watch as they make whoever did this pay." She sighed. "Are you going to tell me who did it?"

"Let's wait until the interview. I don't want to be wrong about this."

"Okay."

I glanced at my phone. "I need to get downstairs."

Someone knocked on the door and we both turned our heads.

Vas carried two cups of coffee and I just about tackled him as I held out my hand. "Gimme."

I took the first life-affirming gulp. "Please tell me Samael didn't wake you up for this."

He smiled. "I was up on business anyway." He glanced at Evie and sympathy gleamed in his dreamy eyes. "I've linked the feed to the TV in the living room so Evie and I can watch from there."

My throat tightened. *"Thank you,"* I mouthed at him and he nodded.

I glugged more coffee. "I've got to get going. I'll talk to you both later."

Danica

Kyla was waiting for me downstairs, outside the interrogation room.

"Thanks for this. You want in on this little chat?"

She raised one dark eyebrow. "I sure fucking do. You know, I wouldn't have guessed it was her."

I thought back to my interview with Caroline. I'd had Misty on me the whole time. And it hadn't glowed once.

"She lied like the fae when I talked to her," I said. "Not outright lying, but dancing around shit. Choosing her words carefully. And I didn't notice."

"I didn't spend much time with her, but I didn't smell any deception. Still, she could've been focusing on her grief, which would've covered up the stink of fear."

I nodded. "Right. She's likely been planning this for years. I bet she was *pissed* Evie wasn't in the house. Take out a few more witches in the next year or so, and she'd be Gail's number two. In fact, she wouldn't even need to take them all out. You bet your ass she'd start campaigning to be made number two based on her stupid healing spells alone."

I rolled my shoulders. "Let's get this done."

I opened the door. Peter Hanson looked very young and very scared. I clamped down on the pity that wanted to rise. Willow had been young too.

His eyes were red, and he needed a shave, the sparse stubble somehow making him look like a preteen boy. He'd obviously slept in his clothes last night, and he met my eyes for one moment before dropping his gaze to the table.

"Do you know why you're here, Peter?"

Silence. His jaw tightened and I readjusted my approach. I leveled a hard stare at him as Kyla slid into one of the chairs on our side of the table.

"I'm going to offer you a lifeline," I said. "I think you're a piece of shit. But you're a manipulated piece of shit. Tell us everything, and I'll arrange for you to be taken to the Mage Council under the condition that they don't hand you over to the High Coven."

He swallowed. "The Mage Council… will I ever see my mom again?"

"That's up to them."

He thought about it for a long moment. Kyla angled her head. "You know what will happen if you're taken to the coven, Peter," she said gently. "But the Mage Council rarely kills humans. They may allow you visitation with your mom."

His eyes gleamed with unshed tears. "She's dying. This will probably kill her."

Not if Eldan had anything to do with it. He'd contacted Samael earlier today. Peter's mom's cancer wasn't going away completely, but she was up and walking. She could probably live for another twenty years thanks to the fae healer.

All while her son was locked away.

I sat down next to Kyla and plunked Misty onto the table. "This dagger will glow if you lie. Tell us what happened."

He shoved his hand through his hair and obviously decided we were his best shot at mercy.

"Caroline caught me. At the hospital. I was just taking something for my mom's pain."

Stealing something. Even now, he couldn't admit to it.

"What did she say?"

"She looked so disappointed. We'd become... friends. She asked me what I was thinking. Told me there were good rehab facilities in the Triangle. I guess she thought I was using. I uh, I told her it was for my mom. Caroline said how it wasn't fair that she had to suffer just 'cause we had no insurance."

The bitch had seen the perfect target. "And what did you say?"

"I said it *wasn't* fair and we didn't ask to be poor." His gaze lifted from where he'd dropped it to the table. "My dad split when I was seven and my mom could only find cleaning jobs. Then she got sick. And she was getting sicker and sicker."

"So Caroline stepped in and offered to help."

He nodded. "She told me she had an idea. There was a witch in her coven who was evil. Real evil. She'd convinced all the other witches in her coven that she was good. Caroline was using all her power to keep her from killing. If the witch was dead, Caroline would be able to use her power to help my mom. She said she was good at healing spells."

I closed my eyes for a long moment. When I opened them, Peter had buried his face in his hands.

"Caroline said the witch I hit was a black witch. That she'd been preying on children. She said no one in her coven would believe her."

"She lied, Peter. Willow was a good person." I shook my head at him. "You knew it, deep down. If she'd been preying on children, her coven would've taken care of it. And if not, either the Mage Council or the High Coven would've stepped in."

He shook his head, wetness gleaming in his eyes. "She said the witch was too powerful. Powerful enough that no one could stop her."

"No one except a human with a van? If she was that powerful, she would've sensed you coming. You would've crashed into her ward."

Realization was dawning. Tears slipped down his cheeks, but I didn't have it in me to feel sorry for him. Mostly, I felt sorry for his mom.

We worked on him for another hour, but he couldn't give me anything else. We'd taken his phone, but Caroline had probably used a burner.

"Witchling?"

"Yes?"

"My people spotted the witch. She is attempting to flee."

I scowled. Of course she was. She knew Kyla and I weren't parked outside the hotel, and something had tipped her off.

"Where is she heading?"

"Toward the bus depot."

"Thanks. How's Evie?"

"I will ask Vas."

Kyla asked Peter a few more questions, making notes on her phone.

"She left the tower to go to the coven," Samael

informed me.

She'd probably had enough of listening to the way Caroline had manipulated this guy into doing her dirty work. My sister *loathed* bullies. She'd be disappointed when she got to the hotel and realized Caroline wasn't there.

"Thank you."

We left Peter crying in the interrogation room. I pulled my phone from my pocket and texted Evie.

Please don't say anything to the coven until I bring Caroline in. I want Kyla to watch everyone closely and see their reactions, just in case Caroline was working with someone else.

A few moments passed and then she replied.

Got it.

I glanced at Kyla. "You look exhausted."

"Are you kidding? I was made for this. Let's go find the bitch."

CHAPTER TWENTY-FOUR

Danica

Caroline was easy to track. She hadn't imagined she'd need to run, so she'd headed straight to the bus station on Pettigrew Street. We found her, ticket in hand, waiting next to a sign that read New York.

I glanced at the schedule. The bus wasn't leaving for several hours, which explained why there were so few people around.

She spotted us immediately and turned to run. My power whipped out and froze her in place.

"Huh," I said. "That's new."

Kyla raised one eyebrow, glancing between me and Caroline. "Why don't you do that shit more often?"

"I can't trust it. My power wants to kill people." She stared at me and I sighed. "I'll explain later."

We moseyed over to the witch. I reached for my power, and it took me a few moments to figure out how, exactly to unfreeze her.

"You're a monster," Caroline gasped. "What are you *doing*, Danica?"

"More importantly, what are *you* doing, Caroline?"

"I have a friend's wedding in New York."

Kyla made a sound like a game-show buzzer. "Try again."

"I need help," Caroline blinked back tears. "I'm being framed, and I was too scared to stay until I cleared my name."

"Better," I decided. "But still crap."

I shoved her against the wall.

"You tried to kill my sister. You killed everyone in that house."

"I didn't. I didn't kill them. They promised they wouldn't kill them all. Only Gemma, Evie and Nellie."

"Why?"

She opened her mouth and then clamped it shut. My power licked at her and I watched with satisfaction as the blood drained from her face.

"Talk," I purred, "or I'll make you wish you were dead."

"Okay, okay."

It all came pouring out of her. How she'd met a guy she'd thought was human at a bar. How she'd woken up at his place, tied to a chair.

They'd threatened to torture her, but instead, she'd made them a deal. They wanted a way into the house, and she wanted the path clear for Aunt Gail to be coven leader. They'd work together.

"Who made them fall asleep?"

Silence. I let another tendril of power wind around

her and she shuddered.

"I did! I uh, I got the idea at the human hospital. Some of the spells we were making were used to help patients get some rest. Others to keep them unconscious if they had a problem with general anesthesia."

"So you stole them."

"I made some of them myself because I wanted to make sure they wouldn't do any damage. The coven was only supposed to sleep for a few hours."

Tears glimmered in her big eyes and I ignored them.

"Why would they kill all the witches?"

She sniffed. "I don't know. Because they could, I guess. I never should have trusted them."

"Yeah, talk about stating the fucking obvious. Who changed out the smoke detectors?"

"I did. The men… they said the smoke detectors still worked, they just had cameras in them so they'd know when to enter the house."

If they'd had cameras, they'd taken them out with them when they got into the house. Either Samael's people or the human authorities would have found them otherwise. But they'd left the smoke detectors themselves as one more 'fuck you' to everyone investigating.

"It didn't tip you off when they wanted the smoke detectors?"

She shook her head and I rolled my eyes. No one could be both this conniving, and this dumb.

"You knew damn well what they were planning. Break the coven, and they're all too busy grieving to think about revenge for killing their sisters."

Her lower lip trembled and she firmed it, eyes hard.

"This was Evie's fault. They targeted our coven because of her. They never would have approached me if they didn't want her dead. Just ask Gemma. The older witches are protecting her from something. It's their fault too."

I clamped my hand around her throat and watched her face turn purple.

"Use me to kill her," Misty whispered in my head. *"I'll bathe in her blood."*

Well crap. I hadn't heard anything from the dagger since it spoke to Evie. I'd assumed it was dormant or sleeping or something. The shock of it helped me push back most of my power, as Kyla elbowed me in the ribs.

"Ease up a little. At least until she's told us everything."

I took a deep, steadying breath and relaxed my hold. "Why did they want Evie dead?"

"I don't know. I don't, I swear. They just said they wanted access to the curvy blonde in the far-right bedroom on the second floor."

"They were watching her."

"I guess. They wouldn't tell me what day they were going to strike, only that it would be while I was out of town."

"They screwed up. Brooke was in Evie's room. That's why they're coming for my sister. You knew they were after Evie. Even after everything you were still focused on covering your ass."

"Please don't kill me."

I laughed. "Oh I won't. Gemma would prefer to do the honors herself, I think."

Kyla used zip ties, clamping Caroline's arms behind

her back, before gagging her with an old t-shirt she found in my trunk. We couldn't have her attempting any spells on the way.

A few humans were waiting for buses at the station. They gaped at us as Kyla pulled my car around and we shoved Caroline in the trunk. I must've had crazy-eyes, because no one dared approach.

Caroline began steadily kicking the trunk as we drove, by the time we pulled up to the hotel's loading zone, I was more than ready to hand her over to the witches.

"You can't park here– oh my God, why is she in the trunk?" the doorman's voice climbed steadily higher as we parked and opened the trunk.

I ignored him, hauling Caroline out of the car while Kyla gave a snarl, low and threatening enough that the doorman shoved his phone back in his pocket, held up his hands, and opened the door for us.

"Move," I told Caroline, and she sent me one vicious look but stepped into the lobby.

The concierge looked shell shocked as we frog-marched Caroline past him.

"Madam. Madam I really must–"

"Stow it. This is witch business."

There weren't many people in the lobby at this time of the early morning, but those who were knew better to get involved in what they would consider infighting amongst a coven.

The elevator doors opened to Gemma's floor and Caroline went crazy, kicking, slamming her head back, and screaming muffled curses behind her gag. I rolled my eyes and Kyla muscled her out while I stalked down the hall to knock on Gemma's door.

Freya answered. "If you're here to implicate Gail some more, you can leave," she said bitterly. "She fell apart after you interrogated her the other day."

I jerked my head toward the elevator and Freya leaned her head out the door. "Oh God."

"Yeah. Give us some room."

"If you've messed this up again…"

I gave her a hard stare "I haven't."

"Shit." Freya closed her eyes. "This is going to kill Gail."

I strode past her into the room. Evie sat in an armchair next to the window, her eyes on Caroline's face.

"What are you doing here?" Gemma demanded. Her gaze slid past me as Kyla pushed Caroline into the room, letting her fall to her knees.

"Are you out of your mind?"

"Nope." I held up my phone. "I have it on record. But I'm sure you'll want to hear it all first-hand."

Evie got to her feet, her gaze burning with retribution as she stared at Caroline. Her eyes softened as Gail stepped out of the other room, her face ashen.

"No. No, please no." Gail's hands were held out in front of her as if she could push this entire scene away.

Freya stepped up next to Gail, rubbing a hand up and down her back. Several other witches filed in, most of them giving me the stink-eye.

Kyla untied the gag but kept Caroline's hands tied.

"They were after Evie. Caroline agreed to let them kill my sister, as long as they also killed Gemma and Nellie. The offshore account was hers, and she was stealing money from her own aunt so she could leave the country if she needed to."

Gemma's face turned cold and hard. "Is that so?"

Caroline sobbed. "I'm sorry." She turned to Gail, who had been helped into a chair and was staring at her niece as if she were a stranger. "I'm so sorry."

"You're sorry you got caught," Freya said. "How could you do this? All those women. Our family. And for what?"

"She wanted Gail to take over the coven," I supplied. "And eventually, when Gail was too old or too weary, Caroline would be right there waiting."

"No," Gail moaned, rocking back and forth. "Please no."

"I'm sorry," I said.

Gemma met my eyes and I nodded. Caroline wouldn't be walking out of this room. After what she'd done, I didn't have it in me to care.

"We wouldn't have discovered this without your help," Gemma said. "None of us could have imagined this. We owe you a debt."

I shook my head. "No, you don't. I did it for Evie."

Gemma glanced at where my sister was still staring silently at Caroline. "We both know you would have investigated even if Evie was out of town."

I shrugged. "Fine." I could always use a favor from the coven.

Gemma nodded. "Now leave. This is for those who have a blood debt."

I had no desire to stick around, and from the sick look on Kyla's face, she didn't either. She was silent in the elevator, only glancing at me when we were walking through the lobby. "You think they'll kill her?"

"Oh yeah. Not only did she kill their people— their family— but she crippled the coven. Gemma may look like a sweet old lady, but she would never tolerate that."

"I didn't realize the witches were so…"

"Brutal?" I glanced at her as we got in the car. "I'd say they have more in common with the way a werewolf pack works than you'd think."

I rubbed at my pounding temple and craved more coffee. "The witches straddle two worlds. They're human, but they have power. They're not powerful enough to go up against the fae or the demons, but when they work together, they can be a power to be reckoned with.

"When the portals opened, those everyday humans suddenly had an influx of power. But when it became public that the McCormick coven had been the ones to open the portals…"

"They were screwed."

"Yeah. They formed covens out of necessity. Humans were less likely to try to burn a witch alive or drown her in their swimming pools if they knew she had several witches ready to back her up. It was a brutal time, and Gemma was around for it. She lived through the Decade of Despair with a target on her back, and she built that coven from the ground up, making it the most powerful in the Triangle."

"She must've been so young."

"Yeah. Caroline could have told her she'd been approached at any time. The coven would have investigated, and they likely would've involved me, even though they would've hated it. They knew I'd use the demons if it would protect Evie. But Caroline wanted the power. So yeah, she's toast."

If the thought made my stomach clench, I ignored it. A last-minute, secret date with a werewolf. That was the only reason why my sister was alive.

I glanced at Kyla. "I couldn't have closed this case so quickly without your help. Thank you."

She turned in the passenger seat, adjusting her belt so she could look at me. "It was fun. Not all of it," she admitted. "The stake-outs sucked. But solving the mystery, getting justice for those witches, saving Riona's life? I guess I should thank Nathaniel for convincing you to take me on."

"At first I only did it so he'd owe me a favor."

"I know."

"But now, if he wanted you to go work for the pack, I'd fight him."

Kyla smiled. "He'd kick your ass."

"I dunno. I'm pretty sneaky. I'm going to dump you at the tower so you can grab your car. I need to swing by Meredith's and tell her we know who was responsible for Jessica's death."

I pulled up outside the tower. "Get some sleep," I said and Kyla nodded. "I will. Good luck with Meredith."

By the time I parked outside the bar, it was 4:00am and close to closing. Her bar stayed open later than most, since she served mostly paranormals.

I slid onto the stool in front of her.

"How are you doing, Meredith?"

She attempted a smile. Across the bar, her light fae

bartender floated several bottles of spirits in the air for a customer to peruse.

"It's been tough. The funeral helped a little. I like to think of her with the rest of the coven now." She reached for a fresh glass and I shook my head. All I wanted was coffee.

"Everything I've heard about Jessica tells me she was an amazing woman. I'm so sorry for your loss."

"Thanks." She sighed and reached for a clean cloth, wiping down the already spotless bar. Across the long, polished wood, an incubus spilled his drink. Mere lifted one hand, stopping the liquid in flight and directing it back into his glass. He gave her a nod.

"We know who was responsible for the fire. For all of it. Well, we know which coven member was responsible."

Mere stilled, slowly raising her gaze to my face. "Who?"

Vengeance shone in her eyes and I shook my head. "She's been handed over to the coven. It was Caroline."

Meredith's mouth dropped open. "That little mouse? The butter-wouldn't-melt witch who was always bragging about her healing spells?"

"That's the one."

Mere blew out a long breath. "I never would've guessed. What about the rest of them?"

"We have some leads. The demons are helping."

She studied my face. "Finally given into him, have you?"

She didn't say it snarkily, but I scowled anyway.

"Yeah, well, the poor guy hounded me until I threw him a bone. Who would've known demons could be so clingy?"

That was my story, and I was sticking to it.

She threw her head back and laughed. "Keep telling yourself that, Dani."

My phone vibrated and I pulled it from my pocket.

Cara. Why, exactly would she be texting at this time of the night?

Get to the Mage Council. It's important.

I scowled and texted back. *The only place I'm going is to bed. What are you even doing up, anyway?*

You need to get here. SOS.

This night was never going to end.

"Problem?" Mere asked.

"Cara texted me. She's a… friend, I guess. She's helped me with a few cases over the years."

And she helped me analyze the arrows when someone was shooting any demons who had a lead to my mother's death. She was the reason I knew about rowan.

"She wants to meet me at the Council."

"Now?"

"She must've found something good. Probably in their library."

"You've got a man on the inside. I like it."

I grinned and got to my feet. "See you around, Mere."

Since the Mage Council facility was so close, I considered walking, but Cara had made it clear she wanted me there fast. I pinched the bridge of my nose as I started my car. All I wanted to do was crawl into bed next to Samael and sleep for about sixteen hours. This better be worth it.

The Mage Council was quiet as I made my way into

the lobby, holding my hand above the spelled water that served as the Council's ID checkpoint. It glowed green, and I strolled toward the elevator, once again thankful that Keigan had put me on his guest list.

Cara was waiting for me in her office.

"Hey, what's going–"

Movement out the corner of my eye made me turn but I wasn't fast enough to duck. Searing pain slammed into my temple, and the ground hit me in the face.

CHAPTER TWENTY-FIVE

Danica

I sat on the floor in the entrance of Cara's office, my wrists wrapped in Naud chains. Thick links connected them together, giving me limited movement with my arms.

My connection to Samael was gone. My powers, gone.

My patience? So gone.

Bruce stood by Cara's side, his expression victorious.

"You're fucking dead," I told him, and his expression turned blank.

Cara glanced at him. "Stop scaring Bruce," she told me as she pulled her gun.

Cara wasn't particularly powerful. But the gun in her hand made all the difference when I was wrapped in Naud chains.

"What the fuck are you doing? I thought you were my friend."

She nodded. "I *am* your friend."

"Then why would you do this?"

"You know why I joined the Mage Council."

"Yeah, so you could be the first female on the Council itself. So what?"

"So what? A few months ago, Albert told me I needed to stop talking about it. Stop giving women hope and do my job. He said there was no way a woman would be joining the Council. Not in my lifetime, and certainly not in his."

She wasn't looking at Bruce, so she missed the sneer of agreement on his face.

I gaped at her. "So this is some kind of twisted revenge?"

She shook her head. "A week later, a demon approached me outside my apartment. One I hadn't seen before. He said Lucifer had an offer for me. He's giving me a position in his court. I'll be sitting next to you when you take your throne in the underworld."

I gaped at her. "Are you high? Lucifer will kill me."

"He doesn't want you dead. He wants you to join him."

"You got played, Cara. You take me to the underworld, and we're both dead."

"Your grandfather is a reasonable man. I looked into that prophecy. You *can* kill him, sure. That doesn't mean you have to. He's got no family, and the underworld is lacking the kind of power you can wield."

I closed my eyes.

"You had me chasing after black monkshood so I could figure out what was in my arrow. You knew about the rowan the whole time."

"I didn't, I swear. I didn't know you had rowan– or even what it was– until I researched it. Lucifer's demon hadn't contacted me then." She sent me a sympathetic look. "He never would've found you if you hadn't read that prophecy. Once you did, it was a simple matter for him to trace the artifact back to the fae and then to you."

"Yippee for him."

She smiled and lowered her voice as if we were gossiping in the breakroom. "Apparently, the big guy was hoping you'd use the arrow on Samael. Two birds, one stone and all that."

Bile crawled up my throat at the thought.

"Weapons," Bruce growled.

Cara slid him an unfriendly look but gestured at me with the gun in her hand. Obviously, girl talk was over.

"Put them on the ground, Danica. All of them."

I ground my teeth. "You won't shoot me."

She fired at my feet and I lunged to the side. "What the fuck? You're batshit crazy. What happened to you?"

"You'll thank me when you're sitting on your throne."

She had a real obsession with thrones.

I hesitated some more and she shook her head. "Don't make me shoot you, Danica. Lucifer's healers will fix it, but you'll be in a lot of pain until then."

How someone wearing such blatant crazypants could sound so goddamn reasonable was beyond me.

I slowly reached for my throwing knives. There are few things more insulting than being stripped of your own weapons. I swear I would've rather been stripped naked, as long as I'd stayed armed.

Cara studied the pile when I was done. "Where's the rowan arrow?"

I ground my teeth. "Samael found it and turned it to ash." I slid my gaze to the wall behind her as if wrestling with embarrassment. If only I could blush on command.

Cara let out a low laugh. "That must chafe."

I ignored her. The only reason I hadn't told Cara I'd managed to get Hannah and the bladesmith to cloak the arrow hanging around my neck? I hadn't had a chance to chat with her in the weeks since. And that may just save my life.

Cara glanced at Bruce and jerked her head. A muscle jumped in his jaw. Clearly, he didn't enjoy taking orders from Cara. Bitch needed to start watching her back.

Bruce stepped toward me. I strained, reaching desperately for even the faintest spark of my power, but the Naud Chains were doing their job.

I watched Bruce, desperate to kick him in the balls. But Cara wasn't faking. She'd shoot me and haul my deadweight to Lucifer with a sweet smile on her face.

When I didn't return to his tower, Samael would rip this city apart looking for me, and the Mage Council would be one of the first places he looked. But it would take a few hours before he noticed I was gone. I didn't exactly check in with him about my whereabouts all that often.

I had to figure out a way to get these chains off so I could save myself.

"Get rid of them," Cara ordered.

Bruce stroked my Nim Cub admiringly and I yearned to stab him in the gut with it. I'd bet he was planning to arm himself with my fucking weapons as soon as I was no longer around.

Bruce walked away and Cara eyed me. "Get up and walk toward the elevator, Danica."

I ground my teeth but slowly got to my knees.

"Faster. I know you're scheming, Dani–"

"Only my friends call me Dani," I snapped. "You no longer qualify."

Silence. Then she stepped a little closer. I glanced over my shoulder.

"I know you're mad now," she said. "But this is all going to work out. We'll look back and laugh at this one day."

I gaped at her. Since I was staring at her, I saw the moment her head exploded.

Fuck. I hit the ground, but I was a sitting duck.

Rose stepped forward. She held a gun in her hand, her face ashen.

"Are you going to shoot me?"

"No. God no." She looked at Cara and swallowed, reaching out one hand to lean against the wall.

"What are you doing here?"

She swallowed. "I don't sleep. I came to catch up on paperwork and heard them talking. I hid under my desk." Her gaze slid to Cara again.

I stepped into her line of sight.

"Don't look at her," I said. If I lived through this, I'd mourn the loss of the friend I'd thought Cara had been. But I had more important things to worry about now. "Do you know where Bruce took my weapons?"

"No." She reached for her knife, still in its sheath and handed it to me.

I struggled with the Naud chains until I could shove it down the back of my jeans, and immediately felt more in control.

"Do you have your phone?"

She shook her head. "They've done something. Some kind of spell or something. There's no service."

"How many others are here?"

"That new contractor… uh… Wes, I think his name is. And Ben."

I rolled my eyes and she nodded. "I know, right." We shared a look. The first time Rose and I had been on the same page in our lives.

"Ben's in charge. They're going to take you to the portal, Danica." She looked slightly sick at the thought.

"Okay. I need you to go and get help."

She gaped at me. "You want me to split up? I knew you were crazy, Amana…"

"When Cara doesn't take me to Ben, he's going to either come looking himself, send Bruce, or both. They need me alive at least long enough to hand me over to Lucifer, but they don't need you. If they find you, you're dead."

She nodded, eyes turning wild. "Oh God, it feels like a nightmare. How could they do this?"

"Let's ask ourselves those kinds of deep questions if we're still alive an hour from now. Here's what we do. You take the elevator, I'll head for the stairs. One of us will get out."

I had to believe that.

"Okay. Okay. God. Okay."

"I need you to contact Samael."

Her face paled and I reached out, giving her a shake. "Tell the demons. Promise me."

"I promise." She took a long look at my face. "Good luck."

"Yeah. You too."

She turned and hauled ass toward the elevator. I gave Cara's body one last glance and then headed in the opposite direction toward the stairs.

The chains hung between my wrists, and I gathered them closer so I wouldn't trip, My knees pumped as I sprinted, and I glanced over my shoulder as Rose stepped into the elevator. Pure, unfiltered relief unwound in my chest.

I choked, falling to the ground. I couldn't breathe. I gasped, rolling as I clutched my throat. Someone had clotheslined me.

Bruce.

I fought to get a single breath into my lungs as Wes stepped up next to him, my Colt in his hand. He fired at Rose and she ducked, wedging herself into the corner of the elevator.

"Jesus, you couldn't hit the side of a barn," I managed to get out.

Wes sent me a look of retribution as the elevator doors slid closed. He took a step toward the elevator but Bruce shook his head.

"Don't bother," Bruce smiled, his gaze on my face. "By the time Rose gets out of here, the demon whore will be tucked away in the underworld and it'll be her word against all of ours."

Samael would believe her.

"Get up," he said.

I slowly got to my feet as Wes trained my own gun on my chest.

"Fucking finally," Bruce said, stepping closer. He leaned down until he was right in my face. "All this time you've swanned around here like you own the place, even after you were fucking fired. Everyone knows you only lasted as long as you did because you were fucking Keigan."

My chest tightened at the thought of Keigan. When he learned exactly what had happened here, it would kill him.

I smiled sweetly at him. "You know, you really need to chew some gum or something, cause your breath smells like—"

He slammed his fist into the exact same temple he'd hit last time.

I leaned over and fought to keep down what little I had in my stomach. The edges of my vision darkened as Wes laughed.

"Walk," Bruce said. "Make any sudden moves and I'll tell Wes to shoot you. And unlike that stupid bitch Cara, I don't care if Lucifer heals you."

I walked.

They took me back toward the elevators. With two of them watching me this intently, there was no way I'd get to the knife in the small of my back without getting shot.

Bruce pressed the button for the 9th floor, whistling a merry tune before smiling at me. This was clearly the best thing that'd ever happened to him.

The doors opened and he pushed me forward.

Both men walked me to Albert's office. "Sit," Bruce said, and I ground my teeth.

Wes pushed me into Albert's guest chair and then leaned against the desk.

"Watch her," Bruce said. "Ben wants to say his goodbyes before she leaves." He glanced at me. "Right now, he's on a call with some friends. An extra little alibi just in case."

I smiled at him. "That's cute."

Bruce took a step toward me, and Wes put out his hand, slapping it against his chest. "Hey, hey. The demons will kill you if she dies before she gets to the underworld."

Bruce stared at him for one, fraught moment, but then he nodded, his gaze sliding back to me. "I'm bringing the car around. Shoot her in the leg if she tries anything."

Wes nodded, leaning back against Albert's desk. Bruce turned and stalked out without another word.

I knew why Ben was having me brought here. He was obsessed with Albert, infatuated with the idea that he'd be in Albert's spot one day. He probably wanted to sit behind the boss's desk while he bored me about how smart he was and how bad my death would be.

I had one shot at this.

I glanced at Wes. "You know Albert's going to kill you, right?"

Wes sneered at me as he picked up the heavy glass paperweight on Albert's desk, idly examining it. "Silence, whore."

I yawned. "You sound like an echo of Bruce. That's embarrassing."

He glanced up. "He's right. You've always been Keigan's favorite. A good for nothing bounty hunter who happened to fuck a demon. You know what?" Wes reached out with one hand, grabbing my t-shirt so he could get right up in my face. That meant that he only had one hand for my gun.

I let my body go limp, sliding off the chair as he leaned closer. It pulled him a fraction off balance.

I struck.

My foot hit his wrist with enough power to send my gun flying. His arm swung toward me but I slid beneath it, leaping at him.

I wrapped the Naud Chains around his throat.

Wes pushed at me, but I had the leverage, my arms crossing the chains behind him as I hooked my right arm around his neck and tightened the chain.

He drove his fist into my ribs. Once, twice. I screamed as a sharp pain took up residence in my side. But if I let go, I was dead.

He clawed at his throat and I pulled the chain tighter. His neck muscles strained, and he dropped his hand again this time burying his fist in my gut.

I'd tensed my stomach muscles but not fast enough. My hands automatically let go as the air exploded from my lungs. I gasped for breath like a fish suddenly on land.

He tripped me, following me down to the ground. "Your turn to learn how that felt," he snarled, one hand wrapping around my throat.

What little air I'd managed to suck up disappeared instantly. My arms were still tangled behind his neck, and I slammed my hand against his head, slipping the chain back toward me. I needed the slack.

My right hand groped beneath the desk. Wes smiled at me, clearly enjoying himself.

I slammed the paperweight into his face.

He screamed, and I hauled back, hitting him in the back of the head. And again. Air whooshed into my lungs, only to be cut off again as the asshole collapsed on top of me.

I pulled the knife from the small of my back and held

it to his throat as I wiggled out from underneath him. No movement. I made it to my knees and gasped at the pain in my side. He had fists like goddamn sledgehammers.

The closet. Get to the closet, and break into the chest. I could do this.

I found my feet and opened the closet door, pushing the blanket off the chest Albert kept in here. My hands shook as I pulled out another blanket and gaped at Albert's hoard.

Weapons, jewelry, cash, and passports.

I recognized some of the weapons, but I dumped them on the floor. My hands shook, my mouth so dry I'd give just about anything for some water.

Bruce was getting the car. Ben would be here any minute.

"Keys, keys, keys, keys, goddamnit!"

Nothing. I choked out a sob. Where the fuck would Albert keep the keys to the Naud chains? My hands touched something soft and I froze.

I pulled the pelt out. It was about the size of a coat, and somehow as smooth as silk, and yet it felt almost like fur. I wrapped it around my neck like a shawl. Then I stepped over Wes, picked up my Colt, and opened the door, peering down the corridor.

Wes groaned and I glanced at him. "Don't make me regret leaving you for the demons," I snarled. He wasn't moving. I took a deep breath and that breath caught in my throat at the pain from my ribs. Okay, I'd try not to do that again.

I just had to get to the 6th floor.

Stairs or elevator?

I crept out of the office, past Albert's receptionist's

desk. My whole body jolted as the elevator doors sounded, incredibly loud in the silence.

Stairs.

I ran. One hand holding my gun, and the other pressed against my aching side.

I hit the stairs at a limp, my ribs screaming at me, but I picked up the pace. Either Ben or Bruce was in that elevator. I'd bet one of them had found Wes, and they'd split up.

If they hadn't, and they were together, I was screwed.

My thighs burned, desperation and adrenaline driving me faster. I kept my eyes on the stairs as I ran down them. If I tripped, I was toast.

Three floors. I had to get down three floors. Each step jostled my ribs, and my breath sawed in and out of my lungs in pained pants.

I almost missed the door to the 6th floor when I hit it. I took one breath, and shot out of the stairwell. The elevator doors opened.

I spun as Bruce came into view, a smirk playing around his mouth.

Our eyes met.

I fired.

He ducked, and I used the two seconds of his distraction to haul ass. My feet slid on the cheap carpet as bullets whizzed past my head.

I wasn't dying tonight.

CHAPTER TWENTY-SIX

Danica

I turned and ducked around the corner, careening wildly through the stacks of shelves, dodging through them at random.

The library was like a labyrinth at night, but I knew the general direction I was going.

"Oh, Danica… you have nowhere to go, you idiot."

I was faster than Bruce. But I was pretty sure my ribs were cracked if not broken, and the heavy chains wrapped around my wrists were slowing me down.

Thirty feet away, Mella's desk lamp glowed like a beacon.

Twenty feet.

Her head popped up from her bed beneath her desk as I sprinted toward her. "Danica?"

I pulled her pelt off from around my neck and her eyes widened.

Ten feet.

Mella rounded the desk and jerked against her

chain, arms outstretched.

Faster. I had to move faster.

Bruce hit me like a truck and Mella shrieked. I stumbled. I had less than a second to decide if I'd use my hands to break my fall or throw the pelt.

I threw the pelt as far as I could.

My gun went flying as my bad side hit the ground and I screamed. Bruce flipped me over, his grin lighting up his face.

"This has been fun, Amana. Chasing you with a gun in my hand is kind of a turn on, to be honest."

He casually slapped me across the face, and I used the momentum to sneak a glance behind me. Mella was crouched beneath her desk. Why wasn't anything happening?

The chains. Maybe her pelt wasn't enough against the Naud Chains.

Fuck.

I turned my attention back to Bruce.

He raised one eyebrow and stood, placing his foot on my stomach. My ribs screamed at me as I struggled, but I was trapped like a butterfly on a pin. I needed to keep him talking.

"Now you're going to die, and I hope Lucifer makes it last for weeks."

"And what do you think Samael will do about that?"

He angled his head. "Not my problem. I have four people who'll swear I'm hanging out with them right now."

"And Wes and Ben?"

Something dark and excited slid into his gaze. "Sacrifices must be made. And those sacrifices will pave the way for a world without demons."

A shiver ran up my spine as a warning siren rang out in my brain. There was something I wasn't seeing. Some bigger part of this plan that I'd missed.

I swallowed. "Think about the worst way you've ever thought about dying," I advised him. "And prepare yourself, because when the demons get hold of you, it'll be worse."

He jabbed his foot into my stomach. I screamed as he jostled my ribs.

"Hey Bruce?" Mella's voice was achingly sweet.

He glanced past me, and I slid my hand beneath me, pulling the knife Rose had given me. Now or never.

Power exploded.

I flew through the air. My body hit the wall and my knee popped.

The air left my lungs, and then a scream was ripped from my throat as an unseen force lifted me, pushed me beneath the closest desk. It jostled my knee further.

Mella. Maybe she was trying to be helpful. I dragged myself further from the selkie, tears streaming down my face as agony ripped through me.

I used my arms to pull myself behind a fallen bookshelf, the movement making my stomach swim.

WHOOSH

A fireball flew past my head. Every window in the library shattered.

Bruce's screams were terrible. He begged for mercy, and while I hated him more than I hated most people, his desperate wails made the hair on the back of my neck stand up.

The building shook as Mella laughed. The entire right wall of the library disappeared.

I was going to die here, crushed like a bug as the building pancaked.

"Mella, stop!" I screamed.

A bookshelf fell on top of me, pinning my legs. My knee was on fire, and I leaned over and vomited.

Someone was snarling. The deep, animalistic sound made me shudder and I peered around the bookshelf, squinting through the smoke. Mella had transformed into something out of a nightmare. Her long, blonde hair had darkened to a blue so deep it was almost black. Her teeth had lengthened, becoming long, lethal fangs, and her face was sharper somehow, her cheekbones jutting out in a way that made the hair on the back of my neck stand up.

But it was the feral, vicious expression on her face that turned my blood cold. I froze as my deepest instincts warned me not to attract the attention of the predator in front of me.

Mella raised her hand, revealing long, black claws, and shoved that hand into Bruce's chest. Bile crawled up my throat as she pulled his heart free and bit into it like it was an apple.

Her gaze met mine and I went still. The Naud Chains were still keeping my magic buried deep down where I couldn't reach it, and I longed for the knife I'd lost when Mella broke free of her chains.

She threw Bruce's heart away and slowly got to her feet. I reached for a long shard of glass and held it in my hand, but if Mella wanted me dead, I was dead.

The selkie wore her pelt like a cape as she sauntered

toward me, crouching down next to my head.

"Thank you, Danica Amana," she said. Pink flesh dangled from her sharp teeth. Bruce's heart. I swallowed.

"You're welcome."

"I would like to help you, but the compulsion is too strong. I must get to the water."

"As long as you don't kill me, you're helping."

The ghost of a smile danced across her face, and the blood dripping down her chin made it even creepier.

"My people owe you a debt. One day, when you need it the most, you may collect."

I nodded.

She reached over and pushed the bookshelf off my legs with one hand and black dots danced in front of my eyes.

"Dislocated," she said. "As soon as a healer arrives, you'll be fine."

If this building didn't come down on me first. Mella seemed unconcerned, already walking away. I attempted to move my leg and a scream ripped from my throat.

I just needed to relocate my knee. If I didn't, I'd burn alive here. The smoke was already flooding my nostrils, so all-encompassing I could taste it as it slid down my throat.

I choked on a sob as I sat up, agony ripping through me. I froze. Someone was walking toward me. I could hear footsteps over the crackling of the fire. I held the glass tighter in my hand and cursed as Ben appeared.

"Well, this is interesting," he said. His gaze found Bruce's body and he shook his head. "You're going to pay for that."

"Fuck you."

"No," he said. "Fuck you."

He smiled, pulled his leg back, and kicked my knee. Pain engulfed me and everything went black.

Samael

Naud chains. Someone had used Naud chains on my little witch.

I hadn't noticed the bond becoming fainter at first. I'd been busy taking a call with the light fae king.

It wasn't until I glanced at the time that I realized Danica should've been back.

And when I reached for our bond, I received nothing back but silence.

She couldn't be dead. I would *know* if she were dead. That only left the chains.

"I want every demon in this city looking for her. Get in touch with Finvarra and tell him I want his people searching as well. He owes me."

I strode out of the room with some idea of hunting for her myself. I'd tear this city apart if I had to.

"Samael."

I turned and Lilith held up her phone. "You need to see this."

The Mage Council Headquarters were on fire. Several floors were mostly missing on one side, as if a huge chunk had been taken out.

"She was in there," I was certain of it. "She was in there and I can't feel her anymore."

"Samael–"

My wings extended, dripping flames. Wrath burned through me, incinerating every other emotion in its path.

Lilith stepped closer, her face pale. "They wouldn't have killed her there. You know that. They'd take her to Lucifer and he'd kill her himself."

She was right.

"I have a call for you," Sitri announced as he walked in, his face grim.

I slowly turned my head at the interruption and the blood drained from his face.

"You're going to want to take this one. It's a witch. Says Danica saved her life, and it's her turn to repay the favor."

I was across the room with the phone in my hand before I knew I'd moved.

"Speak."

"Uh, hi. Is this–"

"You're speaking with Samael. And you're wasting my time."

"S-sorry. My name is Riona. I'm the witch–"

"I know who you are."

"Okay so I had a few drinks with my sister and we ended up at Meredith's. She was about to close–"

"Get to the point, human."

"Um. Mere has a tiny touch of the sight. No visions or anything, but she gets like panic attacks. I mentioned I wanted to find a way to thank Danica properly, for saving my life and she suddenly had this massive panic attack. She just knew Danica was in danger."

I could hear someone cursing in the background,

along with the sound of a car's engine.

"Where are you?"

"Mere said Danica was meeting a friend at the Mage Council. We got there as the top floors exploded and a car drove out of the garage. It nearly hit us. Then Rose ran out and said Danica was kidnapped."

I took a deep breath, reaching for the little patience I had left.

"The taillight," Riona said quickly. "Someone punched out a taillight, and they'd shoved their hand through it. It's Danica. I recognized the bone bracelet on her wrist."

"Where are you?"

"We're taking 40 East. We're following the car."

40 East. They were heading to the closest portal to the underworld which was next to Lake Wheeler in Southeast Raleigh.

I threw the phone to Sitri. "Stay in contact with them." I turned and strode toward the balcony.

"If she's in the underworld, you can't follow her," Ag said.

I ignored him. He pushed in front of me, blocking my way.

I snarled, seeing only an enemy. "I suggest you move before I move you."

"You're dead. If you go into the underworld, your powers are gone."

"Do you think I don't know that? And do you honestly think, even for a moment, that I would allow her to be taken and do nothing?"

I shoved him aside. Both balcony doors flew open and I launched into the sky.

CHAPTER TWENTY-SEVEN

Danica

I woke in a trunk.

Panic clawed at my chest and I slammed my fist into one of the taillights again and again until I managed to shove my hand through, cursing the heavy Naud Chains.

I waved a hand furiously at anyone who happened to be around, but I wasn't hopeful. It was late enough that most people were asleep, and early enough that they hadn't yet started commuting to work.

Ben would hand me over to Lucifer, and then he'd go into the Mage Council as if nothing had happened.

I kicked out with my good leg, smashing it into the roof. My breath came in sharp pants as my hands clawed at the trunk, searching fruitlessly for the emergency release.

Nothing.

Either they'd chosen this car for that reason, or they'd removed it.

My knee wailed at me, and as the car jolted over a bump I fought not to throw up again from the pain. It was now so swollen that there was no way I could relocate it myself.

I took a deep, shuddering breath and forced myself to quit panicking. Why hadn't I told Samael I was heading to the Mage Council?

You just never knew when an insane mage was going to try to send you to the underworld.

Another deep breath. I counted to ten.

Okay. I'd been in worse positions before. I couldn't quite remember when, but one thing was damned sure: I'd die before I let them hand me over to Lucifer.

That decision made it a little easier. There was no outcome where I arrived at granddad's doorstep with cracked ribs and a dislocated knee.

If I ever faced him, I'd do it when I was at my best.

The Naud chains seemed to be draining me— not just magically, but physically too. I had a new empathy for Mella. I couldn't imagine living with this for years. No wonder she'd gone nuclear in the library.

The car slowed and my heart pounded like a drum in my chest. I would've given my right arm for a single throwing knife.

The car stopped. Doors slammed. The trunk opened and Ben smiled at me. Then he stepped back and gestured for Wes to pull me out.

It wasn't often that I regretted *not* killing someone, but I sure regretted it now. I cocked my good leg and kicked him in the face.

Wes cursed, cupping his nose. Ben rolled his eyes, shoving the other mage aside before slamming his hand down on my bad leg.

The edges of my vision went dim. Distantly, I felt myself falling to the ground. The landing jolted both my knee and my ribs, and the sheer misery sparked a fury so deep I was surprised the Naud chains didn't break.

"How the tables have turned," Ben said.

"Your hair charm is failing. I can see your bald spot."

He frowned, and I managed to get my hands under me so I could sit up.

We were in a grass field somewhere, next to water. Less than four feet away, the portal waited. The outsides were a deep merlot, lightening to scarlet and then crimson near the center. It pulsed like it was alive.

I pulled my gaze away and sneered at Ben. "All this time, all the shit you talked about me being a traitor, and you're working for *Lucifer?*"

"I'm working for any demon who will help us remove the blight of those who have made *our* world their home. Lucifer will stay in the underworld where he belongs in exchange for his granddaughter being returned to him."

"Lucifer has to stay in the underworld anyway, you idiot. He's bound to it."

He thought that over for a moment and then shrugged. "You never belonged here, Amana. The demons are too powerful to be allowed free run of our world. With Samael and his people gone, the balance of power will be restored."

I sneered at him. "And by that, you think the mages will be in charge. Are you forgetting about the fae?"

Ben shrugged. "The fae kings spend most of their time in their own realms. It's only the demons who actively suppress our ability to keep humanity safe."

"Oh please. We both know this isn't about keeping anyone safe." I tried a new tactic. The longer I stalled, the better. "Samael will kill you slowly for this."

"You think we're the only ones who know about this plan? The mages are getting us out of here, dumbass."

These guys honestly thought the mages would cover their asses? They would sacrifice them in a heartbeat.

Sacrifices must be made. Bruce's words ran over and over in my head, itching at me.

Ben gestured with his gun. "On your feet, Amana."

"Go to hell."

He grinned and waved his gun toward the portal. "You first."

I met Ben's eyes. "Shoot me," I said. "Shoot me, and deal with Lucifer yourself when I bleed out."

A flash of uncertainty darted across his face before he firmed his jaw. "I don't have to hit anything vital. What do you think, Wes? Should I kneecap her?" He trained his gun on my good knee and the world swam sickly around me at the thought.

"You kill her and I'll die too when Lucifer comes for you," Wes snarled. He was still cupping his hands to his nose, and blood dripped between his fingers.

"Ouch," I said. "Bet that hurts. How's the head, Wes?"

His eyes widened. "You just don't know when to shut the fuck up."

I smiled at him. I'd only have one chance.

Wes dropped his hands from his face. "Get your skinny ass through the portal, bitch." He lunged at me, reaching for my arm.

I let him catch it, only long enough to slide my hand

down his forearm.

I twisted, grunting as I used my good leg to lift my hips, pouring every ounce of strength I had into the throw.

He screamed as he flew over my shoulder and disappeared into the portal.

I turned back to Ben. He looked a little sick as he stared after Wes. I winked at him as he met my gaze.

"Just you and me now, Benny boy."

Danica

Ben aimed the gun at my bad knee. "Looks like this one is ruined anyway. Let's start here."

A roar sounded from above us. It sounded primal, the fury pouring from an ancient creature.

It was the sound a predator would make before it struck.

It communicated that it was the king of the jungle, and you were nothing but prey.

I knew who was making that sound, and it still scared the crap out of me.

Demons landed. So many, I couldn't count them. Samael's wings spread wide, the sparks dripping from them glowing in the twilight.

His eyes met mine. His rage ran so deep it made me shiver, but I was so fucking glad to see him, my eyes stung with it.

His gaze took in the rest of my body, lingering on my knee, and Ben turned, firing his gun.

Oh, you idiot.

Samael raised his hand.

Time stopped, then started up again, this time in slow-motion. Every cell in my aching body seemed to have been jolted into action as I launched myself up onto my good leg.

Bruce's smile flashed through my mind. *Sacrifices must be made.*

No.

No no no no no.

"Don't touch him," I screamed.

Samael waved his hand and Ben's body turned to ash.

It was too late. Ben was nothing but the sacrifice. The lure.

Samael glanced over his shoulder at me. His gaze turned puzzled for a split second. Then a sick kind of acceptance slid into his eyes as they met mine.

"Danica."

One word. I saw him mouth my name, but I couldn't hear him say it over the sound of my own screams.

Samael's wings began to fall to pieces, crumbling into ash. His skin turned gray as I stumbled toward him.

The Spell of Three.

Samael was the most powerful demon around. He'd never seen it coming. *I* should've seen it coming.

"Hold on. Don't you dare die on me."

The demons were losing their minds. Ag was roaring orders at every demon in the vicinity, while Lilith screamed out at someone to get the chains off me.

"You keep him here, girl," she shook me as I crawled toward him, dragging my bad leg.

The chains were lifted away and I was suddenly free.

My power came pouring back, and I screamed as it

burned through the last of the suppression spell. My hand reached for Samael's, and our fingers linked, his eyes turning blind.

He looked like a gargoyle. His fingertips were turning to ash and a pain I'd never felt before swept through me, followed by fury.

"You don't get to make me love you and then leave me here, you son of a bitch."

I reached desperately for our bond, *pulling* it toward me. I could feel him at the end, no longer a raging inferno, but barely a brief spark. I held that spark between cupped hands in my mind, nursing it, keeping it alive as I wept. I fed it my power. All of it.

"Please, please, please, please."

"Holy shit," someone said.

I opened my eyes. Parts of Samael were a blackened ruin. He wasn't breathing, but I could hear his heart beating in my ears. I leaned over and pressed my mouth to his, tilting his head back as I breathed for him.

Someone was pulling me away and I snarled as I smashed my fist into them.

Ag was shaking me. "Stop, stop and look what you've done you stupid girl."

I followed his gaze to Samael's arm.

There, amongst the charred skin, was an intricate gold mark. I knew without looking that it perfectly matched mine.

"You've killed yourself. When he goes, he'll take you with him."

"So be it."

CHAPTER TWENTY-EIGHT

Danica

I sat by Samael's bed, my leg up on another chair in front of me. Soon after the demons had found us, they'd knocked me out and sent me into surgery. Someone pushed my knee back into place, and Eldan healed my various wounds.

My ribs felt fine. My knee would need Eldan to work on it a few times over the next few days.

I'd woken up in a hospital bed, on the floor where Evie had her surgery, and threatened bloody murder until Eldan let me return to Samael's rooms.

His fingertips were gone, his fingers crumbling into ash. His wings looked like someone had set fire to them.

I was mostly too scared to touch him. But I reached out one finger and gently ran it down his cheek. He was so cold.

"You're not going to die. I'm going to fix this."

Silence. Tears burned my eyes but I talked to him. Just in case he could hear me.

"They had to act tonight," I murmured. "They

knew Gloria was on the run and if your people found her, they'd torture their involvement out of her. I'm sorry. I'm so stupid, I've been three steps behind this whole time."

Lucifer had made his first move. And I was the weapon he used to take Samael down.

"Danica?"

"Yeah?" I glanced over my shoulder. Vas hovered in the doorway, wearing mourning black. His dreamy brown eyes were sad, and he carried a canvas bag. He placed it on the chair next to me and I peered inside.

All of my weapons. And my utility belt. My throat tightened and I had to close my eyes.

Vas put his hand on my shoulder.

"We're all here for you," he said. "You're not facing this alone."

I opened my eyes. "Thanks."

"We have some intel from our people in the underworld," Vas said. "The human you pushed through the portal had enough power to make it across. Likely because he was training with the Mage Council. One of Lucifer's generals killed him the moment he came through. He'd also had the Spell of Three performed on him. Lucifer is furious about the general's death."

"Wes." If I'd had it in me to smile, that would've done it. "Lucifer probably ordered Gloria to spell most of the mages with the hope that if Samael killed at least one of them with his power, he'd go down with them."

"Yes. But he obviously knows he can't trust some of the demons closest to him. If he'd told his general about his agreement with Gloria, he wouldn't have dared strike out at a human who came through the portal."

I liked to imagine Lucifer paranoid and increasingly alone. It made my heart all aflutter.

"We need to spread the word. Every demon around needs to know that if Gloria is found, no one is to strike out at her with their power." I sighed. "That goes for all of the mages too. Until Gloria's dead, and her spell dead with her, any mages found to be traitors need to be locked away."

Vas nodded. "We've got it, Danica. It's going to be okay."

No it wasn't.

Vas held out an envelope. "This came for you."

I ripped it open, my chest tightening.

Dani

I don't know if I ever properly said it, but congratulations on your new office. I know you're going to do incredible things here. I'm SO proud of you for everything you've done since you left the Council. They were stupid to let you go, but I'm glad they did, because you were never supposed to spend your life bounty hunting for them.

Instead, you're going to be a badass who runs her own business.

I know you're going to hate this, and I'm sorry. But I can't sit around and wait for you to save me all the time.

I never told you, but Mom tried to call me a few times over the years.

I refused to talk to her. I blamed her. I tried to hate her. And she was doing everything she could to save my life.

I talked to your demon. He told me a few things about Lucifer. About how he's obsessed with breeding for power. How he loves the new and unexpected. Mom knew his people would've been looking for you. And if they found you, they would've found me.

And unlike you, I don't have a kick-ass prophecy attached to me.

I've been doing some research since we found the lab. And I've located the dark fae guy who hung around when we were kids. I'm pretty sure he's related to me in some way, and I know where to find him.

I'm the reason Mom is dead. I know it, deep down in my bones. But even from beyond the grave, she's still saving me.

It's my turn now. I'm going to help you find out who killed her. And we'll make them pay. Together.

For now, the next part is up to me.

Thank you for being the best big sister, and I'm sorry for leaving without warning.

I love you,

Evie

I read the letter to Vas. When I was done, we were both silent for a long moment.

"You want me to bring her back?"

"No. She's a grown woman and if this is what she needs to do, so be it. But she's not okay, Vas. Someone from the coven tried to kill her, she found out she's been tied to the house for most of her life, a big chunk of her family is dead, she's being hunted, and she was born in a lab."

"I'll have some of our people track her. They won't act unless she's in extreme danger."

I blew out a breath. "Thank you."

I studied the letter some more.

She'd left as soon as the coven had dealt with Caroline— probably while I was at Meredith's. There was no way she would've left if she'd known what happened to Samael.

I wished she'd stayed. Wished we could've figured it out together. But I got it.

Vas squeezed my shoulders as Ag stepped into the room. Vas gave his uncle a warning look as he passed, and the ghost of a smile darted around Ag's mouth. It dropped when he looked back at me.

"I don't have it in me to do this right now," I said.

"You don't have the luxury of burying your head in the sand. You're now in charge of the demons in Samael's territory."

If there was any sentence that could shake me from the depression and apathy that called to me like a lover, that was it.

"I don't know what you've been smoking, but that's ridiculous."

Ag took a step closer. He was being very careful not to look at Samael.

"Like it or not, but you're his bond mate. You proved that when you accepted the bond and gave him one of your own."

Yeah, that. I glanced at the burnished gold which warred with the black ash on Samael's arm.

"I didn't know what I was doing. I just wanted to keep him alive."

"You did. And now, you'll likely die with him."

He said it as if completely unconcerned. The smallest ember of fury broke through my numbness.

"Why do you have such a problem with me?"

He sent me a sharp smile. "When you went missing, Samael thought you'd already been taken to the underworld. He's powerless there, but he was going to go anyway. Likely ready to sacrifice himself in the hope that Lucifer would let you live."

My hand shook as I pushed the hair off my face. "He loves me."

"He's known you for months. You're prophesized to bring the downfall of his biggest enemy. The strategic decision, the one that was best for his people, was to allow you to be taken."

"I'm sorry you didn't get a showdown between me and Lucifer."

He merely raised one eyebrow. "You have never been to the underworld, so I will educate you. When Samael's grandfather ruled, it was a place of prosperity. Of course it was dangerous for some— it was still home to demons. The underking had been in power for centuries. Cross him, and you wouldn't live to regret it. But he was a fair ruler. Even his most fervent enemies could never say he was unjust.

"Lucifer was the son of his greatest rival. He was raised to believe the underking was weak and he struck when he least expected it. The damage he has done to our world, to our people, can never be truly put into words."

I swallowed. "I understand."

Ag's face could've been carved from stone. "No, you don't. You are the only hope for our people. A half-blood who has been on this earth for less than thirty years. But now all of us know the truth. In the unlikely event that both of you were to live through this, Samael would never allow you to step foot in the underworld without him. And so, our people are doomed." He opened his mouth as if to say more. Then he clamped it shut, shook his head, and walked away.

I leaned over and gently stroked Samael's cool cheek. My face was wet. I hadn't realized I was crying. Hadn't realized I had any tears left to shed.

I used my t-shirt to wipe my face, took out my phone and opened my notes app.

To do:

1. Save Samael's life (and also mine)
2. Find out who killed mom
3. Kill the underking

They would pay. Every single one of them would pay for what they did to us.

No matter what I had to do to make it happen.

The end.

I hope you enjoyed Inner Demons! Danica and Samael's story continues in the next book in the series: *Luck of the Demon.*

If you'd like to hang out with a fun group of like-minded fans, come check out my reader group on Facebook- Stark Society.

Want to see how Danica managed to fool Samael and steal Misty from beneath his nose? Visit Staciastark. com for your free copy of Fool the Demon.

ALSO BY STACIA STARK

The Deals with Demons Series

Speak of the Demon
Dance with the Demon
Inner Demons
Luck of the Demon
Demon's Advocate
Play the Demon

The Bargains with Beasts Series

Unnatural Magic
Unbroken Magic
Unending Magic

The Kingdom of Lies Serie

A Court This Cruel and Lovely
A Kingdom This Cursed and Empty
A Crown This Cold and Heavy
A Queen This Fierce and Deadly